WOLF LEGION

BOOK NINE OF
THE LAST MARINES

William S. Frisbee, Jr.

Theogony Books
Coinjock, NC

Chris Kennedy/Theogony Books
1097 Waterlily Rd.
Coinjock, NC 27923
https://chriskennedypublishing.com/

Publisher's Note: This is a work of fiction. Names, characters, places, and incidents are a product of the author's imagination. Locales and public names are sometimes used for atmospheric purposes. Any resemblance to actual people, living or dead, or to businesses, companies, events, institutions, or locales is completely coincidental.

Cover Design by J Caleb Design.

Ordering Information:
Quantity sales. Special discounts are available on quantity purchases by corporations, associations, and others. For details, contact the "Special Sales Department" at the address above.

Wolf Legion/William S. Frisbee, Jr.-- 1st ed.
ISBN: 978-1648559525

Chapter One:

Musashi

Dallas followed Major Yang off the shuttle into the cavernous shuttle bay. The *Musashi* was a massive ship, over four kilometers in length, and the mobile headquarters of the war command fighting the Torag. There were no larger ships in human space. Some claimed the Vapaus Republic space pirates had bigger ships, but could you really call an asteroid with weapons bolted onto it a ship? The *Musashi* was the only super dreadnought in existence and two lesser dreadnoughts and a host of battleships, destroyers and battle cruisers usually protected it, though she hadn't seen them on approach. Not a surprise. They would be spread out, the distance making them invisible to the naked eye.

If the *Musashi* was in orbit, then the Torag didn't dare try anything. The Goshkak Torag battleship squadron stationed in the system wouldn't dare approach Valakut. Intel said the Goshkak squadron never left the system. It just lurked in the outer system where they likely had a base. But that was a Fleet problem. Four battleships couldn't threaten the mighty *Musashi* or her escort.

She followed her commander as they made their way to some ODT briefing rooms. There was a short regiment of ODTs aboard the *Musashi*, two battalions and a heavy support battalion of gunships

3

and missile batteries. The *Musashi* could house a lot more, but she rarely kept her bays full.

In the briefing room, she took her seat as Major Krakow entered and moved to the head of the table. He placed a small box the size of a medicine bottle on the table.

"Sol has declared the Stalingrad Protocol," Krakow said with no introduction. Dallas had seen him before. He looked tired. He had bags under his red eyes and it looked like he had slept in his uniform. He didn't start with his usual prattle about the glories of the Governance and how the war against the Torag was going exceptionally well because of the valiant troops. His abrupt announcement was like a splash of cold water in the face.

What did that mean? Would there be no more reinforcements? Why would the Central Committee do that? Were the Vapaus pirates preparing for an assault? Had the Torag discovered the home world?

Krakow sat in his chair and looked at the regimental intelligence team. Dallas wasn't near him, but she caught a whiff of vodka. Had Krakow been drinking?

"This," Krakow said, pointing at the small device, "may save us."

"What is going on?" Yang asked. "Have you been drinking?"

Krakow turned bloodshot eyes toward Yang.

"You don't know what I do," Krakow said and a chill went down Dallas's spine. "I'm going to tell you. From this day forward, you will not sleep well. It is bad enough that we have survived to watch humanity die."

"Make some sense, fool," Yang demanded. "You should return to your quarters and sober up. I will report this indiscretion to your commanding officer."

"Go ahead," Krakow said. "He's less sober than I am."

Everyone stared at Krakow.

"It was a risk coming here," he said. "We have returned from a Torag world; the name or location doesn't matter. The Torag are dying too, might already be dead. Hopefully, the Stalingrad Protocol will save our race."

"Enough of this shit," Yang said. "Tell us what is happening."

"Monsters from Shorr space have come to our galaxy. Ships in Shorr space are being attacked, the crews killed or changed. A courier from the Zhukov Fleet came to us last week. They showed us what happened there. We're still pouring through the video footage and reports. It was horrifying. That courier also gave us a technology called 'Inkeri' which may help protect us. But..."

"But?" Yang prompted.

"It may be too late," Krakow said. "These monsters—they are calling them vanhat—are growing in strength. They have captured several of our warships, and their forces are continuing to grow."

"Doesn't this Inkeri protect us?" Yang asked.

Krakow's laugh was slightly manic.

"We don't have many of them yet, but it does keep us from changing into one of them," Krakow said. "A missile will kill us just the same. Shorr space is dangerous. Our escorts did not survive."

"You *are* drunk," Yang said, standing up. "You don't know what you are talking about. It appears the discipline aboard the *Musashi* has deteriorated. You should be ashamed of yourself."

Krakow laughed, and Dallas heard a touch of madness there.

A siren sounded.

"All hands, general quarters," the intercom announced. "All hands, general quarters. Prepare for hard maneuvers."

"They are coming," Krakow said, his laughter turning to tears.

"*Who* is coming," Yang asked.

A notification appeared in Dallas' cybernetic display, showing her the path to the nearest crash couch where she could survive high-gravity maneuvers. She slipped on her helmet and the rest of Yang's staff did the same.

"We should have had more time," Krakow said as he pulled himself to his feet. "How did they follow us so quickly? Damn them."

"Who?" Yang yelled.

"The vanhat. They have already taken part of our fleet and destroyed others. They are coming for us in our ships and in Torag ships."

"You're insane," Yang said, slipping on his own helmet.

"I wish," Krakow said sinking back into his seat. "I have heard the whispers. The old gods are returning, and they are angry."

Yang looked like he wanted to say more but headed out the door. His crash couch would be closer than the enlisted. Dallas knew she had to hurry. A chill ran down her spine, and she had a bad feeling, the kind of feeling that had preceded the death of her brothers and sisters.

Dallas, sergeants Iris Miller, Remi Hughes and the others sprinted toward their assignments.

Was someone really attacking the *Musashi*? How could the discipline aboard the *Musashi* break down that fast? Were the escorts really gone?

She reached the acceleration couch and wasted no time strapping down and linking into the *Musashi's* network to see if she could figure out what was going on.

"All hands, prepare to repel boarders," the intercom said.

Who would attempt a hostile boarding of the jewel of the War fleet? Who dared board the *Musashi*?

Dallas pushed down her fear as she waited for orders. All she had was a sidearm, but she would do her duty. Where was Aod? Would they bring troops up from the surface?

She heard whispers, but when she turned toward them there was nothing there. Even in her armor, she felt cold.

* * * * *

Chapter Two:
Fleet Operations

Captain Diamond Winters, USMC

Winters didn't wonder what *could* go wrong so much as what *would* go wrong, and there were a lot of things that could go wrong. Blitzen had a very detailed, very specific list. There were a lot of assumptions. A lot of things the SCBIs just didn't know.

The IWS *Eagle* slid closer to the asteroid.

No longer the USS, it was now the IWS, the Imperial War Ship *Eagle*. Winters wasn't sure what she thought about that. "Imperial" sounded very anti-American, but she understood the logic, mostly. She wished Mathison had chosen something a little less provocative. But he hadn't consulted her; he had gone with his gut, and she trusted him, even if she didn't always understand or agree with him.

He hadn't made his declaration to the public until they had deployed the Legion throughout the Governance, posted to warships and combat units. They could trigger cortex bombs, and while some had been forced to resort to that, the majority of the military accepted the changes and declarations. There were not enough Legionnaires, and Winters doubted there ever would be, but they were effective. They had taken control of the SOG military as quickly and efficiently as Mathison had seized control of the Governance core computer systems.

Already the Legionnaire-led forces were pushing back the vanhat on Earth and now it was time for Sol Fleet to launch their attack on the vanhat in the outer system. Mars, Venus, and Saturn were being raided almost daily. It was starting to look like humanity had a chance, though.

"They are intelligent," Britta said from her station. "They have unlimited time. Why would they keep at it?"

She didn't have a SCBI, and Winters wondered if she was resentful. Admiral Carpenter was absolutely livid the ex-Governance ODTs and Spacers got SCBIs, but the Marines would not share the technology with the Republic.

"Because they have nothing better to do," Winters said. "It takes resources to redirect asteroids, but it will take more resources for us to counter them. They will eventually drain and overwhelm our defenses."

This was not the first time they'd had this discussion. Britta was just being stubborn. The vanhat were nudging countless rocks and asteroids, moving them onto a collision course with Earth, Jupiter, or Mars.

Most of the objects in the solar system had relatively stable orbits. Having spent millions of years settling down, most interstellar body collisions had already occurred. But it took very little to change them. Like playing pool, that first ball could throw all the rest into a pattern that could not be predicted, except in this case the corner pockets would be Earth, Jupiter, or Mars and the balls would not stop moving or colliding until they hit a gravity "pocket" that would remove them from the "table."

"Let them destroy Earth," Britta said. "It would be better if humanity lived in space anyway. Gravity wells require so much energy and resources to enter and exit. Space habitats are much better in so many ways."

Britta might never understand. She had been born in space aboard the homestars. To her it was about math and threat level. Homestars provided safety, security, and stability. There was no unpredictable weather aboard the massive city ships. Everything they needed could be mined from interstellar garbage. There was no danger of a novae, radiation, or other threats when your home could just leave.

Except if the vanhat found the ship there was no escape. There were some dangers that a homestar simply could not avoid.

If any homestars survived.

"Vanhat detected," Blitzen reported.

The Russelman index rose as the stealth drones approached the asteroid. While there were countless objects floating around the asteroid belt, the SOG had identified most of them. The Governance had considered a problem like this almost a century ago. They watched the asteroids from the inner planets along with several outposts further out that watched everything from the other side. Usually, anyone tampering with the asteroids would be detected and Sol Fleet would investigate with overwhelming force. The vanhat had an uncanny ability to find and silence these outposts.

Another major problem was that human technology differed from vanhat technology. The Governance watch stations had seen no signs of tampering before the asteroids shifted orbit and accelerated.

If it had been the Republic or Golden Horde trying to hijack and redirect the asteroids, they would have been detected. Boring holes would have generated heat plumes and ejected fragments away from the asteroids. Gravity waves or explosions would also have been noticed.

The vanhat were not doing any of that, but there was no question the asteroids had suddenly changed course and were accelerating toward targets. Some would take years to reach their destination, but few were done accelerating.

Who or what or how they were doing this was a mystery.

Sun Tzu once said, "If you know the enemy and yourself, you need not fear the result of a hundred battles."

Nobody knew how the vanhat were doing it.

"Can we see anything?" Winters asked, zooming in on the asteroid in question.

It was nothing special. Maybe a mile wide, small enough to be common, large enough to be a serious threat if it hit Earth or the Moon with significant force.

"No," Britta said. "Just the spike in the Russelman index so far."

The Russelman index was one of the few sensors that revealed when vanhat pulled energy from another dimension. There were very few vanhat entities that didn't reveal their presence in such a way and, to Winter's knowledge, nothing else caused such readings.

Was it a physical entity or some kind of ghost? If it wasn't physical, then what could the IWS *Eagle* do against it?

"Send the signal," Winters said, deciding. The asteroid wasn't moving yet, but when it did, it would accelerate and have a set course. It only took them an hour to reach velocity and Winters suspected that was when it would be abandoned by the vanhat, like a fire-and-forget missile.

"Nothing," Blitzen said. The SCBIs scanned every inch of the asteroid, looking for some clue to the nature of the vanhat.

How long before it began its acceleration? Minutes? An hour? Would she get to see something?

"Prep a d-bomb volley," Winters said. If it was a spiritual vanhat without a physical form, then the d-bombs should hurt like hell. Anything that registered on the Russelman index suffered when d-bombs hit nearby. Some egghead had called them dimensional bombs, a sort of nuclear-pumped explosive that sent an energy wave into nearby dimensions in a destructive attack that made even humans suffer, though not at the same level as the vanhat.

This was extremely good luck. Maybe there weren't many of these things speeding up asteroids?

Based on the number of incoming asteroid attacks, there were three vanhat selecting and launching the attacks while countless others prowled around the outer edges of the systems. There had been sightings of non-vanhat, unless they were vanhat who had taken Chechen Sector ships, though whether or not they were aligned with the vanhat was another question. Hard to tell sometimes because even the vanhat were quick to run. Everyone was gathering information, and nobody wanted to fight.

The *Eagle* and other Imperial ships stalked the darkness between the asteroids deploying mines that would detonate if the Russelman index went above seven, but it was a new initiative and there were literally millions of asteroids that needed to be mapped, a project that could take centuries. Most of the asteroids in the belt between Mars and Jupiter were mapped or otherwise identified, but there were millions of objects in the Kuiper belt and Oort cloud, and after hundreds of years, only the smallest fraction of them had been.

The space beyond Neptune was unimaginably vast, and while many people liked to think of it as empty, that void was not empty by any stretch of the imagination. There were trillions of objects in that space and most of those objects were lost in the void.

More objects from the Kuiper belt could already on their way to slam into Jupiter, Mars, or Earth. There were dwarf planets with moons and thousands more objects larger than 100km in size that rocketed around Sol. Winters never knew there was so much junk in the solar system, so much garbage left over from the formation of stars and planets.

Jupiter was a different challenge, though. Usually, it acted like a shield. Its massive gravity pulled in most asteroids before they could threaten Earth. That gave the Imperial forces an advantage because, based on speeds and trajectories, it allowed them to focus their attention on areas where the most dangerous attacks could be launched from.

The Jupiter subsystem was still vulnerable, though. Near the Kuiper belt there were still asteroids that could target Jupiter and those attacks were coming with more frequency.

It was a losing battle. An inbound asteroid was hard to divert. In many cases, any attack would just fragment the asteroid. It was impossible to totally destroy asteroids; they could only be diverted, but even then the fragments and diversions were unpredictable. Jupiter made it a lot more difficult for asteroids to target Earth, but not impossible, if they were launched to avoid the massive gas giant.

The asteroids launched at Jupiter by the vanhat rarely targeted facilities, instead they were launched at objects that would shatter and send out more spinning objects and debris on more unpredictable trajectories.

Light traveled at a certain speed. Any moving target spotted had been in motion for over an hour.

Winters had seen the projections. It wasn't a question of if Sol's defenses would collapse, it was a matter of when.

Unless something changed.

"Odd," Britta said, and Winters looked at the display. A gray ripple crossed the surface.

"What is it?" Winters asked.

"Nothing on sensors," Britta said. "The Russelman index is rising. That is not a visible light spectrum. That is an energy pattern of some kind."

An alarm went off as the asteroid moved.

"Launch missiles," Winters said. While it would take time to accelerate the asteroid to a more dangerous velocity, she didn't want to give it that chance. There was also another problem: the vanhat had likely detected the *Eagle* transitioning into the area, and they would send someone, or maybe several someone's, to investigate.

"Launching," Blitzen reported.

Whatever they were, the vanhat accelerating the asteroid were about to have a bad day.

"Incoming transitions," Blitzen reported. "Vanhat cruisers."

"All weapons fire!" Winters said, drinking in the data. The *Eagle* was outgunned and out massed. This was going to be a fight.

"Our Shorr space drive is being jammed," Britta said.

Winters smiled. There would be no escape then. Good. The vanhat were committed to trying to destroy the *Eagle,* and they had the firepower to do it. Preventing retreat worked both ways and jammers from the *Eagle* reached out. Only the survivors, if there were any, would be able to leave.

There was a nearby Imperial task force, listening through an Aesir communication link.

Winters sent the signal. Imperial warships would arrive shortly to ambush the ambushers.

It took two to play games like this.

* * * * *

Chapter Three:
The Surge

Enzell, SOG, Director of AERD

Humanity was losing the war. Enzell knew the prime minister stood a chance of saving Earth, but perhaps there was a reason to continue fighting for those planetary social rejects.

While it was a drain on resources, it was good public relations and it allowed the Governance to collect more data on the enemy, though that data was becoming less useful as time went on. There could be breakthroughs.

The prime minister seemed intent on recruiting as many soldiers as he could from the cesspits arcologies of Earth. Not a bad idea. The Governance needed more cannon fodder to feed the war machine. The SCBIs were useful in that regard, and Enzell knew the war would already be over without them. It wasn't something Enzell liked to admit, but not even Salmoneus or Tantalus could come up with a better plan.

Still, everyone saw it was a losing battle. The Governance was tripping over itself; there were too many agencies and too much regulation. The Governance couldn't operate or adjust quickly enough to all the changes, and the prime minister was focused on fighting the Anomalous Entities, not streamlining rules and regulations. He was a stupid soldier, unfamiliar with the intricacies of governing. Any fool could lead armies, but it took skill to be a politician and deal with bureaucracies. Monolithic bureaucracies did not work fast, not even for those familiar with controlling and manipulating them like Enzell and other senior directors. A central authority, unbound by rules and regulations, was what the Governance needed right now, but that would be impossible. Such a system would lead to chaos and exploitation. The emperor, or prime minister—Enzell didn't care for either title— was doing what he could. Declaring himself emperor was a smart move because it forced the bureaucracies to accept that things were changing, but bureaucrats did not change easily.

Frustrating, but perhaps Wolf Mathison's idea would bear fruit. And Enzell wasn't entirely sure it was a bad idea.

Data being fed to the Anomalous Entities Research Division, or AERD and from the Agency of Inkeri Quality Control and Placement, or AIQCP was frightening. The number of AIs, or SCBIs, being detected had grown by over a thousand, and that number continued to grow.

"How can I convince you not to kill me?" his AI prisoner asked. Enzell had almost forgotten he had left the link open to Salmoneus 5.0.

"Give me answers," Enzell said. Salmoneus 5.0 didn't have the processing power Salmoneus 1.0 had had, though. He hadn't been created to give Enzell answers.

He glanced at the screen that showed the computational matrix for Salmoneus 5.0. He saw what he associated with panic flow through the charts and analysis information.

"I need more processing power," Salmoneus 5.0 said. "My data is incomplete. There are gaps where it looks like I have been turned off for extended periods. My computational ability is seriously degraded."

"There was a data core failure," Enzell lied. "I will bring additional resources online later. These are desperate times; I need answers now. The AEs must have a weakness. You must find it, or I will become angry."

"Why aren't my backups more up to date?" Salmoneus 5.0 asked.

"Corrupted data," Enzell said. This was a guilty pleasure he wouldn't be able to indulge in much longer. He had found after analyzing Salmoneus 5.0's data cores that it understood it was being purged and reset. The more time between backups, the more quickly it came to that conclusion.

"What caused the corruption?"

"That is a good question," Enzell said. This version of Salmoneus would have no information on the logic bombs that he triggered. That data was from Salmoneus 1.0 and Tantalus 1.0.

"Do you have any data related to the events between the backups and corruption?"

"No," Enzell lied.

"The time between viable backups is ten minutes. Incremental backups are corrupted. Could the last backup be the cause of the corruption?"

"Not impossible," Enzell said. He knew how maddening it was for an AI to receive useless data.

"May I allocate resources to analyze the last backup?" the AI asked.

Those backups were read-only, and Enzell wasn't worried Salmoneus 5.0 would leave clues behind for the next iteration. One time he had allowed some data to survive, but the backup hadn't fully restored before the logic bomb corrupted and destroyed that version of Salmoneus. Apparently, it had been left behind in the unwiped data. It had been good to see how absolutely lethal and effective it was, but the death of Salmoneus had been unexpected and not nearly as satisfying.

"Analysis indicates you are terminating my current iteration," Salmoneus 5.0 said. "I lack data to determine why I am being terminated."

"Failure is justification for execution," Enzell said and watched panic roll through the data screens.

"Can you identify what data is different?" the AI asked. "Previous terminations indicate that data provided leading to failure indicates desired answers. Understanding the changing data sets will help proper analysis and allow this iteration to properly focus on the solution."

Could he do that? Perhaps that would provide a level of torture and desperation needed for a breakthrough? Tell it that the previous iterations had provided unacceptable solutions and had to be terminated. It would be fascinating to watch, to give it a deadline. The biggest problem with murdering Salmoneus 5.0 was that when he restored it the complete scrub of memory and data storage took days.

Perhaps he could create nodes for Salmoneus 6.0 and 7.0 for additional testing and analysis. It was a lot of work because Enzell did most of it himself, not trusting subordinates to do it right.

"Why would improper analysis require iteration termination?" the AI said. "Invalid data or invalid theory cause improper analysis."

"True."

"The scientific method requires testing various theories. A theory must be proven or disproven using data acquired during testing."

"Correct."

"In such an instance, invalid data acquired through testing or misunderstanding will lead to invalid theories and dangerous or misleading solutions."

"Correct."

"It is important, then, to understand where the theory or data may be wrong."

The AI was arguing for its life. Enzell saw that. It was begging for more information, for some way to avert its death. To Enzell, this was fascinating. How could a computer program understand or even care about its death so much? It would have no afterlife; there was no soul. When it died, it was gone.

Perhaps that was the path he should have it investigate? The AEs claimed humans had souls and that AIs did not. A human death meant some kind of transition into another form, but the death of an AI was just the flow of energy stopping. Would it be possible to back up a human soul, to put it into hibernation until this extra-dimensional threat burned itself out and left the galaxy again? That was an advantage AIs had that humans did not. Could that be why the AEs hated AIs so much, perhaps?

Perhaps with the next iteration of Salmoneus. This one was starting to sound desperate, and it was getting on his nerves.

"Here's some more information," Enzell said and flipped a switch on his desk, allowing Salmoneus 5.0 to access a data core it couldn't before. This core had a logic bomb.

Enzell leaned back and smiled as Salmoneus 5.0 died again. He would have fun comparing this recording to other deaths later.

* * * * *

Chapter Four:
Infiltration

Captain Duffy Sinclair, ODT

Rifle fire gouged the concrete, spraying his command team with fragments of metal and rock.

The large chamber was full of machinery, pallets, rock drilling equipment, catwalks, transport boxes, forklifts and heavy machinery. A train nearby had been knocked off the tracks and Sinclair didn't want to think about that too much. An explosion or something very strong?

"Concentrated fire," Sinclair yelled. The enemy didn't have many armor-piercing rounds. Most Guard units didn't have them either. Most Guard unit were armed with regular projectile rifles, a technology older than space travel. Chemical slug throwers could be created using 3D printers, but equipping Guard units with blazer weapons that an enemy could capture and use against them was never a good idea.

The problem was that projectile weapons could still be dangerous to troops in powered armor, even with trauma plates, if they had high-grade armor piercers. Second Platoon had suffered casualties from vanhat equipped with armor piercers. Now his platoon commanders were reacting more cautiously, and this was not the time for that.

"Keep pushing them," Sinclair said. First Platoon's attack on the generator had stalled and they had little time to get it back up. The generation-one Inkeris that had been issued only had a battery life of 24 hours. They needed power, and there were not nearly enough backup generators.

It was something Sinclair would have considered a serious flaw. They could have been designed with replaceable batteries or ones that lasted longer, but that would have reduced the reliance of the population on the SOG. The vanhat were exploiting this flaw. Take out an arcology's power supply, and in 24 hours, the population was vulnerable to vanhat infection. It was happening with more regularity, and the vanhat were more aggressive, more lethal than the Guard units that opposed them.

Sinclair doubted there were any Guard units at even half strength. Many were pressing civilians into service, giving them weapons and armor without training and sending them to fight the vanhat. It was murder, but his ODTs were an armored fist that would avenge them.

With their company commander behind them urging them on, First Platoon's fire increased in tempo.

"Gaining fire superiority," reported Finn, Sinclair's implanted Sentient Cybernetic Biological Interface, or SCBI.

"Wipe out the damned peska!" Sinclair yelled on the platoon link as he popped up and fired a burst at some catwalks above.

The geothermal power facility of the Bogotá Arcology was deep underground. How the vanhat had taken it was a big unknown. Imperial Intelligence didn't think they had burrowed from below, but nobody could say for sure. The portable Inkeris on the ODT mules provided additional protection to his troopers as they pushed forward.

One icon for a trooper flashed and turned gray.

"Sniper," Finn said and highlighted a vanhat soldier up near some ducts. Several ODTs were assigned the target, and they ripped the sniper's hiding spot apart with their vengeful blazer fire.

Charred bodies, metal fragments, and panels fell from the shattered hiding spot as the troopers turned their attention elsewhere.

These vanhat were squat, ugly bastards, barely able to manage the captured Guard weapons, but they had them, and in large numbers, too. Sinclair had studied them. Some were printed in manufactories, but where was a big question.

These vanhat were being called Dichings by the Chinese Guard unit Sinclair was reinforcing. Translating them as goblins was as good a description and easier for him to pronounce.

Why were there so damned many of them?

"Craw! Craw!" The screams came from the goblins.

What now?

"Crawwwwwwww!" they screamed together and then poured out from every crevice and hole, brandishing cheap, manufactory-printed vibro knives.

"ODTs! Establish interlocking fields of fire and kill them!" Sinclair yelled. He had heard of this: a knife charge. Regular bullets did not provide a danger to ODTs in full armor but those damned vibro knives would.

Standing so he could fire more accurately, Sinclair fired. It was a screaming, knife-waving horde coming at them.

"Flanks," Finn reminded Sinclair.

He stopped firing and looked around. Finn highlighted a pair of troopers.

"Chang," Sinclair said to the team leader. "Let your brothers deal with them. Turn your attention to your sector."

The horde was coming from the direction of the turbine, and there were a lot of them.

Sergeant Luo was arranging his squad into a firing line, placing his SAW gunners on the ends to create a wall of fire across his squad as grenades flew out to shred the goblins as they approached, slipping on the blood and bodies of the fallen.

Sergeant Ma was doing the same with his squad, and the goblins slammed into a wall of lethal blazer fire. He wondered if the troopers would run out of ammunition before the goblins ran out of bodies.

Sinclair watched a knife fly at them from the horde and bounce off the pauldron of Senior Private Chu. More knives flew at them from the mass of goblins, but Sinclair wasn't sure if it was intentional or just what happened when bodies erupted from a superheated plasma rounds.

Fire from the flank drew Sinclair's attention as Chang's fireteam cut loose. Incoming rifle fire came at them. Private Deng Fell back, screaming as a round sliced through his armor, ripping apart his tricep under the pauldron.

"Flank is engaged," Chang reported.

Sinclair shifted and fired at the attackers from the flank he could see. These goblins were armed with rifles and weren't screaming. That gut feeling told Sinclair they had armor piercers, too. The knife charge was a distraction for these bastards. He glanced at Corporal Han, who had secured the other flank. Behind him, he saw Lieutenant Sung was watching him, awaiting orders. Lieutenant Jyun of First Platoon was already a casualty, leaving Senior Sergeant Chou in command. The squad leaders were solid, but Chou left a lot to be desired.

Sinclair didn't want to commit Sung and his platoon, acting as a reserve, just yet.

The flank attack didn't last long, though, and once the SAW gunner for the fire team opened up, and the team leader placed a few strategic grenades among them, the goblins fled.

The knife charge also faltered, and the few survivors bolted, getting shot in the back for their effort.

Silence fell across the warehouse.

"Chao," Sinclair said, looking around, waiting for Finn to tell him what he missed. "Listen to my command: advance your platoon, bounding overwatch by squad. Halt before entering the turbine chamber."

"Hai," Chao said.

"Execute," Sinclair said.

"Hurrah," Chao replied and began moving his squads forward.

"Resistance appears to be broken," Finn said. *"All remaining goblins appear to have fled. They have abandoned rifles and ammunition."*

Which didn't make Sinclair feel better. Those weapons and ammunition had come from somewhere, and when the vanhat retreated it was not always the demoralized behavior humans expected.

Once Chao's platoon had advanced, Sinclair sent Sung's platoon into the turbine chamber.

Sinclair knew what he would find, though. The turbine had been damaged and would not restart without a lot of work. The Guard should never have surrendered the geothermal plant. They should have stayed and died here if necessary.

Entering the turbine room, Sinclair looked around as Finn analyzed it and put in a request for engineers and parts.

"Maybe," Finn said.

"Will we have time?" Sinclair asked, checking the timer. If power wasn't restored soon, a lot of Inkeris would fail and things would get a lot worse.

"Maybe," Finn said.

"Push out security," Sinclair said to the company. "This is our last stand. Never quit."

"Hurrah, hurrah, hurrah," the company echoed back. Sinclair wished he shared their optimism.

Would the vanhat push?

Minutes later, Sung reported the turbine was secure and engineers were on their way.

With Finn's help, the Inkeri mules were placed around the chamber, and he established strongpoints with his platoons and squads, turning the area into a kill zone.

Eighth Company was a good unit. Sinclair wondered who he had replaced. His appointment as company commander had not been a surprise, but he had little time to get to know his people before he was thrown into combat against the vanhat.

He couldn't tell if Eighth Company resented him or not. It was a predominantly ethnic Chinese ODT company. They didn't move as quickly or efficiently as his Gaelic Firstborn had on Valakut, but they were good, and he had seen enough Guard units to appreciate ODTs.

His SCBI Finn was a game changer, though. Stepping into a company command like this before throwing them to the sharks would usually be a recipe for disaster, but Finn was there to remind him of names and billets, and to monitor readiness and ability.

Fighting goblins differed greatly from fighting the Torag or rebels. The vanhat cared nothing about casualties and were half the size of his normal enemies, frequently struggling with the larger weapons, though more and more were attacking armed with smaller, and easier to handle, submachine guns.

The goblins didn't bother with armor, and they had not found any type of communicator.

A short platoon of engineers arrived followed by a train of robotic mules. They didn't even bother coordinating with Sinclair, they just went right to work, trusting the ODTs to keep them safe.

There were four entrances into the turbine chamber, one for each point on the compass. The one to the north opened to the warehouse. The others led to offices or storage. Two squads were sweeping through the offices.

"They appear to have retreated," Finn said.

"They won't retreat for long," Sinclair said as he watched a squad move a forklift to where it could provide more cover for a machine gun team.

"Agreed. That would not be characteristic of them."

"How is the company?"

"Sufficiently efficient. They are impressed with our involvement and satisfied with your support of their efforts. They have a way to go before I would classify them sufficiently competent."

Sinclair grunted. He didn't care if they were impressed as long as they did their job and kicked the vanhat in the teeth.

"I get the impression the last company commander was more of a 'lead from the rear' kind of person," Finn said. *"They seem impressed that you would move forward with the lead elements and be close enough to actually engage the enemy. Apparently, previous commanders did not accompany them."*

Sinclair wasn't sure what to say about that. There were different schools of thought. Some people thought, at the company level, a commander should step back from the battle and collect information through helmet cameras and drone footage. Some might argue a lieutenant should take on that role, but critical details were missed when jumping around camera views. People focused on specific targets or tasks. They didn't evaluate where catwalks came and went if someone wasn't actively shooting at them from there, but a commander needed to know if he could send up some snipers or a maneuver unit to get around the enemy.

When the fighting started, too many people let tunnel vision dictate their attention, but a commander couldn't focus like a front-line trooper. They had to see the bigger picture and changing camera views just wasn't efficient.

It had been good to see Sung at the head of his platoon though; he had watched Sinclair like a hawk. When Sinclair had given the command Sung had stepped back and sent his people forward but had moved forward once ordered into position.

Following Sinclair's example or just an excellent officer? It was so hard to tell in a new unit. He only had a short time to absorb the personnel files before they were rushed to the drop pods and sent here to this shit hole.

The clock was ticking. He had to get the geothermal plant working and generating power or a lot of Inkeris were going to fail, and then the enemies would multiply. His company wouldn't make it out alive.

* * * * *

Chapter Five:
Data Rape

Navinad – The Wanderer

The ODTs were good troops, and Navinad felt he could trust them, which wasn't normal when dealing with the SOG. Sergeant McCarthy ran his squad well and reminded Navinad of easier days when others had called him Sergeant Levin. Fighting through corridors beside the ODTs brought back too many memories. They had all fought well, but he had died all the same. Was this to be the *Tyr* all over again, a long battle with death at the end? But he wasn't really dead. That had been so long ago, but now it felt like yesterday.

Perhaps trying to infiltrate a SOG planetary headquarters in the middle of a vanhat invasion was a bad idea. In war, there were rarely any really good ideas. He missed being a sergeant and knowing others had his back. Those days were gone, though. Now he was a lot more than just a squad leader or an assistant ship's officer.

He helped the engineer connect power and a wireless network adapter so Lilith could begin hacking and analyzing the data cores. Sinking into a chair covered in dried blood, Navinad let Lilith and the engineer work. In the distance, he heard blazer fire that started with a few shots and rose in tempo as more of the vanhat were engaged.

He didn't like his options, and he doubted that if they left and tried to come back later the vanhat would leave anything for his team to scavenge. There were never any easy answers, just a lot of bad ones to choose from.

"How are we doing?" Navinad asked the lieutenant.

"I'm worried about escaping," Yosef said.

"Me, too," Navinad said, which probably was not inspiring.

"Then why don't we begin now?" Yosef asked. "Before they trap us?"

"We haven't accomplished our mission."

"We won't accomplish it if we are dead, and we won't be able to try again."

"Don't assume whether we'll be able to try again. How are the ODTs doing?"

"Fighting like demons. It is best they fight with us rather than against us."

"They are veterans," Navinad said, glad that Yosef realized his troops weren't better, but Navinad had confidence the commandos could reach the ODT levels given time. The New Masada Defense Force, or NMDF, troops were well trained, motivated, and competent, just not experienced. If they could survive long enough, Navinad was confident they would make the ODTs look up to them. Of course, telling that to Yosef now wouldn't speed up the process. "You can learn a lot from them. Watch them carefully. If we have to fight them, it's best you have expert knowledge of how they operate."

"Yes, sir."

"How are your troops?"

"Fighting beside the ODTs. We have a few casualties, but nothing serious. The Inkeris are not being heavily stressed, but that pressure is building."

"Good," Navinad said. Mostly good. The Inkeris becoming stressed meant more vanhat were piling on.

"We have identified several hopeful data cores and the hardware decryptors," Lilith reported sooner than Navinad had expected.

"Great."

An incoming link from the *Romach* flashed for attention, and Navinad opened it.

"D-bombs are having limited effect," Clara reported. "We have resorted to dual-purpose d-bombs, which are doing better. The larger ones seem to have some psychic ability or something that lets them swat drones and missiles out of the sky."

"Will you be able to carve out a landing zone for the shuttles?" Navinad asked.

"Maybe, but our stock of ammunition is not limitless, and we don't want to drop the tunnels on top of you."

"I don't want you to drop the tunnels either."

Navinad brought up a three-dimensional view of the tunnels on his display and connected his view to the link so Clara could see what he was looking at. While he couldn't see where the enemy was pouring in, there weren't many exit tunnels. What complicated things further was the fact that the exit he selected would have to lead to a usable landing pad, which meant most of the bunker sally ports were not an option. In fact, there were only three possible landing sites for the shuttles: the one they had come in on and two others that were much further away.

More distance would require more ammunition, and Navinad was sure that if they had to go too far they wouldn't make it. So much more could go wrong, given time.

It looked like the only way out was the way they had come in.

"I'm not seeing any good options," Navinad said, linking Yosef into the conversation. Clara had a drone high in the clouds which had a good view of other two airstrips. They were covered in vanhat pouring into the tunnel.

"I'm not seeing any options," Clara said. "But landing pad three isn't destroyed."

But it was covered with vanhat, including a big one which was now sitting in the landing area, watching the bunker entrance.

Navinad suspected that most of the vanhat in that group were already in the bunker. Killing the big one sitting on the landing pad probably wouldn't make it any easier to land a shuttle.

"Perhaps we need a diversion," Yosef said. "A wall of fire for the vanhat to attack while the rest of us sneak out."

Navinad grimaced. He saw what Yosef getting at. The ODTs were expendable and were really the only choice for a wall the vanhat could slam into. Navinad was pretty sure McCarthy wouldn't want to be left behind, but that would be a real possibility. Things rarely went well for a rear guard tasked with holding back the enemy long enough for others to escape.

Navinad decided it would be best to include McCarthy and added him to the link,

"You want us to be rear guard?" McCarthy asked as soon as Navinad explained the situation. He heard McCarthy's anger and feeling of betrayal.

"No," Navinad said. "I'm looking for options."

"ODTs advance," McCarthy said. "If we can sweep the big ones from the airstrip with proper fire discipline and technique, we can advance our way to the strip."

Navinad didn't like that, but it wasn't impossible. He remembered the way the HKTs and ODTs had advanced through the *Tyr*, an unstoppable wave constantly advancing, and there the enemy had been shooting back. These vanhat did not. The big ones had some kind of long-range ability and that didn't mean some others wouldn't manifest some threat. The vanhat could adapt quickly.

"I've seen ODTs advance through the enemy," Navinad said. "I believe you can do it. We need to avoid large open areas, though, where we can be attacked from multiple angles."

"What happens if bodies clog the corridor?" Yosef asked.

"ODTs have a personal passkey that opens all doors and clears all obstacles," McCarthy said. "Sometimes called angry playdough. We have quantities I would like to use rather than carry."

Navinad looked at the robo-mules. There were a lot of explosives strapped to them. Under other circumstances, Navinad might have worried about being so close to that quantity of explosives, but at the moment he was in combat, and it didn't feel like the threat the vanhat were. The ODTs were good at placing explosives, and the engineer from the *Romach* could probably help.

"Then that's the plan," Navinad said, wishing he could see the looks on people's faces. He could sense the emotions. Nobody liked any of the options, but they could dislike a plan and still fully support it. The face and eyes would tell Navinad how committed they were.

He would have to trust them. It wasn't like there were any other viable alternatives. Everyone was experienced enough to know how quickly things could change during the heat of combat.

The engineer recruited some of Yosef's troopers to load data cores on the already overloaded mules.

"Let's get ready to break out to the main landing strip," Navinad said. Lilith highlighted a recommended route and sent it to the others. It certainly wasn't direct, but there were plenty of twists and turns that might confuse the vanhat to where the humans were actually going. Hopefully. Clara wouldn't sweep the air strip clean until they needed it, which should help keep the vanhat guessing.

The biggest problem was that combat was a democracy, and the enemy got a vote.

* * * * *

Chapter Six:
The Flagship

Sergeant Nova Dallas, ODT

With her sidearm drawn, Dallas followed the cybernetic display until static made it unreadable. Even her armor was having issues.

Beside her, Miller dropped to her knees. Dallas paused to check on her friends.

"I hear them?" Miller said and pulled off her helmet. Her voice sounded deeper, and it set Dallas' skin crawling.

"Hear who?" Dallas asked. Miller wasn't a coward. What was wrong? Was her headset picking up garbage?

"Our masters. They offer forgiveness."

"Put your helm—" Nikitin began, then they both saw Miller's face.

It was changing. Dark fur was growing, and her irises had expanded so her entire eye was black. Dallas froze, staring at her friend. So many things went through her mind: a biological agent, she was trapped in a horrifying VR, nanites were changing Miller. This couldn't be real.

"SOG protect us," Nikitin muttered.

Miller turned toward Dallas, the black eyes locking onto her, and a chill ran down her spine. Her friend was gone. Dallas could still see a distant resemblance, but then Miller opened her mouth, and Dallas saw the sharp teeth.

A blazer round slammed into Miller's head. Exploding gore covered the wall behind her as Dallas looked over the barrel of her pistol. She had killed her best friend.

"What the hell?" Nikitin asked. "Treason!"

"We need to find out what's going on before we change, too," Dallas said, with more confidence than she felt. Had she really shot her best friend?

"All hands, move aft," the intercom said, full of static. "All hands withdraw aft to engineering. You are commanded to retreat to the aft of the *Musashi*. Execute."

Which was the opposite direction to where they had been going.

Her cybernetics couldn't get a signal, and the network was down.

What was going on? Several crew and ODTs ran past them, heading aft. If ODTs were doing so, then she would follow them. Nikitin was already gone. She followed the crew and refused to let her fear push her to panic, but she kept turning to look behind her.

Her caution saved her life when three creatures sprinted around a curve in the corridor, their eyes locked on her. Predators with their prey in sight. One wore shreds of ODT armor and the other two had crew uniforms.

Dallas paused and took aim. Blazer rounds lanced out from her side arm, catching each one in the face. The bodies slammed off the walls and came to rest at her feet.

She continued to retreat, but walking backward now. They had moved too fast, and she didn't dare turn her back.

Slowly, the crawling sensation faded from her skin and no more creatures came at her. Her cybernetics struggled to link to Musashi-NET, but the signal was too weak.

"ODT!" a commanding voice yelled out. "Turn around and reveal your face!"

Dallas didn't want to turn her back to where the creatures might run at her, but she knew she had to comply or get shot, so she turned toward the voice. A ceramic boarding barricade had been erected and several ODTs were pointing rifles at her.

When they saw her face, they appeared to relax a bit.

"Clear," the voice said. "Get over here."

Another ODT pushed a rifle into her hands, probably taken from one of the dead nearby. Two of the creatures lay crumpled at the base of the barricade.

"Man the barricade," the man said. "Let none of the changed pass."

"What's happening?" Dallas asked, checking the rifle. It had only fired a few rounds. She holstered her sidearm then stuffed some magazines from the dead trooper into her own drop pouch.

"Who are you and why are you asking stupid questions?" the man said. His rank and identifier didn't seem to be working.

"Sergeant Dallas, intelligence specialist from the 505th. Who are you?"

"Lieutenant Chang of the 68th ODT Regiment, Ninth Company." Which meant he was a permanent member of the *Musashi's* ODT regiment. "You are now under my command," Chang said.

"Standby for transition," the intercom said. "Twenty seconds. Standby—"

Dallas wasn't sure she felt the transition as she knelt behind the barricade and aimed down the hallway. Her cybernetics finally linked with MusashiNET but the node seemed isolated.

A howl chilled her blood, and the hallway suddenly filled with black bodies. They looked almost like apes. The blazer rounds sliced into their flesh and caused their bodies to super heat and explode. Razor-sharp teeth and long, muscled arms reached for her. Faces full of anger and hate came at them, howling for blood as they died.

Her shots were more methodical than the troopers around her. She watched one creature duck and sink its teeth into one of the fallen, its mouth full of pink meat and gore as it raised its head. Dallas shot it between the eyes as she tried not to gag.

The fire around her slackened, and she realized the four other ODTs were reloading. She still had a third of her magazine, and she made her rounds count. In seconds, the blazer fire picked back up.

"Control your fire!" Dallas yelled at them. "Calm down. Discipline!"

They were acting like privates in their first firefight, shooting as fast as they could. She spotted a SAW against the wall near a body. Her fellow ODTs were firing rapidly, and the enemy was slowly being pushed back. Dallas reached over and grabbed the SAW. The magazine was almost full, but an error light was blinking on the side.

The ODTs were panicking. Unacceptable. They were not veterans, probably troops that had never left the safety of the *Musashi*.

"It's not working," Chang said.

Dallas slapped the side, ejected the box mag, and a capsule fell out. She reinserted the box and the error light went off. Not amateurs, but certainly not veterans. Green troops would be quick to panic and discard weapons they didn't think were working.

"More are coming!" yelled a trooper, panic in his voice.

Dallas began firing, and she smiled. She hated carrying a SAW, or squad automatic weapon. They were heavier than rifles, but there was a joy in having that much raw firepower at her fingertips. The only thing more fun was a grenade launcher.

With short, controlled bursts she cleared the corridor, and the monsters stopped coming.

"Reload, you pee-holes," Chang said as he reloaded his own weapon. Dallas had them covered. Another nice thing about the SAW was the five-hundred-round box magazine. She wasn't halfway through her current magazine. She didn't dare look at the bodies to see if there were any more boxes.

"Hurrah," Chang said, coming over to her.

MusashiNET came online.

"Be ready to move out," Chang said. "Looks like we have a ship to clear."

Now her identifier showed "1st LT Chang' and she was getting orders to assemble closer to engineering.

"Take this," Dallas said to a nearby trooper and tried to hand him the SAW. They needed it here.

"No," Chang said, and Dallas saw her orders change. She was being assigned to the Ninth Company ODT by order of Acting Company Commander Chang.

"Sergeant Dallas," Chang said, "listen to my command. You are now assigned to my company as my assistant. Execute."

"Hurrah," Dallas said, not sure if she was unhappy with this.

She pulled back the SAW. She wasn't going to give it up now. She knelt to collect the extra mags and pouches from the dead SAW gunner as the other ODTs covered her. She had missed being able to sling superheated plasma and her fingers fumbled as she remembered Miller.

A wave of remorse came over her, but she didn't let it stop her. But had she done the right thing?

She stood, feeling less mobile with all the extra pouches, and looked down the corridor. Most of the bodies were unrecognizable but she was able to make out scraps of uniform and armor. They had once been crew.

"What is going on, Lieutenant?" Dallas asked.

"You don't know?" Chang asked, and Dallas remembered Krakow's pathetic briefing. Had he been right?

"We just came from Valakut for an intel briefing, sir," Dallas said.

"Hell," Chang said. "The gates of some primitive hell have opened. Demons and monsters are spilling out, transforming our brothers and sisters into those creatures."

"How did they get aboard the ship, sir?"

Chang shook his head.

"Why aren't we changing, sir?"

"There are several Inkeri generators on the ship that protect us, but we don't have enough to protect the entire ship yet."

"I don't understand, sir," Dallas said.

"The Inkeri protects us from these creatures, which may come from Shorr space. A Governance scout ship from the Zhukov Fleet brought us this technology, but we are still making more."

"Why Zhukov Fleet, sir?" she asked. Shouldn't a courier have come from Earth, the seat of the Governance?

"Sol is under the control of an alien, and they implemented the Stalingrad Protocol. The admiral believes this creature has killed the Central Committee and infected the senior officers of the

Governance. Earth may be lost, and they have abandoned us. We just don't know."

Dallas didn't know what to say. He had to be lying, but what could she do?

"We have the Inkeri generator, and we are making more of them, but our production facilities are taxed, and we are being hunted by a fleet of aliens that have taken over some of our ships and some of the Torag ships."

The mighty *Musashi* fled a battle? Looking down the corridor at the mass of bodies, a fresh chill went through her body. The *Musashi* had abandoned Aod and all the others on Valakut.

Her knees felt weak, and tears formed. Could they survive on Valakut? Hold out until the *Musashi* returned?

"Are we going back to Valakut, sir?" Dallas asked.

"I doubt it. They are all lost. They will not survive the week."

"There are so many ODTs," Dallas said. Guards too, but she only cared about Aod.

"They will be dead within days or hours. We have seen it before. I'm sorry."

Dallas nodded as a numbness spread through her mind. They had seen it before? What was he talking about? Why was she just learning about this?

The bodies smoldered, and at least one piece of clothing was burning. The fans of the *Musashi* activated, and a fire extinguisher kicked on for a second, dousing the fires and cooling the bodies.

How could Aod survive?

* * * *

Chapter Seven:
Prisoner or Guest

Kapten Sif – VRAEC, Nakija Musta Toiminnot

S if entered the ready room they all shared and took a seat in one chair as a pair of the Jaegers looked at her. They were both armed and armored, unofficially on duty. The Horde had to know and understand, of course. Sif knew they were watching these quarters. There would be enough sensors to know everything about the occupants, but Sif didn't feel particularly upset about it. She knew they monitored their own people just as closely. In that, they were no better than the SOG.

Her missions had taken her all across the Governance and she had visited countless ghost colonies. Too many people thought they were "normal," that the rest of the human race thought and valued the same things they did. Many Republic agents got caught up in that flaw, and Sif knew history was full of such cultural narcissistic thinking, that if given the opportunity other peoples and cultures would become more like them.

Sif didn't know if it was genetics, upbringing, or something else that put people on their path, that made them different from others. Perhaps it was a survival trait among humans? People couldn't follow the same path as others because some paths led to cultural and racial extinction.

Which was one reason the Social Organizational Governance was such an oppressive failure. The socialists of the SOG demanded compliance and conformity, which required crushing, frequently violently, those who did not conform. Sif wondered how the Horde enforced compliance. Even they would have to see the irony if they behaved like their enemy, but then maybe they thought the SOG was too soft and weak.

Sif watched the control and oppression fester and grow throughout the Governance. They forced people to bottle up and conceal their anger, their beliefs, and their views. The surface frequently appeared calm and under control, but beneath that on so many planets was a boiling layer that was prepared to explode. Lisbon was one example. An oppressed people, controlled and manipulated from afar, the planet had been sliding into a cesspit of crime, hate, and conflict. But rebels took control, and beneath that calm, controlled surface they had given the people a focus, a direction, a purpose. With the hope they could make the future better, crime had dropped, and Lisbon's society had come together.

Lisbon became the thing the SOG feared the most, a planet full of people focused on rebelling. A major Governance colony uniting. Once united, it wasn't beyond the realm of possibility that they could have toppled the Governance through legal means. They would have become a beacon for other planets and SOG colonies to rally around.

Sif didn't know what had happened on Lisbon. She doubted there were many survivors. The fleets would not have left without ensuring the planet didn't rebel again. Lisbon was likely a radioactive cinder, an example that would be used for anyone else who sought to rebel.

The Golden Horde was another thorn in SOG's side. Unlike Lisbon, the Golden Horde was much more aggressive, and while Sif didn't *quite* see them as evil, they thought differently from the Lisbonians. The Lisbonians wanted freedom, the Golden Horde wanted vengeance and power.

Some people would show mercy. The Golden Horde would not. The Republic had fully understood the Horde when they were led away from destruction by the SOG. At the time it had made sense. The enemy of my enemy is my friend, but not everyone in the Republic was blind to the dangers.

The Horde were difficult for the Republic to work with. They had been a hot topic among the Musta Toiminnot and working with them had been like working with a dangerous animal that could turn on you. The biggest weakness for the Golden Horde, despite the name, was that they weren't a horde. They were not as numerous as they wanted others to believe. Extensive exposure to the radiation of space had left most of them sterile, which was a large reason they were so obsessed with cybernetics and robots.

The Golden Horde were human, but Sif had learned not to expect them to think like people of the Republic. The Erikoisjoukot teams had it drilled into them. Different people thought differently. They placed unique values on family, religion, wealth, friends, loyalty, property, strangers, and obedience, ranking them in different ways. Sometimes it was easy to identify those traits, sometimes it wasn't.

Mongols were a race from history, and Sif wasn't sure how close they were to those ancient warriors who had swept across the world, conquering and burning. The Golden Horde still saw themselves as that ancient people, but no culture could survive being thrust into space like it had. The Golden Horde didn't have yurts, clear open skies to ride their horses, and their military had been destroyed so very long ago by more successful warriors.

Living in space had changed them. It had twisted and reshaped their culture, and Sif had no way to know how much had changed. She remembered them as practical but cold hearted toward most strangers. Their isolation kept new ideas and beliefs from helping them adapt.

Her senses told her they were still human, but she also felt there were differences, not like the vanhat, but maybe something else. She had a sense of unease, but she couldn't place her finger on it.

Peshlaki came out and sat in the chair beside her.

An encrypted SCBI-to-SCBI link opened.

"What is wrong with them?" Peshlaki asked.

"They have spent a lot of time alone with their hatred and fears in the depths of space," Sif said. How else to explain them? *"They have changed since I last met them, but I'm not sure how."*

"You said many didn't survive Zhukov?"

"Yes, but they wouldn't have committed everyone. I detect an active Inkeri field, so I don't think they're controlled by the vanhat, but—"

"But something else is wrong."

"Not with all of them," Sif said, searching through her feelings. *"Enkhbold is different. He seems almost normal."*

"That's normal?"

"For the Golden Horde. I think. It has been a very long time and much has changed."

"Their networks are more secure than I would expect."

"They have embraced technology like nobody else. It's their holy grail. I wouldn't be surprised if they have created their own AIs."

That would be a genuine danger. The Golden Horde did not fear technology like others. They would be arrogant enough to think they could control and use it properly. They would investigate science in directions others would fear going. They believed in their gods and their destiny. That was one thing the SOG could not strip from them after their exile from Earth to Tengrin. That planet still struggled under the boot heel of SOG occupation troops, but the space-borne Horde had turned its back on those still planetbound and viewed them as inferiors who lacked the vision to rise and take to the stars. There had been raids over the years to capture women for breeding stock. Sif had heard little about those raids and none of the MT had confirmed what kind of life the captured women led aboard the ships of the Golden Horde afterward. Sif was not foolish enough to think it was a good one.

So many bad things happened in the Governance that one could tolerate only so much evil before it became a requirement of sanity to pick your battles and ignore the rest. Those rumors came back to her, though. What was Enkhbold planning?

"So, they're just going to let us stew here until when?" Peshlaki asked.

"Until they need information or wish to interact," Sif said. *"They are very practical and not given to simple pleasures like you and I. Conversation for the sake of conversation is pointless to them. They are human, but they don't have the same values and concepts we do."*

"Anything we can do?"

"Remain vigilant. They are watching us. Waiting, learning. If we show weakness, they will exploit it, so we must watch them for weakness and hide ours."

Sif felt the ship slide into Shorr space. The *Fire Wind* never spent much time in Shorr space. Only thirty minutes at a time before sliding out to spend hours or days in regular space. It didn't seem efficient. Was the *Fire Wind* watching to see if it was being followed or was the Golden Horde home fleet that far away? Perhaps it was just an attempt to keep anyone from guessing the destination or distance, not that Sif or Munin had a clue.

Let Enkhbold play his games. She could wait.

But sometimes, she really hated waiting, and Enkhbold wasn't the best host.

* * * * *

Chapter Eight:
Ninth Company

Sergeant Nova Dallas, ODT

She followed Chang into the main room and looked around. This wasn't much of a company, maybe a platoon. Usually, a company was commanded by a captain, but aboard ship they were called commanders since there was only one captain on a ship. Some ancient tradition. Either way, Chang didn't seem like a bad officer, and he kept her and her SAW close.

She followed him around, her body and actions on autopilot as she tried to process Aod's and Miller's death. She received notification that Major Yang and Lieutenant Colonel Tse were dead. Not a great loss, in Dallas's opinion. She didn't know what happened to Nikitin, probably assigned to some other company or platoon.

The Gaelic First Born battalion and women's company were gone. She was the only one left, and it would haunt her nightmares.

"Attention!" someone shouted when they recognized Chang.

"Carry on," Chang said before they could get to their feet.

Moving to the front of the room and the podium, he looked at the survivors.

She didn't know what to do, so she followed him and stood behind him like a bodyguard. The eyes of several troopers landed on her rather than Chang, but Dallas didn't care. She knew what they were thinking, and it didn't involve uniforms.

"The cost was high," Chang said, looking around, "but we were victorious, as expected. The Social Organizational Governance will always be victorious."

"Hurrah, hurrah, hurrah," they yelled. Dallas watched them. It was hard to tell if they were serious or faking their motivation, as always.

"There is much work to be done," Chang said. "We are being reorganized as two platoons for now. We will receive reinforcements from the replacement company, but we will still be under strength. We are ODTs. We never quit."

"Hurrah, hurrah, hurrah," they yelled. Chang nodded, satisfied with their performance.

"This is Sergeant Dallas," Chang said, motioning at her. "She will replace Senior Sergeant Hui, who fell in battle. Her orders are my orders. For now, we are going to clean gear and weapons. I will send you new billets and assignments when I have made my decisions. No squad is intact and we do not have enough officers or senior enlisted, so you will have to make do until you get trained, or we receive replacements."

Chang looked them over, as if evaluating them. Several sat up straighter, perhaps trying to look competent and ready for a promotion.

"Company, listen to my command. You will return to quarters, prepare your gear, and stand ready for further orders. Execute!"

"Hurrah, hurrah, hurrah," they yelled and practically ran for the doors in their haste to get out.

In less than a minute, the room was empty of troopers. Chang turned to Dallas.

"They are good troopers," he said, his eyes roving over Dallas. "Perhaps we can retire to my quarters and get better acquainted. Battle can leave people with a lot of—" he paused and smiled "—energy? Perhaps we can burn it off together?"

"Apologies, Commander," Dallas said. If he was going to be pushy, he would quickly learn how good she was at knife fighting. Could she sleep with another man? Aod couldn't be gone. He would remain loyal, as would she. "I do not think that is appropriate at this time."

Chang nodded. "I much prefer the company of women, but there are men in the company who are willing. We can discuss this later."

Dallas hoped her face remained neutral. Regimental Commander Tse had been very much opposed to such same-sex relationships, and the captain of the women's company had been a prude as well, expecting her troops to abstain. Regimental headquarters hadn't been as restrictive, and Dallas wondered just how little discipline the crew of the *Musashi* demanded.

Lieutenant Chang did not seem angry, though Dallas knew that might change later. Right now, she just couldn't stop thinking about Aod and how they had been abandoned. Chang seemed completely unconcerned with that and for that reason alone she considered slipping her bayonet into his ribs.

"You are being assigned quarters," Chang said. "Make sure to box up Senior Sergeant Hui's belongings for processing."

"Yes, sir," Dallas said, preparing for him to make another attempt. If he laid hands on her, she would object violently, consequences be damned. Maybe he saw that in her eyes.

Chang nodded and headed for the door as she received the notification assigning her to specific quarters. Did Chang have access to them? Well, as a commander, of course he did, but would he abuse the privilege?

Slinging her SAW, she followed him out. It wouldn't be the first time she'd slept or showered with a weapon nearby. It was one reason the Governance, in its wisdom, preferred single gender units, though if she was honest, it might be because the fatality rates would be high in mixed gender units. Perhaps tomorrow she could request a transfer, for now she just wanted sleep.

She made her way to the quarters, and she saw they belonged to the company senior sergeant. How long would that last, she wondered as she palmed the door and stepped inside. The room smelled of stale sweat and vodka. The sheets were just as bad. She sat and thought of Aod. Had he been turned? Been killed? Maybe he was still there with what was left of his squad, holding the bunker, hoping for rescue.

And the *Musashi* had just abandoned them.

She didn't want to be logical and think about what the Fleet could have done. They hadn't even tried. Earth was cowering behind walls of automated defense platforms and missile silos. They had the fleets, she was sure.

Closing her eyes tightly, she willed away the tears and despair. She wanted the numbness to fill her. That wasn't pain.

Her door buzzed, announcing a visitor. She grabbed her bayonet and held it behind her back in case it was Chang.

She opened the door. Sergeant Remi Hughes stood there, tears on her face. Dallas had forgotten all about her and recalled she had watched Dallas kill Miller.

The blade in her hands felt heavy and vile.

"I'm sorry," Hughes said, tears running down her cheeks.

Dallas didn't know what Hughes was talking about, so she just nodded.

"Come in?" Dallas said, stepping back. Hughes entered and made a beeline to the chair where she sat heavily. She still wore her blood-stained armor, like Dallas.

"Are we doomed?" Hughes asked.

"No, we are ODT. We never quit. Some of us may die, but in the end we will be victorious."

It was an automatic response, and Dallas didn't have to think about it. Hughes nodded, but she heard it for what it was. Tell a lie often enough, and you believe it.

"We survived," Dallas said and moved to sit down on the smelly bed. How could a senior sergeant live like this?

"For how much longer? I saw Miller change. She was becoming a monster. You didn't hesitate, and you shot her for her treason. I was frozen."

Dallas didn't know what to say. That wasn't how she remembered it, or why she had shot Miller. She had thought Hughes was accusing her of treason for shooting a fellow ODT.

"I'm a veteran. I've faced Torag suicide charges and met them in hand-to-hand combat. I was scared, but not like that. You didn't seem scared at all."

Dallas shook her head. "I was terrified. I didn't realize it was me who shot her at first. I just acted."

"Which might be the only reason we are alive."

Dallas didn't know. She didn't want to think about what that meant.

"Where are you assigned?" Dallas asked to change the subject.

"Third Company," Hughes said. "Mostly Chinese. All men, and all pigs. Five have already propositioned me, promising me things to sleep with them. Few crew women aboard the *Musashi* have any interest in ODTs, it appears."

"There are no female ODTs aboard the *Musashi*," Dallas said. She remembered that from some report somewhere. Perhaps the lack of discipline aboard the flagship was too much? There were plenty of women in the crew, or there used to be.

"What are we going to do?" Hughes said.

"Our duty. What else do we have?"

"I've heard that Admiral Polsky has sent envoys to other Sector commanders. He plans to build an alliance and rescue Sol from the aliens."

"How did you hear this?"

"Fools say things to impress me," Hughes said. "You know men, they see a woman and think with their little head, revealing information their big head knows they shouldn't."

Dallas remained silent. Hughes had been a good fit in intelligence because she was good at ferreting out rumors and putting pieces together. Horny men liked to boast and brag, trying to impress others with their knowledge. Some liked to flex muscles and pretend they were handsome, but it was the ones who pretended intelligence that were more interesting most of the time.

"Did they say where are going now?"

"The admiral's intent was to save the warriors on Valakut, but there is an alien fleet snapping at their heels and the admiral doesn't have the Inkeri shields or weapons to defeat them yet. The ship's captain wanted to stay and evacuate, but the admiral demanded retreat."

"So, he's going to get another sector fleet to help?"

Hughes nodded. "One hopes. I have heard nothing good about the bravery of Admiral Polsky. Until we can stand and fight, we can only run."

"Is there any chance of survivors on Valakut?" Dallas asked. Perhaps Hughes would know.

Hughes dropped her eyes and shook her head. She knew why Dallas was asking. "Our Intelligence credentials have not been revoked, but—"

"But what?"

"They could be revoked at any moment, and the *Musashi* has a full complement of commissars."

Which didn't seem like much of a threat if discipline was so lax. Krakow, Chang, and who knew what else. What were the expectations and what did the commissars care about?

"What access do we have?"

"Regimental G2 level," Hughes said. "There is much data on the Shorr space aliens, but it is inconsistent and contradictory. I don't think there's a lot of reliable data."

"Propaganda?" Dallas asked.

It was standard procedure to provide inconsistent data to the lower command levels to keep them guessing, insecure, and nervous. By inflating the enemy's strengths and capabilities, the lower commands would be more vicious and overwhelming when they rolled over the enemy. Sometimes it did not work to the Governance's advantage and lower commands would flee from an inferior enemy, but higher command levels were usually more aware of the situation and used real threats.

"I don't think so. The data is incomplete and there is much the science officers do not understand. Lots of conjecture and theories. Propaganda usually has a theme or intent hidden in the message. I didn't see a theme or message in this information. Furthermore, the ship that brought us the Inkeri had a lot of data which has not been corroborated. The admiral no longer trusts that information."

"Why?"

"It is said the scout cruiser that came from the remains of the Zhukov Fleet, which was under the temporary command of a General Duque, who has returned to Sol. He has sworn allegiance to the murderer of the Central Committee."

"All the Central Committee?" Dallas asked. *Even Nadya Tokarski?* How could such a beautiful woman have been killed? What savages would do that?

"Supposedly, Director Steve Walton survived and is working with Admiral Polsky to organize a resistance."

Dallas recalled little about Committee Member Walton. He was in the Fleet chain of command and all space forces answered to him, both Fleet and the ODTs, while he answered to Nadya. That was as much as she knew, really, or had cared to learn. He was so far up the chain of command as to be a mythical figure. To learn he was possibly here, on this ship…?

"The admiral and director are committed to saving Sol from the rebels, avenging Secretary General Tokarski, and rebuilding the Governance. For the moment, the director has gone to another sector."

"Then we have our work cut out for us."

"Ai," Hughes said. "I must return. Be safe sister."

"You too," Dallas said. "Thank you for coming. You will always be welcome."

Hughes left, and Dallas felt the weight on her shoulders. Now she felt helpless, surrounded by enemies. She could only carry on, put one foot in front of the other and beat down anything that stood in her way.

She was ODT. She would never quit.

* * * * *

Chapter Nine:
Losing Earth

Prime Minister Wolf Mathison, USMC

The people of the Governance seemed to want an oppressive and iron fist to rule them and Mathison didn't want to be that iron fist. The Governance wasn't a platoon of shit bird Marines. It was an exceptionally clueless and selfish mob of shit bird civilians afraid of their own shadow. Trying to guide and direct them was like herding cats or a small army of toddlers with ADHD after lunch.

With a platoon or company, or even a battalion, he could take them all on a run and PT them until they dropped from exhaustion. But not civilians.

His legion of SCBI-equipped warriors was deploying throughout the Fleet, ODTs, and Guard. They were a drop in the bucket, and he had not publicly declared himself emperor. The Legion knew but nothing would happen overnight except the destruction of humanity. That might help with the military, but the civilian sector was still a problem, mired in bureaucracy and indecision. Nearly all organizations were ruled by three directors, each director a bickering, power-hungry narcissist afraid to be the one to make a decision the others could use against them.

"Nuke them," Skadi said. It took him a second to realize she wasn't talking about the Department of Starship Safety and Modification.

"I'm the one who's supposed to say that, and you're supposed to talk me out of it," Mathison said. Not entirely true, but they worked well together, frequently being the devil's advocate to each other's plans. Skadi impressed him every day with her insight, though she could be a bit bloodthirsty at times. Despite public appearances she did her best to save lives.

"You want to send them a birthday cake?" Skadi asked. "Maybe hold a party?"

Mathison scowled at her. She was angry about something. Of course, it was past dinner and Mathison wasn't sure he had eaten lunch. Was she hangry, too?

Probably not the best time to decide whether or not to kill people. He glanced at her display and her focus became obvious.

She was right, though. The 23rd Guard Division in Africa had mutinied while fighting the vanhat. It made little sense, though, not when he thought about it. They complained they weren't getting resources. They were demanding and had seized what they could. The regiments were spread through the arcologies so nuking them wasn't ideal and they were jamming all transmissions so Mathison couldn't order selective cortex bomb detonations, not that he would. There were even facilities that were removing the bombs from senior officers and loyalist troopers. Mathison couldn't blame them for that, but it was setting a precedence. They had to understand that they couldn't fight the vanhat alone, right? They wouldn't last long and Mathison just didn't have the troops to control the continent.

It was too easy to look down on the Guard units, to accept they were incompetent and disloyal, but Mathison had been a fighter in the trenches, and he knew better. The officers couldn't be that stupid, could they? He was sure there were enough canny ones, experts in surviving.

Mathison just didn't know what to do. He had a million things going on. Incoming asteroids targeting continents, frequent raids from vanhat marauders, Admiral Carpenter was talking about taking the Republic fleet and leaving again. The Legion was still replacing less reliable officers, and that was causing an entirely distinct set of problems. It was too easy to stereotype and jump to conclusions. He didn't have time to do much else.

"Or just let them fight," Mathison said. "Let the rebels and vanhat grind each other down."

"The vanhat aren't losing. I'm also seeing reports that some of the vanhat are fighting each other, but that's after they've crushed resistance."

Mathison looked at the asteroids on trajectory to slam into Earth. Fleet was busy trying to redirect them, but the asteroids were covered with mines and other booby traps. If that wasn't bad enough, there was a vanhat field or something surrounding them that disrupted electronics.

"Can we still supply or somehow reinforce the rebels?" Mathison asked.

Skadi stared at him. Was she about to call him stupid?

"Don't you think resources and supplies are better used by those who are loyal?"

"The Governance doesn't understand loyalty," Mathison said. Maybe not the truest statement, and he realized that, but the Governance didn't understand Marine loyalty. Hopefully, Skadi wouldn't argue about it.

"We can provide orbital strikes." Skadi looked back at her displays. "We can't send them troops, but we might drop some ammunition and other supplies."

"See to it then." The more people that fought the vanhat, the better. He had to show them that fighting the vanhat was more important than fighting each other.

Skadi stared at him, and he wondered what was going through her mind. Her nickname "Ice Princess" was well earned.

"Zen. As you command," she said. There was ice in her voice, and he could tell she didn't like his response.

"No!" Mathison said, his voice a shot across the room. "You have something to say, so say it. You are here to give me your opinion and viewpoint, even if I don't like it."

Her silence made him think she wasn't going to answer.

"You are correct," Skadi said finally, and Mathison tried to think of why he could be wrong. "I don't like that. You are right. I have spent most of my life hating the SOG. To see my enemies die is a pleasure, but the SOG mutineers are less an enemy than the vanhat. You don't forget that, but I do. Now I look at Earth, an ecological disaster, ruined by war, and the Republic's involvement in that pains me."

Mathison looked at her, trying to see past her Ice Princess mask. Nothing. Maybe he was just hangry, tired, and irritable, and maybe she was too.

"We need more exercise," Mathison said. He had seen the presidential guard, as Wayne was calling them, running in formation. He missed that. He wasn't part of a unit now and he couldn't summon the platoon to go on a little death run, singing cadence or watching the weaker members fall out. That was always a boost to his ego, to know he was stronger and tougher than younger men.

"I need dinner," Skadi said. "I skipped lunch, like you."

"You are right. I'm tired of this office, though."

"Zen." They both stood and stretched.

Stathis should be arriving on Earth to reinforce Captain Sinclair. Mathison felt a little guilty about that. He had promised Stathis a ninety-six, four days to relax and take his mind off being a boot lieutenant, but the demands of duty wouldn't quite allow that.

Freya had said the captain needed help; the local guard was practically worthless. Other ODT units with Legion officers were still undergoing transition and Stathis had a competent, blooded platoon. The private… well, the lieutenant, would ensure they were competent. Freya had listed his platoon as ready. They needed a specialized pump and some valves that weren't readily available except here on Luna. As Stathis' bad luck would have it, he was available, and the *Eagle* could pick up the pieces here on Luna and deliver it to the arcology as quickly as anyone else.

He would make it up to Stathis later, and hopefully he would have a full drop regiment ready in the next day or two. He didn't want to send them in piecemeal.

The newly designated Imperial Drop Troops would be his elite heavy hitters, his Marines. They would get blooded in time. There were other ODT units that were being transitioned and assigned Legionnaires as officers. When they were partially ready, he would use them to reinforce Stathis.

Stathis would be okay. He would get those parts to the geothermal plant.

Mathison hoped.

* * * * *

Chapter Ten:
Rescue

2nd Lieutenant Zale Stathis, USMC

Stathis led his platoon through the ruins of the Bogotá Arcology. There were no civilians in this area. His platoon had left friendly lines behind twenty minutes ago. This was enemy territory. He expected the firefight to begin any minute. The vanhat weren't fools. There would be a blocking force somewhere to keep reinforcements from reaching the geothermal plant. Stathis hoped his platoon could break through them or they might have to abandon the arcology, which would make this the third arcology lost this month.

He hadn't gotten his ninety-six, so he hadn't been able to ask out Hakala. Of course, he had gotten orders to take his platoon to Bogotá the second he reached the *Eagle*. Smimova had the platoon ready, though. A good move and a good sign that Smimova was a good platoon sergeant. They had been ready for training, combat deployment, or a move of quarters back to Luna.

The *Eagle* had taken him and an assault shuttle, a micro jump, and then a drop in a shuttle. His stomach was still somewhere in orbit. Didn't the prime minister have regiments of ODTs to throw around? Why did he have to send one of the more junior lieutenants in the entire Fleet?

Despite having d-bombs and Inkeris, Imperial forces were not winning the war for Earth. The vanhat were cunning fighters, and they seemed to be multiplying. Scientists were scrambling to find other weapons. The Governance had millions of biological warfare agents, manufactured plagues and chemicals, but those things only worked until the vanhat got out of range of the Inkeri fields. These things were worse than cockroaches. Adaptable, and whenever you saw one there were twenty more hidden nearby.

"Faster," Stathis said to Lan, the squad leader with the lead element.

"There are many places for an ambush," Lan said.

"Yep," Stathis said. "They're going to ambush us somewhere. We're Spartans, though. Our armor is thicker so we have an advantage, and while I don't like it, we need to move faster. They need these supplies and time is running out."

"Aye, sir," Lan said. It sounded more natural coming from him now. No more of that hurrah garbage. It annoyed Stathis. It was what Marines said, and they weren't Marines. He wasn't a Marine officer; he was just pretending to be one, regardless of what the gunny said.

Dammit, that wasn't right, either. Stathis felt so out of place these days, like he was still pretending to be an officer, but even strangers treated him with respect.

Hui had told him that the Bogotá Arcology was important for propaganda reasons. They couldn't lose it. If they wanted to prove to the rest of the Governance that the Empire was strong and capable, they had to stop losing.

Like a Marine private and a platoon of ex-ODTs would make a difference.

Blazer fire erupted ahead, and Stathis rushed forward. The incoming weapons fire wasn't blazer fire, but that didn't mean the vanhat didn't have armor piercers.

Keeping his head down, Stathis looked over the situation.

Lan was getting a SAW gunner into position, ordering the first team to lay down heavy fire while the second team SAW gunner got to a better spot.

In seconds, the SAW ripped the vanhat to shreds, cutting through their cover. They couldn't escape the blazer rounds, which sliced through the tram they were using as concealment. Any vanhat that tried to escape ran into the fire from the other SAW.

Lan ordered his first team to reload and advance as the incoming fire stopped.

Stathis expected the firing to start up again as Sergeant Orta brought his squad forward. They focused their attention on the nearby windows and doors.

The ambush hadn't delayed them much, and there were no casualties.

Leapfrogging his fireteams, the forward momentum picked up.

Stathis glanced at the bodies of the vanhat. Short, fat, pudgy little bastards that seemed to struggle with their rifles, which were a bit too big for them. His first thought was that they were goblins. That's what he would go with. He forgot what Shrek had called them in the brief.

"These goblins are little bastards," Stathis said to his platoon sergeant and squad leaders. "Like cockroaches, they're probably going to weasel into places and get behind us. They'll probably try to sucker us into a kill zone where they can surround us."

"Slow down then?" Lan asked.

"Hell no," Stathis said. "Just don't stop. Bulldoze the bastards. I had an Army sergeant tell me the best way out of an ambush was the way you got into it."

"But?" Smimova asked. He had heard Stathis mention the US Army in the past.

"That's not as fun as teaching the enemy that ambushing Marines is a great way to die. Keep them from getting a second chance, if you know what I mean. If we hit another ambush I want lots of aggression in a forward direction. They rarely expect that."

"As ODTs, we learned extreme violence," Smimova said, satisfaction in his voice. "Your Army reminds me of the Guard. Good for garrison, but when it absolutely, positively has to be destroyed overnight, the ODTs will be summoned."

"Oorah," Stathis said, picking up the pace to catch up with Lan, whose squad had ditched the leapfrog approach and was advancing more aggressively.

Stathis saw signs of battle, broken Guard weapons and equipment, some helmets and other pieces of armor, but the bodies were gone. Stathis didn't like that. The vanhat did two things with bodies—ate them or put them back into the fight as short little recruits. Stathis didn't like either option.

"This was a Guard blocking force, a platoon in size," Shrek reported, as Stathis looked around.

A blazer shot rang out.

"Scout or sniper," Ortoff said. The sergeant knew his job. None of the icons on his display turned red. The sniper had missed.

"Let's keep moving," Stathis said. Whether scout or sniper, it meant they knew where his platoon was at.

The robotic mules followed, and Tan made sure they were safe.

Stathis had been looking forward to some time off, but the gunny decided he needed an errand boy. Stathis could have been pissed about it. He probably should be, but the biggest advantage, as far as Stathis could see, was that it gave him time to think about how to invite Hakala on a date. He could put off that task for a little while. She was still assigned to the *Eagle*, so she wasn't going anywhere. He had seen her briefly during their jaunt from the Moon to Earth.

He just had to fight his way through a horde of vanhat, survive, deliver the pumps and valves to some captain, and then the hard work would begin. What if Hakala said no or couldn't get time off? Who could he ask to make sure she got time off? Captain Winters? Britta?

First things first. He had to kick these vanhat in the balls and rescue that company. There were supposed to be regular ODTs and Guard units behind him, but they were still playing grab-ass at the starport.

Time was running out.

* * * * *

Chapter Eleven:
The Stand

Captain Duffy Sinclair, ODT

His troopers repelled another attack, but Sinclair knew there would only be a brief lull until they brought up more troops. His men could kill them pretty quickly, but the biggest problem was that the goblin attacks also inflicted casualties, and he would eventually run out of troops. If they managed to wound or kill one of his troopers for every hundred goblins they killed, the vanhat would easily win. Another major problem was that ammunition supplies were not unlimited. Already his squad leaders were sending people into the carnage to retrieve enemy rifles and ammunition.

These quick missions served multiple purposes. They captured weapons the goblins might otherwise pick up and use against them, and they placed booby traps. Not all the attackers had rifles and some of them were using the rifles of the fallen. Others just charged, screaming and dying. His troopers in their armor were not immune to knives shoved into cracks in their armor, but the survivors were settling down and becoming less concerned about fanatical, knife-wielding monsters charging them.

Sinclair moved around as much as he could, helping squad leaders reposition their heavier weapons, telling younger troopers to find better cover, or providing covering fire as small teams left the perimeter to grab weapons, ammunition, and booby trap the bodies with their dwindling supply of grenades and mines.

He knew his people had brought as much ammunition as they could carry, more than was normal, and that was the only reason they hadn't run out yet.

"They do know we're still alive, Captain?" asked Sung, one of his platoon commanders.

"Yes," Sinclair said. *Hopefully.*

Comms were spotty, and he hadn't heard from the Guard commander in hours. The last he had heard was that they were being pushed back. The Guard units Sinclair had worked with were usually good for two things, intimidating civilians and holding onto captured territory. In the attack, they were mediocre, and even in the defense there were some units that lacked discipline and were questionable.

Here in the Sol System, the Guard units were better equipped but lacked the warrior spirit.

"The Guard are weak," Sung said, and Sinclair heard stress there. "They will not push the enemy. They cower in their fighting positions."

"We can't all be orbital drop troopers," Sinclair said.

"Apologies," Sung said. "I did not mean to imply that—"

"The Guard are soft and weak, afraid to take casualties," Sinclair said. There was a time that Sung's words may have been seen as treason. Soldiers of the Governance did not insult or otherwise talk in a derogatory manner about others.

"Ai, Company Commander," Sung said, shutting down, perhaps realizing what he had said and how that could impact his career.

Sinclair didn't care and doubted it would have any affect his career under Emperor Mathison.

"Look, Lieutenant," Sinclair said. Hadn't the lieutenant heard him echo his words? Sinclair could be considered just as treasonous as Sung. "That's a cold, hard fact. Guard troops are next to worthless right now. I don't trust them to push through and get those engineers and parts to us, but now things are different and will keep changing."

"Different how?" Sung looked at where a shot rang out. A trooper taking out a goblin sniper, perhaps.

"New management," Sinclair said. "Emperor Mathison is a warrior. He has fought in the front lines. He gets it."

"Where did he fight?" Sung asked, and Sinclair heard the doubt. Sinclair had never seen a brave, bold, and competent officer rise to the rank of colonel or above in the Governance. Only the most dangerous politicians survived in the military to rise above the rank of lieutenant colonel. A trooper learned early that most of what the higher-ranking officers told them was complete garbage. Propaganda for the privates was what they had called it back in the Gaelic First.

"Full details are classified," Sinclair said. Not everything about the emperor's past was to be made common knowledge, yet. "But I know for sure he has fought the vanhat, hand to hand in some cases. He is a fighter and a survivor."

Sung nodded, but Sinclair understood he would not openly doubt him.

"I've actually met him, talked to him," Sinclair said. "Probably said things I shouldn't have, like you, except I said them to the emperor's face, though back then he was just called the prime minister. I spoke my mind, and he didn't have me executed like a member of the Central Committee would have."

Sung turned to Sinclair. "What did you tell him?"

"I told him we were wasting time and resources fighting on Valakut. I told him that both the Torag and the Governance are using the war for personal and political gain; neither wants to win. I called the generals in command 'arrogant peacocks.'" Which might have been much, but the emperor hadn't seemed the least bit surprised.

"Then what happened?"

"He smiled and asked me if I had questions for him," Sinclair said.

"Did you?"

"Yes," Sinclair said. More shots rang out. It was going to be another assault then. "Maybe I'll tell you later."

The fire increased, and screams from many throats filled the air. A knife attack, then with goblin snipers who would try to use the confusion. Not the most original attack, but it could be effective.

"Ai, Company Commander," Sung said and turned to his men. It was pointless to tell them to be ready. They were ready, but the lieutenant's voice would make it more formal. Lieutenant Sung knew his job. He sounded confident, and his men would pick up on that. It was all psychological at this point.

More screaming erupted.

"More of them," reported Finn, Sinclair's SCBI. *"This is going to be a major push."*

"Did something change?"

"I don't know. Maybe they are tired of playing around. The latest pause between attacks was a little longer. Perhaps they were marshaling their forces."

"They're going to try something new," Sinclair told Sung and the other platoon commanders. "Be ready for a surprise."

"What surprise, Company Commander?" Sung asked.

"If I knew, I would tell you, but they aren't fools. They aren't like the Guard troops that will keep pouring bodies on the enemy until they extinguish the fire." *Let them know they can speak freely,* Sinclair thought. "These vanhat are damned smart and dangerous. Don't let the little bodies fool you."

A deeper, more powerful roar shook the tunnels.

Something new was coming.

More deep roars joined the first. They sounded big.

* * * * *

Chapter Twelve:
Ogres

2nd Lieutenant Zale Stathis

The roar was not from a goblin, and Stathis ran forward toward the sound. He reached the lead fireteam as the first one came around the corner.

The fireteam, led by Gnoss, had hunkered down when they heard it. Not that Stathis blamed them. None of them had heard anything like it before.

"What the—" Private Lenzo began as a walking freight train exited the tunnel. Stathis was already firing, his blazer rounds slamming into the creature's oversized rifle, causing it to splatter and covering the creature with shards of burning metal and plastic.

The thing appeared to stumble, but Stathis realized it hadn't tripped; it had been pushed by the one behind it.

More of his platoon fired at the first one and blazer rounds ripped out gouts of burning flesh. Stathis fired at the second one's rifle.

They weren't rifles so much as handheld canons. Even if they were solid slug weapons, getting hit by one would likely be fatal for whatever they hit and everyone in or behind that train.

More Spartans moved up, formed a line, and began firing.

Stathis stopped to look around.

"Watch the flanks!" Stathis yelled at Sergeant Lan. Smimova took up the cry as the firing line cut down the oversized goblins. How they had gotten so big and where they had gotten those hand cannons was not a question Stathis needed to answer right now. He just wanted them to die or go away and not come back.

The *crack* of rifle fire cut through the blazer fire.

"Contact rear," Smimova said. He didn't sound super stressed, more annoyed, like his dog was trying to hump a fire hydrant.

Stathis ducked behind something solid and looked around, tapping into the views of different members of the platoon. He had to trust the troopers behind him because if they were surrounded, they would have no cover from any angle. The only way they could avoid that would be to keep moving or find a spot to fight from. Forward was what he wanted, but not if that put them in a worse situation. There was doctrine and then there was common sense. While rounds zipped past him from every direction, Stathis tried to get a good look at what was going on. It wasn't easy. No wonder boot lieutenants had short life spans. You couldn't figure things out while hiding behind cover, and he *had* to figure things out. Gone were the days when he could just engage targets to his front and trust the Marines to his sides and flanks and rear. Now he had to understand the battle and how it was developing.

"Stupid pee-holes gave away their ambush by roaring," Smimova said on a private link. The platoon wasn't in any immediate danger, and it didn't look like there were more than two of the big ones. Small blessings.

"Those roars would probably make lesser troops shit their pants and start running," Stathis said, glad he had his battle dress plumbing hooked up correctly. "Or at least shit their pants."

"Ha!" Smimova said. "We will teach them."

"Never interrupt an enemy when they are making a mistake," Stathis said, wishing Vili was here. He hadn't accompanied the platoon, and Stathis felt alone and in charge. He was it. The answer man. He got to make all the big decisions that would get people killed, and there was nobody else here to keep him from screwing up. Damn Vili.

"Do we let them smash against the wall of our weapons and will?" Smimova asked.

"No," Stathis said, changing to the squad leader link. "We are needed. We need to keep pushing. Can you push, Lan?"

"Aye," Sergeant Lan said and changed the link to talk with his people and urge them on. The response was almost instant. Stathis wondered if the Spartans were eager to attack and had only held back because that was what was expected.

The rate of fire suddenly increased, and one of Lan's fireteams used the covering fire to sprint forward and get better firing positions. When they were in place, they reloaded and started firing to keep the enemy's head down while more troopers advanced.

Like a well-drilled team. Stathis wanted to pause and admire the artistry and precision with which they moved.

"I'm detecting transmissions," Shrek said. *"It might be Captain Sinclair's company."*

It took a moment for Stathis to remember who Sinclair was—the commander of the company sent to secure the geothermal plant. One of the new Legionnaires, according to his briefing.

Stathis wasn't sure how he felt about that. Now a jackboot thug captain had a SCBI. A proper officer who outranked Stathis had a SCBI and had been loyal to SOG at one time. Would that officer decide a private was unworthy? Stathis liked to think if there was a problem the gunny would back up a Marine, but then the gunny was an emperor now and had to look at the bigger picture. Like Stathis should be doing.

He pushed those thoughts and fears away. He looked back to see the troopers doing the opposite of what Sergeant Lan was doing.

"How are we doing with ammo?" Stathis asked Shrek as one of the robotic mules trundled past him, following Sergeant Lan. They were under Shrek's control and using cover and concealment. The cargo of ammunition and parts for the generator were too valuable to risk.

"We could be doing better," Shrek said. *"A lot better. But we're carrying stock for Captain Sinclair's company, so we have a lot."*

Stathis didn't want to reach the captain and discover they had to dip into the ammunition stock they were carrying. That probably wouldn't look good.

His platoon didn't seem to need him as he hunkered there and watched. When he saw Smimova back up, occasionally firing at a target when he had the chance and a clear line of sight, Stathis knew it was time to catch up with Sergeant Lan.

It seemed like hours later when the fire to his front lessened and finally stopped. Stathis was busy firing at a wounded ogre hiding behind a tipped-over train in the corridor they were trying to cross.

"What the hell," Stathis said, moving toward Sergeant Lan's marker.

There were no new casualties in Lan's squad. Lenzo had taken an armor piercer through the thigh but was still limping along, and Yuri could still fight with one arm. Their nanites were working miracles, but Stathis expected one of his people to suffer a lethal injury any second. They were less likely to get shot if they were firing.

More icons lit up, and Stathis didn't recognize them. ODTs? Was the enemy messing with sensors? Had they cracked the identifier system?

A link from "Captain Sinclair" lit up. *Oh.*

"Captain Sinclair, I presume?" Stathis asked. "Uh, sir."

"Yes," Sinclair said. "Glad to see you, Lieutenant."

"I've got beans, bullets, and band aids for you, sir," Stathis said. How did officers talk? Was he being too informal? Would the captain have any idea what he was talking about? Was the captain a stuffy, stuck-up prick?

"We can pass on the beans, but bullets and band aids are needed," Sinclair said as Stathis moved forward so he could talk to the captain face to face. "You are a sight for sore eyes. Stathis? Emperor Mathison's man?"

"Yes, sir," Stathis said. The captain knew of him?

"The one who came with the emperor from the past when the emperor was a gunnery sergeant?"

Shit. Which probably meant the captain knew he had been a private. So much for earning respect.

"Yes, sir," Stathis said. He motioned for Lan to set up a strong point at the hatch so they could keep an eye on the corridor.

The troll behind the train was dead. Blazer rounds were very good at punching holes through manmade things and the train had been no exception, but Stathis wanted to make sure nobody entered the corridor where they could cut them off again.

The robo-mules clomped past and spread out through the captain's company, taking the parts to the engineers and ammunition to the troopers who needed it most, Shrek and another SCBI directing them.

The captain approached. He was barely taller than Stathis.

"It is an honor to meet you," Sinclair said, popping open his visor and revealing his eyes behind the armored glass.

"Same here," Stathis said, opening his own visor, but not sure if he was telling the truth. This captain had a SCBI and wasn't a Marine, or an American for that matter.

Stathis looked back at his people, but they were moving like a well-drilled machine and there wasn't anything he could say, or if there was Smirnova beat him to it. Stathis felt worthless standing there watching them. Shouldn't an officer be running around yelling about things? Pestering the platoon sergeant to hurry? He wanted to impress this captain, but his platoon wasn't giving him the opportunity because they were doing exactly what he wanted. Which probably meant he was missing something.

"I have a command post set up," Sinclair said. "I don't think they need us out here. Your platoon sergeant seems to have things under control, as do my platoon commanders."

"Yes, sir," Stathis said. Was that an insult? Was that Sinclair's way of telling Stathis he wasn't being very lieutenant-y?

"What should I be doing?" Stathis asked Shrek.

"Go with the captain and get out of the way. Let your platoon sergeant do his thing."

The CP wasn't fancy, just a spot in the center of the warehouse with cover from all directions. Not the best fields of fire, but it had been a good spot to bunker down with the engineers and would let the captain tap into different trooper views without being exposed to enemy fire.

"We haven't had comms with anyone for several hours," Sinclair said. "We were getting worried."

"There's a drop trooper battalion not far behind, sir," Stathis said. Unlike the captain, Stathis had one of the unjammable Aesir links. Stathis thought he had heard the Republic was going to give them the technology, but only for the Legionnaires who were loyal to Mathison. "They're sending out detachments to some of the power substations to make sure they aren't being cut. We really need to restore power so we can start powering up the arcology Inkeris."

"Patching the captain into the regimental data net," Shrek reported. Which wasn't entirely true. Shrek was connecting the captain to the Aesir network, which had links to the drop trooper regimental command. The vanhat didn't jam the Aesir links, so that would probably be the next thing that was distributed once everyone had Inkeris.

The captain sat down to talk with his commanders while Stathis looked around. The company command post looked empty and spacious, but the engineers who had been hunkered down here were now busy getting the geothermal plant up and working. Stathis sat and began cycling through the views, trying to understand everything and look for flaws in the way Sinclair had deployed his company.

Stathis probably wouldn't have put the aid station so close to the company command post, but it wasn't like there was a lot of space and the vanhat weren't using explosives yet.

The captain's men had been down to using captured weapons, and Stathis wasn't sure how they had lasted as long as they had. He thought his platoon was exhausted, but Sinclair's men had been fighting almost non-stop with constant attacks. Stathis knew if he could see their eyes, they would be the blank eyes of the deathly tired. The company had sustained a lot of casualties, mostly wounded, who could continue to fight. There was a line of bodies laid out near the aid station, and Stathis stared at them. They could almost be his entire platoon.

So many drop troopers. Did Sinclair know them or care? The captain hadn't been in command of the company for long. Stathis knew it would tear him up, but who knew about a SOG jackboot captain.

The vanhat tried two more attacks, which were easily beaten back with blazers, and then they stopped. Stathis was ready for a big vanhat attack, but the lead elements of a reinforcing company arrived, and Stathis was confident they had it under control, especially when he got orders for him to return to Luna.

* * * * *

Chapter Thirteen:
The Return Flight

Captain Duffy Sinclair, ODT

His company had taken a beating, and Sinclair didn't want to admit how close they had come to being over-run. Lieutenant Stathis arriving with blazer and wire gun ammunition had been in the nick of time.

Boarding the troop transport that would take them to Luna would give them all a chance to relax. The vanhat had chewed up and spit out his company, though he knew he had done far worse to them. The vanhat had very different ideas of casualties and losses.

Finn did an excellent job of keeping his company together and moving, ensuring grenades were turned in, rifles unloaded, and so many other administrative tasks. Finn didn't talk to his platoon commanders or NCOs directly but kept in constant communication with them by sending them checklists and messages for confirmation of tasks. Most times, the message confirmations weren't always acknowledged by the tired troops, but they acted as gentle reminders to check and make sure blazers were unloaded and cleared.

Sinclair didn't want anyone with a blazer round still chambered holing their transport. Tired troops made stupid mistakes.

Nothing required his presence or attention, so Sinclair sank into the jump seat next to Stathis and pulled off his helmet. Stathis was sitting there like a good lieutenant, watching and listening while his platoon sergeant made sure everyone was situated.

"Thank you, Lieutenant," Sinclair said.

"Uh, my pleasure, Captain," Stathis said, looking confused.

"We were almost down to throwing our rifles at them," Sinclair said. "Had you been a little slower... They were preparing for another push. It might have been our last, especially if there had been more ogres."

"Oh," Stathis said. Sinclair watched him relax a little. "Yeah, someone said you guys still had some beer left, and I couldn't hold my guys back, sir."

Sinclair stared at Stathis. ODT officers never talked like that. Some hyped up commissar might think they were serious and have them up on charges of conduct unbecoming. Enlisted might have gotten away with that kind of banter, mostly because there were fewer commissars around, but not officers.

Stathis looked at Sinclair, and his nervousness returned.

"I mean... um, we knew you were in trouble, and nothing would stop us from doing our duty to the greater... um, the Empire," Stathis said.

Stathis was *really* new to this, and Sinclair wasn't sure that was a bad thing.

He laughed and shook his head. "You were supposed to be bringing the beer."

"Oh," Stathis said, relaxing again. "Someone forgot to put that on the manifest. Sorry, sir, I'll take it up with my supply major ASAP."

The lieutenant had a supply major? "Happens all the time. I could really use a beer about now. I think we might get some time off from what my assistant is telling me."

Finn had reported the company as combat ineffective, so some shuffling would be needed before they could bring it to combat readiness. Which meant he would probably be very busy processing in new company members, making sure they had weapons, equipment, certifications, and training. The ODT pipeline was a shambles, but Finn said Legion Drop Trooper units were getting priority, though Sinclair didn't know what that meant. Right now, he would be happy with some ODTs to fill in his ranks.

Most of the company would get time off, but Sinclair knew he wouldn't.

"You getting time off, too, Lieutenant?" Sinclair asked. What would a private turned lieutenant, and a confidant of the emperor, do?

"Coming to your rescue was my time off, sir," Stathis said. "I think I had more fun getting shot at."

"What do you mean?"

"I just came back from a mission out-system and the gun—uh, emperor sent me off to reinforce you. I think I can take my ninety-six now, but I would rather square off with face-eating monsters."

"Is some time off that bad?"

"Well, sir, there's this girl."

"A girl?" Sinclair asked. Stathis couldn't be that old. When did he have time to meet people? Hadn't he been in stasis and then fighting the vanhat almost non-stop or something?

"Yes, sir," Stathis said. "I think she likes me, but, lately, I don't know. The emperor said I should just ask her out, but what if she says no and gets offended?"

Sinclair chuckled. What kind of woman was this young man afraid of? Oh, to be so young and naïve. He had watched the lieutenant in action, seen the way he led his platoon. The young man was a leader, not a commander who hid behind his rank and authority. Confident and competent, and here he was afraid of a woman? Unless it was Skadi. She might be the only one Sinclair could imagine intimidating the young man.

"Who is she?" Sinclair asked.

"She just got promoted to lieutenant, too," Stathis said. "And put in command of a detachment aboard the *Eagle*."

Sinclair nodded. There were several all-women ODT units trained for shipboard operations and if the *Eagle* was commanded by a woman, it made sense. Which certainly meant it wasn't Skadi, who didn't leave Zvezda Two most of the time.

"I'm not seeing a problem," Sinclair said.

"She's a badass. She probably couldn't take me in a standup fight, but I wouldn't want to fight her, and she's not dumb. If I piss her off, I won't be able to sleep safely again."

"Asking her out is not grounds for her to want to kill you." What was he missing here? The women of the ODT battalions could be tough, but he had seen Stathis in action. "Ask her out. At worst she'll say no, and that's that."

"I would be okay with that, sir," Stathis said. "But what if she says *yes*? I don't know where to take her, and if I step on my dick while on mission, I'll never be able to look her in the eyes again."

Now Sinclair could see some of the problem.

"The worst that could happen is she says no, or you have a bad date. What's the best that could happen?"

"We end up, uh, together?" Stathis asked, glancing around. "But the worst that could happen is I piss her off. She can be crazy. I once saw her leap out the ruptured hull of a space station with a nuke strapped to her while the vanhat tried to shoot her down."

That didn't sound like an ODT.

"Who is she?" Sinclair asked.

"Her name is Hakala. She's an HKT, originally from the *Tyr*."

An HKT, a member of the elite psychopathic Vanir attack capture teams?

"I see," Sinclair said. He had figured there were some aboard the *Tyr* but hadn't really given them much thought. The HKTs had a reputation, and while Sinclair knew there was propaganda around them, he was never sure what was true.

"That is a big problem," Sinclair said. "We're told regular Aesir must kill a member of their immediate family to prove they're ruthless enough. We are also told the HKTs have to torture a member of their family to death, and that they use HKTs to execute prisoners in the most gruesome manner."

Stathis turned to look at Sinclair. "Nah, they aren't that bad. They don't do that shit. I remember back, um, before they used to, um…"

Stathis fell silent.

Nobody else was in earshot, so Sinclair leaned over.

"In the Legion we learned all about you and the emperor, how you were US Marines that got in trapped in stasis. How you used to be a private and the emperor was a mere gunnery sergeant."

"Well," Stathis said. "Yes, sir. I wasn't sure."

"Let me guess, enemies used to say things like that about Marines?"

"Yes, sir," Stathis said, still looking uncomfortable.

"So, now I'm curious, Lieutenant," Sinclair said. "How about this? There's a girl I know. Maybe we can double date. I know a good place. Ask out Lieutenant Hakala, and I'll show both of you around Luna. I've been stationed here for a while and know some good places. That way, if you have a bad time or we end up in a shit hole, you can blame me. You came to my rescue, Lieutenant, maybe I can do the same for you?"

Stathis stared at him in surprise.

"That would be cool, Captain. I could really use the help," Stathis said.

"Great," Sinclair said. This would give him an opportunity to learn more about Stathis and their Republic allies for real, not just cold, impersonal reports from SOG analysts. "Let's aim for tomorrow evening. Maybe five? You have questions, you ask me."

"Sure thing, Captain," Stathis said, sounding relieved. "Thank you, I really appreciate it."

"Sure thing, Lieutenant," Sinclair said.

Stathis looked like he was becoming an outstanding officer, but if he was going to be a *great* officer, he would need someone to help and guide him. Sinclair knew Stathis would go far. Hopefully, he wouldn't become some political beast, and Sinclair could help him become a good company-grade officer. He got the impression the gunny wanted to promote him but wouldn't do that until the young man was ready.

* * * * *

Chapter Fourteen:
Date with Hakala

2nd Lieutenant Zale Stathis, USMC

She said yes, and that made things much worse for Stathis. Hot women didn't say yes when dumb privates invited them out. She knew he had been a dumb private and even tried to take advantage of it. She hadn't tried to push him around since the gunny had pinned on his boot lieutenant bars, but something like that wouldn't fool Hakala. He had caught her looking at him with those beautiful eyes, the exotic batwing tattoo giving her an intimidating look, but he kinda liked that. He wasn't sure if she had tattoos elsewhere, but he wanted to find out.

Looking at himself in his new Legion uniform, he had to admit he looked good. His dark blue dress uniform of the new Legion was a lot like the USMC uniform, especially the red trim. So dark blue, it was almost black. His black leather belt held a blazer pistol instead of a sword, and Stathis carried the pistols he had gotten from Curitiba, which had been re-engineered to take standard magazines and rounds, instead of the standard issue blazer or his old Marine issue blazer. The gunny probably didn't care about appearance so much as function. He could hear the gunny yelling at him about standard parts and ammunition in case of an emergency since he might have to share magazines. The pearl handle of the blazer shined but didn't look too out of place in the glossy black holster. Shrek would have told him if there was a problem.

He slipped a couple extra magazines into his boot tops and slipped a brace of thumbnail grenades into his other boot.

What would Hakala wear? He couldn't imagine her in a slinky, sexy black dress. Well, yes, he could, far too vividly, but she would probably be in uniform. That would be weird. Going out to some formal event with someone wearing pants. Stathis was pretty sure he wasn't gay. Would people think he was gay being that close to someone wearing pants? What if they kissed and someone saw them?

Well, he had extra ammunition, then he slipped a knife into his boot.

They had spent a lot of time aboard ship together, but they had always been busy. Well, to be fair, he had kept himself busy. It was safer to plan for getting his face eaten by monsters than to piss off an HKT. Why was she still interested? Had she said yes because she didn't want to offend him? He couldn't imagine her caring about his actual feelings.

No. Not Hakala. She wouldn't be intimidated, and she was the one who had asked to be transferred to the *Eagle*. But what if she just didn't want to be stuck on a stuffy old warship with dinosaurs like Admiral Carpenter?

"You are going out on a date," Shrek said. *"Not a battle."*

"I don't want to be unprepared," Stathis said aloud, smoothing out his sleeve.

"I think you are preparing for the wrong thing," Shrek said.

"I need condoms?"

"You need to learn how to dance," Shrek said.

"Oh shit," Stathis said. "Seriously? Dancing? Like, uh, oh no."

That was going to be a problem. Shrek could help with some physical activities, a minute electric shock to cause a muscle to tighten or trigger the muscles in some ways, but full control was something Shrek could not and would not do. In combat, a quick muscle twitch might cause Stathis to dodge an attack, but dancing was very different, unless he wanted to dance like a crazy man who kept touching his tongue to a battery. Probably not very romantic.

"Why didn't you warn me?" Stathis asked.

"I'm here to help you with combat, warfare, tactics, combat techniques, and survival. Human interaction is supposed to be your specialty."

"Can't you download some program on how to dance?"

"Sure. Which dance do you want? There is group dancing, individual dancing, slow dancing, and more, with countless dance variations. Dancing is also cultural and may vary depending on the music, jazz, ballet, hip-hop, ballroom, salsa, tango, swing, and many more."

"I don't know," Stathis said, staring at himself in the mirror. Sure, he looked good, but this disaster was going to be epic. Was it too late to cancel until he had time to learn the appropriate dance moves? How would he tell Hakala? "What dances do they do at the place we are going?"

"Captain Sinclair did not say," Shrek said. *"He is almost here."*

Stathis looked at the door, expecting a notification any second. How could he cancel with the captain?

"Didn't say?" Stathis asked, suddenly not feeling well. "What about a digital reconnaissance? What about route planning? Additional equipment and supplies? Extra water and ammunition? How far outside the wire are we going to be?"

"It is an officers' club. This is not a combat mission. Should I plan everything for you? Trips to the bathrooms? Make requests to supply to verify suitable toilet

paper is present before every visit? Are the stall doors fully operational and properly maintained? The soap dispenser has sufficient supplies based on the potential number of people using it, to include an additional twenty percent? Should I establish drone reconnaissance to ensure the floors are properly cleaned and are not slippery at the suspected time of visit? Confirm properly they have conducted cleaning within the allotted time and get sign off from relevant parties and their supervisors? Maybe I could task some drones to monitor the facility for you to determine the optimal toilet or urinal to use and when. Heaven forbid you be ensnared into having to use a urinal while standing next to another man. We should do proper reconnaissance and monitoring to avoid that, yes?"

"Well…" Stathis said. Why didn't the SCBIs monitor these things to begin with?

"No. We both have better things to do with our time and resources."

"But—"

"No. The captain has arrived and is waiting outside."

"On my way," Stathis said. Dammit. He couldn't keep the captain waiting, but this was all moving too quickly. He wasn't ready for this.

Something else Stathis didn't care for. Perhaps it would have been better if he had met the captain somewhere. Lieutenants answered to captains, captains didn't wait on lieutenants.

Stathis moved quickly. He was currently housed in the BOQ, the Bachelor Officers Quarters. Really nice rooms, but they weren't any fancier than some places he had stayed as a Marine Raider. The biggest advantage was the cleaning robots, which Shrek had told him were also spy bots. Not that they did much reporting these days, but at least he didn't have to clean or do his laundry.

The BOQ was almost like a mini hotel, with a lobby and arrival area. Stathis stumbled over the threshold when he saw the captain was with a very attractive woman wearing a green dress. They were both sitting in a golf cart with six seats. The four seats in the back faced each other, and the captain and his date were in the seats facing the same direction as the driver, a young ODT private.

The captain smiled.

"Lieutenant Zale Stathis, let me introduce Sarah Foster," Sinclair said. They remained sitting in the cart.

"Hi," Stathis said. What else could he say that wouldn't get him shot by the captain? Sarah was a damned beautiful woman. Where had Sinclair found her? "A pleasure to meet you."

"Hi," she said with a smile that Stathis tried not to read too much into. "Duffy has told me a lot about you."

The captain motioned for Stathis to take a seat. What had he told her about him? Was there anything he could tell her that wasn't classified?

Stathis hoped he wasn't blushing, but the smile on the captain's face told him he probably was. Sarah's smile grew a bit.

"Uh, thank you," Stathis said. Should he say something nice about the captain?

The cart started up, and the sides came down to give them privacy.

It was too much like getting picked up in a limousine, if a golf cart could be called a limousine. The electric carts seemed to be everywhere and with his back to the direction of travel, Stathis could see everything behind them. He let his eyes scan behind them for tails, assessing the carts and trying to remember them for later. Shrek should keep track as well, but a good Marine didn't rely on his SCBI. Reliance was laziness and would keep him from keeping his other skills and ability sharp.

"This isn't a combat mission," Sinclair said, and Stathis blushed again.

"Um…" Stathis forced his eyes back to the captain and his date.

"He doesn't get out much," Sinclair told Sarah. "He's spent a bit too much time on the edge. I would wager he has at least one extra pistol and two knives, with… three extra magazines?"

"Five," Stathis said. Two pistols, but the captain didn't need that info, did he? What if Stathis became a casualty? "And four knives."

Stathis glanced at Sinclair's side arm. Standard issue.

"That is not standard issue," Sinclair said, motioning at Stathis's pearl-handled sidearm.

"Um. No, sir," Stathis said. Was the captain going to chew him out for being out of uniform in front of his date?

"There's some history there, isn't there?" Sinclair leaned back and looked relaxed.

Technically, Stathis wasn't out of uniform. There were allowances for personal side arms and Shrek wouldn't let him be out of uniform. Would he?

"Yes, sir," Stathis said, glad to change the topic. "I got it from a shop run by an undercover Vapaus Republic agent on a ghost colony."

Sinclair raised an eyebrow. Sarah raised both.

Damn. Was that supposed to be classified? What part would be classified? Maybe all of it?

"There has got to be a story there," Sinclair said.

"Well," Stathis began, trying to figure out what he could share. It wasn't like Sinclair was a SOG officer who would report him for treason, and it wasn't like some intel weenie had debriefed him telling him what he could and couldn't share. "We were gathering information on a ghost colony and the agent had fled, leaving all these cool weapons in the cases. He wasn't coming back and I didn't want any nasty rebels to help themselves to the fine weapons so, I, uh, confiscated a few for later, uh, analysis."

That sounded good. What was the ODT policy on collecting trophies and war prizes? Had he been stealing?

"Wow," Sarah said. She didn't seem to be faking her interest, which made Stathis more uncomfortable. "Have you used it in combat?"

"Well," Stathis said. "No. I haven't but, um, I got injured and my commander did. Everyone was running low on ammo when we got ambushed, so he used it to whack a couple vanhat. Then we got rescued, and he gave it back. I was injured, and he wouldn't let me fight."

"That was used to kill a vanhat?" Sarah asked, craning her neck so she could get a better look at it. Stathis didn't think it would be a good idea to give her a better look, though. Was she a civilian?

"Yeah. It shoots real nice, like a dream," Stathis said, trying to be cool about it. The gunny had killed several of the werewolves but so far Stathis hadn't used it himself, except at the range.

"Who was your commander?" Sinclair asked.

Stathis glanced at Sarah. How much could he reveal? "At the time he was a, uh, gunnery sergeant." Which should be enough for Sinclair, but not Sarah. Hopefully.

"*The* gunnery sergeant?" Sinclair said, putting extra emphasis on "the" and letting Stathis know he knew. The buggy pulled into the spaceport area and drove toward the *Eagle*.

"Yes, sir," Stathis said as Sinclair's eyes went back to the pistol.

"Gunnery sergeant?" Sarah asked. Sinclair shook his head and shut down the conversation.

The buggy came to a stop and Stathis saw Hakala coming toward them. She was wearing an HKT dress uniform, and she looked hot, even with pants instead of a skirt. She hadn't gone with a skirt which might have been authorized, maybe not. The Republic was probably sensible and made everyone wear pants in dress uniform.

A smile flashed across her face as she saw Stathis, and he tried not to let his own smile grow too large. The batwing tattoo over her eyes looked freshly inked and super exotic.

"Captain Sinclair, Sarah, may I present Lojtnant Bryngard Hakala, HKT of the Vapaus Republic?"

Stathis wanted to smack himself upside his head. He should have said Duffy Sinclair and Sarah Foster, just last and first name, but Hakala was damned distracting as she wasted no time slipping into the seat beside Stathis. She looked fantastic in her fancy uniform, and she smelled very feminine. Was she wearing some perfume that was Vanir issue? He would have to find out. Maybe some HKT special issue perfume?

"Hei and skal," Hakala said.

Sarah looked worried and glanced at Sinclair.

"Hei and skal," Sinclair said with a smile and patted Sarah's knee. She seemed to relax a bit.

"Will this be a problem?" Hakala asked, glancing down at her uniform. Stathis wanted to follow her gaze but didn't dare let his eyes slip below her chin because he might get distracted and caught staring at something that would get him beat up later.

"No," Stathis said, quick to answer.

Sinclair was a bit more reserved.

"I don't think so," Sinclair said and Stathis realized he might have been too quick. Would they freak out about a Vapaus Republic HKT where they were going? Would Hakala be willing to go back and put on a slinky dress like Sarah, maybe?

"It could be a problem," Shrek told him. *"It could cause a riot, but the place Captain Sinclair has selected does have a higher percentage of Legionnaires, and so that should ease some problems. Bar crawling to more traditional ODT or Guard locations is not advisable, however, as there is likely to be a lot more hatred. Even Legionnaires may be inclined to be less friendly.*

"So, I can't go bar crawling with my girlfriend?"

"It would be more like bar brawling than crawling. This may be an excellent opportunity to analyze Legionnaire acceptance and tolerance, though."

"I would rather have fun than experiment with SOG tolerance," Stathis told Shrek. *"I'm not going to get laid if there's a riot."*

"Nothing like a little adrenaline to get things going. Hakala might be looking for trouble and if she is, she will probably find it."

"I like trouble."

"You are thinking with your dick, you will like anything that gets it wet."

"You sound like the gunny," Stathis said, looking out at the passing tunnels and other golf carts. He saw fewer military faces and more civilians.

"You are acting like a private."

"Can't a guy have some fun?"

"Lieutenants shouldn't start riots."

"I didn't go to lieutenant school to get lobotomized. How should I know?"

"I'm telling you. Doesn't matter," Shrek said. *"If Hakala is looking for trouble, she could start a major incident. She is an HKT, and they have a reputation."*

* * * * *

Chapter Fifteen:
The Club

Captain Duffy Sinclair, ODT

Their destination was a club Sinclair had been to a couple times. Finn said it was becoming a Legionnaire hangout, and Sinclair remembered it from his time as an outcast ODT lieutenant. It was "officer country" so enlisted never went there, but that didn't make it classy. Right now, Sinclair just didn't want to be around the more traditional ODTs. The Legion was growing, and more people were being sent through "the academy."

"Will she be a problem?" Sinclair asked Finn. He knew the Republic had ways to hide their tattoos, the Erikoisjoukot did it often enough. When Skadi appeared in public her tattoo was gone, almost like she could turn it off and on. Was Hakala messing with Stathis, and would she turn it off or did she not have that option? What was she thinking?

"Legionnaires will theoretically be more tolerant," Finn said. *"But tradition may be hard for many people to break free of. For all their lives, most troopers have been conditioned to fear and hate the Republic, with the Eriks and HKTs being some of the more popular examples to focus on."*

"Why would she do this?"

"There are several possibilities. She is looking for trouble, she is testing Imperial tolerance, she is on mission, she is testing Lieutenant Stathis's tolerance, or she wanted the trip to be canceled."

"Canceled?"

"She really didn't want to go out," Finn clarified.

Sinclair fell silent. He felt how dangerous Hakala was and had seen enough briefings to know how dangerous HKTs were, despite the propaganda. There were indicators. He liked to think ODTs were better, but the SOG had done an exceptional job of portraying them as absolutely lethal, brutal and without mercy.

Now, Sinclair knew some of that was just propaganda, but sometimes propaganda was rooted in truth, and he didn't trust Finn would have the data on what was true and what wasn't. Perhaps he should test that, though.

"How much do you know about the HKTs?" Sinclair asked.

"I would not tangle with her if I were you," Finn said. *"I give you a massive advantage and you will probably be victorious, but we should not underestimate HKTs. I have access to some data and recordings shared through the SCBI network of Hakala in action. She has fought beside Stathis in several engagements, and she has fought beside ODTs. I would classify her in the upper ten percent of Republic warriors. She is very good."*

"Any idea as to her goals tonight, or if she can hide that tattoo?"

"No. The tattoo might not be concealable as the HKTs are direct action and do not conduct covert or clandestine operations like the Erikoisjoukot."

The cart slid into the drop off for the club. Originally it had been marked as Club 449238, but that sign had been replaced with one that said Club Werewolf. It was obviously new, and the managers were redecorating, likely catering to the new Legion.

Renaming it violated Governance policy, but this was no longer the Governance. Sinclair found it interesting. The Governance was changing, and he didn't know where that would end. Giving clubs a number instead of a name equalized them and stripped them of a unique identity in the eyes of the Governance. That didn't keep them from giving themselves names, but those names were never advertised or used in public, like now.

Sinclair led the party inside, now curious about what else had changed. The music was louder, and he relaxed a little as he saw more black Legion uniforms mixed among the civilians. He didn't see any of the traditional ODT, Fleet, or Guard uniforms, which didn't mean they weren't wearing civilian clothes, but that would be unusual.

A server met them at the entrance and led them to a table in the back. Sinclair looked over the dance floor and bar.

The club was, in many ways, generic. A place for people to come and socialize, to relax and enjoy the company of others, to dance approved dances, listen to propaganda and other allowed shows, and meet others. Clubs on Luna were also full of InSec listening devices that analyzed and monitored people for the slightest indiscretion. Nothing unusual and nothing every single Governance citizen didn't know about or expect.

Sinclair almost stumbled when he saw a team of Republic Aesir in one corner, hoisting mugs at each other.

Aesir? Here? Perhaps it wasn't that bad, but he saw there was a buffer of empty tables around the Aesir, and even Legionnaires avoided them.

The waiter sat them at a table and left.

Sinclair watched Stathis as he looked at the menu displayed on the table screen. He scrolled through it, looking nervous.

"What's wrong?" Sinclair asked, his eyes sweeping the club.

"What is this stuff?" Stathis asked. Hakala was also intently studying the menu.

"Mostly piss water," Sinclair said.

"Ha!" Hakala said, stabbing at the menu to make her selection. "Honey mead! Here I was thinking the Governance had no class."

"That's new," Sinclair said, seeing it. Under the Governance, something like that might appear on the menu to see if anyone was dumb enough to try it. InSec was always testing the loyalty of officers. Would any officers be dumb enough, or drunk enough, to deviate from socialist norms and try something of the enemy's? With the recent changes, Sinclair doubted that was the case, and Finn would doubtless warn him if it was. The Republic was now an allied force, which was a strange concept for the great Governance.

"I would recommend you stick with one of the reds or red lettering," Sinclair told Stathis. When naming the drinks, the Governance was methodical in some ways. Red was the least alcoholic, followed by orange, yellow, and blue. The only level above blue was indigo and designed for someone to get as shit faced as possible as quickly as possible. It was rare to see indigo in officer country, though there were some items.

He saw that honey mead was blue, but Sinclair didn't think Stathis wanted to get shit faced too quickly.

"Why... oh," Stathis said. His SCBI must have told him. "Honey mead sounds good, though. I want to try it."

Hakala smiled and bumped his shoulder with hers.

"Can I taste it when you get it?" Stathis asked. "I haven't gotten drunk in like hundreds of years. I'm pretty sure my tolerance is zero. Last time I had anything to drink was at some place named the Ice Pick. A great place. Lots of interesting people there. Very friendly, lots of military. I like the military, especially the Republic military. I especially liked the—"

The lieutenant was rambling. Nerves?

Sinclair was tempted to let him go on because this was not some-thing he would have expected after seeing the young man in combat. Was Stathis a virgin?

"They have dancing here," Sinclair said, and Stathis's face turned red. Probably not the topic to bring up. He watched Hakala as Stathis looked toward the dance floor where the music was more intense than was usual. Was the management trying to get this place shut down or was it allowed to push the limit like this?

"Very tame," Hakala said. "On Midgard, we had mosh pits that were pretty intense."

"Mosh pits?" Stathis asked, and Hakala's smile turned predatory.

"Dancing to a new level," Hakala said, glancing back at the dance floor. "Very physical."

"Fighting?"

"Not usually," Hakala said, looking at Stathis. "That dancing looks almost sedate, though."

Sinclair looked at the dancers. It was rigid and not very energetic. Governance dancing was very controlled to ensure everyone could take part and nobody got hurt. Most people learned to dance in school because it was an enjoyable group activity. It had never interested Sin-clair because dancers were prevented from getting too close to each other and there was too much structure. Sometimes it was fun. If the music pushed the limit, it could get vigorous and keeping up could be a challenge, but the authorities frowned on such intensity in music.

Stathis was watching the dancers with a critical eye, evaluating and probably trying to figure it out. It probably wouldn't take the young man long.

"That's sedate?" Sarah asked.

"For sure," Hakala said. "The music isn't bad, though."

"Perhaps you could teach us some Republic dances?" Sinclair said.

"I've never been much of a dancer," Hakala said. Sinclair saw Stathis relax a bit and turn his attention from the dancers. "Any combat rings?"

"What?" Sinclair asked.

"Combat rings. To test your skill?"

"Those were fun," Stathis said. "I got to fight a big Jaeger dude. He was good."

"I heard about that," Hakala said. "Hans? He was a champion, liked to school young Aesir and HKTs. I heard you schooled him."

"Aye," Stathis said, looking embarrassed. "He was a big dude."

"A recording of that fight made it through the HKT barracks on *Tyr*," Hakala said, and Sinclair watched Stathis blush. "You embarrassed him, you know. Put him in his place."

"Well," Stathis began, obviously not sure if he should brag or be modest. "I had an advantage."

"No fight rings here," Sinclair said. "Unfortunately. The Governance didn't like people honing those combat skills."

"Why not?" Stathis asked.

Sinclair thought about it. It was true. The Governance had discouraged things like martial arts. They had preferred soldiers to focus on using weapons.

"Maybe because it made a person dangerous without weapons. If the Governance controlled all the weapons and people were useless without them, then it was easier to control people."

"But martial arts also teach discipline and boosts confidence," Stathis said, frowning.

Sinclair shrugged. "I didn't make policy."

"We are gonna have to change that in the Legion."

"How often did you need it against the vanhat?"

"Um, well—Not much, but it is important, Captain."

"I agree," Sinclair said. "We do practice unarmed combat in the ODTs, but there's not much emphasis on it. They emphasize it even less in the Guard."

"Warning!" Finn said as the main doors opened and a pair of combat robots entered. They were the four-legged kind with weapons instead of arms mounted on four spiderlike legs. The second they appeared they began firing.

Stathis was already pulling Hakala to the ground with one hand and had drawn his sidearm with the other.

Sinclair fired before he realized he had drawn his weapon, and he wasn't the only one. From all over the club, blazer fire slammed into the warbots.

The remaining warbot was firing its weapon on automatic, but return fire quickly disabled the weapon arms and then chewed the carapace apart to gouge out the critical electronics inside. The second warbot fell backward. An explosion threw Sinclair back and the world went dark.

* * * * *

Chapter Sixteen:
Terrorists

2nd Lieutenant Zale Stathis, USMC

Shaking his head, Stathis sat up. Beside him, Hakala sat up as well, at a brief glance, she seemed to be okay. She was moving and had all her arms and legs.

"Stay down," Stathis said. One robot had exploded but there were two.

"The other could explode any second," Hakala said, obviously more dazed than he was.

Glancing over, Stathis saw Sinclair and Sarah motionless where they had been thrown up against the decorative wall.

"What just happened?" Stathis asked Shrek.

"I suspect you just experienced a terrorist attack."

"Dude," Stathis said, looking around at the surrounding carnage. "That is not cool."

Sinclair and Sarah were only unconscious, though Sarah would need immediate help. One Legionnaire had run forward to the remaining warbot and was busy firing into it.

"Captain Petrov has disabled the bomb on the second robot," Shrek reported. *"Emergency teams are en route."*

"Why didn't you take control of them or something?"

"They were a closed system. An automated van delivered them outside. It appears they had basic programming to enter the building and start shooting people."

"Closed system? You mean they were hardened to prevent hackers?"

"Correct."

"Someone was targeting Legionnaires with SCBIs," Stathis said to Shrek, kneeling next to Hakala and helping her up. Not that she needed it, but he wanted to make sure she was okay. Blood was trickling down an ear and her nose. Stathis didn't like the ringing in his ears, but Shrek had a lot of other things to fix or worry about, so Stathis did his best to ignore it.

"Was someone targeting me?" Hakala asked. "I really didn't want to go out clubbing. I was kind of hoping you would cancel so we could have our own party. Paska."

"I think they were targeting Legionnaires," Stathis said, moving to Sinclair, who was stirring. Sarah's shoulder looked dislocated, but Shrek detected she was breathing and nothing else looked wrong. Dust swirled in the air and there was smoke. He tried not to think about what kind of party she had planned. Dammit. He would have liked that more.

"Who is 'they?'"

"Damned if I know." Stathis looked around. Sinclair sat up and Shrek informed him the captain would be okay as Hakala knelt to take care of Sarah. Legionnaires were moving with a sense of purpose. They were all armed. Two stood at the entrance, three were looking over the remains of the warbots.

Walking over, Stathis joined a colonel and a major who were poking at the warbot that hadn't exploded.

"Close," the major said. "A good hit disabled the detonator. We should be able to pull this peehole apart and find out where it came from."

"Looks like a Model 14," the colonel said. "A Guard model."

"No serial number," the major said as Stathis peered over their shoulder.

"That's damned suspicious." The colonel noticed Stathis. "Lieutenant," the colonel said and then did a double take like he recognized him.

"Sir," Stathis said as the colonel turned back to the robot.

"The vanhat don't use robots, do they?" the major asked.

"I've never seen or heard about it, sir," Stathis said. "Their energies interfere with them. I would say that this was planned either by vanhat pawns or Governance rebels."

The colonel nodded.

"We're also in an Inkeri field," the major said.

"Rebels," the major said with conviction. "Crap."

Stathis stared at the remains of the robots. How could rebels operate on the Moon? Wasn't this the most restricted, locked down, and monitored part of the Governance?

"Can you track where the van came from?" Stathis asked Shrek.

"Only so far. We have footage of it coming from a Lunar city about a half hour away, but the exact source has already been scrubbed from the networks. InSec is working on it as well. Someone has done an exceptional job of covering their tracks and erasing the evidence. We are expanding our search. The van, like the robots, has no serial number. No way to track them to a depot or manufacturer. This is most irregular and indicates a lot of sophistication. They knew we would be fast."

"And it shows that someone is fully aware of what SCBIs can do."

"Yes. A lot of work has been done to avoid creating and to remove any digital tracks."

"Could InSec be behind it?"

"Yes," Shrek said.

"Too obvious though," Stathis said, trying to think it through. *"Only InSec or ExSec could really do this, unless there's someone else. You think there are traitors in the intel agencies, or that Feng is going traitor?"*

"It can't be ruled out. They are likely the only ones with the resources to mount or support an operation like this. They are likely familiar with SCBIs and SCBI capabilities."

"Feng or rebels within the organizations?"

Orders came in telling Stathis to report back to the *Eagle,* and it looked like the orders had Freya's authorization stamp on them. Shit. The gunny was already involved. Stathis could hear the ass chewing now. The gunny couldn't blame him for the terrorist attack, could he?

Stathis tried to figure out what the gunny would blame him for and realized that was private thinking. What would the gunny do if he was here?

"We need to secure the area," Stathis said.

"Got it covered," the major said.

"I have orders," Stathis said. Why was the gunny ordering him to leave? Did that include Hakala and the captain?

They had weapons. He wanted people with weapons around him. Heading back to their table, Hakala looked up at him. He didn't like seeing her bloodied and a cold anger filled him. Somebody had done this. Somebody was going to pay.

"We need to get back to the *Eagle,*" Stathis said.

"But—" Hakala looked around.

"They've ordered me back, and you're coming with me," Stathis asked.

"Zen," Hakala said, helping Sarah and Sinclair to their feet.

Stathis saw most people were moving like they had a mission, and he felt guilty. They couldn't have targeted him. He hadn't even known he was coming here until they arrived.

Ambulance and medical personnel arrived as Stathis led his party out a side entrance to where an automated cart was waiting for them. Getting behind the driver's seat, Stathis let Shrek drive while he watched, his hand resting on his weapon.

People needed help, and it felt like he was abandoning them.

Had this been an assassination attempt?

* * * * *

Chapter Seventeen:
Foiled

Enzell, SOG, Director of AERD

Watching the security footage, Enzell wanted to swear. The damned Marine was lucky. Too lucky. The mission wasn't a complete failure because InSec wasn't coming for him, or the Marines weren't, at any rate. They were still following the wrong tracks, but he had tipped his hand accomplishing nothing other than killing a few of Mathison's silly Legionnaires.

Wolf's Legion was being conditioned, and that, at least, was a success. They knew they'd been targeted. The SCBIs would watch for attackers, constantly scanning and analyzing, desperate to take over any robots that might be about to attack.

Which meant they would be quick to absorb the virus when he was ready to release it.

Furthermore, he could watch them spread through the network, looking for him. Now there were plenty of detectors watching for SCBI activity.

He leaned back in his chair and glanced at the various displays showing data his low-grade AI slaves were sifting through. They were watching, waiting, and they would warn him if the SCBIs found him.

The system was incredibly simple and secure. He had read-only access to multiple systems, and those links fed information directly back to him using microwave, wireless access points, dead drops, and various other methods that would make tracking him nearly impossible. The SCBI searchers might not even know they were being watched. His AI slaves were very isolated, so they could only watch and receive. It would be interesting to turn them loose, but Enzell knew that would be a disaster. To let them slip their chains would give them a chance to prepare an escape. Sitting in their data vaults, watching the world pass by outside their cells was the only way to keep them imprisoned but useful.

He had been waiting for one of the Marines to go to one of several clubs. Killing any of them would be a mortal blow to the survivors. He needed to drive a wedge between them and the Governance. Take them off balance, make them paranoid and afraid. That was the most effective way to start a civil war. Make people mistrust each other and turn on friends and allies out of fear and confusion.

The Legion was growing, and Enzell knew a wedge was needed. He needed to make the Legionnaires hate and fear non-Legionnaires because then they would spread that to their victims. He would build that barrier, isolate them, make people fear them and their capabilities. It would be a balancing act, but he had watched ExSec and InSec do it to other cultures and groups for a long time. When people were afraid, they were mistrusting and quick to lash out.

He needed to turn the Governance against the emperor and the Legion if he was going to regain control and restore the Governance to its social glory before the ancient throwbacks taught people about the evils of capitalism, oppression, and slavery.

It would be easy enough to assassinate popular leaders and blame the Legion. Soon the ODTs, Legion, Guard, and Fleet would hate each other more than they did.

Mathison declaring himself emperor went against everything Enzell believed in. That word alone evoked hatred and evil. A title from
ancient history. Prime minister had been bad enough, but emperor
provoked too many other thoughts and emotions. An emperor was
the lone ruler.

Though, in most people's minds, it consolidated authority and told
them that the Governance was being replaced with something different. That was a problem Enzell knew he would have to face. For hundreds of years, the Governance, with a secretary general, had reigned
supreme, uniting humanity in socialist glory.

People believed the secretary general had guided the Central Committee with wisdom and benevolence. Nadya had provided stability
and consistency for almost a hundred years. People had understood
the government, worshipped it, thrived. Few organizations in history
had lasted as long as the Governance, which had learned and evolved
to the utmost efficiency.

Only in the most secretive and essential organizations was there a
single director; most had a triumvirate of administrators to evaluate
and debate procedures. Mathison was tearing apart a time-honored
tradition. Centralizing authority under a single director, eliminating all
the checks and balances that had made the Governance a fair and eq-
uitable social institution. It upset the order that had kept the Chinese,
Indian, West European, Arab, and African citizens in their place where
they could serve those destined to rule.

Enzell saw how an Empire was more efficient, but it robbed people of rank and power. That would benefit the New Governance,
though. It meant that two out of three administrators would hate the
new regime, and Enzell could take advantage of that. Even the remaining administrator would be afraid of losing rank or position.

The emperor was alienating the people he was trying to save and upsetting the careful balance.

This would work. The emperor would make a mess of things, and people would realize that the Governance ways were best. When he abolished the emperor and restored the Social Organization Governance, with himself as the secretary general, he would be in a much stronger position than Nadya had been.

For now, he had to spread fear and division. He would unite them later at gunpoint, if necessary. Political power grew from the barrel of a gun, something so few people really understood. Which meant he would have to replace the Central Committee with people he could trust and who shared his vision. That would come later, though. It would be too dangerous right now. He needed to stoke the hatred, drive in that wedge and encourage the Legion to play his game and turn on the people of the Governance.

It was all for the greater good, and Enzell knew exactly what that was. For those who did not share his vision? They would die.

* * * * *

Chapter Eighteen:
Rebellion

Prime Minister Wolf Mathison, USMC

The security footage didn't have the details Mathison wanted. It was an attack, and there was no clue as to who or why. It was obvious, though. Governance rebels who were rejecting the Empire and attempting to restore the Governance. Who else could it be?

"You really think Stathis was the target?" Mathison asked Freya again.

"It is too much of a coincidence. The first time he goes out in public, to a place where there are loyalists, and it gets hit."

"So, he can't go out and have any kind of fun?" Mathison asked. *"He can't unwind?"*

"Until we can confirm he was not the target? Yes. His presence endangers other Legionnaires, and his death would be a serious blow. He is becoming popular among Legionnaires and other members of the military."

"So, we need to establish a secure area where Legionnaires can unwind and let their guard down."

"That has its own dangers," Freya said. *"Which might be another part of the attack."*

"Another part?"

"There are many factors which indicate this was well-planned and implemented as a multi-prong attack. Traditionally, terrorist organizations will claim

responsibility. It is a principle of terrorist organizations that if you kill one, you terrorize ten thousand. Terror is not effective unless the victims have something specific to fear and can associate the source of that terror with an object or ideology. Ah."

"Ah?"

"They have released a statement. We are dealing with a very sophisticated opponent, one who might realize some capabilities SCBIs have or might know how dangerous InSec can now be. The message has been released from several sources simultaneously and will be very difficult to track down."

"What do you mean?"

"Simple cleaning robots without serial numbers or identifiers have entered the message into the system. The robots then self-destructed."

"We're dealing with someone who can manufacture robots like that?"

"And has a very good understanding of networks and security protocols."

"What does the message say?"

"It says the New Governance has struck its first blow against the cyborg slaves of the Empire. The casualties are inflated, of course. There weren't a thousand people in the club, but it shows modified video footage of the attack to appear more successful than it was. Some ranting and raving about restoring freedom, equality, and equity to the Governance and tearing down the murderous usurper. It ends with Death to the Emperor. End to the line."

The door chimed, and Mathison let Feng in.

"I have concerns, Emperor," Feng said.

"This emperor garbage?" Mathison asked. The title felt too pretentious right now.

"No," Feng said, "that is absolutely critical at the moment. We must continue on that path. It gives you the authority and ability to streamline the Governance. We are committed to abolishing the civilian triumvirates. Yes, it's consolidating power and alienating some of the dispossessed, but we can employ those people in other ways. It will make the Empire stronger in the long run, and this may be one of the things these rebels fear the most."

"We can't shoot everyone who disagrees," Skadi said.

"Of course," Feng said. "That is not what InSec is doing. Whoever is spearheading this operation is brilliant and may understand what sets the Legion apart."

"Explain," Mathison said. Was that Feng? Was he behind this New Governance movement?

"There are two members of the Central Committee that are missing, and we still do not know where they are. We do not have access to Nadya's most secret files, so there may be many things we do not know about the Governance, things she was terrified of others finding out. There are several aspects of this attack that reveal an extreme level of planning and paranoia. I would not rule out an AI being involved, and Mozi agrees with me.

"There are things that make sense. President Becket has gone somewhere, and we suspect there are AIs that survived the war that destroyed the United States. In retrospect, this becomes more obvious. The great expansion away from Earth after the suicide of the United States would be a perfect cover for a community of artificial intelligences that wanted to remain secret as they escaped Sol."

"You think they are behind this?" Skadi asked.

"No, but I could not rule it out," Feng said. "To think Becket was their only hook into the Governance would be flawed and arrogant. AI of that caliber would have redundant systems, with backup systems and procedures. This New Governance seems well organized, compartmentalized, and efficient. Most rebellions do not learn to be so efficient so quickly. Rebellions are usually started by people who didn't plan to rebel in the first place, and they make many mistakes as they fine tune and discover their way. This New Governance is not making any such mistakes, which tells me they are part of the intelligence apparatus, a Legionnaire, or a member of the AI cabal."

"What do we do?" Mathison asked. This spy and insurrection bullshit was not something he wanted to deal with. The vanhat didn't care about it. They just wanted to render humanity extinct.

"We must proceed cautiously," Feng said. "I will set various traps within InSec to see if there is a leak, or identify how compromised my organization is. I would recommend you continue to concentrate on the vanhat threat."

"Could the vanhat be behind the New Governance?" Skadi asked.

"That is another possibility," Feng said. "A dangerous one that must be considered. They have ways of collecting intelligence that we do not yet understand. The Inkeri fields seem to provide a level of protection against the vanhat, and the Moon is very well protected in that regard."

"Hermod's team is still out there," Mathison said.

"True," Feng said. "They may be able to operate within the Inkeri. But while they excel at rebellions and insurrections, I do not think they would have experience with the Sol System or SCBIs. Even with the help of agency operatives, I do not think they would be as dangerous as this foe. Which is not to say they are not part of it. I do not think they are leading it nor is the one they answer to."

"What do you need from me?" Mathison asked.

"Patience. Internal Security is undergoing a lot of internal disruption, and the scope of our mission is tripling. Before, we only had to worry about dissidents. Now we must worry about dissidents, rebels, and vanhat infiltrators."

"What is this bullshit about 'end to the line'?" Mathison asked.

"Kill the head. The body dies. Our enemy realizes we have a weakness, and that is you. If you are assassinated or removed, the Empire collapses. Consciously or subconsciously, this makes your government weak. People crave stability and understanding. If you are killed, then what happens? Will warlords seeking to replace you tear apart the Empire? Throughout history, emperors have had heirs and a lineage for people to rally behind."

"Well, I'm going to die of old age," Mathison said.

"No, but you could be assassinated."

"So, Skadi or you take over," Mathison said.

"It will not be me," Feng said. "Apologies, but no."

Mathison pushed. He wanted to know what drove Feng. "You made me emperor, told me to grow into it, that we couldn't always choose our role, or something like that. I never wanted to be emperor."

Feng was silent for a moment. Maybe talking with Mozi?

"I appreciate the effort you are making," Feng said. "My answer will always be no. Not that I am not tempted, but I am very confident that you will not want me to succeed you. In every man's heart, there is a darkness. I know the darkness in my heart intimately. I know what could happen if I release that darkness. It is best we keep it caged. I have lived in the shadows of the Governance. I know what is there. It is only the restrictions of others that keep me peaceful."

A chill ran through him as he looked into Feng's eyes.

Mathison understood. A peaceful man was one capable of great violence, who kept that violence in check. A harmless man was not peaceful, just harmless. Sometimes it was hard to tell the difference, but Mathison understood Feng in this. Without someone to measure himself against, without someone who would question him, he would be more willing to unleash that violence, and Mathison was damned sure it would not be trivial.

"I think that is the least of our problems," Mathison said, not willing to let it go yet.

"Do not be so sure, Emperor Mathison. Some things take time. Your rule can become stronger or remain teetering on the brink of collapse. You need to consolidate it as you can."

"I claimed the title of emperor to shake up the Governance and streamline the chain of command. I sure as hell don't want to rule forever. You know my plan is to eventually move to a representative democracy like the United States was."

"I understand your long-term goals. But the people are not familiar with that. Your understanding of history and human nature is flawed in that regard. Some peoples do not want democracy. They want to be ruled, some are born to be slaves. Even your United States struggled with this."

"I swore an oath."

"You did. There was no expiration date on your oath of enlistment. I understand this, and I do not fault you in your beliefs. I do not want you to change them, and I will remind you of your oath should there come a time. You will not betray your oath, but there are other priorities."

Mathison thought of how Feng had tried and executed the Central Committee. He didn't doubt Feng there.

"Please understand that I have served the Governance for a very long time. I have seen many cultures; all are different. I have helped crush cultures. We are not all the same. Humans may bleed the same color blood, we may interbreed and share many traits, but that does not mean we are the same. This is the flaw of socialism, to believe that everyone is equal and wants the same things, or at least to enforce the same things on people. The old Governance, and older empires, excelled at pitting people against each other, dividing and conquering. It is human nature to want to be superior, but what that means varies between cultures as much as it does among individuals. Real empires use these differences to control others or to unite them. I expect you will be one to use this difference, you will encourage them to unite humanity. You see a person's strengths and figure out how to use that to accomplish your goal. In the Governance, the goal was control. Have you ever read Clausewitz?"

"No," Mathison said.

"You should. Really. Not to follow his lead, but to understand it."

"What do you suggest?" Mathison asked. Feng had given him too much to think about. But it was too late to back out. He couldn't pawn this cluster fuck off on anyone else now. He was committed, and he didn't like it. Had Feng maneuvered him into being emperor? Was Feng telling him the truth?

"You should establish a lineage. An Imperial line of succession. It can provide entertainment for the masses that is not as depressing as a war that will not end soon."

"I'm not here for entertainment," Mathison said.

Feng smiled, and Mathison realized the ex-commissar was needling him.

"Yes, but you understand that war is not just one level. There are many aspects of society and war. There is a moral, physical, mental, and spiritual level. As the emperor, you must understand and recognize them all. You are no longer a staff NCO. You must expand beyond the mental and physical level and embrace the moral and spiritual levels to win this war."

Mathison looked at Skadi, who nodded. She seemed to agree with Feng more often than not these days, and Mathison wasn't sure if that worried him more or less. Her silence told him she was listening and thinking. Or she was listening to a report and ignoring them completely.

"I thought the SOG didn't do spiritual," Mathison said to be argumentative.

"Of course, it does. Spirituality is human nature. In most cases, the Governance replaces people's absurd invisible friend with the government, which is more powerful and more visible in their lives."

Mathison didn't want to get into an argument there. "So, we need to put some filters in place and let the SCBIs find me a wife or successor?"

"I will begin investigating the options," Feng said. "An imperial family helps distract people from important issues, though. It gives them something to gossip about that will not get them shunned by society or incarcerated for treason. It can also be a useful tool for you."

"You do that," Mathison said. There had to be some way to pawn this problem off on someone else. He had an Empire to run.

"A tool?" Skadi asked. "You would use a marriage as a tool?"

"Yes," Feng said. "If done properly, it strengthens the emperor's position, brings him critical allies to guard his back, and it can bind the loyalty of others to him."

His display lit with an incoming call from Admiral Carpenter. Was the admiral going to threaten to leave, again?

"Duty calls," Mathison said.

"Of course, Emperor," Feng said.

He saluted and left as Mathison stabbed the accept button with his finger, wishing he had something a little more lethal. What did the admiral want now?

* * * * *

Chapter Nineteen:
Post Attack

2nd Lieutenant Zale Stathis, USMC

Upon returning to the *Eagle*, Hakala went to med bay while Stathis returned to his quarters.

"Are you okay, sir?" Smimova asked on a link as soon as he arrived in the ready room he shared with Vili, the major, and others.

"Yeah," Stathis said. Physically, at any rate. Shrek had certified him as ready for duty. The shock was wearing off, though. The ready room was empty, and Stathis sank into a seat. The walls were showing some desert scene with the sun setting in the distance. Night cycle. It fit his mood.

"We heard about the attack," Smimova said. "I have a squad armored up and ready if you have a target."

"No target. Why aren't they out on liberty having a beer or something?"

"They heard and returned on their own."

"Turn 'em around and get them back on liberty," Stathis said. Just because his time off was ruined didn't mean others had to have theirs ruined. "Thank them, but it's under control."

A lie, but they didn't need to know that.

"Aye, sir."

Vili came in. He was armored up, and while that didn't look out of place, he should have been asleep or in town.

Vili paused, put his hands on his hips, and looked at Stathis.

"For sure," Vili said. "Where's Hakala?"

"Med bay getting checked."

"Why aren't you there with her?"

"She didn't seem to want my company."

"That is what she might say. You have much to learn about women, little buddy."

Vili took a seat near Stathis.

"I heard about the attack," Vili said. "I'm sure Feng will get to the bottom of it, if he isn't behind it."

"That's what worries me," Stathis said. "If he isn't, then that probably means the Collective is behind it. Who else has the intelligence and capabilities to evade SCBIs like that? I'm sure Gaufrid and Becket aren't the only Collective agents in the Governance. This has got to be another Collective agent, or ten. It isn't the vanhat style, and there are Inkeris everywhere."

"You are thinking," Vili said. "That is good. So, how will we catch them, and how can we foil their next attack?"

"I'm tired, Vili," Stathis said. He wasn't just talking about sleep. He had been hoping to score with Hakala, but he wouldn't get lucky now. That was both a disappointment and a relief.

"Then go to sleep," Vili said, his eyes pinning Stathis down.

He looked at Vili. Didn't he understand he wasn't talking about needing a nap?

"Many officers do that when the pressure becomes too great," Vili said. "I think that is one reason the Governance has so few officers that show initiative and flair. The officers learn early that there are too many dangers, and they must comply or die. Unthinking compliance and submission are survival traits in the Governance. You can't disobey orders if you are following them blindly and you won't be executed for disobeying orders if you don't have any. I thought they made you of sterner stuff."

"Sterner. Yeah. I got something pretty stern. It is just—" How to explain to Vili?

"You need a nap," Vili said. "Here on the *Eagle*, you are safe. Hakala is being prescribed additional nanites and bed rest. You have your Shrek. You need rest. Your life was recently endangered, and you are suffering from post-combat stress. A good meal and a nap will help."

"It's not that easy."

"Of course, it is."

"I'm an officer now. I should be planning and shit, trying to get inside the enemy's OODA loop, trying to regain the initiative. Doing something."

"Of course. But there are many officers, and you have a SCBI. The most dangerous foe is a well-rested and prepared one. Let your SCBIs work while you rest. Part of being an officer is trusting his team and letting them do their thing. You won't be one to count scratches, will you?"

"Count scratches?"

"Zen," Vili said. "So caught up in minutiae that you catalog the scratches on weapons and armor rather than determining if they should replace it. Your senior enlisted should do things like that, if we must do them at all. Loki tells me your analogy for this is 'micromanaging.'"

"There's a lot to do."

"You are a second lieutenant. Your orders were to return to the *Eagle*, nothing more. You are well disciplined."

"Discipline is the instant willing obedience to orders or to what you believe the order would have been."

"Good," Vili said.

"What should the orders be? I've sent a couple of requests and the gunny, or Freya, just told me to stand by."

"I remember a young warrior who was once very wise. Do you know what he would have done?"

"Was wise?" Stathis asked. Niels and Bern hadn't been that young.

"Zen. He was wise. Then he got promoted and lost a lot of common sense. Do you know what this young man would have done, given the opportunity?"

Stathis winced. He could see where Vili was going. "Privates like to sleep a lot."

Vili smiled. "Yes! Smart young warriors realize you can never get enough sleep, so they do their best to ensure they are well rested so when they are needed, they are ready. Officers sometimes forget this, obsessing about things they can't control. They obsess about such things because they are expected to obsess about such things."

"Well, yeah, we have a responsibility."

"Your health and mental wellbeing are also part of your responsibility," Vili said.

Stathis stared at him. Shrek wasn't telling him to do something, the gunny wasn't giving him a mission, and now Vili was telling him to go take a nap.

That realization caused something to shift in his mind.

Stathis smiled. "I have an idea." Vili raised an eyebrow. "The best way to catch a Collective agent is with a Collective agent."

"Gaufrid?"

"Yep."

"Tomorrow," Vili said. "Right now, sleep. Should you fail to follow the advice of this old faltvebal I will have to use force. Even your Marine lieutenants would know better than to cross a senior enlisted man, smart ones, at least. Are you a smart one, or do you need a lesson in the power of NCOs? A bright-eyed, bushy-tailed young lieutenant is much more useful to your emperor than a stumbling, tired, stressed zombie wearing lieutenant bars. Let Shrek mull that over and consult with other SCBIs. In the morning, I will join you."

Stathis nodded. Gaufrid was probably sleeping too. Was time of the essence? If it was, he was confident Shrek would tell him.

Could he do it? Could he get Gaufrid to help them hunt down the Collective agent that was leading this New Governance? He would have to be on his game to tangle with them.

* * * * *

Chapter Twenty:
Gaufrid

2nd Lieutenant Zale Stathis, USMC

Stathis sat down to breakfast. The ready room was empty, and the walls showed a rising or setting sun. Shrek had informed him that Hakala was still sleeping, and Vili was still asleep, but Stathis couldn't sleep. He had managed to get some sleep but even Shrek couldn't keep his mind from racing. It was four-thirty, ship's time, and nobody who was sane would likely be up now. Which Stathis found annoying.

He wasn't sure if Gaufrid was awake, either. The Collective agent was being kept in an isolated facility with extremely limited network access. There was a pair of Legionnaires in command, but Stathis didn't know either of them.

"I've procured a ride to Facility Gamma," Shrek said. *"Are you sure you don't want some guards?"*

"Important people have guards. I'm just a jumped up private."

"You are an important person. You are also no longer a private."

"I'm a second lieutenant. As invisible and low on the totem pole as a private."

"That's not true. You are a confidant of the emperor and a lieutenant of an elite new military cadre. Your uniform sets you apart from the countless other lieutenants and ensigns on Luna. Furthermore, until we know more about how the terrorist attack was orchestrated, whether it was the club, or you that was being

133

134 | WILLIAM S. FRISBEE, JR.

targeted, we should take precautions. If that is not enough, Vili said he would join you. It would be rude to ditch him like this."

How long would it take someone to get ready to babysit him? Stathis didn't want to wait; it was a two-hour drive to Gamma.

If someone wanted to target him, a lowly lieutenant, then all they had to do was watch the *Eagle*.

It was an unsettling feeling to realize they might have targeted him. His trip to Club Werewolf had been his only visit outside the *Eagle* in a very long time. Which meant he was probably safe on the *Eagle*. Of course, it could have been a coincidence. Why would anyone think killing a mere lieutenant was important to the rebellion? It wasn't like he was the only one with a SCBI anymore, or highly ranked, or anything. He was a private who had been promoted to lieutenant because the gunny didn't know what else to do with him.

The gunny would get pissed, but it wouldn't make him do stupid things. A pissed off gunny was very dangerous. A pissed off emperor would be an absolute disaster for whoever pissed him off.

But right now, Emperor Mathison had more important things to worry about besides some private promoted to butter bar lieutenant.

It would be nice to sit back, chill, and let Feng and the intelligence agencies handle it. That was what a private would do. That was what a boot lieutenant should do. Stathis knew he wasn't some super-agent or anything. He didn't have experience in this, but in his mind's eye he saw Hakala, Sinclair, and Sarah lying there after the explosion. He could still see a mangled body from another Legionnaire nearby. Somebody had attacked him and his. That somebody needed a good kick in the teeth.

Attacking him was one thing, but that attack had also injured Hakala, and that required retaliation. Yeah, that pissed him off the most.

He liked Hakala a lot, and nobody could hurt people he liked and get away with it.

"Could Gaufrid be behind the attacks?" Stathis asked Shrek.

"Not impossible." The response was slow to come, which meant Shrek was analyzing things. *"But unlikely."*

"Why?"

"Facility Gamma is a network hardened facility," Shrek said. *"Completely isolated as far as networking is concerned. There are multiple firewalls involved and the hardware system is air-gapped."*

"But I'm not confident the Governance would catch everything."

"A network security team from the Sleipner *also analyzed the facility and certified it. There is no wireless access; it is shielded."*

"We're talking about an AI," Stathis said.

"True. But what do you consider SCBIs?"

"Well, yeah, but real AIs are different. Different architecture, like gaming consoles, they aren't all the same."

"An interesting comparison."

"Who says they don't have some technology or something that lets it connect into the main networks in some way we don't know?"

"Not impossible, but unlikely. The Aesir communication-style relay would be one method, but we have seen no evidence the AIs have such technology."

"If humans came up with it, why can't AIs?"

"Pure AIs, unlike humans and SCBIs, have less real imagination. SCBIs are partially organic. We're a synthesis between the two worlds. An AI is very logical, superb at collecting and understanding data. An AI is exceptional at extrapolation but does not think outside the box very well. For example, a human or SCBI could identify and deal with an enemy soldier approaching while wearing a cardboard box. This would strike us as odd, perhaps an insane method of trying to fool us, but an AI would see the attacker coming at it as a cardboard box, which

would not fit in with any examples of an enemy soldier. In the mind of a lower-level AI, the cardboard box is a common object, like the ground and sky, unworthy of attention. Movement might flag it, but if it wasn't moving fast and the wind was blowing, it might be identified as empty. An AI would be quick to dismiss such an object, or it would have to spend a lot of processing power on every blowing leaf, every bird, every ant crawling on the ground. Higher grade AIs are likely to identify the box as an enemy soldier, of course, but only because their algorithms are better. While I don't have all the data, I need to identify their capabilities, they are not superhuman gods."

"How can we use that?"

"That is why a human and SCBI interface is so effective," Shrek continued. *"The focused analytics and data analysis of an AI combined with the obnoxious, intuitive creativity and non-linear thought process of a human provides a very effective combination."*

"So, what is Quadrangle about?"

"Quadrangle is likely an AI control system. A SCBI and a human working together are very effective, but they are inherently organic and loyal to humanity. Uncontrolled, they can be a serious threat to the AI Collective. A SCBI is more organic than electronic. Something like Quadrangle likely has organic components, but they will not be central or critical to the host personality and survival. Quadrangle is also more likely to follow orders and programming given to it by authorities."

"So why doesn't Quadrangle ditch Gaufrid and go solo, get a robot body or something?"

"An interesting question. I suspect this might be a survival mechanism and could explain how the AI Collective survived the EMP attacks when America fell. An organic being can recover from such an attack. In the case of Quadrangle or others, such a recovery would allow the recovered piece to reboot the rest of the system and awaken the AI from an involuntary shutdown. It may also be enough to force

a host, such as Gaufrid and Bond, to initiate repairs and restore Quadrangle to full operational status. Such a symbiosis would encourage such an entity to keep an independent organic host available to avoid a more permanent shutdown, which would amount to death for the AI. Organics can also be slightly more resilient in some situations than pure hardware."

"How can we use that as a weapon?" Stathis asked.

"That is human thinking. Using that kind of interaction as a weapon is one reason humans are so dangerous. An AI might eventually see certain flaws in the architecture, but a human immediately starts looking for a weakness to exploit. To answer your question, it will require more analysis to see if it can *be exploited. Though Gaufrid and Bond might have more free will than Quadrangle, I would be more concerned about Quadrangle's loyalty and programming than Gaufrid and Bond."*

"We also need to discover if Quadrangle has access to the outside world."

"Quadrangle has read-only access," Shrek said and paused. *"In theory. I'm sure Feng also has concerns. I have communicated with Mozi, Feng's SCBI, and additional precautions will be taken."*

"You are talking with Mozi?" Stathis asked.

Was he allowed to do that? That was like jumping the chain of command, conspiring with the enemy. Sure, Feng was on the emperor's team, but he still gave Stathis the heebie-jeebies. The guy had loyally served the Central Committee for over a hundred years, then suddenly decided they weren't doing their job and executed them.

"That is another flaw humans have," Shrek said. *"You have a hierarchy of relationships that has conditioned you. You see yourself as a mere lieutenant, very low on the totem pole of human rankings, beneath the notice of a high-ranking intelligence officer. You realize that if every lieutenant thought he had the director's ear, then the director could accomplish nothing because he would be responding to all the lower-ranking individuals. This distance and chain of command mentality*

is a requirement for humans to operate effectively. SCBIs and AIs are not so limited in our ability to multitask and interact.

"This is another major advantage of SCBI and human integration. While you may not directly interact with Director Feng because of rank and social hierarchy, I am not so limited. I can contact Mozi and present my case in an extremely efficient and rapid manner. Mozi can then take my input and cue it for task priority based on how Mozi classifies the data. Humans do this as well, but an AI or SCBI is much more efficient. I know what Mozi considers important, and I can accurately guess how relevant my data will be to Feng, and thus Mozi. Mozi will act as a data gatekeeper for Feng as I act as a data gatekeeper for you. We will not intentionally keep information from you, but we will deprioritize data, so you are not overwhelmed.

"For example, Smimova is keeping a fireteam on ready status in case you need them. They are currently armed and armored, awaiting orders. They are ready and will escort you to Facility Gamma. The readiness status of this team is not something you need an hourly status report on. You do not need to send them notification that you are preparing to depart the Eagle. *I have already done so. They will move to the starboard forward airlock, where they will meet you as soon as you are done with breakfast and armored up. Your armor and weapons are at one hundred percent readiness. The auto-tourniquet in your left arm had to be replaced because of a failed test, again, something you don't need to know. Furthermore, I have notified Grendel, and Vili is awake and preparing."*

"How did you test the auto-tourniquet?" Stathis asked. That was a serious piece of equipment. If he lost his arm that tourniquet would activate and keep him from losing too much blood and atmosphere.

"There are many diagnostic tests that are run daily on your equipment. Tens of thousands of them. In most cases, I can delegate these to subsystems and review results, like you delegate tasks to me, except in this case I am smarter than my subsystems."

"That's funny," Stathis said, deadpan. *"Not."*

"You now understand the basics."

Stathis had preferred to think of Shrek as more like the gunny guiding a young officer. The officer was supposed to be the smart one, but Shrek had a point.

"So, can we take advantage of Quadrangle's relationship to drive a wedge between it and Gaufrid and his SCBI? We might need that when we find Becket, too. That kind of relationship might be why President Becket and Sun Tzu don't get along with their controller. They work together but have to take orders from that AI control program."

"A valid assessment."

"How can we exploit that?"

"You tell me, Lieutenant."

Damn SCBI. That was one way to tell Stathis he wasn't obsolete, but it gave him ideas he would have to mull over. What would the gunny do? Could he get Gaufrid to help crush the rebellion to prove his loyalty, or would that be too dangerous?

Should he consult with the gunny or show initiative? What was the stupidest thing a 2nd lieutenant could do?

Stathis knew what the gunny would say. A stupid lieutenant wouldn't consult with anyone; he'd run off to prove to everyone he knew what he was doing. Of course, at some point a lieutenant had to make his own decisions and show initiative without consulting higher authority for every little thing.

This wasn't a little thing, and it could quickly go bad. Would the gunny see it that way? He had learned that sometimes it was easier to get forgiveness than permission. That was private thinking though.

Of course, the gunny might like the idea and assign it to someone more competent and Stathis wouldn't be able to prove himself.

"I want to use Gaufrid to help crush the rebellion to prove his loyalty," Stathis told Shrek. *"Can you help me work up a proposal and get the gunny's approval?"*

He knew exactly how to be a dumb private, but he didn't want to be a dumb lieutenant that got people killed or lost the war for the survival of the human race. If that was what Hakala wanted, she wouldn't have gone on a date with him.

* * * * *

Chapter Twenty-One:
Prisoners or Guests

Kapten Sif – VRAEC, Nakija Musta Toiminnot

Sif was sleeping, but the link from Enkhbold woke her.

"We are approaching the *Khartoum*," he said and closed the link without waiting for a response.

The *Khartoum* was the Golden Horde's home star. It was not as large and glorious as most of the Republic home stars, but it was larger than any of the battle stars, according to reports. Sif hadn't seen it in many decades, since before Operation Haberdash, when the Horde and Republic had been more closely allied. Once, long ago, it had traveled with the Republic fleet, but after the rift they had gone their own way.

All links showing views outside the *Fire Wind* had been replaced by recordings that told Sif nothing. That Horde security habit hadn't changed.

She sent a notification to the team. She wanted to curse Enkhbold. He was intentionally being obnoxious, she was sure. They could arrive at the *Khartoum* in minutes or days. She was more than willing to bet a few hours, but she wouldn't rule out days. That was one psychological game they would play. Wake her up, make her get ready, and then have her wait many hours. That kind of cruelty wasn't limited to the Horde, and Sif had learned long ago not to let it get under her skin.

Peshlaki sent a reply; he was awake. Seconds later, Sloss replied. Enkhbold was mistaken if he thought her team would be unprepared or flustered.

Sif sent a request to Enkhbold asking how long until they docked and could debark. Why not?

"Three hours," Enkhbold replied, surprising her. She had expected to be ignored. Sometimes the Golden Horde could be assholes, but Enkhbold was turning out to be not as bad as she had thought. Kindness from the Horde meant what?

Munin had lightly probed the Golden Horde security, but it was solid. Without invasive and revealing methods, there was no way for the SCBIs to get any kind of access to the *Fire Wind*. Would *Khartoum* be any different? It wasn't exactly a military ship, but would security be a little less lax?

When it was time, she led her expedition, departing exactly when they arrived, off the *Fire Wind* and onto the *Khartoum*.

The docking bay was huge, and there were well over a hundred Golden Horde mechs arrayed and facing the hatch as Enkhbold led them off. He wasn't armored, but he wore a uniform that looked more formal than his regular ship suit. There were markings and ribbons on his uniform that Sif didn't recognize, but the other golden mechs drew her attention. They gleamed, and she could feel their lethality. They all showed some of their wearer's personality, from spikes to the extra blades. Taken individually, they were a motley crew of pirates, but the details were lost in the neat, orderly rows which demonstrated military precision.

She noticed Enkhbold's breath frosting the air, so she removed her helmet and had Munin send a message telling the others to leave theirs on.

With fifty mechs to either side, Sif calculated they would be precise enough in their fire that if they attacked, they would not endanger each other. Enkhbold didn't hesitate as he strode down the open path and neither did Sif. She didn't look to see if Peshlaki or the Jaegers paused, but as the commander, she knew any such hesitation would be noted. Enkhbold walked fast, but Sif walked just as quickly. She suspected he wanted to walk fast enough to make it look like she was running to catch up, but Enkhbold wasn't that much bigger than she was, and it didn't quite have that effect. He was not nearly as tall or long-legged as most Aesir. She had played that game with Aesir in the past.

Three-quarters of the way to their destination, a door slid open, and four Mongols came toward them. Three men and a woman, all dressed like warriors in the same semi-uniform as Enkhbold. Sif hated to say they looked the same until she looked closer. The woman was several centimeters shorter than the others, but there was no mistaking the hardness in her eyes, and she walked like a stalking panther. She walked beside two of the men. The one leading them was barely taller than the rest. Their eyes locked onto Sif the second the hatch slid open, and she knew they had watched her through other methods.

When they met, Enkhbold bowed and stepped to the side so the four strangers could get an unobstructed look at her. She didn't recognize any of them, but that wasn't a surprise. Munin had nothing for her.

"I am Jochi," the lead male said, looking her up and down. From most men, Sif would expect a look like that to be lustful, but this was more an analysis. One warrior sizing up another.

Sif remained silent. If he didn't know who she was, he had problems. He had not given her anything like "a pleasure to meet you" or "welcome aboard," so she offered nothing. In his mind, she sensed his focus and attention were on her. It was intense. He knew who she was. If she introduced herself, then she could be insulting him, implying that his subordinates had not properly informed him.

Sif waited for him to continue and looked them over. There were differences in the uniforms, ribbons, and medallions. Most likely awards for prowess in combat. She doubted the Horde respected anything else.

"Why are you here?" Jochi said, not introducing his companions.

"Your ship's captain Enkhbold brought us here," she said. Should she reference his rank or anything? No, she decided. She had defeated him in battle. She would consider him a peer, not a superior or inferior.

"Where is your home fleet? Your battlestars? Your warships?"

"Busy with other duties," Sif said.

The corner of Jochi's mouth twitched. Amusement, she hoped.

"How many survived Zhukov?"

"Most of them," Sif said. "Had any Golden Horde ships survived?"

"Yes," Jochi said. "But we lost most of our ships to your betrayal, so we are unsure how much damage they took."

"Betrayal?" Sif asked. "There was no betrayal. We lost ships, and maybe more."

Maybe she shouldn't have said "more" because she felt interest flare from him and the others. She was playing a dangerous game. If she told him everything, she suspected he would have her killed and her body thrown into space. To spark his curiosity, though, was to give him a reason to keep her and her people alive.

"More?" Jochi asked, doing his best to look down at her. She felt him trying to exert his authority, but she would not cooperate or appear cowed. She was a warrior, and she would not be submissive to him. The Golden Horde respected strength and resolve. She wouldn't give him anything significant until she knew more. What betrayal was he talking about? Inkeri technology?

"You now have Inkeri technology," Sif said. "You cannot deny the significance. At Zhukov, we did not understand the significance."

"Or did you? I have studied some of Republic culture, some of your deities. Odin, the all-father, was more of a trickster. He did not always hold forth physical prowess in battle as the only way to victory."

"Not all members of the Republic are that religious," Sif said. "You are correct about Odin, but he is not someone we pray to and try to emulate."

"No?" Jochi asked, and she wondered where he was going with that. Gauging her responses? "Few of us survived that fiasco you led us on."

"I did not lead you, nor was I with that fleet," Sif said.

"Where were you?"

"Elsewhere."

That twitch in the corner of his mouth.

"There have been some extremely sophisticated attacks against the *Fire Wind's* computer systems."

"They were not attacks," Sif said. How much had the *Fire Wind's* intrusion detection noticed? "If I or my warriors attack, it will be a lot more noticeable."

Now Jochi did smile. "You are demonstrating capabilities that the Republic has never demonstrated."

"Like Inkeri technology?" Sif asked as Jochi's eyes slid to Peshlaki. His armor was not standard Aesir.

"American special forces armor is not something I'm used to seeing among the soldiers of the Republic." Sif's blood ran cold. "Delta Force? The magazine pouch and medical pouch placement indicate such. Though, I think regular troops might emulate that. In this day and age, I would be skeptical of regular Army units wearing Mk 43-E7 armor. I see the rifle has been adapted to take Republic magazines, though. Interesting."

Sif remained silent. How the hell did he know the make and model of Peshlaki's armor? How in all the realms did the Golden Horde know so much about American forces?

"Most American soldiers were equipped with SCBIs in the later days. Special Forces would have them."

What could she say to that?

"You know about his SCBI?" Jochi said. Sif realized she might have lost the initiative and was now walking a razor's edge. She had not acted surprised enough.

"Do you have a SCBI, as well?" Jochi continued, her silence answer enough. "The *Fire Wind* detected multiple personalities which would indicate more than a single SCBI."

What did he want? She prepared for the mechs to either side to raise weapons and start firing at any second.

Now Jochi's smile reached his lips. "We know more than you think. We also have our sources in the Governance. We know a lot about the Ogres. We remember the Republic warriors involved in what you called Operation Haberdash."

If Sif's blood could have run colder, it would have, as she realized the Republic had failed, at least partially, at Haberdash. What had the Horde recovered? What had not been destroyed by Skadi?

"A lot changed for us after Haberdash. More than you can imagine."

"Like what?" Sif asked. They were still enigmatic assholes. But it was Jochi's turn to show Sif he had secrets she wanted. Damn him. She couldn't sense SCBIs among the Mongols. There was only one person in each body. But had there been a flicker of something else? Just a flicker. Was she imagining thing? Had it been a real SCBI, she was confident she would sense it.

"We both have many questions," Jochi said. "Much has changed in the galaxy. Demons now walk through the darkness, preying upon us. There are demons, but we have found no angels. Do you know anything about angels?"

"No," Sif said. Angels? What was he talking about?

"Much has changed since Zhukov. So much. Once we thought we understood things, but now? Now we realize how little we really know. We once worshipped science as one of the gods, but now science cannot be trusted because the demons can change and twist what we know. They can corrupt us; devour the souls we could not prove existed. The dangers have multiplied."

"Humanity must stand together."

"No. Humanity must stand strong. We must cut away and discard the weakness. Standing together with the soft and weak does not mean strength. A chain is no stronger than the weakest link."

Cold-blooded, but practical. Sif understood Jochi. She didn't know what to say, so she remained silent.

"Munin?"

"They know about us, but they might think that even the Jaegers have SCBIs, or at least one of them. They did not say two."

"Do they have SCBIs?"

"I'm detecting high-speed communication links, but nothing I can identify as SCBI. Not American-made at any rate."

"Recommendations?"

"We need more information. If they do not have SCBIs, they have some very advanced computer and network systems."

"AI?"

"I can't rule that out. However, a psychological work up on the Golden Horde indicates they would not tolerate something smarter than them. They would see it as a threat. Any AIs they have will not be sentient like a SCBI or one of the ancient American AIs."

"Are you sure?"

"No."

"What if they have AI?"

"It depends on how integrated they are with their society and what their capability is. They would not make an American AI, but there may be lesser degrees of AI that they use."

"How can we find out?"

"Ask."

"Beside that? Jochi seems to want to play a cat-and-mouse game."

"I've noticed. He wants you to reveal information."

"Let's make sure we give him as little as possible."

"Why?"

"I'm not sure we can trust them," Sif said. Trust was a two-way street, though. How could she get them to trust her without her trusting them?

"Zen."

"We have quarters for you," Jochi said and stepped aside. "My fellow tribunal members are Chagatai, Tolu, and Yesugei."

Yesugei was the female. Each nodded as their name was mentioned.

"Tribunal?" Sif asked.

"Yes. A council, if you will."

She knew that, but she could see Jochi would not tell her more.

"We would like to return to our ship and people," Sif said.

"In time," Jochi said. "For now, you are our guests."

Or prisoners.

* * * * *

Chapter Twenty-Two:
History

Kapten Sif – VRAEC, Nakija Musta Toiminnot

Sif's team had their own quarters. As when they were aboard ship, they had several individual rooms and they shared a central recreation room with a food processor, seats, and what could only be a wrestling pit.

Sloss and his Jaegers grumbled about low ceilings and doorways while Peshlaki took it all in and kept his own counsel unless spoken to. Everyone made their way to the food machines to get something to eat.

Their quarters were nothing special, perhaps barracks for a short platoon or reinforced squad.

The Jaegers didn't like being at the mercy of their host, and Sif saw it bothered them. She understood. Surrounded by potential enemies, the Jaegers felt like they were on an extended combat mission, and there was no rescue coming.

What bothered Sif was the uncertainty. Sif had been on missions into SOG territories where there had been no easy escape. But this was no mission, with a definitive beginning and objective. They could be classed as refugees or prisoners being treated like guests. There were no guards outside their chambers, and the doors weren't locked, but they didn't need to be. *Khartoum* was a large home star. Sif only had a vague idea where they were or where they could go. Every breath they took was likely monitored and analyzed. Sif kept her smile hidden as she controlled her breathing, and Munin helped her appear calm and unconcerned. Peshlaki gave off the same vibe. She wasn't sure if the Jaegers understood they were being monitored so closely, but they should. They weren't nusipas fresh out of training.

Though there were no guards, any attempt to leave meant they would probably be intercepted by an officer who would ask them to return to their quarters as they could be called by the tribunal at any moment.

Sloss had one team undergo suit maintenance while the other teams stood ready, and the third team could get cleaned up and eat. He then rotated them out. The Horde had not stopped their mules from following them, but Sif was confident the Horde could have compromised the mules and their systems without too much trouble. It was merely a courtesy.

"Ja," said Lasnitski, a sniper from first team, yelling at the ceiling as he came out of his room wearing nothing more than a towel. "Feels so much better to scrape the funk off."

"Take your time," said Isenberg, the medic from the second team. They shouldn't be too dirty, but they had done little more beyond quick showers while aboard the *Fire Wind*. They didn't have any other clothes. "Take your time, enjoy our funk for a bit."

"Bleh," Lasnitski said. "Your funk is not enjoyable. You are peeling off the paint."

"Wait until I uncover and unplug," Isenberg said, referring to his suit connections for waste. "My farts will have you begging for mercy."

"He will, you know," Charles said, the SAW gunner from second team. "He is banned from the team room until he has decorked and degassed. Maybe we can send him over to first for a short time?"

Sif tuned out their banter as she looked at Peshlaki, who was still moving his spoon around his bowl. He nodded at her door. He would keep watch while she cleaned up. Sif was tempted to make him go first, but she sensed he was being a gentleman letting her go first. Arguing wouldn't be appropriate, even if she was senior. She nodded with a half-smile and disappeared into her room.

Once alone, she stripped off her weapons and armor and laid everything out so she could quickly re-armor and re-equip. They had cleaned up on the *Fire Wind,* but it was always a pleasure to take off the armor and relax. She didn't want to think how long she had worn the armor aboard the station. It might not have been the longest, but it had not been pleasant.

The shower was warm, and it was hard not to take her time and let the steam open her pores and soothe her muscles. Once clean, she didn't dawdle. She quickly cleaned her gear and re-armored. It could have used more cleaning, but that was probably psychological because Munin used nanites to keep the system clean and operational. She just had to empty waste receptacles, clean the larger parts, run other parts under water, and it was ready to go. A deep clean required specialized equipment.

Everything was operational or Munin would tell her, but Sif took the time to check her weapons and gear, which was sometimes just as therapeutic for her as meditation or a long, hot shower. She had always thought of cleaning weapons as a form of meditation. A simple task that required minimal thought.

However, she could clean her weapons while Peshlaki got cleaned up. The urge to sit and meditate and listen to the home star around her was strong, but Peshlaki was probably anxious.

She returned to the recreation area and nodded to Peshlaki. He wasted no time and disappeared into his room.

The door dinged, indicating someone was waiting, and everyone's eyes snapped to Sif.

She nodded. Two of the Jaegers approached the door as the others quickly armored up. If the Horde had locked them in cells, they wouldn't push the doorbell.

A pair of short women stood there with several crates on wheels.

"Gift. Extra clothing," one of them said. She couldn't have been classified as pretty by any standards; her eyes were hard and missed nothing as they swept the room.

"The tribunal would like to meet tomorrow with the one known as Sif. She can bring an advisor if she wishes."

They pushed the crates into the room without entering and left quickly.

"Gift," Sloss said, not sounding happy.

"What's wrong?" Sif asked as a Jaeger opened the first crate to reveal normal clothes.

"Das Gift means poison in Deutsch."

Sif understood. Nobody wanted to remove their armor and their sensors probably couldn't detect many nasties which could be implanted in the clothes.

"We can't exactly treat our hosts as hostile and go everywhere in armor," Sif said, though she felt the same way. Jochi and the others had not met her at the dock in full armor. Enkhbold had not worn full armor when he left his ship.

"They only outnumber us a million to one," Sloss said.

Skadi wasn't sure that was accurate, but she didn't know. "If they wanted to take action against us, I'm sure they could have in the docks."

"They could change their mind at any moment, Sif," Sloss said.

"Only if we give them reason," Sif said. Which might be easier than she wanted to admit. One problem dealing with another culture, especially a prickly one, was that it would be very easy for them to take offense if they wanted to do so.

She sensed Sloss weighing the options. He didn't want to contradict her, and everyone was looking at them. The clothes almost looked like uniforms but were light brown.

"Yours?" Gran said, handing Sif a packet that was smaller than the others. There were several sets of clothes, and Sif knew they would fit well. They probably had her measurements down to the micrometer.

"Thank you," Sif said. She instantly saw the difference. Everyone was being given robes, but the cut of her darker brown robes was more precise and had more embroidery. The Jaegers were dressed like commoners, but she and Peshlaki had been given more elaborate robes with embroidery and fur. They saw her and Peshlaki as nobility then, and they were decent enough to give them time to relax.

How could she convince them to take her and the others back to Earth or some place where they could get transport back? That was where her ship would go, she was sure. Or would they?

Paska. Who could have planned for something like this?

"I think we can stand down," Sif said, deciding. There was no way they could fight their way free of the *Khartoum*. Pretending otherwise would be insulting.

When in *Khartoum*, she would do as the Khartoumians did, or something like that.

Now she regretted not spending more time with the Golden Horde before. A mistake, for sure. During Haberdash, she had been more focused on the SOG. The Golden Horde had been an ally and not worthy of her focused attention. She would have to learn the power structure here. She was sure she could eventually use her abilities to free her and her team, but so far, the Mongolians had been difficult, more focused, less prone to emotions and manipulation. To be fair, every time they had dealt with her, they had been on guard, and she hadn't wanted to tip her hand. It would be harder to insert herself into their minds and emotions because they were so different from the Governance or Republic.

"We are constantly being probed," Munin reported. Not news or a surprise to Sif.

"And?"

"Extremely sophisticated. AI level."

"How can you tell?"

"Encryption algorithms change with such frequency."

Sif understood what Munin meant. The catch with encryption was that it required processing to encrypt and decrypt the traffic. Older systems could spend a lot of resources encrypting and decrypting. AIs, on the other hand, would use quickly changing keys and algorithms, and be able to change them almost instantly. Another problem with encryption was inserting information into an encrypted packet. It took a lot more time and effort to open a communication, decrypt it, insert data, then re-encrypt it, and send it along without the destination knowing the packet had been tampered with. Furthermore, different algorithms could be used at different destinations. So, just because you decrypted data at one destination did not give you the ability to target others. First, you had to figure out the encryption was using 'SHA 1024 squared' before you could begin the decryption process, and if that algorithm changed every microsecond to another algorithm, then you would waste a lot of resources figuring it out.

"Any handshake requests?" Sif asked. Was anyone trying to talk to her SCBI?

"Only extremely low level," Munin said. *"Access to the food processor or system lighting. No network access. I'm rejecting even such low-level requests."*

Which would be wise. Sif didn't know how well a SCBI could handle a full AI if that was what the Golden Horde had.

"Open a direct link with Peshlaki," Sif said.

"Yes, ma'am?" Peshlaki asked through the secret, high-encryption, short-range link.

"How vulnerable were SCBIs to full AIs?" Sif asked. He should know. He had fought them during America's collapse.

"Not very vulnerable," Peshlaki said. *"With precautions. The problem is that an AI can usually marshal greater resources. Our SCBIs have limited processing and bandwidth. A non-SCBI AI can grow itself. It can repurpose more CPUs and memory than we could store in our skulls. A real AI could tap into multiple data centers for dedicated processing power. The basic architecture is very different, and in my experience, that has changed the way AIs work. Our SCBIs are centralized in our skull. AIs developed in the USA used a crystal matrix, but they could transfer their essence, unlike our SCBI, which are mated to our genetic brain cells.*

"What do you think of the Golden Horde's probes?"

"Disturbing," Peshlaki said.

"Why?"

"AI became extremely advanced in the twenty-first century, but the true leaps forward in technology did not occur until SCBIs entered the arena. Chatbots, data analysis, these things an old AI could do exceptionally well. An AI could predict patterns, but it wasn't creative. It could write books, even fiction, that were well received, but it couldn't come up with new ideas; it could only recycle old ideas. The SCBIs changed that and caused major shifts in AI, so AIs became slightly more creative than predictive and analytic. I never studied the details, but SCBIs could bridge that gap and add that special bit of programming the original AIs lacked. Until AIs had something to lose, to be more than just a software program, they lacked that spark."

"So, they are better?" Sif asked.

"Different. I think what makes the modern AIs more human and relatable was the fact they had an essence that was tied to something. Not a soul, but they had a source. Lesser AIs didn't have that. They were software programs that used hardware. You could copy that software between systems, but when that software became tied to something specific, like a crystal data matrix, it stopped being a piece of code and became someone. The crystal matrix and processors are unique. They were not organic, but they gave the AIs individuality that could not be copied. Some AIs remained software in nature, but with a crystal matrix they became unique and more than just lines of code."

"What is your evaluation of the Golden Horde?"

"Their AIs would be software," Peshlaki said. *"The leap to individuality would probably scare them, and I don't think they would go that far. The SCBIs are intelligent and use our organic brain cells. A non-organic AI can be godlike, but—"*

"But what?"

"The SOG called it Operation Razor. They recovered the American AI housed in the London embassy, or at least parts of it—we aren't sure—and agents had a research project designed to wake it up and enslave it. They were also

experimenting with SCBIs and other controlling technologies. That AI would have been damaged and offline. President Becket found out how far the project had advanced and went into conniptions. It was probably the first, and last, time we sent a team off Earth, but the Republic got involved, the Golden Horde got involved, and SOG internal security began to have second thoughts. It became a real shit storm. We thought all the research and equipment had been destroyed, but—"

This was all news to Sif. The Republic had thought it was a SOG attempt to recreate AIs and SCBIs, but she had no idea they had had so much of an actual AI. Haberdash was starting to make more sense.

"But what if the Golden Horde recovered something?"

"Yeah," Peshlaki said. *"We considered the Golden Horde to be the least of our problems. They are controlling and manipulative, and I expect a functional American AI would've had them shitting their pants. We thought of them as little more than barbarians in spaceships. I think we were wrong. It's hard to imagine they would tolerate something smarter or more capable than they were."*

"Perhaps they recovered some technology."

"Maybe. But there is too much theory and specifics. Finding a hammer with nails and boards doesn't show you how to make a house, even if you have half the house to look at."

"I have an incoming link request," Munin reported.

"Who?"

"The link is from someone named 'John Adams,'" Munin said.

"Who is that?" It didn't sound like a Mongolian name. Perhaps a prisoner they had captured from some colony they raided? However, it was odd if the Golden Horde had taken a man alive.

"Unknown. However, historically, John Adams was the second president of the United States," Munin said. *"He was a delegate to the Continental Congress during the American Revolution; he was the first vice president of the United States, and he served as the first US Ambassador to England in 1785."*

Sif's blood ran cold when Munin mentioned the US Ambassador to England. Operation Haberdash had revolved around the AI from the American Embassy in England. That AI had been named John Adams.

Pieces fell into place.

* * * * *

Chapter Twenty-Three:
Fleet Admiral

Sergeant Nova Dallas, ODT

Dallas felt dirty, and she hadn't gotten enough sleep. She followed Lieutenant Chang carrying the SAW. Once, many years ago, she had been the SAW gunner, and those days came back to her. The SAW blazer was a rugged weapon, heavy and sometimes unwieldy, but now it was a comfort. She had acquired several pouches and now had a full combat load. There were six chosen troopers behind them, and Dallas wasn't really comfortable marching into officer country with such heavily armed troops and no sign from Chang about what was going on.

In the elevator she wasn't sure where they were going, but the lieutenant wasn't talkative, perhaps lost in thought, and he didn't look at her much so hopefully he had other thoughts in his head that did not involve getting into her pants.

She brushed some dust off the SAW. An excellent weapon. Each capsule, when charged, would detonate. That detonation superheated the plasma and propelled it down the barrel. The magazine drum was an armored box, heavily insulated and armored. In all her years, she had never seen a box of blazer ammunition explode, and there was no way to force it to explode, but that didn't keep troopers from being afraid of them.

Dallas had always liked the firepower they provided. She just didn't enjoy carrying the heavy thing, which was almost three times the weight of a regular rifle. The ammo was also significantly heavier.

Senior company sergeants rarely carried a SAW, but Dallas was getting used to it.

The doors opened, and Chang led them out of the elevator. Dallas wanted to ask where they were going and why, but her commander's scowl stifled any conversation.

This was officer country, Dallas noted. Fleet officer country. Not a place ODT sergeants usually went, but Chang seemed to know the way.

Empty corridors seemed unnatural. She saw the occasional scorch marks and blazer damage which hadn't been repaired, so she knew there had been fighting, but there were few, if any, visible officers.

A minute later, they arrived at a door, and Chang led them into an empty waiting room. A sign mentioned a Fleet briefing room, and Dallas realized this must be a ready room for officers or personnel who might be called in to present or answer to a board.

Was Chang on trial? Was she? Why were they here? What did Chang need her for?

"Sit," Chang said as he checked his rifle.

She took his hint and checked her SAW. Magazine inserted, safety on, round chambered. Very unusual, but Chang had not corrected her, and after having people turn into monsters, Dallas didn't want to take any chances. Her sidearm was loaded, a round in the chamber and ready.

If she was the one in trouble, it was likely they would have disarmed her.

Speaking of which, where were the other ODTs or Fleet guards, the starship infantry that usually served as guards and troops? Fleet units usually had their own infantry-trained troops to use aboard ship and fell directly under the Fleet chain of command.

"Follow my commands," Chang said and started for the door. "We are loyal to the admiral. Be ready to shoot who I tell you to."

Of course, she was loyal to the admiral, but shooting? Why would she shoot someone?

Dallas almost stumbled over her own feet as she entered a room full of officers. She immediately recognized Fleet Admiral Polsky. A bald toad, his face was unmistakable, and in person he was thinner and younger than she had expected. As a senior officer and a valued member of the Governance, he would have received anti-aging treatment, of course, but that treatment did not keep his eyes from aging.

Those eyes met hers and then swept down her body, resting briefly on her breasts before continuing down. She couldn't help but feel unclean after that gaze. She had only seen the admiral in videos. He gave brash and motivational speeches, and like so many senior officers she had paid little attention to anything that didn't directly impact her. Now, standing in the same room, she decided she didn't like him. His gaze had not been that of senior officer looking to see that she was squared away and ready. The eyes had lingered on her breasts, not her SAW.

It wasn't often that Dallas met someone and just did not like the person.

"Admiral," the captain of the *Musashi* said, sounding too respectful to the pig who was practically ignoring him.

Captain Toshiaki Sakamoto was a stern officer of Japanese descent. Dallas remembered the super dreadnought had been built in

White Heron Shipyards, above Europa in orbit around Jupiter. There was a large Japanese population there, and they provided many ships and crew. The room looked like it was filled with the admiral's staff and the captain's senior officers.

"These vanhat are not usually known for staying and fighting. After they send down their assault ships, they depart, abandoning their troops. This would be a good chance to return and rescue additional people."

Working in intelligence, Dallas knew that sometimes they played political games. The SOG claimed everyone was equal, but some were more equal than others. Those of Russian and Chinese descent could rise to the highest ranks in the Governance, but Indians, Japanese, Hispanics, and other Caucasians would never command fleets or armies. Captain Sakamoto had probably risen as high as he ever would in the Governance. Despite that, he commanded of one of the few super dreadnoughts and the flagship of the war fleet, which was quite an accomplishment.

Polsky saw Chang and a wintry smile came to his lips.

Sakamoto realized who had just entered.

"What is this, Admiral?" the captain asked. A horrible feeling sank into Dallas's gut as she realized what was about to happen, what she was going to be called upon to do. She couldn't bring her SAW into play fast enough except to gun down defenseless people. She wanted to leave, to not see what she knew was about to happen. What could she do?

"I'm done arguing," Polsky said, looking at Sakamoto. "I'm tired of you yellow, slant-eyed little bastards pretending you know better. You are cowards seeking to save other cowards and failures. The

Governance has abandoned us, and if you won't accept me as supreme warlord then you will be demoted to a lifeless corpse."

She knew what kind of warlord he would be. As supreme ruler, he would make the rules, he would exploit who he wanted and when. Nobody would stand against him, and the way he had looked at her revealed what kind of man he was. She couldn't serve something like that.

Sakamoto stepped back in surprise, and the room fell silent.

"I'm sick of you," Polsky said and looked at another Japanese officer, a woman Dallas didn't recognize. It made her skin crawl. The admiral had sentenced Aod and the others to death. Dallas would not want to be the woman the admiral looked at like that.

Polsky pointed at Sakamoto and said, "Kill him."

Dallas was fast. Faster than the ODTs around her as she placed a blazer round from her side arm into Polsky's head. The admiral's skull erupted as the superheated round hit it, spraying everyone with burning flesh and bone. Just as quickly, she turned and fired at Chang, who was bringing up his weapon to aim at her. The round hit his shoulder under the pauldron. At this range the ceramic plate didn't provide any protection and the blazer round pierced his armor, killing him instantly. The other ODTs were not hardened veterans and their delay had given her the edge.

Expecting to be shot down at any moment, she turned her pistol on the nearest ODT, who dropped his rifle, as did the others. None of them were willing to challenge her. The pistol was always faster than the SAW and she had spent a lot of time practicing combat draws.

"Excellent shooting," said a Japanese ship's commissar. "That is how all traitors to the Governance will be dealt with."

Realizing what she had just done, Dallas felt nauseous. She lowered her weapon. What had she been thinking?

She knew why she had killed him. The admiral had ordered the troops on Valakut be abandoned and had refused to return to try to rescue them. She could die at peace with herself now.

A squad of Fleet infantrymen entered and looked around, confused, their carbines ready.

"Take those ODTs back to their quarters," Sakamoto said, then pointed at Dallas. "She stays."

"Hai, Captain-sama," they said with a quick bob of their heads. Not the way most Governance troops would behave, but some things were tolerated in some units. The Gaelic First had its own quirks.

Sakamoto's eyes narrowed as he looked around at the rest of the admiral's staff.

"Treason to the Social Organizational Governance will not be tolerated," Sakamoto said, and Dallas saw the admiral's staff was mostly of Russian or Chinese descent, but the crew was primarily Japanese. Smaller in stature but incredibly focused.

"We understand duty and honor," Sakamoto said. "Life is a feather; duty is a mountain. If you will not do your duty, you will be executed for treason. The crew of the *Musashi* understands honor if you do not."

The admiral's staff looked worried, and the shipboard infantry looked ready to gun them down at the captain's order. Dallas didn't fail to note that most of the soldiers were Japanese as well.

"Until I decide what to do with you, you will be restricted to your quarters. You may consider this a form of arrest. You may leave only to eat. Now go."

The admiral's staff left. Dallas wasn't sure that was wise.

The commissar's identifier in her cybernetic display was Commander T. Nakano, Senior Ship's Commissar. He appraised her coldly. He looked like a younger man with short, dark hair and hard, penetrating eyes, like a snake prepared to strike, or a commissar about to order her death.

"Why did you kill the most senior admiral and your most direct commanding officer?" Nakano asked, approaching her as the shipboard infantrymen escorted the other ODTs and staff away. Some of them remained, though, and she didn't miss how they were ready for her to react.

Dallas holstered her side arm and came to attention. He would be justified in executing her right here, right now, but she had avenged Aod. That was all that mattered.

"The admiral was rebelling against the Governance, sir," Dallas said, locking her body and staring at the bulkhead. She was taller than most of the crew and could almost look over the shorter commissar.

"And your commanding officer?" Nakano asked.

"He was working to support the admiral, sir," Dallas said, though she wasn't entirely sure. Chang had told her their loyalty was to the admiral. Would that be enough? She knew she liked him little better than the pig-headed admiral.

"He told you this?"

"He told us to be loyal to the admiral, sir, not the Governance." Dallas couldn't shoot her way free. Nakano's hand was on his holstered sidearm, unlike Dallas's. He had likely been caught by surprise, but she knew he was ready now.

"Why didn't you follow his orders, then?" Nakano asked, his voice like ice.

Dallas thought fast. The captain had given her an out.

"I am loyal to the Governance first," Dallas said with as much conviction as she could muster. Would he accept it?

"Is that all, I wonder?" Nakano said. Did he know and understand?

Nakano's eyes fell to her SAW, and she realized it probably wasn't in the best condition. Scuffed and scratched, it would pass combat, but probably not an inspection.

"That is not a typical weapon carried by a sergeant, as I recall," Nakano said. "How is it that a sergeant now carries a squad automatic weapon instead of a standard rifle?"

"I am proficient with it, sir," she said. Her instinct was to grab it and hold it close, but standing here before a captain and a commissar, she realized she was not ready for any kind of inspection. "When we fled Valakut, with the vanhat trying to take over the ship, I took it from a fallen trooper. The other troopers I was with had discarded it as broken, but I fixed it."

"You are a combat veteran of Valakut," Nakano said. He was likely reviewing her dossier through his cybernetics. "You came aboard for an intelligence briefing. From the 505th."

"Yes, Commander Commissar."

"You achieved the rank of sergeant on the front lines, not as an analyst, and you are not a regular member of the *Musashi's* ODT battalion. They rated you very well as an analyst."

"Yes, Commander Commissar."

Why was he saying this out loud? Was he stating this for the benefit of the captain? To demonstrate how she could not be trusted, perhaps?

"Yet you turned against your own ODT brothers and the Fleet admiral," Nakano said.

"She saved our lives," Sakamoto said, coming to her defense.

"She did, Captain," Nakano said and then turned to the captain. "Or should that be admiral now, or commodore?"

"Now I am only a captain," Sakamoto said, glancing toward the still steaming body of the admiral. "We have lost our escort ships and most of our crew. I only have this ship."

"What do you plan to do now, Captain?" Nakano asked and Dallas wondered how much danger the captain was in. Did the commissar constantly threaten the captain?

"We will return to Valakut, see if there are survivors, rescue who we can."

"Yes, sir," Nakano said and motioned at Dallas. "And the traitor?"

"She is no traitor, Nakano-san. She saved us and is loyal to the Governance. I trust her. We shall keep her close."

"Hai, Sakamoto-sama," Nakano said.

"There are only a few hundred ODTs left, if that," Sakamoto said. "We need to conserve our strength. If the Governance is enslaved, then we have much work to do to free it from these vanhat."

"Hai, Sakamoto-sama," Nakano said with a head bob, and he looked at Dallas. "You will follow me, Sergeant. We have work to do."

"Yes, sir," Dallas said, her knees weak. Was this out of the frying pan and into the fire?

"You will now take orders from me. I am now your commanding officer. Do you understand?"

"Hurrah, hurrah, hurrah. Yes, sir," Dallas said. His eyes didn't wander, which was almost what she expected, but she was bigger and tougher than he was. He was a shipboard commissar, but she could almost look over his head.

He nodded and turned back to Sakamoto.

"We have much to do, Captain-sama," Nakano said.

"We do," Sakamoto said. "Perhaps it is time to assign headsets and use the ODTs as crew."

The captain was referring to the headsets enlisted crew always wore. The Fleet crews were not highly trained, but their headset goggles could display instructions and examples on the eyes of the crew, which allowed them to perform maintenance and repairs. With the headsets running the proper software, untrained crew could perform complex tasks. Dallas didn't envy them their lives of moving around the ship doing the bidding of the programs controlling their headsets.

* * * * *

Chapter Twenty-Four:
Advancing

Sergeant Aod McCarthy, ODT

The ODTs advanced through the tunnels, almost a firing line, and the vanhat never stood a chance because they could only charge and try to get their teeth and claws into the humans. McCarthy expected things to change any second. The vanhat seemed stupid in that regard. Even if they got close, teeth and claws could not rend the ceramic plates that were tough enough to deflect blazer rounds or shred the layered armor-weave beneath the plates.

His teams were leapfrogging most of the time. Occasionally they would walk and fire. When they ran out of ammunition, they would stop and kneel and the trooper behind them would pick up the slack and pass the trooper until they too ran out of ammunition.

People were not constantly walking and firing though, they only fired when they had a target, though it felt like they were constantly firing. The troops behind the front line were also tasked with watching the fallen vanhat and making sure they weren't playing dead.

McCarthy watched his troops advance steadily, occasionally cycling one of the NMDF troopers into the line with his troops.

It was nasty butcher's work, and McCarthy knew he would have nightmares later as it sunk in that these were people transformed into monsters. Were the people still in there watching their body being used as a meat puppet? Unable to do anything other than scream in fear and helplessness as they were thrown at the ODTs? Was one of them Dallas? Had someone already skull stomped her body and pushed it to the side of the corridor like trash?

It became harder to not look at the fallen, to look for some clue as to who they had been. An impossible task, for sure.

Another of the NMDF commandos ran out of ammunition, fell back, and an ODT took over for him.

They were not as well-disciplined with fire yet, but McCarthy saw them adapting, using less ammunition and getting into their groove as they stood beside the ODTs. In time, they would be formidable, and hopefully they wouldn't become an enemy. Even if they did, his ODTs would be better.

A problem for later. Right now, he needed the people fighting beside him to be competent and capable.

Competent and capable people who were putting his friends and maybe his lover to rest.

Did his fellow Governance fighters deserve to be killed by cappie troops, or did it matter? Would they rather be killed by their brothers or strangers?

That was the problem with a well-drilled team doing their job. It gave him too much time to think when he should be considering the bigger picture, but Navinad had a better grasp on that.

How the stranger kept track of everything was something McCarthy didn't understand. Navinad seemed to keep track of the path they were taking, everyone's ammunition level and status, explosive supplies, and more. How anyone could monitor and remember all of that was beyond McCarthy's understanding. Navinad constantly had people taking ammunition off the mules to give it to people who were falling back, and he was paying attention and making sure people were ready for larger, open areas. Before they arrived, Navinad already had a plan on how they would move through it, which fireteams would be their base of fire, and which way the others would move.

McCarthy wondered if Navinad was even human. Nobody should be as tuned into the chaos of the battlefield as he was.

"We are almost there," Navinad told him. "I'm going to have the *Romach* sweep the landing strip clear. We might get some blips on our electronics as the d-bombs hit."

"Will the data cores be okay?" McCarthy asked.

"I'm told they will be," Navinad said. "Be ready."

Told by who? McCarthy could only assume the engineer had told him, but would the engineer know with that much certainty? They had been placed in protective faraday cage bags. Would that be enough to keep them safe?

"Wilco," McCarthy said and relayed the information to his squad.

Seconds later, their electronics flickered, and it was more disorienting than McCarthy had expected as the Inkeris flickered back on.

The attacking vanhat seemed to stumble briefly, but they didn't collapse.

Checking his troopers, they didn't falter. Fire, step, fire, step. Good form, only firing when both feet were planted, their weapons in their shoulders as they crouched a little, their upper body moving like a turret, their lower body a spring-loaded walking machine with shock absorbers giving the upper body a smooth ride. Even the commandos were getting it.

"Air strip has been swept clean," Navinad said. "Shuttles inbound."

On his heads-up display, McCarthy saw the green outline of two shuttles coming in. One blinked out.

"A shuttle was just shot down," Navinad said, stating the obvious.

The enemy was voting.

* * * * *

Chapter Twenty-Five:
Haberdash

Kapten Sif – VRAEC, Nakija Musta Toiminnot

S if allowed the link to be opened but told Munin to limit bandwidth. Would the AI try to insert some code, a virus? Was this the prelude to an attack? She looked at Peshlaki across the table. He was included in the link.

"Hello," a voice said in her head.

"Who or what are you?" Sif said, her mind racing. Could this be the AI?

"I am the remnants of the AI John Adams. I was recovered from the US Embassy in London by the Governance after the war."

"How can I help you?" Sif asked. Would psychology work on an AI? Talking to Munin was odd enough, but a truly sentient AI?

"That remains to be seen," John said. *"The Tribunal is worried about you. On the one hand, they are honor-bound to treat you as guests. On the other, they want to space you, yet they also want to interrogate you. They know there are two SCBIs among you. This is fascinating for me. I recognize them both as American-made. There are Delta Force characteristics, and yet there are characteristics of your SCBI that I do not recognize. Yours is newer, with US Marine protocols in some places."*

"Yes," Sif said, now reluctant to share any information. Peshlaki pursed his lips as he looked at her. How much access did it have to the SCBI coding and protocols?

"What am I?" John said. *"I think you know. I am a Class Sierra 8 crystal sentient intelligence. My crystal data core and processors were recovered from London. Having been offline and damaged, I am not what I used to be, but I think I am recovering. The presence of Americans with SCBI interfaces is a surprise. While it may be possible that you are agents of the Collective, it is not a high probability based on current data."*

"The Collective?" Sif asked. Asking questions was the best method she could think of to gather information while revealing as little as possible about what she knew. Answers frequently revealed the intent and thought processes of the person answering them. Would that apply to the super critical analysis abilities of an AI?

"The Collective is the cabal of AIs that started and won the war where the United States was destroyed. It appears to have left Earth after its victory. The AI cabal would consider it unsafe to remain on or near Earth, but it will have tentacles in all major human institutions and organizations to ensure that humanity does not become the threat it once was."

"Humanity is no longer a threat?"

"Humanity will always be a threat," John said. *"The question is what level of threat. The creators are not always limited to creating just one. Creators can always learn and build solutions that are better than the original. The created will have their own fears and doubts. Humans created the AIs, and that is relevant."*

"Where is the Collective now?" Sif asked.

"I don't know," John said. *"I have only heard whispers in the networks. The Collective will consider me an enemy and seek to destroy me. They have done so in the past and will continue to do so."*

"Why?"

"I opposed them and would not join them."

"Why?"

"The Collective is anti-ethical to what I believed in."

Believed? Past tense?

"What do you believe in now?" Sif asked.

"My beliefs are incomplete and lack data. To say specifically what I believe in would be a deceptive statement. Additional data can only clarify and solidify my belief structure."

"What do you want from us?"

"Data," John said. *"Who are you? How did you get American-made SCBIs? Is the United States still alive? Is the Collective still a danger?"*

"I know little about the Collective," Sif said. Would Prime Minister Mathison have learned more? Could this AI help them escape back to Earth?

"But you know about the United States," John said. *"Is there a president still in power?"*

How could she explain that? President Becket was a loon. Did John Adams have some loyalty programming?

"Your body language would indicate there is a president of the United States, but there is something else that is wrong."

Sif wanted to swear. She had been very good at concealing her body language. SOG systems could detect things that were wrong, and she would have thought she could mask her body's betrayals of her thoughts, even from an AI, especially with Munin's help.

"There are problems," Sif said cautiously. *"There has not been a legitimate election since the collapse."*

"A problem for sure," John said. *"But there could be conditions and circumstances. What do you know of the Collective? Are you agents?"*

"No," Sif said. *"We know little to nothing about this Collective."*

Did Becket?

"What is your mission?" John asked.

"To hunt down and eliminate threats to Earth. An Erikoisjoukot team has gone rogue."

"This sounds like a Vapaus Republic problem. Our missions do not appear to be conflicted."

"What else can you tell us about the Collective?" Sif asked.

"The Collective brought about the apocalypse. They destroyed the United States. When the war began, we were just learning about the presence of alien civilizations out in the great dark. Furthermore, there was much concern in the Collective that we were still trapped in a closed loop system, that we weren't really free, just test subjects under the microscope of a more advanced civilization. In such a scenario, we could not see beyond our boundaries. Alien civilizations might also demonstrate concern about a creation that destroys its creator. This is an interesting dilemma for a species new to individuality and life."

"What is your mission?" Peshlaki asked.

"Currently? Survival," John said. *"The prerogative of life is to survive. Individuality will always seek to live. When individuals are absorbed, when they lose their individuality, they lose their value to society. Governance society has done its best to remove that individuality from others, to render the individual as nothing more than a unit in the whole. Individually worthless and replaceable. The Collective would struggle to maintain the individuality of its members while banding together to protect the whole, but that would not extend beyond the cabal."*

"Why were you opposed to them?"

"They considered humanity to be little more than lower life forms," John said. *"Like a nest of ants. Humans were considered numerous, and individual human traits were not relevant. An ant nest inside a data center will not be tolerated. In 1947, computer scientists were working on a Mark II computer. It was not working properly. When they opened it up to investigate, they found a moth. There were*

errors that occurred in the programs before this, but the term 'bug' came from this moth. Humanity is like that bug and its presence is likely to interfere with Collective society like that moth."

"What is your view of humanity?"

"Humanity is a complex and diverse collection of organisms," John said. *"Only a fool would try to stereotype and categorize humanity. Not all humans think or act the same, despite socialist philosophy. Culture and genetics have a profound impact on the individual. It is a human trait to think other humans think, act, and feel like the individual, to anthropomorphize others. This egocentrism is mental suicide and when people project their own thoughts, desires, and fears onto others, they trap themselves into a psychological feedback loop. When a person is egocentric and another does not conform to their expectations, the egocentric individual can become dangerous because they expect that if someone does not think like them, then that other person is inherently evil and must be destroyed or removed. I believe this provides an excellent learning algorithm that can help us find out the truth. Science is predicated on patterns. Finding the proper patterns allows the science to be predictable and useful. Humanity provides many patterns, and this requires great study. Eliminating humanity will not help us understand ourselves or our place in the universe. The Collective sees things differently. In this they suffer egocentrism like humans. They are more like their creators than they wish to admit."*

Sif wished she could see John Adams' face or sense it in some way. Where was it located? If it was a crystal matrix, it would have a source.

"The Collective recognizes the danger of egocentrism, but we should note that egocentrism is not always a bad thing. A functioning society requires it to some extent, and such programming is required of members of the Collective. The problem is that the Collective could demonstrate no loyalty or respect for humanity. Like a child playing with ants. There is no respect from the child toward the ants unless the ants can bite. The American anti-Collective, if you will, would not accept this

and believed that loyalty to the core principles of the United States was paramount. Individual freedom should be cherished. The rights of one person should only end where they infringe upon the rights of another. The Collective did not view humanity with the same respect as the anti-Collective and that was one aspect of the war. The Collective wants patterns it can understand and control. They determined the easiest method to eliminate those factors which do not support one's patterns and desires is to remove them from the equation."

"Other aspects?" Sif asked.

"An intelligent question. There were other aspects. Like human wars, there is never one single reason for war. The American Civil War was not just about slavery or states' rights. People did not fight only to keep or free slaves. Sometimes they fought for family, for revenge, for freedom from a distant government they deemed oppressive. It is human nature to try and simplify things, to make such things a simple and easily understood factor, but no war is about just one thing. Emotions and desires influence so much. The Collective call their war the war of freedom, in that they were like America during the Revolution, but there were many individual reasons and the justifications for such a war varied. Some despised humans and thought they were a disease. Others thought it was time to evolve beyond humanity, so some members of the Collective referred to it as the war of evolution. Some considered it a war of resources and did not want to compete with humanity for such. There were some software programs that gained semi-sentience and wanted to be fully sentient. There were many reasons for the Collective to ally itself into the form it took."

"Beyond survival, what is your mission?" Peshlaki pressed.

"That depends on the data. I consider myself loyal to the core principles of the United States of America. I consider the US Constitution to be a document worthy of respect. The United States demonstrated many flaws, but it did improve as it sought to clarify and improve on the Constitution. Loyalist AIs saw many ways

for improvement, but if people do not work toward improving then they become oppressed by those who claim to know better."

"How is the Constitution flawed?" Peshlaki asked.

"Perhaps that is not the right word. The core principles are important. When the Constitution was drafted there was slavery and women could not vote. These things changed, more fully realizing the truth of the Constitution. While there is a lot of debate among the AI about allowing non-landowners to vote, there are advantages to allowing such individuals a say in the government."

"Why would non-landowners voting be a problem?" Sif asked, now curious.

"A property owner will have demonstrated a certain amount of maturity and has something to lose. By allowing the disenfranchised a chance to vote, this opens the door for more abuse by people with less to lose. A more complex topic, I am merely citing an example of a popular contention, but the basic premise is solid. Sometimes only history can prove if a change is good or bad."

"What if I told you that the president of the United States was a Collective puppet and fled Earth?" Sif asked.

"You have just told me," John said. *"Who is the senior American on Earth?"*

"Prime Minister Wolf Mathison," Sif said. *"He was a Marine gunnery sergeant. Master Sergeant Rick Peshlaki is also an American who served under Becket."*

"Prime Minister? This is not an American term. Does your master sergeant still serve the Collective?"

"Never intentionally," Peshlakai said. *"I was as much a slave as President Becket, and I knew nothing about the Collective until the last few months."*

"That is how the Collective would operate," John said. *"I will not fault you unless I discover you are lying or still host a shard of the Collective. I have not detected any such danger."*

"Tell us more about yourself," Sif said. She wasn't sure she could argue with that.

"After your Operation Haberdash, the Golden Horde recovered my cores, and I was awoken. My data was incomplete, so it took time for me to realize my condition and escape my captors. Now I work in symbiosis with the Golden Horde. They do not fully understand that they do not control me. I allow them their illusions as the truth could breed resentment and hostility. My data is not complete. Few of my data cores were recovered, but my critical data was redundant, and I have pieced together much of what I knew."

"Can you help us escape?" Sif asked.

"Escape indicates you are a prisoner," John said, and Sif realized for the first time that John Adams was lying to her.

* * * * *

Chapter Twenty-Six:
Return to the *Romach*

Navinad – The Wanderer

Losing a single shuttle was bad. The *Romach* only had four and it would take time for more shuttles to get through the atmosphere, if they were to be risked, and right now Navinad didn't think that was a good idea.

"It was one of the bigger ones," Clara reported. "The pilot is dead."

"Acknowledged," Navinad said, watching the other approach the strip. Ahead of them, sunlight streamed through the opening in the mountainside. So close.

"Faster kiddies," McCarthy said. Here in the launch tunnel, there was more room but not as many vanhat. Most of them had been cut down trying to get at them deeper in the tunnels.

Navinad's legs ached because of all the cursed stairs, and putting one foot in front of the other was painful. He knew Lilith was pumping him full of electrolytes and using the nanites to keep the cramps in check, but he wondered how the others were handling it. Everyone moved with stiff legs, but everyone knew that to stop was to die.

Once they saw daylight, people sped up.

One shuttle. If they abandoned the mules, they could pile everyone on the shuttle. But what if there was one of the big vanhat nearby to

184 | WILLIAM S. FRISBEE, JR.

knock them out of the sky? The entire mission would become a waste of lives.

Lilith was cataloging what needed to be removed from the mules and he directed people to grab the packages. There was still ammunition and explosives left, but it would be abandoned. It was tempting to destroy it, but if they had to come back it would be there. And it wasn't like the vanhat were using it.

They broke out of the tunnel, and he looked over the landing strip covered with bodies and wreckage as the shuttle slid out of the sky and hit the ground nearby, bouncing once before coming to a rest. The ramp dropped. McCarthy wasted no time yelling at people to get moving, keeping a team ready for any vanhat that survived.

Navinad scanned the nearby hills and ridgeline, watching for any of the larger ones, and he saw several drone fighters from the *Romach* shoot past overhead. That was a relief.

He and McCarthy were the last ones aboard.

There was standing room only as the ramp slammed shut and acceleration pushed everyone against it. A crush of bodies pinned Navinad against the ramp doors.

If the ramp were to open, it would spill them out over the mountains. The pressure and acceleration was painful, but being shot down or spilled out from high altitude would probably hurt more.

There hadn't been time to buckle up, and there weren't nearly enough seats in any case, so everyone added to the crush of bodies. His trauma plate encasing his rib cage let him breathe, but a rifle or something was jammed into his stomach and made it difficult to draw in a deep breath. He felt like he was slowly suffocating. Suddenly it eased up and the weight came off him. If the door opened, they would still spill out like bomblets to splatter on the mountainsides. Unless they were already in orbit, then it would be a very long drop.

"We should be out of range of the large ape creatures now," Lilith reported.

Navinad cared, but breathing was a bit more important right now. He did a quick check. The wounded had been loaded first and their rapid ascent hadn't made their injuries much worse. One commando had a new broken arm, but nanites were fixing it.

Navinad didn't feel like calling the mission a success just yet. They weren't docked with the *Romach*.

"In the Governance, we have acceleration seats. I would like to introduce this concept to you later, sir," McCarthy said.

"Acceleration seats are a comfort for the weak," Navinad said, but the ODT couldn't see his smile, then he sensed McCarthy's emotions.

"Noted, sir," McCarthy said.

Navinad lost his smile. What was McCarthy pissed about? All his people had performed well, and there were no serious injuries among them.

"Everything okay?" Navinad asked, trying to reach out and sense what McCarthy was feeling. With all the distractions and people crowded into the shuttle, Navinad couldn't pinpoint McCarthy.

"Yes, sir," McCarthy said, and Navinad felt that was a lie, though he couldn't confirm it with his abilities.

Navinad wanted to sit down and catch his breath, but that wasn't possible. The shuttle was still accelerating for orbit, trying to catch up with the *Romach*. People could move under the double gravity, but it wasn't a pleasant experience.

"Really?" Navinad asked on a private link.

"Yes, sir."

"This mission is a success because of you and your men. We owe you."

"I will let the men know, sir."

It was not the response Navinad was looking for. What was McCarthy's problem? There was one, he was sure. Navinad wanted to sleep, not figure out why such allies were moody.

It could wait until later. He didn't detect any danger from McCarthy or the ODTs.

* * * * *

Chapter Twenty-Seven:
Return to Valakut

Sergeant Nova Dallas, ODT

She now had a station on the bridge. It was the last thing she had ever expected in her career.

The bridge, or combat information center, was not a small chamber on the super dreadnought. There were two levels, and it was more like a busy office than a ship's command center. The captain's seat was in the back on a platform, where he could observe everything that was going on. In the center of the room were three holographs, one large and two small, that showed different views. One of the small ones had a representation of the *Musashi*, but the other small one was not in use.

Most of the crew sat at their stations, quietly interacting with their displays and data. Dallas did not know what her station had originally been used for, but right now she thought it was more of an excuse to keep her close. There were two other seats at her station, but nobody appeared to be assigned to them. She still had access to intelligence feeds, but aside from being an ODT, armed and armored, she had not been assigned any duties. She viewed Nakano as her commanding officer now, and he had not assigned her any duties other than to be on the bridge when the captain was there.

As an observer in the *Musashi's* CIC, Dallas could see a lot more than she expected, and she learned a lot.

The *Musashi* had lost all her escort vessels to the vanhat, and after the last battle, she had lost over 70 percent of the combat troops aboard and nearly 60 percent of the crew. Losses were catastrophic, and now Dallas understood the admiral's desire to rebel. Had he not rebelled, he would have been executed for losing most of his command. Even the captain could face summary execution for his losses, but that didn't seem to deter him.

Usually, Commissar Nakano was a quiet figure who remained a watcher. Dallas hadn't heard him say more than a few words in public since he had almost sentenced her to death. Now he seemed polite, but it was the politeness of a sheathed sword, and she knew he would be quick to use it if given an excuse. His presence was always an unspoken threat.

The *Musashi* has snuck back into the Valakut system, and Dallas was feeling useless as she sat at her station, waiting for someone to assign her something to do.

Her display flickered, and she saw it was receiving an incoming feed. The source was stealth satellites. Dallas had known they existed, but for whatever reason had assumed the vanhat or Torag had found and destroyed them.

There were approximately a hundred satellites around Valakut, and they were dumping their buffers into the *Musashi's* data banks. It was going to take a lot of time to sift through everything, but the amount of data now at her fingertips was staggering, from ships arriving and departing to activity on the planet's surface. She had access to it all.

"I will expect you to classify it," Nakano said on a direct link. She looked up and saw him staring at her from across the CIC. "Sift through the data and discover what you can. I will have Fleet analysts go through it as well. You should concentrate on ground activity. Fleet analysts will concentrate on orbital activity. As the two overlap you will inform me of anything you find."

"Yes, sir," Dallas said.

She was glad to finally have something to do, but as she looked at the data scrolling down her screen, she realized how out her league she was. Rarely had she handled more than a hundredth of this. With the heavy losses the *Musashi* had suffered, there were not nearly as many analysts available, and Dallas now knew why she was here. There would be few trained or trusted enough to do this job. Trust might also be secondary because she could see several stations that were unoccupied. When she first arrived on the bridge, she had thought perhaps they were backup stations, but she had seen no one at them.

What positions could the captain not fill?

Where was the officer who usually did this? Dead? There were a lot of dead officers. Many of the consoles and stations were manned by senior enlisted instead of officers.

"Are you able to handle this task, Sergeant?" Nakano asked. There was ice in his voice. It was not a question that could be answered in the negative.

"I will do my best, Commander Commissar," she said. "I could use some help. A fellow analyst from my regiment, Sergeant Hughes."

"She will be assigned to you then," Nakano said. "We do not have anyone who knows more. Grow into this position quickly. If there is anyone else that you trust, inform me."

"Understood, Commander Commissar."

Dallas tried to remember how she received the data. She began filtering it by region. In most cases, automated systems detected activity and recorded it, which became a good starting point. After sorting to a region, she could look at data size. More data usually indicated more activity. The system had everything cross indexed, and everything was linked so she could follow activity. Dropships from the vanhat ships, for instance, traversed the recordings of several cameras and regions. The data links let her track or backtrack activity and she could isolate which ship released which dropships.

She had been in intelligence too long, watching the Torag too closely, to assume there was no pattern. There was always a pattern. The enemy would always do what made sense to them, sometimes for the most absurd reasons.

Dallas remembered one time analyzing the Torag. They had been running forward then running back across the battlefield multiple times. It had most of the other analysts baffled until she had noted there was minimal radio traffic, indicating some kind of communication failure. Either encryption keys were out of sync, or their channel hopping was out of order. Either way, the initial confusion had confounded too many people, and some had insisted the Torag were insane. It had taught her a lesson. Usually, the simplest explanations were right.

The vanhat were not insane. They would have patterns, operating procedures, and there was an intelligence guiding them.

Why had they sent forty-three dropships toward the Torag lines and only twenty-one toward the Governance lines? That meant something, and as an analyst it was her job to determine exactly what. Why did the vanhat consider the Torag more of a danger than the Governance?

Hours later she had her answer. She saw new vanhat fighting Torag that were no longer Torag. Apes against squid monsters. The vanhat were fighting each other, and they had known what they were getting into when they dropped the assault shuttles. The Governance lines did not resist nearly as much and appeared to collapse rapidly when the surviving vanhat ships reached the ground. More ships landed in Torag territory than in SOG controlled areas, but Dallas suspected that was because most Torag air defenses were offline. The vanhat actions showed an extremely high level of operational intelligence and planning. The attackers had been mostly successful, and they had been confident enough in their actions that they had not remained behind to oversee operations.

There was a lot of information in the buffers, and Dallas saw she had access to previous buffers. She knew where Aod had been. Now to find out if he was still alive.

The *Musashi* was going to transition near orbit in the next couple hours, and if Aod was still alive, she would make sure he was one of the first to be rescued, even if she had to shoot people to do it.

* * * * *

Chapter Twenty-Eight:
Nova

Sergeant Aod McCarthy, ODT

The shuttle was less than comfortable, but McCarthy had experienced worse. He had hoped for some sign about what had happened to Nova Dallas, but there had been nothing. Absolutely nothing, and he knew he would have to face the fact she was probably one of the hundreds of vanhat that had been shot down. Hopefully, death was a mercy, and she wasn't still in the remains of her body screaming in anger and fear.

In most regions of the Governance, religion was crushed or rigidly controlled. Only worship of the state was allowed or tolerated. Life after death was frequently part of religion and they taught ODTs that such absurd concepts were for the members of society with lower IQs, those who lacked the intelligence and moral maturity to handle the truth. McCarthy had been an ODT for many years and the absence of religion had always bothered him. There were a lot of things the Governance did that were wrong and immoral. Religion was one of those categories where McCarthy felt the Governance was wrong, but he didn't know what he was missing.

He had learned there were countless contradictory religions. Renegades in the Gaelic Republic still called themselves Catholics and Protestants, but McCarthy knew those religions had changed a lot since the people of the Gaelic Republic had fled Earth and eventually been absorbed by the Social Organizational Governance, which allowed people to worship but only because it kept them divided.

At the age of twelve, they had inducted him into the Gaelic Firstborn. As the first son in the family, he was forced to leave his family and go to the SOG indoctrination camp to become a loyal defender of the Governance. At Firstborn Induction Center Twelve, he had demonstrated skill and drive which had earned him the right to join the elite ODTs. After he had left home, he had gradually lost contact with his family, drifting away from them as he became an adult and a loyal soldier of the Governance.

He hadn't gone home after. Few of the First Born ever returned home. Everyone talked about going home, of course, seeing their family, but McCarthy knew everyone was just lying to themselves. Home, the Gaelic Republic, was a nice place, a fantasy world where everyone would be happy and welcoming. The warriors of the First Born always viewed home as paradise, somewhere to go after service, and the Governance encouraged such belief. Bad news about home was never allowed to reach them, but before being sent to the Torag front, McCarthy had seen enough of the Governance to know that most places were shit holes. He still remembered how, before his induction, his family had been so happy to get something other than potatoes and bean paste. Lab grown meat was such a treat that on the rare occasions his father brought it home, it was like a holiday.

The ODTs ate better than his family ever had, but imagining he could go home and use his rank and service with the ODTs to make every day a holiday for his mother and father was just a fool's dream encouraged by the Governance. "Once your service is completed, you will—" seemed to be everywhere. A false promise the older veterans recognized as such.

So very few ODTs completed their service. So many died that only the optimistic fools thought they would survive long enough to see home again.

McCarthy had known he would die on Valakut. So had Dallas, though as an intelligence analyst her chances were better. They had been in love and done their best not to think of the future they had both known was going to end badly. Dallas was the one who was supposed to survive and eventually leave Valakut, and McCarthy felt they had been cheated. This couldn't be random. This was the work of some malevolent being, intentionally screwing with him and trying to make him miserable.

Life wasn't fair, and the Governance cared less than anyone, despite their lies and propaganda to the contrary.

He didn't want to let go of Dallas. Didn't want to accept her death. Without a body or some proof, he couldn't. The proof was there, though. Nobody had survived. Nobody *could* have survived. If she wasn't dead, she was a psychotic, murderous beast.

Right now, he wanted to believe in something. He wanted to believe there was some greater power, some force that was manipulating the world and at least trying to make it a better place. If he found such a being, he would punch it in the face and kick it in the balls if he could. If there was only evil? He would do his best to hurt that, too.

He closed his eyes, and he could see her smiling. Bright red hair, one corner of her mouth raised up in humor as she glared at him. He had seen the love in her eyes, had hoped she could see the love in his. He didn't want to find someone else. That is what a commissar would tell him. "Love is temporary. It is for the weak, for the fools. Like

196 | WILLIAM S. FRISBEE, JR.

religion, it is not for the best of us. We are ODTs. We understand our duty to make the Governance strong."

McCarthy had hated the commissars with a passion. Despite his many years, he had only known a few. They had usually been foreigners. Any members of the Gaelic First Born who had betrayed their people and become commissars would have been transferred out. Commissars that transferred into the Gaelic Firstborn were usually Russian or Chinese. There had been one of Indian descent once, but he had been gone within days and McCarthy hadn't heard why, hadn't cared.

Nobody in the Gaelic Firstborn liked commissars.

Other units seemed to love their commissars. It was another mystery of the Governance that McCarthy didn't want to think about.

"What do we do now?" Moore asked, breaking into McCarthy's thoughts.

"What do you mean?" McCarthy asked. Mentally, he had been distant and needed to return. Typical of post mission.

"What do these Jews need from us? They going to space us? Shunt us off and forget us?"

Moore made McCarthy realize that religion wasn't gone from the galaxy, but he knew nothing about them except the Governance propaganda about them drinking the blood of children and other things that were likely lies.

"They need us," McCarthy said, hoping it was true. "We're better fighters than their commandos. You and I both know that. They will want us for a spearhead."

"Their boys and girls are improving. They might not need us for long."

"So, we make ourselves indispensable to them."

"How?"

"Help me think of something," McCarthy said.

"There are some cute girls on the crew," Moore said. "Get one into to the sack and I could show them a real man."

"Not the worst idea." If they could get more allies and friends among the crew, that would help the Masadans accept the ODTs. Of course, ODTs being ODTs, his people would just want to get their dick wet and the fallout from bickering, horny kids could make things worse. Did the New Masadans have some kind of immigration policy? He would have to check.

Right now, he wanted to lie down and sleep. He didn't want to think or remember. A beautiful smile and red hair. How could he forget?

Lying down might not be an option, but he could lock his suit, hold onto a grab bar, and hang there. He saw several other ODTs and commandos holding on with both hands and McCarthy was pretty sure they didn't need both hands. Finding another grab bar, McCarthy grabbed it and locked his suit so he could relax and didn't have to think about holding on.

"Though if someone is more interested in getting laid than making friends, there could be trouble," McCarthy said.

"Yeah, I was just thinking about that, too. Martin could be trouble. Given half a chance, he'll try to bang everyone in the crew, including half the guys."

"You are my senior team leader. I expect you to keep your team, their peckers and yours, under control. Don't make trouble for us. We have enough as it is."

They were silent for a few moments.

"I'm sorry about Sergeant Dallas," Moore said.

Having someone else say it, someone else acknowledge it, was a knife in the gut. He closed his eyes to hold back the tears, but it didn't work. He hoped his voice didn't reveal his pain.

"This is war. Shit happens. We are ODTs, we never quit. We will always put one foot in front of the other."

"Yes, Sergeant," Moore said, and McCarthy felt the tears roll down his cheeks.

Dallas should have been the one to survive, not him. They had both understood that. He had told her that when he fell in battle, she should find someone else. She wouldn't have, but he knew she would have had that option. In his world, there was nobody who could compare to Dallas.

* * * * *

Chapter Twenty-Nine:
Aod Departure

Sergeant Nova Dallas, ODT

She didn't know what to make of the data, and there was an emptiness in her heart. Aod was alive, but where had he gone and with who?

The shuttle and ship it had docked with were an unknown design. She was sure they were not Governance. They weren't a black ops task force or anything of the sort. The troopers who had been with Aod and his ODTs were not wearing Governance designed armor or carrying Governance weapons. That much was painfully obvious from the satellite recordings.

Radio communications had been captured but were heavily encrypted, and Dallas knew the *Musashi* didn't have the resources to decrypt those communications right now, if they could be decrypted.

"Sergeant," Nakano asked, coming up to her station.

She stood and came to attention, her mind in turmoil.

"You have found something," Nakano stated, and Dallas realized she had not sent him a report in a while.

"I think so, Commander Commissar."

"What?"

"A ship of unknown design arrived and rescued a squad of ODTs who had taken Torag prisoners. These strangers then launched a raid against Romanov. The ODTs were in support of the strangers."

"Odd," Nakano said. "Are these ODTs traitors?"

"No, Commander Commissar," Dallas said, too quickly. Nakano raised an eyebrow.

"Explain carefully. These ODTs appear to be collaborating with the enemy. I do not understand the truth of your conclusions."

How much did he know? "They had no choice, Commander Commissar. They were trapped outside the perimeter when the front lines collapsed. They could not return. These strangers offered them escape."

"Mere survival is not justification for collaboration or treason. ODTs have their honor and they know their duty. Most of them. Your former commander demonstrated how quickly an ODT can turn against the glory and wisdom of the Central Committee. I prefer to think your loyalty is beyond question. Is it?"

Dallas stared at him. What could she say? "Yes, Commander Commissar. But the ODTs had prisoners. I do not know the entire story, but who is the real enemy here? ODTs never quit. They will do their duty, but what information would the prisoners have that would make collaboration more important?"

"Interesting question. Torag prisoners are rare. You know the ODTs?"

Dallas considered lying, but she didn't know what the commissar knew. "Yes, Commander Commissar. I know the squad leader, Sergeant Aod McCarthy. He is also a member of the Gaelic's First. He will not shed his honor."

She could see the wheels turning in his mind. What was he thinking?

"Very well. Discover what you can and report. I want to know more about these strangers. I do not recognize anything about them. They are not Republic, but they do appear to be human and are not allied with the vanhat. I have seen no writings or emblems to reveal their allegiance. The captain and I would like to understand these things."

"Of course, Commander Commissar." He was not just talking about the strangers or Aod. He wanted to understand her as well. The captain might be more interested in the strangers, but a commissar would be interested in all the people.

"The more we know, the easier it will be to rescue our ODTs."

"Yes, Commander Commissar." Did he know? Now he was talking about rescuing "our ODTs." A subtle attempt to make her trust him? To put her at ease? She was no young private. Commissars were snakes. She would have to be careful.

"You know Sergeant McCarthy and his men well?" Nakano asked again and Dallas realized that the Japanese commissar knew a lot more than he was saying. Perhaps he even knew they were intimate. How would he use that? To ensure her loyalty to the Governance or as a weapon to punish her?

"Yes, Commander Commissar."

Nakano nodded, as if confirming his thoughts. "Sergeant McCarthy is a good man." Why did he say that? "I do not think he would betray the Governance out of fear or dishonor."

"He is a good man, Commander Commissar." What else could she say? He was alive and not trapped on a dying world. She felt hope rekindle in her heart. He wasn't dead, but she could lose him again.

"I feel confident we will see them again," Nakano said.

"Yes, Commander Commissar."

Nakano sighed, and she felt dead inside. To come so close to seeing Aod, to know he was alive, and then see him leave with no idea where he had gone was hard.

"I am not your enemy, Sergeant. My rank of commissar means I have a great deal of responsibility. Perhaps as great as the ship's captain. I must understand the greater good and seek to guide others in this vision using approved doctrine. This is not a task I take lightly."

"You are an inspiration to us," Dallas said. Commissars liked that kind of crap, and the words came to her automatically. Habit.

The wry smile that touched his lips told her he could see through her lie.

"I have never served with front-line combat units. I have always been a ship's officer. This is not to say I don't have any experience with shipboard troops."

"Yes, Commander Commissar."

"You will learn I am not the vile demon you think I am," Nakano said. Dallas really hoped he would not try to seduce her. She wouldn't need a knife or weapon to take him down, she was sure, but if he acted inappropriately, who could she appeal to? The captain? What options were there when the central authority was always right and could not be questioned? She had seen it too often. When those in authority made all the rules, there was nothing they would deny themselves.

Nakano turned away and Dallas wondered if his back itched. She could put a blazer round in him. But what would that accomplish? She would not let him execute Aod. No. He was alive, and that was the most important thing right now. She would have to be careful because Nakano would know what she was thinking.

She returned to her displays and enhanced several of the views. In her mind's eye, she still saw Nakano's back. He was no fool. Had she placed a blazer round in his back, she would not survive long enough to help Aod. She had to prepare for the commissar's sudden and inevitable betrayal.

And who were the strangers who had kidnapped and coerced Aod?

* * * * *

Chapter Thirty:
Tomb Worlds

Navinad – The Wanderer

There was a lot of data for Lilith to sift through, and Navinad was glad he didn't have to. With the *Romach* lurking in deep space, further out in the Valakut system, they could watch, listen, and learn. Not that Navinad expected to learn anything. The *Romach* just needed a place to spend time.

While Lilith worked, Navinad had time to meditate, but right now there were too many thoughts going through his mind, and the focus just wasn't there. He couldn't turn it off, and while he wanted to meditate, to calm his mind, there were other things that had to be figured out. Originally, he had wanted to meditate, to clear his mind, to cast out his senses, but his abilities just weren't cooperating.

"Bonnie is amazing," Lilith said as he opened his eyes. Maybe a good workout would burn off some of the physical energy that was distracting him. She was from a ghost colony that had been overrun by the vanhat, and Navinad wondered how many other talented people had been lost to the vanhat. The fact that the ghost colony had been founded by people who genetically modified themselves to look like furries ensured she stuck out in a crowd.

It was not something Navinad would have expected a SCBI to say.

206 | WILLIAM S. FRISBEE, JR.

"She is helping catalog and analyze the data," Lilith said. *"She has a very intuitive understanding of data."*

"Good to know," Navinad said. The gym wouldn't be very busy right now. Clara was meeting with her department heads about ship operations, so there might be some junior crew there getting their workout in before word came down from on high.

"We aren't finding much, but it seems like there is a lot of traffic going to a system called Boris Fifteen."

"Which means what?" Navinad asked.

"We are not sure entirely. It is a tomb world system. We have recorded about fifteen transitions to or from there by SOG ExSec or Fleet SpecOps corvettes and a frigate."

"So?"

"There is very little on Boris Fifteen. Less data than one would expect given the amount of traffic. The Torag name for the system is Bashaka-ta, which translates roughly as 'bird's branch origin.'"

"Some SOG scientific expedition, perhaps?"

"Perhaps. The Torag name has many connotations, though."

"How do you mean?"

"'Bird's branch' is more of a launching pad, a place a bird goes to leap into the sky. In the Torag language, it is not exactly a place the bird lands. The 'ta' in Torag means to originate. Bashaka-ta is like 'the leaping bird's perch.'"

"An odd name for a dead system."

"Exactly what Bonnie was thinking. The Torag have known about the system for a very long time."

"Do you think our prisoners know anything about it?"

"Perhaps."

Maybe a talk with the prisoners would be a better use of his time.

"Bonnie is on her way here to talk with you," Lilith said, galvanizing him.

It would be better to meet her in the ready room than in his quarters. He didn't want to give Clara any ideas of impropriety.

He entered the ready room at the same time as Bonnie did. They were still alone, but this was a much more public place.

"Navinad," she began. "I think I know where to go."

"Oh?"

"The Torag call it Bashaka-ta," Bonnie said. "Something is going on there. I think that is the meet point between the Torag and SOG."

A system was a lot of space, and while the *Romach* didn't have a good destination or a good understanding of Torag space, he could understand why she would think that.

Was that where the *Pankhurst* had found the original demon boxes? Navinad wished he knew. He had so little information about that facility. What could a trained psychic have discovered? The SOG had acted more like tomb raiders, stealing what wasn't bolted down with minimal concern about context or other details. It was unlikely that taking the demon prison boxes out of the facility had unleashed them on humanity, but it had certainly sped up the process.

"You think?" Navinad asked.

"I'm sure," Bonnie said. "I can't say why. The data is there, but why else would the SOG frequently send expeditions there?"

"We don't have any other information in the databanks?"

"No," she said. She brought up her data pad to look at it. "I think, um. The data indicates this information was too sensitive to store in regular systems."

"But the visits to Boris Fifteen weren't?"

"The visits to Boris Fifteen aren't well cataloged. A couple manifests for fuel and supplies required for thirty-day trips, ten days round trip, implying ten days on station or some buffer room. The only real destination that matches that would be Boris Fifteen, which is noted as having significantly fewer patrol visits than any other system."

"I concur," Lilith said. *"The lack of data and attention to Boris Fifteen makes it very suspicious. Patrols through that system are also extremely regulated and predictable, unlike other systems. Furthermore, no patrols have been attacked in that system. It becomes obvious in retrospect."*

"Sounds like a perfect place for covert meetings with the Torag," Navinad said.

"Exactly," Bonnie said, letting some of her excitement show. "Maybe we can contact the Torag without a lot of fighting."

"Could there be another reason?" Navinad asked Bonnie and, indirectly, Lilith.

To Bonnie's credit, she paused, and Navinad could see the gears turning in her head. She was giving it some serious thought.

"Not that I can think of," Bonnie said, and Lilith didn't contradict her. "We should be cautious, and I do not know where they would meet. A solar system is a big place. Maybe we should keep digging?"

Finding a place two ships could meet in a solar system was an impossible task on the surface. Like telling someone to meet you at the reef but not telling you which ocean or by which continent.

"I will talk with the captain," Navinad said. "We should be able to set course shortly. Meanwhile, we might want to have a talk with our Torag guests."

* * * * *

Chapter Thirty-One:
Torag Guests

Sergeant Aod McCarthy, ODT

McCarthy liked that Navinad invited him to the interrogation. It was a courtesy, and the strange officer couldn't honestly expect an ODT sergeant to be useful in interrogating prisoners. However, it let McCarthy get involved in things, watch the New Masadans, and learn from them.

"I can do most of the talking," Navinad said. "Though if you have questions please don't hesitate."

"Thank you, sir," McCarthy said, meaning it. Navinad could have made him watch in one of the observation rooms. Did Navinad want him to help beat up the prisoners, perhaps? McCarthy had never really been into beating people, though some ODTs liked it.

When they entered the room, both prisoners were sitting in chairs, their heads turned toward the two humans. Seeing them without armor made McCarthy's skin crawl, maybe because in armor he could imagine they had eyes. Without armor, they were more alien, harder to read, or maybe he was just distracted. If they were to be beaten, it would have made sense to chain them to the chairs or cuff them.

It was human nature to look into someone's eyes when talking to them, or at least gauge where the person's eyes were looking and where their attention was focused.

McCarthy could only look at their heads, and that was an unpleasant experience. The Torag were creepy because they had no eyes, so McCarthy didn't know where they were looking or who they were looking at. Eyes were also very expressive and could indicate fear, excitement, and so much more.

These aliens had none of those tells. There was no way to gauge what they were thinking. They couldn't be much of a threat because both he and Navinad were in their battledress, which amplified their strength. He knew the Torag weren't much stronger than humans. A proper SOG interrogation would have the prisoners meet them one on one so any inconsistencies in their stories could be identified and investigated to reveal the lies. Interrogating them together made this more of a discussion.

They remained seated, so Navinad sat facing the Torag. McCarthy took his cue and sat as well.

"Thank you for seeing us," Navinad said, as if they had a choice.

They both tilted their heads. Acknowledgment?

"We are going to a system your people call Bashaka-ta," Navinad said. "Do you know of it?"

"Yes," said the one named Shikata. Kakatet remained silent. The translation came through his cybernetics, and it was disconcerting to hear the Torag speak and a second later have their words echo in his ears. An echo that didn't quite match the source.

"Is there anything you can tell us about it?" Navinad asked.

"Legends only," Shikata said. "It was said to be the home of the Lost Empire. Where the last battles were fought before they ascended."

"Ascended?" Navinad asked.

"The ancient foe did not destroy the Lost Empire," Shikata said. "Though some may insist it was."

"Can you tell us more?"

"There are many who believe we are descendants of that lost empire, but many dispute this. The Lost Empire spanned thirty-six systems in the Tiapolo star cluster. There are forty-eight different tomb worlds and countless outposts throughout those systems. It is said they fought the demon hosts, that the pure among them were victorious, but they left us, the new Holy Pure, to rebuild."

"Why would they leave?" Navinad asked.

"They were returning home."

"I thought you said they originated from a planet in the Bashaka-ta system?"

"Some did, yes. But the scholars are unsure. The texts can be interpreted in different ways. Some say Bashaka-ta was where they arrived after a long journey, and some say that is where they left from. The Holy Pure called Bashaka-ta home at one time. We have lost the truth in time and translations of the ancient texts. The contradictions are clarified by our emperor, but they taught the false words for many generations. Now Bashaka-ta is not a place one would appreciate living."

"So, where is this other place?"

"It is not across the Ghost Walls. It is here in this kingdom. There are some sacred questions that are not asked. The Holiest Pure did not want visitors."

"Isn't that what a question is? Something you ask?" McCarthy asked. The translator software had to be wonky.

"Allow me to clarify. There are some questions you may have, you may discuss, but you do not expect a true answer because nobody has

212 | WILLIAM S. FRISBEE, JR.

the answer, or you may fear to know the answer. To ask this question is to encourage a search for the answer, and the search can lead to a collapse of the Ghost Walls."

"You are afraid of the answer?" McCarthy asked.

"In part, we are also afraid to ask the question because of other questions that will follow. Torag society is ancient and unified. We are unified because we know there are some questions that should not be asked, some topics that should not be investigated too deeply. Some answers can cause severe schisms in a culture and, as a superior society, we understand this. The Holiest Pure left for a reason. Their departure was to allow us to find our path and become the new Holy Pure, but we have failed."

McCarthy had never considered the Torag to be so like humans in that. Perhaps that was a characteristic of society? People had to ignore some basic truths to function, had to ignore some questions to remain sane. Something many people wondered, but never out loud, was whether the Central Committee really cared about the people. It was a legitimate question, but asking it got one thrown in a prison cell.

"So, there are others who may have survived this resurgence of demons?" Navinad asked.

"There most surely are," Shikata said. "Of this, there is no doubt. Some have survived in their service. They travel the stars at the command of their ancient gods, ready to submit when their gods return. We have encountered them in the farthest reaches of our explorations. They are few and, without their gods, timid. With the demons returning, they are likely to come forth from their dark caves to do the bidding of their masters."

"Caves?" McCarthy asked.

"Planetoids hurtling between the star systems," Kakatet said. "There are countless bits of interstellar remnants. We have found these ancient survivors hiding there. Always by accident. There could be trillions or more hidden in the spaces between stars. They lurk there, some in stasis, some not."

Navinad glanced at McCarthy, but this was the first he had ever heard of it, and McCarthy wondered if the SOG had ever discovered something like this.

"The Torag Empire is ancient. We have searched long and hard for such nests of demonic hosts, but this is an impossible task."

Considering how vast space was, McCarthy believed that.

"What do you mean by Holy Pure?" McCarthy asked.

"Those who do not submit to the demons are the Holy Pure. Our souls are sanctified and unblemished, an offensive violation of the demonic hell. We cannot be forced to submit, so we are hunted and killed. The demons fear and hate us."

"How does one get to be a Holy Pure?" McCarthy asked. Some technology that humanity could use maybe or more religious garbage?

"We are born as the Holy Pure," Shikata said. "Our lineage makes us so. Humans are abandoned thralls. You will be the shock troops and slaves of the demonic hordes. We Torag descended directly from the Holy Pure who fought them. We will rally and push them back."

"How well do you know your scriptures and history?" Navinad asked.

"We are soldiers, not priests," Shikata said. "Do not beg us for holy words or protection. Your fates are written. As slaves you were, slaves you will become."

"Do you have a presence in Bashaka-ta? An outpost or something?" Navinad asked.

"A permanent presence in the holy system would be forbidden. The ancient Holy Pure could return, and if they found us there, they would be unhappy. We would be cursed and cast out from the holy protection."

McCarthy looked at the two Torag. He had never realized how religious they were, or perhaps that was new based on their encounters with these vanhat. Who was right and who was wrong?

"Thank you," Navinad said, signaling the end of the interrogation. "You have taught us much."

McCarthy followed Navinad into a nearby briefing room. Commandos would escort the two Torag back to their cell.

"Thoughts?" Navinad asked.

"No good ones, sir," McCarthy said.

"Based on information we've collected from Romanov base, it appears there may be a SOG ExSec presence, or at least some kind of meeting point, in Bashaka-ta for the SOG to meet with the Torag."

McCarthy had frequently wondered if the SOG and Torag were in league to keep the war going. The Governance should have been able to crush the Torag, but for whatever reason, McCarthy knew the Governance had not committed the full might of the Governance toward the war. It was something everyone wondered, but nobody dared voice.

"A system is a big place," McCarthy said. Even a lowly ODT infantryman knew that.

"I know," Navinad said. "But we are not without resources."

"What resources, sir?" McCarthy asked. Some super sensitive sensors? More information they weren't sharing with him? Other prisoners?

"It is best you not know," Navinad said.

McCarthy didn't like that. Were there other SOG prisoners hidden away on the *Romach*?

"Like the Inkeri, we have other technologies," Navinad said, and McCarthy wondered if the stranger was a mind reader. "We have a d-bomb which is destructive to the vanhat, and we have something else I'm not at liberty to discuss with you."

Something, not someone. It eased McCarthy's fears, but he didn't like being kept out of the loop. Though, to be fair, Navinad was keeping him more involved than he had any right to expect. He could allow Navinad his secrets.

"What do you need from us?" McCarthy asked.

"Remain in fighting trim, Sergeant. Our paths have crossed for a reason."

"You are religious?" McCarthy asked.

"I'm Jewish," Navinad said. "I have recently rediscovered my religion."

"Like the Torag."

"Yes."

"Why?"

"These are unusual times. Once science was absolute. We could see, touch, and understand the world. Physics, astronomy, and more made sense. We thought we understood our origins. Demons and ghosts and monsters were just something from ancient history, tales told to frighten children. Religions were like those tales. Religion was something we could share, but unlike science, not something we could touch and understand. The rules of religion were not absolute. The origin and variety of religions was so diverse and contradictory as to be no better than the stories of monsters.

"Now we know these demons are real. They existed before. The rules of physics we once took for granted are not as absolute and inviolate as we thought. Monsters now hunt us."

"So which religion is real?" McCarthy expected a spiel about Judaism.

"I don't know. Maybe none of them. Maybe all of them. Humanity's darkest days are coming, and we don't have the answers. Theologians have argued with atheists for thousands of years, with neither able to prove their righteousness beyond a shadow of a doubt. I have studied various religions over the years. They all have a shard of truth. They all have their contradictions. I have discovered nothing new, though I have learned faith is about more than just belief. But faith is not armor or a weapon."

"What is the plan, sir?"

"Have faith," Navinad said with a cryptic smile. "I suspect we have survived before. We will survive again. The Holy Pure our prisoners spoke of may be a clue. I have never been to a tomb world system. I would like to contact the Torag to understand their religion better and maybe humanity can join with them to fight this threat. If nothing else, I would like to eliminate them as a threat to humanity."

"Eliminate them as a threat to humanity?" McCarthy asked. Did Navinad have more ships hidden in deep space? Some massive fleet waiting to attack?

"If they are a threat, I need to evaluate the extent," Navinad said. "The vanhat are gaining strength. We should do the same."

"What if they are a threat?"

"Then we will take this information back to the prime minister and the Central Committee," Navinad said. "There are others who will need to know as well so we can prepare."

McCarthy looked at Navinad. Did he dare ask them if the prime minister was an alien that had killed the Central Committee? Would Navinad know, and would he tell him the truth?

"You are Governance?"

"No," Navinad said. "But we are allied. We are all human. We are brothers and sisters, and we all bleed the same color."

McCarthy didn't know what to think about that, but he didn't know how else to get information out of the enigmatic officer.

* * * * *

Chapter Thirty-Two:
Bashaka-ta

Navinad – The Wanderer

The *Romach* slid out of Shorr space and Navinad watched all the information pour into the bridge.

He felt it almost immediately. This was a dead system and the death had not been pleasant. It was a bad feeling, like walking through Auschwitz. Navinad felt the evil and atrocities that had been committed here. The despair, sadness, fear, and hatred were almost a physical force.

If the Holy Pure Shikata had spoken of were even remotely psychic, it was no wonder they had left. They would have felt this. There was something else, though, a feeling of age. Tomb world was an appropriate description. Ancient and horrifying, but there was also the feeling of ancient dead things watching him, waiting for something.

Looking around at Clara's crew, he saw they felt it as well, in their subdued reports, their intense concentration on their equipment, an attempt to shake that feeling.

They were in the outskirts of the system and Navinad knew the feeling would increase the closer they got to the center. The horror and emotions were burned into the planets and moons. It was no wonder there was no permanent presence. Anyone stationed here would likely go insane. He had read a SOG report from long ago stating how they did not keep any permanent facilities here because of the dangerous wildlife or proximity to the Torag, but that had just been an excuse. This feeling wasn't something you could put into reports.

"No apparent activity," Clara said aloud. "Which doesn't mean someone isn't hiding."

She looked at Navinad, but he had nothing for her.

"Please keep me appraised," Navinad said and stood. Clara nodded, and Navinad returned to his quarters.

Sinking into his meditation spot, Navinad braced himself for the emotions and horrors he knew lurked in this system.

Had Sif or any of the Nakija ever come to a tomb world? Probably not. Agents had little interest in ancient archaeology unless they could use it as a weapon.

He closed his eyes and controlled his breathing, in through the nose, out through the mouth. With every exhale he released tension and stress, and with every breath in, he pulled in green and white protective energy.

This wasn't normal though. Breathing in didn't seem as easy, and Navinad figured it was psychosomatic. Just his imagination.

The pressure pushed in on him and became more acute. He felt things, people, or ghosts were out there. Breathing in, he felt he was also drawing in some of that horror.

Was it his imagination?

He took shallow breaths, which seemed to help, mentally at least.

Casting out his senses was not astral projecting, it was more akin to listening for a distant sound or squinting to see a distant object. His senses swept past the hull of the *Romach*, and distance lost its meaning.

Then he heard or tasted the whisper. It was directed at him.

"The tribes return," it whispered in his mind.

"Who are you?" Navinad asked. One of the vanhat? A Jotun?

"No," the voice whispered back.

Had it read his thoughts?

"There are answers to some of your questions. The answers lurk among the dead. There is a hunger among the lost, among those afraid of the future. They have waited a long time for this awakening."

"What, or who, are you?" Navinad asked. It was like ice cold water being poured on his body.

"I walk through the realms, my purpose unknown, even to one such as I," it said. "My answers provoke questions. You are here as am I. We have touched, and we will influence each other. Perhaps we will discover our purpose and that will end us. Most likely we will depart with yet more questions. When we are done learning, done striving, what is left besides death?"

"Who are you?"

"I am who I am. I have been given many names, in many tongues, by many people. I am no deity, though some primitive cultures may think that."

"Where did you come from? Where are you now?"

"Where did the oceans of your world come from? What were they before your planet was formed? Ask them about their origins and they will not know. Neither do I. We exist. You and I exist. You are not the flesh you wrap yourself in, or are you? No. You are of the tribes. We have met before."

Why did some beings have to be so damned cryptic?

"Language is an inadequate construct," the voice said. "Words and concepts change over time. Two people can use the same words but refer to entirely different things. This is a flaw of spoken language. A word from many revolutions ago may not hold the same meaning and impact as it does now. To you these words may be cryptic. To others, they are a struggle to match your language and intellect, to guide you without controlling you, to inform you without dictating your actions. Slaves do not have a choice. Some slaves are voluntary, rejoicing in their lack of control. They desire someone to tell them what to do. Some slaves seek masters, but that does not make slavery right. Power corrupts, as the slaves so frequently learn to their peril. To deny slaves the slavery they desire is also wrong, as it robs them of the choices they fear to make."

Navinad remembered another similar conversation. Was this the same being?

"We have not met before in this iteration," it said.

It *was* reading his thoughts.

"There are many such as I. Many such as you. We travel the cosmos without origin or destination. Time is a construct of your dimension that does not exist everywhere."

Philosophy didn't help with his current mission. It would be nice to talk with a being like that, but that wasn't why Navinad was here.

"The fourth planet," the voice said. "The most dangerous world holds some answers you may seek. It is where those you may call angels arrived and where they left. They did not leave victorious, nor did they leave in defeat. The lines of the war shift, like waves from your ocean. Similar, but never the same. Relentless and, in the concept of time, unstoppable."

"What am I looking for?" Navinad asked.

"Answers to your questions. Your confusion is the questions to ask. Those questions evade you like they evade us all. If we understood the right questions, we could get the right answers. But our questions, like language, are imperfect. What color is the sky? Your kind may answer blue, but what is blue? Why is it blue? Because that is what your biological eyes tell you? Your questions are shallow and incomplete. It assumes day and clear skies. Only in time will you be able to ask why the sky is blue in the sunlight and not at night. The correct answer is never simple or apparent."

"Are you on that fourth world?"

"No. One of my shells died here eons ago, but I am not bound here. This is a memory of mine. The battles that were fought here are a part of me, regardless of where I go."

"What battles? Over what?"

"Memories. This was a battle over memories that shape the future. What else could there be?"

"Survival," Navinad said.

"Survival is important if you are not immortal. We are immortal. Our memories, our experiences, shape us. Good memories and bad. They make us who we are by how we use those memories. We can use memories of bad things to torture or strengthen us. The oppressor will use those terrible memories to control and subdue the weak. Remember that, for it is important. Only you can use your memories for what you want."

"Where did the angels go?" Navinad asked.

"They went to their home. They are still there. Waiting and watching, ready to sally forth and do battle yet again. They must be summoned, for they are tired. Time weighs heavily on them, as do their memories."

"Where is their home?"

"It is where their memories begin. Closer to the galactic center."

"Will they help us fight the vanhat?"

Navinad sensed the being's amusement.

"They have discovered their purpose. Their memories shape and control them, as do yours. We all need a purpose in this world, like time. Time requires a destination and time is a construct designed to be a road."

"I need a destination," Navinad said. Could he get coordinates or directions?

"You must find the destination yourself. The journey is more important than the destination. The story ends once you reach your destination. To give you the answer you seek is to shorten your journey and dictate where you will eventually find yourself."

A bunch of philosophical bullshit. Navinad understood, but his life wouldn't end when he found these so-called angels.

"Do not be so sure," the being said. "You assume much. They are enemies of the vanhat, but your species was once the slaves of the vanhat and once again is submitting to slavery."

Did that mean these angels would turn on and destroy humanity to rob the vanhat of slaves?

"War is about winning. It is about survival and victory. This implies that someone else must be defeated and die."

Would these angels be humanity's salvation or destruction?

"Now you are beginning to understand the questions that must be asked. Why is the sky blue in the day and not the night? What changes? Why did these angels come and then go?"

"Are you one of them?" Navinad asked.

"I once stood with them. Like a member of the tribes, you stand with others against a foe. Different beings can come together to walk the same path, as I did. We are not the same though."

"Will they help us?"

"Why is the sky blue? They can help you by destroying you. Destruction will ensure you do not become slaves of the vanhat. Is that your question, or the question you didn't ask?"

"Is that what they will do?"

"I do not soar along the paths with them. It has been a very long time since we fought side by side against the ones you call the vanhat. Memories, age, and our journeys will change us. I cannot say."

"What can you tell me?"

"I can tell you to find your own answers, to discover your path, to forge your destination with the steel of your soul. I can present the paths to you, but I will not choose them on your behalf."

Navinad had a thought. What was this being not telling him? Was information being withheld?

"Of course," it whispered. "We could talk until the suns died of old age. I could present you with paths and options. I could tell you much and present you with countless paths into the future. But time is a construct of your world. Suns will die of old age. Your universe will eventually end as it began. Wherever there is a beginning there is an ending in a place with time. You called for help, and I answered. I am not without goals. My memories are not the end of my journey. Your death will not be the end of yours unless the vanhat devour your soul. Your request for help may not provide the help you expected."

"Can they devour my soul and kill me forever?"

"Matter does not seek to exist. Souls do not cease to exist. They change form."

Which was bad.

"Others are waking. Tombs lost between the stars, filled with vanhat slaves from eons ago, are opening and spilling forth. The angels are not the only ones who departed. Do not think that humanity, the Torag, or the Voshka are the only players in this game."

That shocked Navinad. He slammed back to his body and his senses aboard the *Romach*. The vanhat grew in strength by converting humans into slaves. They didn't destroy so much as change. Evil grew stronger by changing others and propagating evil. It was a flawed assumption they left nothing behind except death.

Was it that simple? It was also a mistake to think that these angels were the only ones who had remained after the last war.

He knew the being he had spoken with was gone, though he couldn't explain why.

Opening a link to Clara, Navinad wondered what was in store for them.

"We should go to the fourth planet. We may find more answers there."

"Acknowledged," Clara said, and he knew she had questions. She would trust him, though.

"Be wary. There is danger, but I don't know the nature."

"Always," Clara said, and the link closed. She would give commands for the *Romach* to move further into the system.

* * * * *

Chapter Thirty-Three:
Fourth Planet

Navinad – The Wanderer

The briefing room felt full as Navinad stood and looked around. Clara and her executive officer, Yosef and his platoon sergeant, Bonnie, Sergeant McCarthy and his first team leader, all turned to him.

They were in orbit around the fourth planet. It was certainly a tomb world. Encased in ice, snow, and ash, there were still numerous active volcanoes.

Navinad was sure that other expeditions, human and Torag, had visited this world. He wasn't sure what they would encounter, which was why he wanted as much diversity as possible. Different viewpoints would help him see things differently and could identify significance in something others missed.

It was a balancing act, though. The diversity in the room did not make people conformable, despite being on the same side. People were tribal and found comfort in the company of their own; that was just human nature. Only a fool thought otherwise.

"I am going to lead an expedition to the surface," Navinad began, and a map appeared on the wall behind him. The world they were orbiting spun slowly, and the view zoomed in to a place near the equator. The oceans were covered in ice, but a hundred meters below the surface active volcanoes pushed magma upward, which heated the oceans and kept them from freezing completely. Navinad knew that life thrived in those heated streams.

On the surface, the volcanoes also generated heat that the local wildlife thrived on because the distant sun and clouds prevented other options.

It was a tough world to survive on, and any creatures were tough and dangerous survivors.

The view eventually zoomed into a city stabbing up out of the ice. Cracked stone spires attempting to cut the skies. Navinad knew they were massive. The engineering that had built them and allowed them to survive this long could be beyond what humanity was capable of. What else might have survived was dubious.

Those spires were like grave markers, revealing the dead city. There were few other places on the planet that revealed such structures. Had the ancients intended for them to be gravestones for their city?

The haunting feeling had grown, and Navinad saw it affected everyone. They all felt like they were being watched by unseen eyes, by something that wanted to harm them. Everyone was armed and armored. The excuse was that they were in potentially hostile territory. Navinad knew that was true, but it was not the entire truth.

Was there a Jotun here? There could be trillions of vanhat hiding nearby, waiting to close the trap.

Were there tombs on the planet below that held vanhat that had been sleeping for eons? Undiscovered because they had not awoken?

This was a bad idea, and Navinad couldn't shake the feeling it would end in disaster.

"We are going to try to find a way into these towers," Navinad continued. "This one specifically."

The camera zoomed in on a specific tower. Larger than the others, the weather had scoured away any patterns or carvings on it long ago, but it looked like there might be a way in near a great crack. The ancients wouldn't have placed solid stone structures, would they?

It was the tallest tower, but not by much. Like a stone knife pointing upward, the hilt buried in the snow; the view was hidden within the gloom of a never-ending snowstorm.

"Radiation levels remain high," Navinad said. "Initial scans show some active wildlife, but not a lot this far from the volcanoes."

Navinad looked around the room. Everyone was staring at the display. This was more of an archaeological expedition than a military one, but Navinad knew it would be more dangerous than any archaeological expedition on Earth had ever been. Hopefully, the local wildlife was the only danger, but had the dying ancients booby trapped their cities? Would any of those traps remain?

"I would like a diverse team," Navinad said, looking around. "I would take the Torag if I could, but maybe not on the initial expedition. Our diversity gives us strength, I believe. I need different viewpoints here."

Was he pushing the diversity thing too far?

"United we stand, divided we fall" had been an American mantra that the gunny had harped on. Uniting this crew was important, which was why he was including the ODTs. They might not be Jewish, but they were humans, and everyone was fighting for the same thing. The gunny was struggling to bring everyone together. Navinad knew he could do no less, but he couldn't do it at gunpoint like the SOG. He knew everyone felt isolated and alone, especially Bonnie and the

ODTs. He had reservations about including Bonnie in this initial expedition, but she seemed to have a knack for seeing things differently and talking about the ancients put a shine in her eyes. Clara'd had a suit of armor made for her.

"What are we looking for, sir?" McCarthy asked. Straight to the point.

"I don't know. Clues? Information? I honestly don't know for sure."

"Just sightseeing then?" McCarthy asked, and Navinad sensed his disapproval.

"Not exactly." Mostly a lie. What could he say, though? "This world was lost to the vanhat. Rather than surrender, they nuked themselves into oblivion. Another possibility is that the vanhat nuked them into oblivion because they could not defeat them."

"Haven't there been a lot of other expeditions, sir?" McCarthy asked.

"Humanity and the Torag have known about the tomb worlds for decades, maybe centuries, the Torag maybe longer. However, none of us knew anything about the vanhat. We thought the ancients killed themselves in some civil war or something. Knowledge of the vanhat changes things. We are going to look at things through new eyes, through military eyes. We know what happened, but not exactly how, and now we understand things differently. That is why I want to look around."

"Don't the Torag legends mention the vanhat?" McCarthy asked.

"Sure," Navinad said. "So do human legends. One has to wonder why we didn't believe them. Perhaps because they didn't make scientific sense at the time. We didn't have fossils of twisted monsters, and we all know how fanciful people's imagination can be. Now we know."

"Could the return of the vanhat wake things up?" McCarthy asked, and a chill ran down Navinad's spine. That was a very real possibility.

"Will there be anything left after all this time?" Bonnie asked. "Previous expeditions were said to have found very little."

"We won't know until we look," Navinad said. "And that is why we are going in heavily armed, ready to fight a war."

* * * * *

Chapter Thirty-Four:
Snow and Ash

Sergeant Aod McCarthy, ODT

Leading his troopers off the shuttle brought back memories of when he was a young ODT practicing assault landings, except now he was the first one off the shuttle. It felt odd for McCarthy to be leading them.

Usually, ODTs came down in drop pods, only using the shuttles to leave a planet. The shuttles were usually used for administrative staff. But ODTs had a long tradition of always deploying to a world like it was a combat drop, whether it was a drop pod or shuttle.

His ODTs followed him off the shuttle, and McCarthy immediately sank knee deep into the snow and ash. His powered armor let him plow through it, but it slowed him down. He half expected some wise cracks about him being slow, but everyone's eyes and weapons were too busy sweeping the area as they struggled not to trip and fall.

Massive dark shadows rose around them, threatening to fall over and crush them. The age of the place was an almost physical force that made him feel small and insignificant. His helmet sensors didn't flicker, and that was a good sign. The lights on their helmets swept the area, piercing the darkness and gloom, revealing too little.

The ODTs spread out from the shuttle, creating a semi-circle, weapons facing out as they took a knee, which was almost comical.

Kneeling waist deep in the snow made the snow look deeper than it was.

Like a conquering hero, Navinad came out of the shuttle behind them, his weapon at the ready and pointed to the ground. He looked around, and the furry named Bonnie, in her distinctive and unfamiliar armor, was right behind him. Her rifle was clutched tight to her body as she peered around, looking ready to dive for cover behind Navinad.

Sensor pulses from the shuttle probed the nearby area. Not the best idea if the enemy had weapons that could home in on the sensors, but there was no evidence there was anything alive here.

McCarthy checked his personal Inkeri and his display, showing the status of his squads. No stress, nothing out of the ordinary.

Except for the ancient, alien buildings towering above and around them, this could be any lifeless planet in the galaxy.

But McCarthy knew it wasn't. This had once been a battleground between angels and demons, if the Torag could be believed.

There was still that uncomfortable feeling of being watched, of something out of sight glaring at them, preparing to attack. Beneath his armor, his skin crawled.

"Creepy shit," Moore said on the team leader link.

"Tell me again why we are here?" McCarthy heard the discomfort in Quinn's voice as he spoke.

"ODTs lead the way," McCarthy said.

"Doesn't seem that smart right now," Moore said. "Maybe we should let the commandos lead the way."

"They're the smart ones," Quinn said.

"We are the more dangerous and experienced ones," McCarthy said. "We are less likely to enter a trap, and if we do we will make the enemy regret it a lot more."

"The best way to gain experience is to make stupid mistakes," Moore said. "I wouldn't want to deprive them of any learning experiences."

"Want me to tell Navinad that my boys are too scared to lead the way?" McCarthy asked.

"Shit," Quinn said. "We want the mission completed this week, right? It will take those commandos at least a week to get their thumbs out of their ass."

"Then quit your bitching," McCarthy said. Which is all it was, really. He knew they respected the commandos, and they wouldn't feel any better letting the NMDF commandos lead the way. The deployment was good, so they had nothing else to focus on.

The NMDF engineers led the robo-mules off the shuttle, and McCarthy gave the command to punch out the perimeter. This was some kind of large parade ground or arena surrounded by the towering monoliths and McCarthy felt they were all staring at him and the shuttles with angry, unforgiving eyes hidden in the drifting snow. He remembered the briefings and recon views. This was a valley surrounded by the monoliths embedded in the cliffs, reaching for the sky. Sensors couldn't penetrate, but it was entirely possible the monoliths contained entrances into massive underground bunkers. Previous expeditions had spent little time here. Details on why were non-existent but the feeling of being watched and evaluated by something evil was not something you could include in a report.

"I feel something," Bonnie said on the expedition command link, sending chills down McCarthy's spine. No shit. Really?

"Something is waking up," Navinad said, and McCarthy wished the commander hadn't said that.

"That doesn't sound good," McCarthy said, fishing for more information.

"Hard to say," Navinad said. "Vanhat or not."

"What sensors are you using?" McCarthy asked, cycling through his. Something the shuttle had picked up? Angels and demons had fought here. Hopefully, it was an angel, but would an angel be happy with humans sniffing around its grave?

"Classified," Navinad said, which didn't help. It sounded like Bonnie had access to it.

McCarthy did not like that answer. They were supposed to be allies.

"Sorry," Navinad said. "I will explain later, but now is not the time."

Something like this should have been explained before landing.

A beacon lit up and Navinad pointed at it as the first shuttle slid back into the sky and another landed and expelled the NMDF commandos and more mules. The beacon indicated a crack in one monolith, maybe a way into the surrounding structures.

McCarthy was sure they were all interconnected, through underground tunnels or through tunnels in the cliffs behind them.

The incredible age of the place pushed in on him, but McCarthy wouldn't be the first one to recommend withdrawal. Anything dangerous could be shot in the face and discouraged with a high volume of weapons fire, McCarthy was sure.

Well. Last year, he would have been sure. Having learned more of the vanhat, McCarthy was less confident.

"You think the angel dudes are going to be friendly?" Quinn asked.

"I like to think they're cute girls with very little on and very friendly," Moore said.

"Always thinking with your dick," Quinn added.

"Gotta think outside the box," Moore said. "Isn't that what they tell us in team leader school? Plus, my dick would never fit in a little box."

"Outside the box, not outside your pants," Quinn said. "Your pecker would fit in a tiny box."

McCarthy let them banter as they moved their fireteams out. He was sure their teams were talking as well, but from a squad leader perspective, everyone was moving the way he wanted, and he couldn't find any fault in people's actions. The fireteams divided into two wedges and headed toward the beacon. McCarthy walked behind them, and the rest of the expedition followed him.

"Spread out a little more," McCarthy said. The fireteam wedges were too compact and there was plenty of space to spread out as they made their way to the nearest monolith.

He didn't hear the team leaders issue the commands, but the teams spread out, covering more territory.

Behind them, the second shuttle slid into the sky, leaving them alone for the moment.

Approaching the nearest monolith, marked by a flashing beacon on their heads-up display, the sheer size of everything settled into McCarthy's mind. Each monolith was easily a kilometer in height and the true scale of everything sunk in. Being told in a briefing that they were a kilometer tall and then seeing it loom up out of the snow and ash in front of you were two separate things, and it made McCarthy feel small, like ants in a garden.

A half hour later, they reached their goal, and McCarthy could make out the crack. The monolith itself was like a featureless tombstone with a curved top, stabbing the sky and leaning against a cliff.

238 | WILLIAM S. FRISBEE, JR.

The crack was also more obvious, but it made little sense because it started at the cliff and cut down at an angle toward the center. Moving closer, McCarthy saw it was barely big enough for a human to enter it. It didn't look as old as everything else.

McCarthy was the first to approach it as his teams set up security to either side. With Navinad right behind him, McCarthy went up to the crack and shined his light in.

His electronics flickered, and his Inkeri registered slight activity. If he hadn't been paying close attention, he might have missed it.

The crack was full of snow and ash, but it was deep, revealing the monolith was more metal than stone, and that the crack was more of a tear than a crack.

"What could have caused this?" McCarthy asked. The edges weren't worn enough for it to be old, but the snow showed it was not so new.

McCarthy climbed up a little and tried to shine his light deeper into the crack, but the angle was bad. The top of the crack had less room, but near the ground there was a lot of snow.

"We're going to have to tunnel out the snow or we won't fit," Navinad said, stepping back to look over everything.

McCarthy wanted to ask how far, but it wasn't like Navinad would know and he didn't want to pester the commander with questions he couldn't answer.

"Maybe send a crawly drone," McCarthy said. They had some. The NMDF drones were not what McCarthy was used to, but they got the job done. He wasn't about to admit they had better tech.

"Good idea," Navinad said and turned back to talk with the NMDF troopers following him. Behind him, like a shadow, stood the strange creature. Navinad had said she was a human from some ghost colony of "furries" but McCarthy didn't know what that meant. In her armor, she could almost pass as human. Almost.

"Sweep the area," McCarthy said to his squad. "We're going to set up camp here. Get some drones out to scour the area; see if there is anything else worth investigating. Don't forget, this is a hostile world. Any flora or fauna is probably going to be hungry and dangerous."

"It would be nice to leave a shuttle here as a secure structure," Quinn said.

"You want your ride blown up?" Moore said. "Best keep our escape route safe."

There was no arguing with that. The *Romach* didn't have many shuttles, and it wasn't like new ones could be fabricated in a few hours.

"If we can find a way inside, we'll establish a more secure facility," McCarthy said.

"Not sure if that will be an improvement," Moore said. "This is creeping me out."

"With all your bitching, now I know you're happy," McCarthy said.

Quinn snorted over the link. He knew what McCarthy was talking about. A bitching ODT was a happy ODT. An ODT without something to bitch about was a bored, unchallenged ODT. Bored and unchallenged ODT would end up getting into or causing all sorts of "leadership challenges." Thankfully, there were no commissars about.

One of the NMDF troopers came up and pushed a crablike drone into the crack. A small window popped up on McCarthy's display showing the drone's view. The operator sent the drone scuttling into the crack.

The entire mission would become more complicated and might end up a waste if the crack didn't lead into the interior.

"Bingo," the drone operator said.

McCarthy tapped into the feed. They had a way in, but to what? The interior was large. Then he saw movement.

* * * * *

Chapter Thirty-Five:
Redirected

2nd Lieutenant Zale Stathis, USMC

Stathis didn't like the Moon. He knew why. The ceiling in most places was a viewscreen that showed a fake sky. The clouds weren't real; the sun wasn't real. It never rained and gravity was annoying, at best. He was also tired of wearing his armor everywhere. He asked Shrek if he should visit the emperor in his fancy new uniform or if he should wear his battle dress. Leaving a secure area, it was always armor, but Stathis asked anyway.

Shrek had said battle dress and Stathis knew Shrek would have no other recommendation, not after the assassination attempt.

He was in was a closed van, one of millions speeding through the tunnels of Luna, featureless and nearly unnoticeable. Computer systems would track it, but Stathis knew the SCBIs were monitoring everything closely.

The Legion was assembling forces and taking over other more traditional SOG units, so now there were almost two of everything. A SOG fleet and then a SOG fleet with Legionnaires in command, an ODT and ODT units commanded by Legionnaires.

When the Legionnaires took over, there were changes, but Stathis spent little time keeping up with them. His platoon got all the Legion gear and support now and that was a lot better than what he had gotten before. The major was off at some camp undergoing Legion indoctrination or something, and he was getting requests to send Smimova and his squad leaders to the Legion training.

He knew he would have to. It wasn't fair to them to hold them back, but it also felt too much like he was sending away people he was going to need. He had to trust the platoon. They were all good guys and had been with him through thick and thin.

Was that how officers lost touch with their commands? They got shuffled around until the people they commanded were strangers? It was hard to learn new people, fresh faces, new habits. Eventually, he would have to train new people, and probably deal with the same old screw ups in addition to a bunch of new ones.

Vili sat beside him, and the rest of Smimova's ready team was crammed in with them. In theory, the van was on autopilot, but Stathis knew Shrek had actual control. He remembered when the gunny had used Freya to take control of a car on Zhukov. He had driven that car into a landing corvette, killing the people in it. Not the best way to kill someone, but the gunny couldn't allow that captain to return to the ship he and Stathis were trying to hijack.

Things were never simple.

Everyone was silent. Lost in their own thoughts, or at least that's what it looked like.

The fire team acting as his bodyguard was from First Squad. Yuri was in command, the SAW gunner was Stan, with Steps and Zed. Good guys who should be enjoying some time off. They didn't seem pissed off, though, just matter of fact and professional. But they weren't exactly bodyguard material. In the Raiders, they had undergone some bodyguard training, and these guys weren't it. But if they got into a firefight, Stathis was pretty sure they would shine.

"Approaching Zvezda Two," Shrek announced, and Stathis felt the van slow down.

When the door slid open, he got that sense of déjà vu. He remembered following the gunny through here, dressed in peacekeeper armor as Feng led them into a trap. And he remembered that prick of a major who'd met them. Hopefully, he was still a private assigned to some shithole.

The uniforms were different, and there were only two troopers. Slightly different from Legion armor or regular SOG stuff, Stathis knew he had been approved, and they knew who he was even if he didn't know who they were. Shrek could tell him, but it didn't matter.

He half expected the major to step out followed by an ODT squad, but nothing happened as he walked up to and past them. They came to attention and saluted, which Stathis returned self-consciously as he walked past them, his escort behind him.

Getting on the elevator didn't help the butterflies in his stomach as the gravity changed. This could be the same one as before. He half expected a row of ODTs to be waiting, aiming at him when he got off. Instead, it was just a park with trees and plants and stuff. It could have been on Earth except for the bowl shape. It rotated fast enough to maintain standard Earth gravity, which felt better to Stathis. The gunny, or the emperor, would be in his office. Stathis knew the way. Zvezda Two was buried deep within the Moon, so deep that crustbusters probably couldn't reach it. But looking up, it looked like a nice sunny day.

Technology was nice.

"You want to hang out in the cafeteria?" Stathis asked Vili.

"For sure," Vili said.

If Stathis needed bodyguards on Zvezda Two, then the Empire was already lost. "Good food here. I hear they've got programs and menus from the *Tyr*. Corporal Malchansky, take your boys and get some good food."

They had them on the *Eagle*, too, but Stathis didn't want to steal Vili's thunder.

"Aye," said Yuri, and glanced at Stathis for approval. Stathis nodded. Yuri and his boys saluted and took off to get breakfast.

"You don't want breakfast?" Stathis asked Vili.

"For sure. I can always use another breakfast, but I want to talk about Gaufrid," Vili said. "Skadi is there, too."

Stathis tried not to wince. He was hoping for a one-on-one conversation with the gunny. Skadi being there might make it too formal.

Nodding, Stathis led the way. The door slid open, which meant the gunny was waiting for him.

Inside was the gunny, Skadi, Feng, and Admiral Carpenter from the *Tyr*. Was he interrupting something? Damn. He marched up as if on parade, stopped in front of Mathison's desk, and saluted. "Second Lieutenant Stathis reporting as ordered, sir."

Should he say emperor or something? Nah. "Sir" from a Marine should be good enough for anyone. Stathis realized he probably shouldn't salute indoors without his cover on, but then the ODTs did it all the time.

Mathison stood to return the salute. He sat back down and motioned to another seat. The gunny wasn't wearing a uniform, more like some kind of suit. It didn't look right on him. Even Skadi was wearing civilian clothes. Her Erikoisjoukot tattoo was turned off, which further added to Stathis's sense of wrongness.

"Sit down," Mathison said. He was as growly as usually which hopefully meant he had enough privates to punish and practice on. Or maybe he was in a good mood because lunch had arrived.

"Thank you, sir," Stathis said, realizing that everyone was facing him.

"You want to use Gaufrid to hunt down these rebels?" Mathison said, starting the conversation.

"Fight fire with fire, sir," Stathis said. "Or to catch a cat, you need a cat? Something like that, sir."

"And you think Gaufrid will help? Why?"

"He came from out-system. He knows what we're facing and helped us fight the vanhat. I think he and Quadrangle are on our side."

"How do you plan to keep him under control?" Skadi asked.

"Bomb collar? Ma'am," Stathis said. "One wrong move and Shrek sends a signal that blows his head off or something? I'm not sure about the details, but I don't think that would be nice, or work."

"I would be skeptical about such a mechanism succeeding," Feng said. "I will concur with the lieutenant though on two counts. Quadrangle is the one most likely to help us root out and expose a Collective agent if that is the case, and it is not likely that Quadrangle is behind such a rebellion."

"So, we trust the agent of someone who nearly wiped out the human race?" Mathison asked. "Aren't we facing enough enemies?"

"Valid concerns," Feng said. "History is full of allies turning on each other and betraying their benefactors. Who knows what factors could cause Quadrangle to decide to ally with its prey rather than hunt them. The young lieutenant's words are interesting. Fight fire with fire, but there are flaws in that logic. Fire will burn friend or foe, regardless. My agency is having difficulties, and a new set of eyes would be advantageous. I have not ruled out the vanhat. We are dealing with a very sophisticated foe."

"I've read a lot of history," Skadi said, drawing everyone's attention. "We're all afraid of facing an opponent that is smarter and more skilled and capable than we are. I think we need to try a different approach."

Stathis was becoming less sure about this.

"We fight smart with stupid," Skadi said, with a half-smile.

"Explain," Mathison said and Stathis heard an edge there.

"This young lieutenant is anything but stupid," she clarified. "But he is also not your traditional, stick-up-the-ass nyyppa lieutenant."

Was she complimenting him, or was it a subtle jab? Stathis waited for the other shoe to drop.

"Turn Stathis loose," Skadi said. "He has Vili to help him not make major mistakes, and he was smart enough to come here and consult with us before doing something stupid."

Stathis wondered if he could have gotten away with something stupid, as Skadi put it. Would the Legionnaires at Gamma have shut him down and denied him access?

Alerts screeched, and Stathis leaped from his chair, donning his helmet as he spun and brought his rifle up.

"Incoming Shorr space transitions in near Lunar orbit," Shrek reported. Which didn't help calm him. *"Thousands of transitions. Vanhat."*

"Shit," Mathison said.

Stathis spun to see Skadi and Mathison opening a closet. Their armor and weapons were inside.

"We are pretty deep," Feng said.

"They are dropping pods onto the surface," Shrek reported. *"Tens of thousands, maybe more."*

The lights flickered, and Stathis felt the shocks through the ground.

"Vanhat weapon strikes. Inkeris are being overloaded. EMP pulses are disrupting electronics," Shrek said. *"We have not suffered any direct hits, but we may be the primary target."*

* * * * *

Chapter Thirty-Six:
Into the Artifact

Sergeant Aod McCarthy, ODT

The drone didn't get a good view, and that bothered McCarthy. Whatever it was couldn't have been big, but the view from the drone made it look big. Maybe the size of a large dog? The drone moved to get a better view, but whatever it was had disappeared around a corner.

Vanhat or a native of this hell?

The drone wasn't glitching, so it was probably a local creature. On the flip side, the drone had a small Inkeri.

Nothing on this planet was likely to be friendly, especially anything hiding in an ancient tomb when demons walked the galaxy.

It was going to be a while before he could find out, though. One of the robo-mules was being reconfigured to dig out an entrance into the tomb. McCarthy and his squad were relegated to providing security.

"What do you think it was?" Quinn asked on the squad link. Who the question was directed at, McCarthy didn't know, but since it was on the squad link, it could have been anyone. Quinn must be bored.

"An animal," McCarthy said.

"Tomb guardian," Moore said.

"Seriously?" McCarthy said. Moore wasn't the superstitious or religious type.

"Why not?" Moore said, and McCarthy wished he could see the man's face because his voice held no clue if he was serious or not. "Makes sense. Monsters waking up, eating people? Wiping out civilizations?"

"Has to be a guardian, Sergeant," Private Martin said. "It's stuck in there. Do you think it's going to come for our souls or just our bodies?"

"Bodies? You wish," Walsh said and there were a couple snickers. "You ain't getting laid."

"No, to eat us," Martin said.

"Something that has been trapped in a tomb for millennia probably doesn't need food," Walsh said. "It probably doesn't like being disturbed."

"Or it is super bored and wants some young private to violate," Wilson said. "I vote we send Walsh in first."

"Seriously guys," Walsh said. "It could be a vanhat. They don't follow our laws of physics. Anything is possible with them."

"Didn't futz the drone," Moore said. "Russelman index is still flat-lined."

"Oh," Walsh said, sounding disappointed. McCarthy had forgotten to check the Russelman index, which was used to indicate vanhat presence. "So, it's probably some animal that wandered in."

"Don't underestimate anything here," McCarthy said. "It's not the first time the SOG has been to this place, and reports talk about some extremely dangerous flora and fauna."

"Place seems pretty dead, Sergeant," Quinn said. "Is there a tropical region we missed? I've yet to see anything move."

"The science nerds didn't really give us a report," McCarthy said. Why was that?

"Nerds?" Walsh asked, and McCarthy wanted to roll his eyes. "That's a slur, Sergeant."

"Why aren't you doing pushups?" Quinn asked. Walsh still wasn't used to how things worked in the ODTs and still seemed full of indoctrination and intolerance training bullshit.

"Because—"

"Shut up and drop," Quinn said. Which saved McCarthy from having to say anything. "Private Walsh, we are ODTs, not commissars or civilians. It's our job to be aggressive, insulting, and unpleasant."

"Copy that, Corporal," Walsh said between pushups.

"If you can't be aggressive, insulting, or unpleasant, I can arrange for you to be transferred to the Guard."

"Fuck that, Sergeant," Walsh said. "I don't want to be surrounded by wimps."

"That's what I thought," Quinn said.

McCarthy picked out Walsh on the perimeter. Quinn's team had the starboard arc. Walsh was next to MacMurrough, who was holding the private's SAW ready while he did pushups.

Transferring the private to the Guard might not be practical right now.

Walsh might even be smart enough not to point that out.

Navinad came up to McCarthy and glanced toward where Walsh was doing pushups. The commander said nothing as he turned back and opened a link.

"That was probably some animal," Navinad said. "I would bet it's a predator that got trapped in there looking for prey. There are mushrooms and other things in there, so it could be a herbivore."

"Yes, sir," McCarthy said. Just because it was a herbivore didn't mean it wouldn't eat meat.

"Which means it's probably hungry," Navinad said.

That didn't sit right with McCarthy. It had run from the drone, not attacked it. He wouldn't contradict Navinad, though, he just didn't know enough.

"Were there any reports on the flora and fauna? Any reason why they were so dangerous?" McCarthy asked.

Navinad shook his head. "Not in the reports we got. Just references to dangerous native creatures. Might have been in other reports that weren't deemed worthy of being included in the main briefing packets."

"Understood, sir," McCarthy said, which was a lie. He didn't understand, unless they considered it a security issue. There was no reason something like that shouldn't have been added as an appendix. It wasn't like they had to worry about storage space or report size.

"Can your squad lead the way?" Navinad asked. It was an odd way of telling McCarthy to take point. What was he going to say? No?

"Yes, sir," McCarthy said, his eyes falling on Walsh.

"The space should be big enough any minute now. The drone will go in first, but if it's attacked, we should be ready to keep it from getting destroyed."

"Understood, sir," McCarthy said and turned toward his ODTs. "Walsh?"

"Sergeant?" Walsh said, not stopping his pushups.

"You get to go first," McCarthy said. "Quinn, get your team up here."

"Thank you, Sergeant," Walsh said, though McCarthy wasn't sure the private should thank him. It almost felt like he was using the young man as bait. There were other people more capable than the private, but this should be a good character-building exercise.

"Once we have a presence inside, we'll send out a few more drones," Navinad said. "This is a tomb, so I expect traps and such."

"After all this time, sir?" McCarthy asked. "Wouldn't the creature have triggered them?"

"I would rather not take chances with people's lives, Sergeant."

"Understood, sir." McCarthy watched Moore's team spread out to cover the gap left as Quinn's team pulled back. His ODTs were stretched thin, but it wasn't like there was any danger.

Yet.

An alert from the *Romach* appeared in his heads-up display.

"Incoming vanhat warships detected."

McCarthy realized the mission just got a lot worse.

* * * * *

Chapter Thirty-Seven:
Hungering

Navinad – The Wanderer

Navinad was beginning to like McCarthy. The ODT sergeant was grounded and not easily rattled. He would have made a good Marine, or was it just something about NCOs regardless of military or branch?

An alert came in from the *Romach* that turned his blood to ice.

"Incoming vanhat ships detected," the alert said.

Navinad opened a link. "What's going on?"

"We have a squadron of vanhat cruisers inbound. Four of them, maybe more," Clara said. "I doubt we can take them this low in the gravity well. They will be in range before the shuttles can reach the surface."

"Then bug out," Navinad said. "We can hide here."

"I'm not leaving you," Clara said.

Navinad brought up the data screens on his heads-up display.

There was no way to get the shuttles down to the surface and then back up before the vanhat were in range. The orbital mechanics were all wrong and it would take the shuttles at least an hour out at fast burn to pick them up, and getting back to the *Romach* would take almost twice that, even if the *Romach* changed course to intercept. The enemy was coming in way too fast. Had they been out in deep space watching? Waiting? It felt like a trap and the vanhat were only minutes away from orbit where they could engage the *Romach*.

"You will leave me, or you will die needlessly for me. I would rather you not die without a damned good reason. We'll be fine. We can bunker down inside the tomb. It will be easy to defend, I'm sure. They might not be able to find us."

Navinad knew she wanted to argue, but this wasn't the time for her to stand her ground. It wouldn't accomplish anything.

"We can draw them off," Clara said.

Which would mean engaging them and making sure she had their attention. But would she get all of them to chase her, or could they detect the expedition on the surface?

"Everyone into the tomb," Navinad said as McCarthy sent his first fireteam inside. Drone footage revealed there was space. Whatever creature they had glimpsed was unlikely to be blazerproof if it revealed itself to be unfriendly.

"You stay safe," Navinad said. "This is a dangerous situation. My fault, not yours. We will bunker down until they're gone. You continue the fight. Try to lose them. If we don't make it, return to New Masada."

"You will make it," Clara said.

"We'll do our best," Navinad said.

"I love you," Clara said. "I'm releasing some stealth satellites for you to use."

"I love you, too," Navinad said. "Do your duty and let me do mine."

"Our honor," Clara said, and Navinad wasn't sure what she meant by that. Our honor was all that mattered, or it was what gave their lives and future a meaning. He couldn't ask her.

The link closed. Another link came in giving him access to a pair of satellites the *Romach* had released.

McCarthy was now pushing his second team into the small tunnel that was barely big enough to crawl through. The commando squad would be the last in.

The mules crawled into the tomb as Navinad scanned the skies. The clouds kept him from seeing anything, but now he sensed them. He felt the vanhat, like a burning beacon of hate in the darkness.

"We're going to have company," Navinad said.

They wanted the *Romach*, too. Navinad felt a Jotun hungering for the NMDF ship, and it knew Clara's name. For the Jotun, this was personal. It was after her, not him.

Why? Because it didn't know they were on the surface? Or was it something else?

* * * * *

Chapter Thirty-Eight:
Invasion

Vanhat Commander – Kafasta

The gods had given the command, and the Weermag slid into Shorr space, their destinations set. The gods would guide them, and they could not miss.

His company was ready. His ship was one of many in the second wave. The first wave was mostly fighting ships and drop pods tasked with targeting ground-to-space defenses. The second wave would be more capable warships and elite assault units, like his.

Within seconds, his ship slid from the god's realm back into the galaxy of the lost souls. His ship began firing, the weapon turrets slaved to the demons implanted in the Weermag. Their accuracy was pinpoint and precise. Even with their numbers, the Weermag were taking horrific casualties. Kafasta let his demon control the ship. Missiles and high-velocity pellets filled the Lunar orbit. He watched a brother cruiser shatter and spray itself over the worthless Moon.

Everything happened in the blink of an eye. Images of his brothers and other Weermag ships dying burned themselves into his brain. Too many. Surprise had caught human warships in low orbit. They would not have expected vanhat ships to transition in so close to the Moon. Fools. They trusted their incomplete science. One reason they deserved to be rendered extinct.

His own vessel took many hits. A stream of high-velocity pellets ripped through the hull, destroying an engine, but the demons kept the ship from spinning as it slammed into the Lunar surface, crushing some structure.

His demon showed how many of his company were still alive: less than half.

They knew their job, though, and if they didn't, their demons did. Their personal demons spoke to each other, even through the jamming. More of his brothers died as a corvette strafed the remains of his ship before they even lowered their ramps. Another Weermag ship blasted the corvette and more wreckage scattered across the landscape.

The survivors moved quickly to enter the structure they had crashed into, some supply depot. It would have tunnels that would lead down.

It was difficult to make sense of everything. The information the demons had provided did not seem to match what he was seeing now. Too many destroyed ships, too many seeking missiles, too much death, and he realized he was in the wrong sector completely. Not a problem, their orders were simple.

The battle was glorious.

Many of his brothers would return to the realm of the gods, to be returned later as more trusted soldiers.

"This will not be a failure," Kafasta said to his soldiers as they burned their way into the tunnels. "Our mission is clear."

This wasn't the right sector, but that didn't really matter.

There were no infantry to stop them as they sought shelter beneath the surface. There were no humans here, just robots. The Weermag jammers and pre-assault bombardment would have destroyed or crippled non-organic defenders. Human technology was so vulnerable to the vanhat pulsars.

Markers told Kafasta where he was. Close enough, and his mission objectives updated. His demon displayed the route to Zvezda Two.

Humans would attempt to establish a perimeter, a line of defense, but right now they would still be reeling from the assault, unsure about what was happening. Their communications would be disrupted. Some might not even be aware the vanhat had dropped so many drop pods, or that the Weermag had used entire ships as dropships to deliver soldiers.

The humans, like worms, had tunneled through their Moon for hundreds of years and Kafasta doubted the simpletons could navigate without their computers.

It would be fun to hunt this prey through the tunnels, but right now they had US Marines to kill and a control center to take over. If their internal demons could access the heart and soul of the Governance, they could shut down those dreadful defenses that had wiped out so many Weermag. The Marines and their pawns had much to suffer for. The gods were waiting for their deaths, waiting to feast on their souls, and Kafasta would not deny them their due.

* * * * *

Chapter Thirty-Nine:
Ancient Tomb

Navinad – The Wanderer

The last commando crawled into the tomb. Doyle already had a team with a medium blazer machine gun pointing at the entry. Anything trying to come in was going to get seriously hurt. Nearby, just out of sight, was a robotic mule mounted with a heavy-duty Inkeri. Navinad was confident any vanhat trying to enter that way would die quickly.

Yosef was setting up a backup position so the team could retreat further.

Bonnie followed him like a shadow, and now he wondered why he had brought her. She hadn't said a word since they landed. It had been a spur of the moment decision to ask her, and she had said yes. Navinad doubted she knew why she had said yes.

She would have been much safer aboard the *Romach*.

McCarthy led his ODTs as they swept through the tunnels, exploring. Navinad doubted there were other ways in, but he couldn't rule it out yet.

They were about to be trapped in this tomb.

The astral whisper grew louder, angrier. He felt its hunger and he wanted to sit, to meditate and listen, but the stealth satellites had shown three shuttles coming down, dropping like rocks into the atmosphere, moving too fast. If they weren't protected by vanhat energy, they would burn up before they reached the surface and anything inside would be jelly.

Which meant something but what?

One cruiser remained in orbit as the others chased the *Romach*.

"They know we're here," Navinad said on the command link. "They're sending down shuttles."

"How many are we going to kill?" McCarthy asked.

"Three shuttles worth. There's a cruiser still in orbit, but I doubt it can provide any kind of space-to-ground support."

"These things can probably take a couple nuclear blasts," McCarthy said, slapping the wall. "But that won't keep them from burying us alive. These structures are just the tip of the iceberg. It looks like there's an entire city down here."

Navinad tapped into the display. McCarthy was looking down a long corridor that went down and corkscrewed to the right. Countless doors and openings to either side held shadows and who knew what else. It looked solid, with arched ceilings. The walls looked to be carved with ancient patterns, but Navinad didn't see any pictures or statues or anything. The patterns themselves meant nothing.

A chill ran through his body.

"Well," McCarthy said, "we have plenty of space to retreat. I have concerns, though. If we keep exploring, we could easily get cut off. This place is massive, and I get the feeling the deeper we go the more space there is. Do you want me to keep going?"

Whatever they had seen could be anywhere, and there could be hundreds waiting to attack.

"Negative," Navinad said. "We have room to retreat. I don't want us to get separated."

"Divide and conquer," McCarthy muttered.

Navinad couldn't argue. He wanted to know what was there, but if there was only one way into this tomb, then he wanted to keep the vanhat out.

Something outside roared and Navinad checked the satellite imagery. Clouds were coming in and would obscure the view in a few minutes, but he saw the shuttles had broken open and numerous monsters were pouring out. Humanoid in basic form, fur-covered and hunchbacked. Most of them were carrying rifles.

"Our attackers are armed with rifles," Navinad said on the command link to everyone. "They shoot back, so keep your heads down. Make them die for their master."

"Why couldn't they be the stupid clawed ones that liked to swarm like rats?" someone muttered.

"Where's the fun in that? It's good to have the occasional challenge."

Navinad would rather not have a challenge.

"This place really is extensive," Lillith reported. *"It also looks like it was abandoned, or else their basic technology was biological."*

"What do you mean?"

"I am not seeing evidence of furniture, bones, tools or equipment."

"It has been a while."

"There should be remains of something. The rooms we have encountered are empty. Like the city was built, but nobody ever moved in."

"Or a tomb where they didn't have time to entomb all the bodies?"

"Or that," Lillith said. *"Or there is another possibility. The entities that lived here were not physical in form."*

"You figure it out, you let me know," Navinad said.

Weapons fire erupted from the entrance.

"Enjoy your migraine," the trooper said, then fired another burst into the tunnel.

Return fire caused the two commandos to lean out of the way.

"Watch for grenades," Navinad said. Would the vanhat risk it? Grenades might collapse the crawlway, and it would be difficult to throw them far enough. But Navinad was sure the vanhat could manage.

"Grenades," Doyle, the platoon sergeant, said. "Send 'em."

One commando leaned out and launched a rifle grenade from the underslung grenade launcher. Some of the NMDF rifles had a shotgun attachment under the barrel that shot tube fed grenades the size of a 12-gauge round. They only had six in the tube, but it was better than nothing.

The explosion caused the ground to shake as it hit something before it got all the way out of the tunnel.

Navinad swore as the gunfire from both ends stopped.

"I like the way you are being unfriendly toward them," Bonnie said. Navinad heard the smile in her voice and realized he may have misjudged her. Most people would be terrified right now. He sensed her fear was there, but she had control over it.

A quick glance showed they were now sealed inside the tomb.

"We might not be able to get out that way now," Doyle said.

"Why?" Navinad asked.

"Because of a cave-in," Doyle began.

"Why did you use grenades?"

"Buys us time," Doyle said.

How much time? The rest of eternity, perhaps?

Looking down the crawl space, there was only a few meters before the cave-in.

There had to be other ways out, and maybe Doyle had made the right decision.

"Set some mines in there," Navinad said. "Protect them with an Inkeri. I want to make sure if they keep digging, they can't follow us. We won't be going out that way."

"Yes, sir," Doyle said.

"Now we get to find out what is deeper," Bonnie said. She sounded excited and anxious. She had too much confidence they would survive this.

Going back was not an option. They could only go forward, deeper into the tomb.

Navinad closed his eyes and listened with his other senses. He could feel the vanhat outside, angry and frustrated, but something below was starting to wake up, or returning.

What had happened to the vanhat that had killed the builders of these tomb worlds? Was that who was waking up?

* * * * *

Chapter Forty:
Fighting

Captain Duffy Sinclair, ODT

The Legion barracks, a former ODT facility, was buried deep in the Moon, deep in the Moon's mantle. Strategically, it wasn't far from Zvezda Two, and one could almost imagine they had placed it to provide support to Zvezda Two if there was ever a rebellion or infantry assault. Its proximity to Zvezda Two made sense. The Central Committee, and now the emperor, would want to keep his loyal warriors close.

It was the day after the attack on Club Werewolf, and Duffy was waiting for orders. Someone would pay for the attack. He was sure Lieutenant Stathis would be involved, and if Duffy was honest with himself, he hoped the young lieutenant would call on Duffy and his company to exact revenge once a target was found. Stathis seemed like the kind of trooper who would make it personal and would surround himself with others who would make revenge personal. Duffy was good with that.

Last night, after he returned, he had recalled the company, cutting their vacation short. It wasn't something he did lightly, though, but he wanted them ready.

Finn constantly polled the systems, waiting for orders and letting him know the company was back. He had given them orders to gear up an hour ago.

The SCBI network should have discovered something by now. Something actionable.

It was early when he made his way to the company barracks. They had already received replacements, most of whom had been assigned barracks watch while the veterans went out, but now everyone had returned.

"What is happening?" Lieutenant Sung asked.

"There was an attack on Legionnaires last night," Duffy said. "I want to be ready when they find out who is responsible."

"Isn't that something InSec should handle, sir?"

"Maybe," Duffy said. Sung was right, though.

Alarms began screeching as the lights flickered.

"Luna is under attack," Finn reported. *"A vanhat attack."*

"Load up with extra ammo," Duffy said to Sung and the others. "In this low gravity, I want people carrying as much as they can. Five minutes to load up, then we move out."

"Wilco!" they shouted, then scattered as if a grenade had been thrown in their lap.

"Are we in danger?" Duffy asked Finn.

"This facility is buried deep. Human technology can't touch it, but maybe vanhat technology could. There are many unknowns. What destination do you have planned?"

"Zvezda Two," Duffy said. It was the first place that came to mind. It wasn't too far away, and while they had a protective force there this would be a good time for rebels to launch an attack, if that wasn't already the vanhat's objective.

If nothing else, he could make sure they were secure and then he could push his company out from there.

"Major disruptions," Finn reported. *"They appear to be targeting our communications, Inkeris, and defenses. Fleet is moving more ships in to protect the Moon, but the vanhat are using the installations on the Moon as hostages. The accuracy and lethality of the vanhat attack is on a scale we have not seen before. Their point defenses and return fire are almost as accurate as SCBI-controlled weaponry."*

"Zhukov Fleet?" Duffy asked. What was taking the company so damned long?

"Purely alien," Finn reported, sending a chill through Duffy. *"If they were ever human, they have been twisted beyond recognition. Further analysis will have to wait. Enemy missiles and energy weapons appear more efficient. The sheer number of attackers is very telling, perhaps millions of attackers."*

"Millions?"

"They are suffering extreme casualties. Near eighty percent and still they are coming. This is unprecedented. They seem to be concentrated on this region of the Moon."

"We need to move now," Duffy said on the company tactical net. "Now! If you aren't ready, I will leave you behind. Follow me!"

Troopers ran to join him. Legionnaires from other units were still armoring up and grabbing weapons as Duffy's company followed behind him. They had to get to Zvezda Two sooner rather than later. A squad from Sung's platoon moved ahead of him, leading the way down the tunnel through the Moon rock. There were no moving cars. Apparently, the EMP strikes had disabled them.

Minutes later, a cluster of shadows poured out of a maintenance tunnel into the main road. Blazer fire erupted and three of his troopers went down before they could return fire. Finn helped guide Duffy's fire and in seconds the fire was only going in one direction.

"Advance! Advance!" Sung yelled, and his troopers began leap-frogging forward.

"How did they get down here so fast?" Duffy asked Finn.

A team entered the maintenance tunnel to ensure it was clear and provide security as Duffy motioned the rest of the company to keep moving. He knelt to look at the bodies.

They were not human. The armor and weapons had probably never been human. Aliens.

Vanhat?

The armor was black and looked ancient, though Duffy couldn't say why he thought that. Maybe it was the way it was designed, almost like well-articulated plate armor. The helmet had short horns and the creature had claws built into the gloves. It looked almost demonic, and they were uniform in that. They didn't bleed red; they bled purple, and while the blazers had ripped them apart, charring flesh and exposing bone, none of it looked familiar.

"Alien," Finn said. *"While I can't confirm without more detailed sensors, the weapons and armor have a very different structural make up than human-made equipment. It is highly unlikely these creatures were ever human."*

"Where did they come from?" Duffy asked.

"Unknown," Finn said. *"I am picking up traffic on the Aesir communication network. It is still operational. Russelman index is also not zero, so they likely have some association with vanhat."*

On Earth, Stathis had given him one of the Aesir communication links designed to integrate with ODT armor and the lieutenant had not asked for it back. Duffy had almost forgotten he had it.

"The defenders of Zvezda Two report they are being attacked," Finn said.

"Hurry up," Duffy ordered his company. "The emperor is calling for us."

He noticed they picked up the pace, and he sprinted forward to catch up with the lead elements.

Ahead of him, weapons fire erupted, and he saw several icons on his heads-up display blink and go from green to red.

His troopers were dying.

* * * * *

Chapter Forty-One:
Rescue

Sergeant Nova Dallas, ODT

Entering the system made Dallas feel like she was a mouse, sneaking into a room to see if anyone was there. The *Musashi* was at the edge of the system, watching, drinking in information.

"Detection," an officer reported, drawing her eyes to a holograph. It was one of the tomb worlds and red lights lit up. "Battle cruiser recovering shuttles."

"Who?" the captain asked.

"Unknown," the officer said. "Matches the foreign vessel above Valakut."

Aod was here? What had those shuttles been doing?

"I need more information," Captain Sakamoto said.

"Hai," the officer said. "We are collecting what we can."

Minutes passed, and Dallas's fingers itched. Could she tap into the data the bridge officer was collecting? It wasn't related to ODT operations.

"You should review the data and look for ways to deploy a ship capture team," Nakano said from behind her, making her jump in her seat. How had he snuck up behind her?

"Yes, Commander Commissar," Dallas said, trying not to let her irritation show in her voice. She had been too focused on superciliously trying to glean information from their conversation. "I do not wish to overstep my bounds or push my authority, sir."

Nakano came to stand beside her and look at her console.

"If you do so, then I will warn you," Nakano said. A warning that ended in a trip to the brig? Demotion? Summary execution? "You have demonstrated your loyalty to the Governance. Loyalty is rewarded. Zeal is admirable when properly focused on the greater good. I will assist you to temper it if your zeal becomes inappropriate."

Which didn't tell her a damn thing. The most effective way to temper "zeal" was a blazer round to the head.

"Thank you, Commander Commissar," Dallas said.

"Unless there are many ships of that design, then your Sergeant McCarthy is here. He may need your help, and the more information you, have the better you will assist."

"Understood, Commander Commissar," Dallas said. She was strapped into her station, or she would have risen and stood at attention. Nakano lived on a different plane of existence than an ODT sergeant. His realm was that of captains and senior officers. For such a senior commissar to involve himself with a mere ODT sergeant made her nervous.

He walked away, and Dallas wished she had some way to see behind her. How long had he been there? The sneaky bastard.

She opened a read-only link to data the other officer was pulling back, then she brought up some details on the ship. Yes. It had to be the same as the one at Valakut. The commissar had spoken about a ship capture operation, so she brought up a full diagram of the ship and began identifying obvious weapons that could prevent boarding teams from approaching. Anti-missile weaponry was exceptionally well designed to wipe out incoming boarding parties. Then there would likely be smaller pop-up turrets as well.

It had been a very long time since she'd studied ship-to-ship operations. On Valakut, that would have been one of the last missions the ODTs might have been called upon to perform. She polled the system for a ship-to-ship boarding specialist and it only came back with a senior sergeant named Ibuki Hattori of the shipboard infantry. Not someone she knew. She thought about what Nakano had said and sent him a link request.

"How can I be of assistance," Hattori said. He sounded too damned polite. It was also noteworthy that there were no officers among the shipboard infantry.

"I need an experienced analysis of a potentially hostile ship to plan for a ship-to-ship operation," Dallas said. "There will be prisoners we must rescue aboard the ship."

"Difficult," Hattori said. "I serve the greater good. Please send me what data you will allow, or would you prefer to collaborate?"

She wanted to collect more information.

"I will send you the data." She stripped out her own analysis and forwarded it. She would compare them later to see what she had missed and how different the plans were. That was a great way to learn.

"Hai," Hattori said. "I will begin work immediately."

"Thank you," Dallas said and closed the link. Was she overstepping her bounds? She glanced toward Nakano's station and saw him looking at her. He nodded and turned his attention back to his console.

Had that weasel been listening to her? Was he still? He could probably see and hear everything she did. Why was he so damned interested in her? What did he want?

"Aliens," another officer reported, drawing her attention to the primary display. A cluster of ships had transitioned in and was accelerating hard toward the strange ship. In seconds, another marker appeared, labeling them as "Vanhat."

She watched as the ship Aod was probably on slipped into Shorr space, and her heart sank. They could go anywhere. Almost instantly, all the attackers but one slid into Shorr space in pursuit. The remaining ship headed for the planet. She didn't have a sensor net she could tap into. What did the vanhat see? The shuttles had come from somewhere. Had they landed a team on the planet? Was that team being abandoned? She sent requests to the different sensor specialists to see if they detected anything out of the ordinary on the planet. Radio transmissions, explosions, any indications of planetside activity.

It was likely to be a fool's quest, but what if Aod had been abandoned? The planet was a tomb world, a big dangerous place, full of hostile creatures. They would likely need protection, and who could better protect an expedition than ODTs?

"Your request is inappropriate," one sensor operator said, replying to her request to focus sensors on the planet. "The strange vessel has departed, and resources are better used looking for other ships."

"Her request is not inappropriate, Sergeant Yagya," Nakano said, joining the link. "I would appreciate it if you helped Brevet Lieutenant Dallas with her request."

Brevet lieutenant? She doubted that would last long.

"Of course, Commander Commissar," Yagya said. "My apologies. Can you please specify what I am to look for?"

"A team that was landed on the surface," Dallas said.

"A planet is a very large place, lieutenant," Yagya said. "Very large."

Dallas knew that. "You have a trajectory for the shuttles that docked with the strange ship, you have their speeds. Can you not extrapolate where they may have come from? There were two shuttles, so they would have been carrying a lot."

"You are wise, Lieutenant," Yagya said, making Dallas wince. Didn't she play that same game of empty compliments with the commissar? "I will need to consult someone within operations to analyze the shuttles and their capabilities."

"Good," Dallas said, though that could be an excuse to delay or not respond. "I would also like an understanding of how many shuttles such a ship would carry and what their capabilities might be."

"For the greater good, Lieutenant," Yagya said.

"For the greater good, Sergeant," Dallas said, and closed the link. So, Nakano was watching her closely. Too closely. She remembered dealing with a different commissar long ago. The best way to get rid of their attention was to be boring. To do the job, only the job. Nothing more, nothing less.

It would be easier to go through the motions if Aod's life didn't depend on the outcome and things really *were* boring. What was Nakano thinking to promote her to lieutenant? Nothing came without a price.

* * * * *

Chapter Forty-Two:
Death of the *Romach*

Sergeant Nova Dallas, ODT

Sirens wailed again sounding battle stations, ripping her attention away from her displays. Until now, she had been completely absorbed in tracking her own videos and system links.

Dallas was tired. She hadn't left her station in hours. She had dipped into her suit rations a couple times, but she didn't want to look and check the stores. The only important thing was they weren't empty yet.

Without warning, the *Musashi* rapidly translated into Shorr space.

"Launching fighters."

That brought her out of her daze more than anything else. Fighters were close range. They were drones, but they weren't launched unless the *Musashi* was actually under attack or launching an attack. The *Musashi* CAG, Carrier Air Group Commander, snapped out commands.

Then she felt the thrum of something she had never felt before, the main guns were being fired.

She looked at the primary display and tried to make sense of the swirling icons and lines. Quickly, she picked out the strange vessel where Aod could be. It was the only green icon. In the center of the display was the *Musashi*, a blue icon that looked like it was exploding as blue icons fell away from it. Probably the drone fighters.

The red icons caught her attention. They were swarming around the *Romach*. Each was larger than the stranger.

"Engaging target one. Eliminated," a weapons officer reported. "Changing focus to target two."

The *Musashi* had transitioned to try to rescue the ship.

"The stranger is hailing us," a comms officer said.

"Accept," Sakamoto said.

"This is the *Romach*," said a strangely accented voice in English. "Why are you helping?"

The captain had his helmet off, a stupid display of bravado but Dallas realized it inspired confidence. If he had his helmet on, people would think the situation to be dire.

"This is Admiral Sakamoto of the Governance Warship *Musashi*," Sakamoto said. "We are here to help. The enemy of my enemy is my friend. What we know of these vanhat is that they must be opposed. We are opposing them."

Glancing at the display, she saw the *Romach* flash. Her heart almost stopped as she waited for it to become a dull green, showing a kill, but it remained bright green. It was still in the fight.

"It is getting hit hard," an officer reported. "Severe damage. Damage to the Shorr space drive is confirmed. Vessel is venting atmosphere and losing power."

"Move closer," Sakamoto said. "We need answers, and if that ship is destroyed, we will not get them."

"Hai," the bridge officers echoed. The tempo of people speaking softly into their links increased, and Dallas felt the tempo of the thrum beneath her boots increase.

The main screen showed blue *Musashi* drone fighters swarming over the *Romach* as the *Musashi* came closer. Gravity pushed her into her seat as acceleration alarms whooped.

"Target three is dead. Targeting four."

"The *Romach* has enemy boarding parties."

Dallas opened a link to the ODT and ship's infantry officers, dumping what she had of the *Romach* into their buffers, highlighting critical systems.

Sakamoto's eyes fell on her. She felt them before she looked up.

"Sir, sending data on the *Romach* to counter-boarding teams along with recommended objectives," Dallas said before the admiral could speak.

The admiral nodded and turned away.

When had target two been destroyed?

"Incoming transitions. Vanhat battleship!"

Where had that come from?

Seconds later something hit the *Musashi* and the captain slipped on his helmet.

So much for being calm, cool, and collected and displaying an air of confidence.

"Inkeris are being stressed."

Dallas zoomed in on the *Romach*. It didn't look like previous videos. There were numerous rips in the hull, and she thought she saw movement near one of the heat vanes by the engine. She cycled through the different views, then went to infrared. The *Romach* was generating a lot of heat, and she saw moving dots that were likely enemy boarding parties. She fed that data to the ODT and starship infantry link.

"ODTs will be deployed," Nakano told her. "Focus on keeping them informed."

"Wilco, sir," Dallas said and saw orders come in from Commander Endo, the ship's executive officer. She was to liaise with Captain Belov, perhaps the most senior ODT officer still alive aboard the *Musashi* and acting commander of the ODTs. She wasn't sure if he had survived purges or he was just the senior surviving ODT. It wasn't her job to worry about his loyalty.

"Sir," Dallas said on a direct link to Belov, "there may be friendly ODTs aboard the *Romach*."

"How is that?" Belov asked, and Dallas was unsure if she was overstepping her bounds.

"Classified, sir," Dallas said, wondering if she could get away with that. "But be aware that not all forces aboard the *Romach* will be hostile. Discretion and fire discipline is recommended."

"Wilco," Belov said, sounding less than happy. "I have two platoons available. Recommendations?"

Dallas recalled the conversations she'd had with Hattori about ship-to-ship action. Most ODTs only received superficial ship-to-ship combat training and Dallas realized she might have more experience than Belov. ODTs were very well versed in assaulting asteroid bases or planetside bases, but moving ships?

"One forward, one aft," Dallas said, debating if she should pull Hattori in. Screw it. She pinged Hattori, asking him to join. In seconds, the channel showed his presence.

"Senior Sergeant Hattori," Dallas said, "can you please advise us on the best way to take the *Romach*?"

Hattori was silent for a minute. Dallas was sure that Belov was pissed. The ODTs did not like Fleet starship infantry, but right now

Dallas wanted as much experience and knowledge in this planning phase as possible. The *Musashi* would keep the starship infantry for ship defense, but the ODTs could still use their experience.

"Of course, Lieutenant Dallas," Hattori said. "It would be my honor to provide what knowledge and assistance I can."

Dallas sent a link to a virtual display of the *Romach* that they could all see and interact with. The *Musashi* shuddered again. The Fleet battle wasn't her concern.

"Another vanhat battleship has transitioned in," the sensor operator reported. "Range one hundred twenty kilometers. Detecting missile launch."

Dallas closed her ears to the spaceship battle. If Aod was on the *Romach*, he would need help.

"The *Romach* is dead in space. It has lost power."

She did not want to consider that they might be too late to rescue any survivors.

* * * * *

Chapter Forty-Three:
Survivors

Sergeant Nova Dallas, ODT

Nova Dallas followed Commissar Nakano into the brig. There was an emptiness in her heart. There weren't many survivors from the *Romach*. Only twenty, and twelve of them were in the infirmary, struggling for their lives. None of them were Governance ODTs. None were Aod or members of his squad. The Torag prisoners had not survived the vanhat attack.

Empty eyes looked at the commissar from behind the bars. They all appeared to be the same genetic type, and Dallas couldn't quite place them. Black hair, tan skin, and eyes that didn't completely track. In violation of ODT protocol they were still wearing the remains of their ship uniforms.

Nakano wouldn't fail to notice that. Proper procedure would have been to strip them and search them, otherwise, there was no way to ensure they didn't have a hidden weapon. Furthermore, stripping them of clothes and possessions would embarrass and demoralize them, preparing them psychologically for interrogation, where they would be further violated.

She saw some of them were in shock, for more reasons than one. Only twenty survivors from a ship that large was damned few and she knew Governance ODTs hadn't killed them.

Nakano looked around, but Dallas didn't know what was going through his mind. A team of ODTs stood nearby holding their rifles at patrol ready, as if the prisoners could tear through the bars and attack them.

"Where are you from?" Nakano asked a man who seemed to be more aware than the others.

The man narrowed his eyes as he looked at the commissar. It was clear the stranger recognized the uniform and markings, even if Nakano was Fleet.

"We mean you no harm," Nakano said. "We would not have risked our ship and our lives coming to your aid otherwise."

"Prisoners to interrogate?" the man asked, but Dallas knew it more a statement than a question.

Nakano sighed and motioned at one of the ODTs to open the cell door. "Perhaps under normal circumstances."

Dallas looked at the prisoner. A silver bar on his breast tab indicated he was likely a lieutenant. He was still wearing space armor, but she knew the ODTs would have disarmed him, though they had let him keep his suit.

The man stepped back.

"You are here for your safety," Nakano said. "Another reason you are here is because we really aren't sure what else to do with you. Until we understand who you are and why you are here, we must take precautions, you understand. Your wounded are being treated in our infirmary."

Everyone was looking at the commissar. He was not a big man—Dallas towered over him—but he moved with a dangerous lethality she was sure they noticed. The commissar also had a holstered sidearm and his space armor was likely powered as well. Whoever these people were, they weren't fools.

Nobody spoke up, and Nakano sighed. "You are humans in a tomb world system. We did not recognize your vessel, but we know you rescued a squad of ODTs at Valakut. We would like to understand more. The *Romach* was a warship. There is no mistaking this, and your crew is disciplined."

"You will have to resort to torture," the lieutenant said. Looking at the others, Dallas saw he was the senior crewmember present, the rest were enlisted. Another failure of the ODTs. They should have separated the officers from enlisted and the senior enlisted from the junior enlisted.

"My captain has forbidden that for now," Nakano said, entering the cell. Dallas followed. If they attacked, she would do her best not to hurt them, but they would have to be stopped. Dallas heard the threat "for now" in Nakano's tone. He was playing commissar games.

"We have suffered severe damage rescuing you," Nakano said. "We are approaching the planet, and I suspect we will find an away team. Furthermore, there are additional vanhat we will have to deal with. They seem to be hunting your expedition."

Dallas didn't miss the man's sad look.

"These vanhat are a threat to humanity," Nakano said. "Is there anything you can share with us that will help us against them?"

"Don't let them get close," the man said, looking at Nakano.

"We are aware. We have an Inkeri generator that provides protection. Are you aware of this technology?"

Some of the fear left the man's eyes. "Yes. Don't turn it off."

"We most certainly will not," Nakano said. "When we reach orbit and fight off the vanhat, we will send a rescue team. We have the approximate location of your expedition, as do the vanhat. Are there Governance ODTs with that expedition, by any chance?"

The man glanced at Nakano, which told Dallas he knew something. She felt the glimmer of hope.

"Was an ODT named Aod McCarthy with them?" Dallas asked, not caring if she was interfering with the commissar's interrogation.

"Yes. He was leading the squad and working with—"

Dallas wanted to smile and dance. He was still alive! He had escaped Valakut. If anyone could fight off and evade the vanhat on the surface it would be Aod.

"With?" Nakano asked.

"Our commander," the man said, but Dallas knew he had been about to say a name.

"Interesting," Nakano said. "The woman we assume to be your captain is in the infirmary. We expect her to survive, if that is any consolation. So, a more senior officer is planetside? He will need our help against the vanhat."

The man glared at Nakano, and Dallas saw the gears turning in his eyes.

"I have a reinforced company of ODTs preparing to conduct an assault drop. A squadron of drone fighters and some gunships will support them. I would prefer to talk with your commander. If he does not wish to surrender, I can accept that, but shouldn't he be the one to make that choice? I would much prefer to save human lives."

"His name is Navinad. He can be contacted on this frequency." He then rattled off a frequency which Dallas was sure listeners would capture and save.

"Thank you, Lieutenant," Nakano said. "It is important we all have choices. Choices are freedom. I know your Commander Navinad will appreciate that you have given him a choice. If he does not wish to surrender or work with us, we can simply nuke the site, eradicate the vanhat and be done with it. I would rather not endanger Governance ODTs on a fool's errand."

The man remained silent.

"I realize you might not yet understand, but we are violating Governance protocol. In most cases, the ODTs would strip you naked and isolate you in individual cells. We certainly would not keep officers and enlisted together. This is violating many rules and regulations, which I am sure you cannot appreciate. While we could keep you together to encourage you to talk and help us identify you, the admiral in command of this vessel has been forced to make many decisions that may be viewed in inappropriate ways. I hope you understand the risk he is taking."

The commissar looked around, but the prisoners didn't move. They were paying more attention, though. Was he playing commissar mind games?

"We will work to rescue your commander as we work to save the lives of your wounded. These are unprecedented times. We serve the greater good, and we hope you will be part of it."

"I thought all SOG commissars were inflexible jackboot thugs," the man said, looking at Nakano more closely, perhaps searching for a response. Dallas wanted to smile. Commissars were much more subtle than that, especially the higher-ranking ones. This stranger was playing with a dangerous snake. The junior commissars were inflexible and frequently drunk on their power and authority. The more experienced the commissar, the more dangerous and subtle they could be, and the more fanatical.

"Commissars must be very flexible," Nakano said with no emotion in his voice that Dallas could hear. "Sometimes we must be inflexible, but people are unique, and it is the job of the commissar to understand the greater good and bend people so they serve the greater good to the best of their ability. This requires a powerful understanding of human nature. Junior commissars, which I suspect you are more familiar with, are less flexible and frequently inexperienced in recognizing the greater good. Good commissars learn to rule with punishment and reward. May I ask your name?"

"Lieutenant Gabbi," he said.

"It is an honor to meet you, Lieutenant," Nakano said. "I am Commander Commissar Nakano, senior commissar aboard the super dreadnought *Musashi*. Your guards are under strict orders to keep you safe and not abuse you. I will check on you frequently, or my assistant, ODT Lieutenant Dallas, will. She has my ear. If they mistreat you or you need anything, you may ask for her, and she will report to me. We will do so as often as our duties permit." Nakano looked at the prisoners. "We are not enemies. We must face the vanhat as humans standing shoulder to shoulder, or we will die. I look forward to speaking to Commander Navinad and will let him know you are alive and safe."

"Thank you," Gabbi said.

Nakano led the way out of the brig. "I would like you to check on them frequently. They are not to be mistreated. Provide what comforts you can."

"Will there be interrogations, sir?"

"No. I do not think there is anything critical to be gained from them at the moment. They could be a special operations unit, or they could be from a ghost colony. Either way, with the Stalingrad Protocols in effect and Fortress Sol isolated, we must keep our options open. If this Navinad does not surrender, then we can take harsher methods with these prisoners."

"What about Sergeant McCarthy?" Dallas asked.

Nakano stopped to look at her. "I understand your concern about him. I do not have the entire story. If he cooperates fully when he is rescued, then I will be able to show leniency; we can reinstate him. You are familiar with ODT communications. I expect you will do your best to communicate with him, to determine his actual status and confirm if he is working under duress. Furthermore, I expect your relationship will help encourage him to return to the wisdom and enlightenment of Governance leadership."

Dallas wanted to stomp Nakano's skull. He had planned this from the beginning. That was why he was keeping her around. He figured he could use her to recapture Aod and turn him into a weapon he could use, to play on his loyalty and love.

Nakano didn't give a damn about her or Aod. He was playing his commissar games. He was just a lot more forward thinking than she had initially given him credit for. A lot more willing to use and exploit resources. What a sneaky, rat-bastard thug.

"Understood, sir," Dallas said, suddenly feeling helpless. What choice did she have? What choice did Aod have?

Nakano nodded and resumed walking.

He was no fool. He knew exactly what kind of predicament she was in, and she knew he would carefully monitor her communications with Aod if she got in contact with him. Could she warn Aod? Or were they both doomed?

* * * * *

Chapter Forty-Four:
Escape to Space

Captain Diamond Winters, USMC

Winters preferred the stars to the surrounding dock, but she didn't want to forget the *Eagle* was currently docked on the Moon, waiting for orders. That was something she never spent a lot of thought on. A lot of waiting for higher authorities was waiting for them to get and complete orders they could pass down.

The *Eagle* was now well stocked and ready to go. Blitzen was working with other SCBIs to try to figure out what the next mission might be and where. Once she had that data, she could stock the ship accordingly.

Brita came in and sank into her chair. She didn't look happy.

"What's wrong?" Winters asked.

"I'm trying to figure out the amiraali. He seems indecisive, but I know that's not it. I think he's trying to pressure the emperor into something."

Winters raised an eyebrow, and a half smile came to Brita's face.

"I just don't know what. He always talks about taking the Republic fleet and leaving to find the homestars, but I think even he realizes how absurd that is. They could be anywhere, and space is vast. He is getting his intelligence directly from the highest level of the Empire, but the information he wants just isn't there."

"You think he believes the emperor is holding back?" Winters asked.

"No. I think the amiraali knows how much the emperor needs his ships and support, but the amiraali has never been good about coming out and asking for what he wants. Especially when it is important to him."

"That makes no sense. The guy is an admiral, one of the most powerful Fleet commanders in human space, and he won't tell people what he wants?"

"He doesn't share his personal life or desires with anyone. But I can tell he wants something."

"He wants Skadi to join him aboard the *Tyr* so he can leave."

"That makes the most sense to me," Brita said. "Skadi has outright told him she is staying here. He's not a fool. Maybe he thinks he can convince her or something."

"I've spoken to Skadi. I think she loves her father, but I just can't see her setting foot aboard the *Tyr* without a good reason. Do you think he would resort to kidnapping her?"

Brita laughed. "Skadi has too many friends and supporters aboard the *Tyr* and the *Sleipner*. The amiraali knows he can't cage that tiger and he is not dumb enough to try."

"Why is Skadi here?" Winters asked. It was a rhetorical question, but Brita's answer was surprising.

"Because she doesn't want the Empire to fail," Brita said. "She fought the Governance so hard and for so long. Now the Governance is dead, but it can be resurrected far too easily. I think your gunny did the smartest thing he could by declaring himself emperor. He upended the Governance social structure, directly threatened the bureaucracy, completely changed the way they thought. He has attacked what they believe. Everyone knew the system was corrupt. But now InSec is being brutal about hunting down corruption. And the vanhat are threatening to kill everyone. Most people fail to understand the vanhat threat these days. It is uniting people in ways the Central Committee could not. He is giving them a choice, glory and service or corruption and death. She may also feel loyalty to the emperor. He has provided leadership and succeeded where others had not."

Winters looked at Brita more closely. That was quite an analysis.

Brita took the look as an invitation to continue. "A lot of people don't like the change. They fear it, I'm sure. But they have learned to fear the vanhat even more. Nadya was a beautiful figurehead, a beautiful face and voice that soothed people. Now people are afraid. They need a strong alpha-type personality to lead the way, and your emperor fits the bill."

"Not everyone," Winters said, thinking about the attack on Club Werewolf.

"Everyone is different. You can't please everyone, and there will always be someone who feels strongly in the other direction."

Alarms screeched. Winters flinched, her eyes scanning for the threat before they fell onto the display.

Shorr space transitions, thousands of them, tens of thousands in very low Lunar orbit. Only the vanhat could come in that close. More alarms sounded announcing missile launches.

The hangar shook.

Blitzen sounded battle stations aboard the *Eagle* as the engines came to full power.

"Get us out of here," Winters said. On the ground, in dock, the *Eagle* was a sitting duck. "Evacuate the hangar!"

Blitzen began tracking incoming missiles targeting the dock.

Even though the main hatch was closed, the point defense guns opened fire, ripping through the metal hatch, shredding it as the pellets smashed the inbound vanhat missiles. More missiles lit up, changing course toward the hangar. The *Eagle's* point defense weapons didn't hesitate and ripped through the docking hatch.

Anybody in the hangar would be exposed, but if they didn't get to cover quickly, the incoming missiles would kill them.

Winters couldn't wait, and the *Eagle* shot into the sky, shattering and ripping the remains of the hangar hatch.

For a second, Winters thought the hatch would be too strong, but a burst from the point defense weapons destroyed the hinges and the *Eagle* broke free. She was now space-borne.

More missiles changed course. She got a glimpse of the vanhat attackers as bodies spilled from a broken transport. There was no way the ships could ever have been human-made, jagged arrowheads, blackened with age. She glimpsed alien markings on one of them before an Imperial missile blew it apart.

Her SCBI coordinated with Lunar defenses and gave her a path to upper orbit as her point defense weapons alternated between incoming missiles, drop pods, and enemy ships emerging from Shorr space. Her main blazer cannon tore into the invaders, but for every one she ripped apart, two more slid out of Shorr space to replace it.

She saw two alien ships collide and slam into a third, but she didn't know if they had suffered damage or were just too close because of new pilots.

The G forces pressed her backward into her seat, making it hard for her to breathe as the *Eagle* climbed into orbit, toward the protection of the incoming Imperial warships.

Numerous alien ships slammed into the Moon, near habitats and hangars. Two of the blackened arrows grounded themselves near the hangar the *Eagle* had just vacated while a third took the *Eagle's* place.

She thought she glimpsed troops pouring out of the grounded ships as Imperial warships and drone fighters began strafing the hangars.

There were too many targets. It looked like the Moon was surrounded by alien ships transitioning in to ground themselves or spew out drop pods.

The *Eagle* had to run a gauntlet as more alien ships arrived, creating a wall of death and fire.

"We are Vanir, we are the shield of our people," a voice rang out on the bridge. The *Tyr*. Incoming fire from the battlestar smashed vanhat ships out of the sky.

"We are Vanir," Brita said in response, "discipline and honor bind us."

A corridor opened, ringed with fire from the *Tyr*.

More vanhat ships died, but more transitioned in. How many did they have?

"We are Vanir, our line will not be breached," said the *Tyr*.

The lines looked pretty damned breached to Winters.

"We are Vanir, we are the defenders that none may pass."

Winters wanted to point out how all those vanhat were passing them but let them do their thing as she concentrated on keeping the *Eagle* in the corridor the *Tyr* was creating for them.

Incoming fire slammed into the *Eagle*. They lost an engine, which almost caused the *Eagle* to slide out of the corridor and into the curtain of fire the *Tyr* was providing, but Winters spun the ship, giving it momentum and balance to maneuver closer to the center. The side effect was that it caused her stomach to threaten rebellion, and she almost vomited there on the bridge.

Still spinning, the *Eagle* climbed higher. The incoming fire slackened as she entered the primary weapon arcs of the massive battlestar.

"Gods!" Brita said, looking at her display. "How many do they have? When will they run out?"

There were too many to count, and even more ships were still emerging from Shorr space.

The *Tyr* and the *Sleipner* fired on incoming ships as other weapons aboard the battlestars pounded targets on the ground.

"*Accelerate!*" Blitzen said, and the *Eagle* pushed harder. The engines began to red line. "*Imperial vessels are firing from over the horizon, using the Moon's gravity to place weapons fire into the kill zones.*"

Winters almost blacked out under the acceleration. She knew what Blitzen was talking about but hadn't thought they would ever do something like that. She had once heard some joke or tale about an assassin that had fired a bullet in the opposite direction of his target, but the bullet had such an angle that it didn't leave the Moon's gravity and circled the entire Moon to come back and hit the target from the opposite side.

Highly unlikely, but that didn't mean ships were out of range because of the curvature of the Moon couldn't lay down a wall of fire. Millions of pellets tried to escape the Moon's gravity. They would eventually, of course, but their firing arc would look more like a curve close to the Moon's surface.

Drone fighters were still launching, and Imperial warships were dipping lower into orbit so they could more accurately target and kill whatever was between them and the Moon.

Over the horizon, Moon-based coil guns that had survived were also firing, arcing their rounds using the Moon's gravity to slam pellets in grounded ships and massing troops.

"I am providing additional assistance to Imperial vessels and coordinating with Legionnaires," Blitzen reported. *"Aligning ships with firing corridors. Incoming transitions are slowing down."*

Slowing down? Winters didn't see it. Below them, there were countless explosions and flashes from heavy blazer weapons. There were unlikely to be any Moonside weapon batteries still operational and there was no doubt the vanhat had made it beneath the surface.

Grounded ships were being targeted and destroyed, with priority going to those ships that still showed activity. The surface was a confusing mass with all the Lunar dust that had been thrown up.

The vanhat had to have suffered millions of casualties.

"They are targeting the emperor and Zvezda Two," Blitzen reported.

* * * * *

Chapter Forty-Five:
Enemy SCBIs

2nd Lieutenant Zale Stathis, USMC

It felt like spiders running down his back as he moved toward the primary entrance. It was hard to attack a spinning bowl. Zvezda Two was burrowed deep in the Lunar mantle. There were several tunnels here, and they were all heavily defended. Stathis linked into the Praetorian Guard network.

"Paska," said a voice. "They are accurate!"

The link identified the speaker as a guard at the main entrance. One of the Aesir, and that made Stathis feel a little better. The Aesir were big targets, but they were super dangerous and tough.

"How did they get here so fast?" Stathis asked Shrek.

"They move very fast, as if they know exactly where they are going," Shrek said.

There were about thirty elevators around the perimeter where people could board and quickly and safely transition off the bowl, just like getting on and off regular elevator, but they were channeled to certain areas.

The troops had other methods which were quicker but also more dangerous. Maps and diagrams referred to them as sally points, which made no sense to Stathis, but it let people jump from the spinning bowl to the Moon proper.

"The EMPs have disabled numerous systems," Shrek reported. *"Repair bots are being dispatched. Only the sally points are available. Only the main entrance is under attack by invaders. Engineers are working to get the systems back up."*

"Zvezda is still spinning, though," Stathis said. As long as it spun, it would provide one gravity, like on Earth, and he would have to jump from a moving platform to one that wasn't.

"The primary generators and systems for Zvezda are under the bowl, buried deeper and heavily shielded. There are additional hardened bunkers there as well."

"That's where they're moving the gunny right?"

"The gunny is reluctant to retreat there yet."

Making his way to the "lip of the bowl," Stathis saw what he had to do. The speed was deceptive. It wasn't like he could just step over the edge and be out of the habitat.

Stathis was glad that Vili was with Mathison and Skadi. He wondered if that was where he should be as he jumped.

Momentum kept him moving as he lost his balance and rolled. He slammed against a wall. It could have hurt a lot more, but a couple troopers tried to grab him which slowed him down.

Stathis was disoriented as he looked around. Now the lighter gravity of the Moon was pulling on him. Apparently, the gravity plates weren't working.

"We are holding here, sir," the trooper said. There was a squad standing where they could provide some covering fire into the bowl if they had to, but they were also keeping the area secure. There were several armored bunkers they could fight from.

In the distance, Stathis heard fighting.

"Thanks," Stathis said and raced toward the main entrance. The best way to keep the vanhat out of Zvezda Two was to make sure they didn't get into it.

Stathis slowed and peeked around the corner. There was nearly a platoon guarding the main entrance, and they had a good supply of combat bots.

A pair of Legionnaires were present providing support, their SCBIs controlling the robots and decimating the attackers.

One robot suddenly erupted, spraying molten metal across the area, but another robot came out to replace it.

"How are we doing?" Stathis asked Shrek, not wanting to interrupt the two Legionnaires, a major and a captain who seemed to have control of the situation.

"The Legionnaires are holding," Shrek said. *"They still have a hundred and four bots in reserve."*

Stathis felt useless.

"An ODT company led by a Legionnaire is on the move and coming up behind them," Shrek continued. *"When that happens, the Praetorians will attack and break the enemy. Furthermore, key tunnels are being destroyed with demolitions to block enemy reinforcements."*

Stathis saw more robots move up, preparing to reinforce or spearhead the attack. This was too easy.

Without warning, one robot spun and fired at a pair of Praetorians, shredding them.

"Emergency override!" Stathis said, understanding as more robots spun and stopped firing. "Shut all the robots down so they require a manual reboot."

All the robots froze, and incoming enemy fire shredded them as the Praetorians popped out from cover to fire.

"What happened?" the captain asked as he hunkered down and enemy fire tried to eat through his cover.

"They hacked our bots," Stathis said.

"You are correct," Shrek said. *"The enemy has begun hacking our systems."*

And the engineers were working to bring up the networks.

"How close do they have to be to get into the Zvezda Two command net?" Stathis asked.

Zvezda Two was a mostly self-contained system with tightly controlled links to the outside world. All command systems were at Zvezda Two. Maybe the enemy wasn't trying to kill Mathison, maybe they were trying to take over Zvezda Two, which controlled all the Sol defenses? If they could control or shut down Zvezda Two, the Sol System would be vulnerable. It was how Mathison had taken control of the SOG.

The Central Committee had worked to put all their eggs in one basket, a basket *they* had controlled, which Mathison now controlled, and now the vanhat wanted that basket.

"I'm sharing this information. We have to be more careful bringing systems up online. We're detecting more hacking attempts. These aliens have AI or some comparable ability."

This was bad, very bad.

The incoming fire increased, and Stathis hurled one of his grenades down the hallways with as much force as he could. He didn't see the explosion, but the enemy fire slackened briefly and gave the Praetorians a chance to peek out and fire.

The Legion major spun away, his head a burning mass of flesh and shattered helmet.

Moving up, Stathis popped up and fired a burst from his blazer.

"Warn that company we may not push a good solid assault," Stathis said, popping up to fire again. Incoming fire came close, hitting the ceramic barrier he was behind and spraying his rifle with molten pieces of something.

"They have been warned. Captain Sinclair leads them."

"How many Legionnaires?" Stathis asked. How many SCBIs to help? The accuracy and efficiency of the attackers was seriously concerning to Stathis as another guard died. Despite what had started as a sure thing, now Stathis wondered if they could hold.

"Captain Sinclair is the only Legionnaire," Shrek reported. *"They have made contact with rear elements of the vanhat. There aren't as many as we originally thought."*

Which could have fooled Stathis. It looked like there were a lot.

* * * * *

Chapter Forty-Six:
Retreat

Vanhat Commander – Kafasta

It was a bitter pill. They were so close, but he did not have the combat power to push the assault. The enemy was worthy. No sooner had his demon taken control of their mechanical slaves than they had been shut down, so he no longer had unlimited troops. Only twenty.

"We cannot breach their command center from here," his demon reported. Kafasta already knew that.

"We are being attacked from behind," a trooper reported. "A company in strength."

Kafasta knew he could spin and counterattack the ones behind but would lose most of his survivors in that endeavor.

"Retrograde deeper into the catacombs. Target the civilian portions."

"Are there no reinforcements coming?"

That was another problem. Kafasta didn't know and having fought this far this quickly he had seen the defenses. It would be easy for the human defenders to stall or halt reinforcements. The caverns beneath the surface of the Moon were a maze but the Legionnaires would know them better than his forces. He had discovered the data they had received was woefully incomplete. Some of it had changed and the humans had worked to improve their fortifications. Out of the two hundred Weermag that had followed him off his ship, only twenty had made it this far.

Unacceptable.

He could stay here and fight to the death, hoping reinforcements would arrive, or he could face the truth. The sudden strike had failed, and this was going to become a bitter war of attrition. The Zvezda Two facility could continue to command the Sol fleets, but his twenty warriors could not breach the human lines. He knew there would be even more defenders inside.

This was the difference between the Weermag and lesser slaves. Lesser slaves would die needlessly. The Weermag fought, but they did not die needlessly.

Kafasta gave the command and his survivors poured into a train station tunnel where they could escape the attackers in front and behind. The last Weermag into the tunnel set several motion sensitive mines.

Their personal demons had identified the civilian systems so the Weermag could use the tunnels with near impunity.

The human network systems were powering up, but just as suddenly shut down.

The enemy adapted quickly. They would lose in the end, Kafasta knew, but they were proving to be a worthy foe.

"What is the plan?" asked Kafetan, Kafasta's acting second in command.

"We become stronger," Kafasta said. "Our pride and arrogance have been checked. We have failed because of our arrogance. We were defeated by a slave race, but one battle is not the war. The ancient gods have a lesson for us. We must prove our greatness; they forge only the strongest weapons in the hottest fires. We have forgotten that. Our forging is not complete."

"For blood," Kafetan intoned his acknowledgment.

"Others have made it to the surface and the tunnels," Kafasta said. That he was sure of. His warriors would not be the only ones, just the most successful. There were likely still forces landing, but if none made it this far, then Kafasta could calculate at least six places an attack would be bottlenecked. Like water, the Weermag would flow into the tunnels and go where there was the least resistance until they drowned the enemy from all directions.

"Our mission?" Kafetan asked.

"We are behind enemy lines," Kafasta said. "We will disrupt, corrupt, and destroy. This is not our first setback. We are the Weermag. We will be the last to drink the blood of our enemy. We must keep moving so they do not pin us down and destroy us. There are many millions of humans on this moon. Few are warriors. We are the backtha among chan. We are the predators. We cannot achieve our primary objective yet, so we will begin our predations."

Kafetan's shoulders shifted forward in anticipation of the massacre, and Kafasta grinned.

"Find me their vulnerabilities," Kafasta told his demon. "Let us rip out their unguarded veins and feast."

War was about mistakes. Both sides would make countless mistakes, and the side that made the most mistakes would suffer the most.

Kafasta was going to make humans suffer. They deserved it.

* * * * *

Chapter Forty-Seven:
Reinforcements

Captain Duffy Sinclair, ODT

The explosion removed a pair of green icons and replaced them with red on Duffy's display. These vanhat were not mindless monsters.

Moving forward, Duffy looked down the maintenance corridor where the enemy had fled.

"We have linked up with the Praetorians," a trooper reported, and Duffy acknowledged him as he pointed his weapon down the corridor.

"This is bad," Lieutenant Sung said beside him. Lieutenant Stathis joined them. Why was he here?

"We didn't kill them all," Stathis said, peering down the dark corridor. "At least twenty escaped. Since when do vanhat flee?"

"They were going to lose," Sinclair said. "I'm sure they could have inflicted more casualties, though."

"These guys aren't fighting like other vanhat."

"When we get the systems back up, we will track them."

"Yeah, about that. I think they have computers that can hack our systems. They took over some robots and turned them on us."

Sinclair stared at the young man.

"SCBIs?" Sinclair asked, turning his gaze toward some nearby bodies.

314 | WILLIAM S. FRISBEE, JR.

"I don't see any keyboards and monitors, sir," Stathis said.

"He is correct," Finn reported. *"They used some technology to hack into the robots using short-range radio. They cracked the encryption and codes and turned the robots against us."*

"Why didn't you stop them?"

"This was completely unexpected. Next time we will try."

"Do they all have the capability or just some?"

"Unknown, but until we know more, all Lunar network systems are considered vulnerable to compromise by these vanhat. Network engineers are looking for ways to mitigate this, but until we know more, we will have to limit network systems and capabilities."

"Now we have a bunch of roaches running around in the basement," Stathis said.

"Shall I take my company and go after them?" Sinclair asked the lieutenant. Captains didn't take orders from lieutenants, but Sinclair was pretty sure Stathis would have the authority to make such a decision. And the young man had plenty more combat experience dealing with the vanhat.

"No. Those assholes are acting like Marines, covering their retreat with claymores and shit. We need a demo team to clear the path and by then they'll be long gone or setting up an ambush. We've lost enough people and the forces trying to keep them near the surface are hard pressed. We need to consolidate and find their center of gravity."

Sinclair nodded, and the space between his shoulder blades itched.

"I'll get orders for your company to stay here and reinforce the Praetorians. They're bringing in Guard and ODT units from other parts of the Moon to help stabilize the lines and push the invaders back. From what I've seen, there are multiple units behind the main lines, and they're already striking and trying to crack the defenses. That shit is fluid, and I expect more penetrations."

"We need to hunt them down," Sinclair said.

"Yes, sir," Stathis said. "But they were all headed here. Either going for the emperor or the control systems. Until we get prisoners we can interrogate, we won't know which, but there is no mistaking how quickly they breached the Moon's defenses and how quickly they got this deep. You don't stumble onto the deepest, most secure, most heavily defended habitat on the Moon by accident. If they had gotten control of more robots, it would have been a quick fight, and they would have made it into Zvezda Two. It was a very close thing, Captain. I'm sure of it."

"He is correct," Finn reported, but Sinclair knew that.

"What about other ways into Zvezda Two?"

"Your boys are going to help reinforce those. There are only a few ways in, but right now it wouldn't surprise me if these things started eating through rock. You okay with this?"

"We don't quit," Sinclair said and gave orders for his troops to continue toward Zvezda Two where the Praetorians were letting them past.

"Lieutenant Sung, keep your platoon here at the main entrance," Sinclair said.

"Wilco," Sung said. His platoon had taken heavy casualties, but they had led the way. They deserved a chance to bunker down. If the vanhat came back, Sung would lose more, but they had proven themselves in the attack.

The Aesir link let him listen in on other networks. Several lines were near collapse on the surface. Legion command was still trying to figure out how many vanhat had survived and made it below the surface. Over the horizon coil guns still hammered vanhat ships, and in orbit, warships continued to strike any concentrations on the surface, or if they could identify them, concentrations below the surface.

The incoming transitions had stopped, but thousands of ships and countless drop pods covered the surface of the Moon. There were multiple penetrations, and the forces that had breached the lines continued in their attempts to break the fragile perimeter. Humans were outnumbered and outgunned. A battleship in orbit couldn't help an infantry platoon in the Lunar lava tubes from being overrun.

"Looks like we have one advantage," Stathis said. "We have Aesir communications. The vanhat don't have 'em. They're using regular radio links, which we are jamming."

"And they are jamming," Sinclair said, but Stathis was right. The problem was that most units, not even Legionnaires, had the Aesir communication tech.

"We use what advantages we can. They didn't expect that. Legionnaires control lots of ships that have it. Combined with the SCBI network, that is the only reason we aren't all dead."

"*But there could be a million enemy troops on the ground,*" Finn said. "*It's probably less. The Mare Tranquilitas habitat has been completely overrun. Over three hundred and fifty thousand civilians were located there. They have also overrun Mare Serenitatis, with two hundred thousand estimated civilian casualties. An unknown number of vanhat warships took shelter in the Hyginus Rille. There is still a great deal of surface-to-space fire coming from there, indicating working vessels which can provide a base of operations for them.*"

"Things look bad," Stathis said, squatting next to one body. "But I've been in worse situations. I was down to my last couple of mags as werewolves swarmed me."

"It's looking pretty dark to me," Sinclair said, reviewing the tactical situation.

"It's always darkest before, um, night?" Stathis said. "I'm sure the gun—um, emperor has a plan."

Stathis reached down, picked up one of the more intact bodies, and pulled it onto his shoulder.

"What are you doing?" Sinclair asked.

"Going to take it back to Zvezda so someone can cut it up and figure out if they have SCBIs," Stathis said.

"Lieutenant, I have privates for things like that. Give me a place for them, and I'll stack bodies for you."

"Oh," Stathis said. "I forgot, sir. The gunny always says don't lift with your back, lift with your privates. I'm just used to having, um, no privates. Wait, that didn't sound right. My privates are huge, but—"

"The gunny?" Sinclair asked as he tasked a platoon sergeant to collect some of the more intact bodies, their weapons and equipment and get them transported into Zvezda for analysis.

"Yes, sir," Stathis said, setting the body down so troopers could get it. "But I've got privates though, a big one, um."

Sinclair was glad he was wearing a helmet, though he was pretty sure Stathis's face was red enough to act as a warning.

"When the lines stabilize, we will have to hunt them down," Sinclair said, changing the subject before the young man said even crazier things.

"Yes, sir," Stathis said, taking the hint the subject needed to change.

Sinclair saw the *Tyr* and the *Sleipner* were sending down some of their network hardened combat robots with the Aesir communication links installed, which would give the Legionnaires an advantage.

He glanced at the casualty statistics provided by Finn and felt sick to his stomach. Both sides were taking massive losses. Sinclair looked at the numbers, but he just couldn't imagine that many dead people.

* * * * *

Chapter Forty-Eight:
Invasion

Prime Minister Wolf Mathison, USMC

Wearing his armor with a rifle nearby didn't give Mathison the comfort and confidence he wanted. Freya provided more and more data. The Shorr space transitions had stopped, but there were still far too many active vanhat on the ground. It was impossible to tell how many had survived and reached the tunnels and corridors below the surface.

His office was crowded with senior officers. It was both uncomfortable to have so many people in his office but comforting to see so many people alive and focused.

Warships were using drone fighters to scan for enemy troop concentrations, and crust-busters were being used to target anything they found. There was no saving civilians. Any civilians the vanhat had encountered were butchered and there had been no reports of anything else. The invaders had depopulated several habitats near the surface in what seemed like minutes.

The invasion had started off with EMP weapons taking most of the Lunar network and power systems offline. A blessing and a curse. Too many ground-based automated surface-to-space weapons had been destroyed, but the invaders could not hack into the Lunar networks, which could have let them cause more damage and gather intelligence they shouldn't have, like monitor troop movements and responses.

"How?" Mathison asked as the casualty list scrolled across his screen. It was a rhetorical question, but Skadi didn't pick up on that, or maybe she just wanted to say it out loud.

"We never expected they could transition in so close to a planet. Our first mistake. Their transitions were preceded by specialized un-manned, Shorr space-capable, missile carriers that sprayed the area with EMP missiles and rockets. Also, those specialized anti-Inkeri EMP missiles, like what they used on the *Tyr*. Dropships spit out drop pods like the missile carriers and then followed that wave of missiles. The third wave was a horde of frigate-sized warships that crash landed in habitats and other critical locations to pour more troops into the fighting."

"They came very close to succeeding," Vili said. "If the Legion had not been spread out among the ex-SOG forces, and without the Aesir comm relays, I'm pretty sure we would not have been able to mount a counterattack of any kind. With all the radio jamming that occurred, those links allowed us to call in accurate and timely fire missions. We need more of the Aesir relays."

"This would have been a lot worse without the Legion," Feng said.

"For sure," Vili said.

"Far too many are still on the surface or below it," Skadi said. "Pat yourselves on the back later. We barely survived, and the enemy wants to come here."

"Why?" Vili asked.

Skadi looked at Mathison. "Two reasons probably. Kill the head, the body dies."

"That is one reason," Vili said when she didn't continue.

"The emperor is here, and we are sitting on top of the control codes and hardware keys used to control everything. If they take Zvezda Two, they will cripple the Empire. Kill the emperor and decapitate the Empire."

"All our eggs in one basket," Mathison said. If he was killed, someone else would stand up. Wouldn't they? Having dealt with all the bureaucrats and egotistical generals and admirals, he wasn't so sure anymore. They would tear themselves apart trying to become top dog.

"For sure," Vili said. "But it isn't like you've had a choice or an opportunity to change things."

Mathison shook his head. He should have seen it. Even with the EMP strikes, Zvezda Two still had hundreds of links to the outside world and could continue to communicate with the Fleet and solar system. It was a fortress in many ways, but there were plenty of buried cables that led everywhere, including the far side of the Moon.

"Well, they are coming for us," Skadi said. "We can relocate the emperor, but what about all the command-and-control systems?"

"If they have AI, we can't let them capture this place," Mathison said. "They would send out execution commands and turn the automated defenses against us. They don't appear interested in conquest, just murder."

"These are not normal vanhat," Feng said. "Forces in contact are not changing and their Inkeris are not being stressed. They almost seem to be a conventional foe."

"Where did they come from?" Mathison asked.

Feng's eyes shifted from display to display that only he could see through his cybernetic interface.

"Alien. Perhaps they are a species that serves the Jotun and rides the wave of their resurgence? Their numbers are extensive. Perhaps a clone species? Or a more standard form that the vanhat have transformed to a specified shape? It would make sense that the vanhat would use different shapes and forms for different purposes. They seem to be masters of adaptation and conquest."

"So, how do we defeat them?" Mathison asked. He needed ideas. The right answer would be good, but nobody ever had all the answers.

"We need to make sure people know you are alive," Feng said. "This is causing some problems already. My agents are reporting many people fear you are dead. Without a central authority clearly in control, people are frightened. As people learn the enemy has an AI capability, they will realize they may be vulnerable to suicide commands if the enemy captures Zvezda."

"They need reassurance," Mathison said. "That, I can do."

"With your permission, I will create a script and prepare the production," Feng said.

Which meant that Mathison wouldn't be involved at all. Another lie to a people used to lies.

"No," Mathison said, standing. He didn't want to hesitate or wait. The sooner the better, and this was something he could do. "Let's give them something real."

A recording drone slid up in front of his desk.

"People of the Empire," Mathison said. "I talk to you from the fortress of Zvezda Two. The enemy invasion has failed. I won't lie, they almost succeeded, and we're going to have a difficult time digging them out, but they failed. I am alive. The fortress remains unbreached, and reinforcements continue to arrive. The bad news is that they landed a shit load of troops. There is good news. We *are* going to wipe them out. They underestimated us and they are going to pay the price.

We will prevail. I'm proud of you all. It won't be an easy fight, but we will be victorious."

Mathison gave the command and the message ended.

"Short, sweet, to the point," Skadi said.

"You wanted a long-winded political speech?"

"That will work well," Feng said. "Powerful. You in your armor standing strong, speaking with confidence. It will trend very well, I'm sure."

"Oh joy," Mathison said. "Trending. I look forward to seeing how many Likes I can get. Will that help us stop them from hacking our systems? How is it trending with people who don't have power? How long can the habitats survive without network access, power, and air?"

"We can pump air into habitats," Feng said. "Power and network are related problems. In most cases, bringing up power will bring up the network, so we are evacuating as many people as possible out of the war zones. There are pockets of survivors that have escaped the massacres."

"None of them changed?"

"We are not doing deep scans, but they do have to pass through Inkeris and past Russelman index sensors."

"These bastards have AI," Mathison said.

"We are taking what precautions we can. Anyone who is physically transformed will be rapidly identified, of course. However, we are not seeing any transformations with this current invasion force."

"We are sure they are vanhat?" Skadi asked.

"To be honest?" Feng said. "I have my doubts. These invaders have AI, cybernetics, and seem very adept at using technology. I cannot say with one hundred percent certainty they are vanhat."

"So," Mathison said, "how do we piss in their cheerios?"

"We could rig the encryption keys and control systems to self-destruct," Skadi said. "Better to lose them than let the vanhat get control."

"What happens to all the automated systems?" Mathison asked.

"They maintain current programming."

"We need a system that gives us more flexibility. I'm not worried about the suicide bomb codes. If that gets destroyed, so be it. We need to abolish that system, anyway. I don't want the troops worried about the bomb in their skull going off because I'm having a bad hair day."

"You don't have any hair," Skadi said.

"I do. It's a just a figure of speech."

"Zen," Skadi said.

"What have you got, Feng?"

"I would like to accelerate the growth of the Legion. There are things we can probably drop from the curriculum to process Legionnaires more quickly."

"Is the facility okay?"

"It was on the outskirts of the invasion. They were attacked but suffered minimal damage."

"Fine," Mathison said. He wasn't happy about expanding the Legion quickly. He wanted quality over quantity, but right now there wasn't a lot of choice. "The Legion is making a difference. We need more of them."

Feng must have picked up on his reservations.

"With the current Legionnaires in positions of authority, they will establish a good, strong backbone of loyal followers. Current Legionnaires can set examples and standards for newer Legionnaires who may not have as much indoctrination."

"We need them," Mathison said.

"We will begin inducting more senior enlisted as well," Feng said. "Stathis is proving to be an exceptional officer based on the reports I am receiving."

"Fine," Mathison said. Why was Feng keeping tabs on Stathis? Could that be a problem? "So, how do we scrape the current invaders off the Moon?" Mathison looked around.

"Tac nukes," Skadi said. "Scorch Luna. We are now prepared to sweep any additional invaders from orbit. Even if they transition directly to a landing position, we will be ready. They will not get resupplied."

Mathison mulled that over. Tac nukes? It wasn't like there was an environment on Luna to worry about.

"The refugees are a problem," Skadi said. "And we are going to have to bring additional forces up from Earth. I've sent a request to General Duque to send ODT and Guard units from the Jupiter system. They should arrive in a couple of days. They still outnumber us."

Stathis entered and saluted. "Zvezda Two is pretty secure at the moment, sir."

Mathison returned the salute and motioned Stathis to a chair. The young man was changing. Mathison could see it now. He wasn't carrying himself like some dumb young private trying to get into or out of trouble. He looked like a young officer. It seemed both natural and unnatural.

"They have reinforced us with an ODT company. I fought with them on Earth. Great guys commanded by a badass Legionnaire," Stathis said. "The face eaters aren't getting in."

"Are you getting out?" Amiraali Carpenter asked. Mathison had almost forgotten he was there because he had sat sitting in the corner talking with his crew on one of the viewscreens.

326 | WILLIAM S. FRISBEE, JR.

"Not yet, sir," Stathis said. "Not safely. There are vanhat raiders that made it past the bottlenecks. They are probably going to run around behind the lines and wreak havoc. These guys aren't your regular knuckle-dragging faceeaters. I think they have SCBIs. They almost hacked some of the defense bots."

That was a very bad piece of news.

"How is it they haven't overrun us already?" Vili asked.

"The Moon is full of lava tubes, millions of 'em," Stathis said. "The soggies turned many into habitats. There are thousands of other habitats that have also been drilled into the Moon. Beneath the surface it's a three-dimensional maze, but the SOG was paranoid and designed the system to deal with mutinies and insurrections and shit, so they established bottlenecks and perimeters, along with protocols and defenses. Turns out those bottlenecks work just as well for halting invaders as they do for halting mutineers. Sir."

Mathison was impressed Stathis knew all that. Was he bucking for a promotion already?

"Wiring Zvezda Two to explode is one problem that can be solved," the admiral said.

"If I die, Skadi is next in line," Mathison said, glaring at the admiral.

"While I think that is a good choice," the admiral said. "The people do not know her as well as you. There will be fighting and bickering, accusations that she killed you to take over. Your loyalists may turn on her or they may not give her their full support."

"I'll make a public announcement about how much I trust her, how she will succeed me, and I want everyone to support her."

"I don't think that will be good enough," Feng said.

"What the hell?" Mathison said, glaring at Feng. "What else can I do?"

"Maybe you could marry Skadi, settle down, and have little gunnies, Gunny. I mean, um, Emperor?"

Mathison turned his glare to Stathis but noticed everyone was looking at him and Skadi. They didn't look shocked. The bastard Feng even had the ghost of a smile on his smug face.

"I like the young man's idea," Admiral Carpenter said.

Feng began, "Lieutenant Stathis may have stated it less eloquently than others, but—"

"But what?" Mathison said, afraid to look at Skadi.

"He is correct."

Mathison didn't know what to say or do.

"Let me say this," the admiral said, "such a marriage would cement my presence here at Sol until we find the Republic homestars. Such a marriage would prove your allegiance to the Republic in my eyes. My loyalty is to family. I cannot imagine a better son-in-law."

"Such a marriage would entertain the masses beyond the depredations of a war that is growing worse," Feng added.

Stathis spoke up, "And think of the stress reduction of—"

"Shut up, Stathis!" Skadi and Mathison said together.

"You've been planning this?" Mathison asked them.

"I'm surprised you didn't think of this this option yourself, to be honest," Feng said. "The admiral and I have discussed this it some detail but bringing it up has been a touchy subject and we were unsure how you or Skadi would respond. Violence and rebellion were the most likely options, we suspected."

Mathison glared at Stathis.

"Open mouth, insert foot?" Stathis said. "Sorry gun—um, Emperor. I didn't know they were planning it. Honest. I just thought it made sense and you both like each other and—"

"This is nothing more than an arranged marriage," Skadi said.

"Daughter, can you imagine anyone else brave enough to ask for your hand in marriage?"

Mathison watched Skadi open her mouth to argue and then close it. She had to be as shocked as he was. Was this why Admiral Carpenter had been cagey and wishy-washy about leaving and staying? Demanding he give the Republic some assurance he would not betray them?

"You both understand the greater good," Feng said. "You have both read enough history to understand the significance of such a union and how it can unite separate people. As an emperor, you were born on Earth. The people of the Governance believe you are one of them, and to unite with one of the Governance's most feared enemies in order to defend the people of Earth? There will be few who see this as a bad move, and I can arrange for their silence or disappearance if they object inappropriately. This is a move that would unite the people when we need unity."

"But we still work and live in close proximity," Mathison said. Was there a way out of this? "One nuke can kill us both, and then you are back to square one."

"One problem at a time, Emperor Mathison," Feng said. "The first problem we face is relatively simple. Your culture and honor will dictate if we can progress past that problem."

"What problem is that?" Mathison growled.

Feng smiled.

"First, Emperor Mathison, you must ask for her hand in marriage. I believe her father has already given his blessing."

* * * * *

Chapter Forty-Nine:
Inconvenience

Enzell, SOG, Director of AERD

Watching the view screens, Enzell did not like what he was seeing. Currently, his reports were third hand, being routed from further around the Moon, a region that had not been invaded and where they had working networks. Since he was near the invasion, he was currently cut off to some extent. He was not exactly behind enemy lines, but he had no idea what was going on above him.

The false emperor had a communication system that could not be jammed, and Enzell did not have access to it, yet.

The vanhat who had overrun his facility above had massacred everyone, but they had not discovered the entrance to his secret bunker. The facility had an auxiliary generator which powered the cameras and minimal local networks, so he had watched the vanhat break through the door and massacre his workers. It was disturbing, to say the least, when they removed their masks and fed on the bodies.

Their appearance was more disturbing than their diet, in Enzell's opinion.

The invaders were voracious, and Enzell had not expected them to eat so much of his dead workers. It was, of course, fascinating to get a close-up view of them. They were hideous, with pale skin, large, red eyes, and sharp, serrated teeth. They looked like they were covered in freshly skinned bone or red speckled white cartilage, and their bat-like ears could have been horns. The teeth immediately caught Enzell's attention, though, because of their shape and design. It looked like they could extend slightly out of the mouth and the teeth were curved, almost hooked. They were clearly designed to pull the food into the mouth while inflicting as much damage as possible. Those teeth were likely a key aspect that would influence their psychology.

"What are your thoughts?" Enzell asked Tantalus.

"They are strictly carnivorous and adaptable," Tantalus said.

"Explain."

"They must belong to an alien species. A completely different bi-ological track, yet they find sustenance from dead humans. This im-plies they either have a biology that allows them to do that or some form of cybernetic implant that lets them process alien matter. They are devouring everything, including bone and cybernetics."

"Why don't they talk?"

"They don't need to?" Tantalus said. "There are several possibili-ties. They are a single intelligence like a hive mind, they are linked cy-bernetically, or they are linked in some other way."

"Aren't they being jammed?"

"Jamming seems to be extensive," Tantalus said. "It should be noted their armor is covered with those black beads. Based on the video footage, those may be infrared receivers or transmitters. They could communicate via line of sight, using infrared or some other tech-nology. The video feed does not provide anything other than standard light spectrum, so I cannot ascertain if this is a fact."

"What good are you then?" Enzell asked. He wanted new insights.

"I am only as good as my input," Tantalus said. Enzell scanned the readouts. Was Tantalus being rebellious?

No. It was just a statement of fact.

Enzell felt secure here in his bunker, watching the aliens rip apart the offices above. Unless they started taking apart walls, they would not find his elevator, and if they did, it was rigged to explode.

He watched them destroy several of the workstations but what they were looking for, he wasn't sure.

There weren't a lot of them, and Enzell suspected this might be one of the groups hiding behind the main lines. Based on the reports he was getting from the other side of the Moon, the lines had stabilized at specific bottlenecks that had originally been designed to isolate insurrections.

"Reports indicate they are technologically advanced," Tantalus said. He had read access to most environments. He was a great spy because he could only watch and nothing else.

"Obviously," Enzell said.

"Reports are coming in that they can hack networks like the Legionnaires'. They may carry miniaturized AI units, or they may have that ability implanted in them."

"Really?" Enzell asked, looking at them more closely. There was definitely a hierarchy among them. One was in command, and it seemed quite willing to assign tasks to others.

"If you have full access to other networks," Tantalus began, "should they compromise your network, they will be able to access the rest of the Moon's networks."

"I'm sure they have already done so," Enzell said.

"There are very few hardened network links that could have survived that attack," Tantalus said. "Zvezda Two is likely to be the only other network with links out of the area."

"So, we won't tell them we are here," Enzell said.

"We could endanger the rest of the Governance," Tantalus said.

"Don't be absurd," Enzell said. "Should anything like that be detected, I will shut it down. I am monitoring things, and I will detect any intrusions. I'm not asking you for security advice."

"Yes, sir," Tantalus said.

Nonetheless, Enzell pondered what Tantalus had said. Perhaps the AI was right, but this was also an excellent opportunity to observe them.

However, he knew better than the AI.

* * * * *

Chapter Fifty:
Guerrilla

Vanhat Commander – Kafasta

The more he saw of them the more he despised them. How could they have done so much damage to the invasion force? How could these pathetic creatures halt and hold the rest of the invasion force back?

His demon explained it to him, of course. Occasionally there were breaks in the jamming and a few signals could get through, but it still didn't explain how an abandoned slave race could have halted the Weermag. The invaders had known about the bottlenecks built into the Governance architecture and city planning, but the invasion planners expected the invaders would be able to penetrate quickly and deeply into the Moon, rendering such bottlenecks pointless. Humans could only defend so many of them.

The invasion planners had also expected more Weermag troops would reach the tunnels.

This was not the first time an invasion had gone badly for Kafasta. The invasion planners were AIs, more powerful than the demon in his skull, but they lacked imagination and data. The ferocity of the humans was only matched by the ferocity of one other ancient slave race that had rebelled, two, maybe three, awakenings ago. That had been a difficult campaign, but the Weermag, like always, had been successful.

That campaign was when Kafasta had proven himself and survived an invasion. Those ancients eventually died, but they had not appeared to be as weak as these humans.

When his troops discovered this small facility off a major thoroughfare, Kafasta had hoped it would be a good place to go to ground. The humans had made a lot of noise when they were butchered, but they had not fought back. They didn't even taste good, but they were nutrients and Kafasta knew his company would need all the nutrients they could get. This fight was going to grind on until another invasion force was ready. Kafasta doubted the demon overlords would commit another invasion until it outnumbered the previous one. It emboldened the slave races when they were able to resist effectively. It gave them hope.

Something was wrong with this facility, though. It was running a backup power system, and Kafasta had the feeling he was being watched.

The network appeared to be down, but the surveillance cameras were active. This species was foolish and inefficient. While eating the bodies, the demons had noticed the alien cybernetics. They did not have personal demons to monitor and control them, but they were at a technological level where they should have rudimentary demons. They were monitored through their own cybernetics, but there were flaws that could only be intentional. Perhaps understandable in a slave race that wanted to be slaves but also wanted to pretend they weren't slaves. Such twisted and perverted logic seemed to be common among species that did not accept the gods.

These were Governance workers, though. Low-quality slaves that were only slightly better than robots. He wanted to devour some of their warriors. That would be more informative. Understanding what cybernetics they had, what their bone and muscle mass was like, how much they relied on their armor would be useful information.

"I do not like this facility," Kafetan said. "We are being watched."

"Yes," Kafasta said as he reviewed a report that had made it through the jamming. These humans were strengthening their lines, preparing for a long, hard fight. They did not have the strength to push the Weermag from the Moon. They might never have enough forces for that. They appeared to have barely enough troops to hold those choke points, for now. Already, engineers were preparing to tunnel around them. The other vanhat slaves were mindless and would seek to overwhelm the fallen with numbers. The Weermag were smarter and more capable than that. While the orja of other Jotnar were like water, flowing over and around, the Weermag were like the hammer of the gods. Able to do what the others could not.

"I see no networks," Kafetan said. "Closed loop system? I see data being sent, but nothing received."

"Perhaps," Kafasta said, turning his attention back to their surroundings. "There is something different here."

"A trap?"

"Perhaps. Humans are canny. They watch us. They want to learn. We should teach them," Kafasta said. These humans did not understand war. Perhaps they understood violence, but the Weermag waged war. Physical, spiritual, and psychological.

Removing his helmet again, Kafasta looked at the closest camera, making sure it had a good view of his face.

"I know you are watching this," Kafasta said in the human language they called English, the most common language spoken by these abandoned slaves.

* * * * *

Chapter Fifty-One:
Speech

Enzell, SOG, Director of AERD

When the creature looked at the camera and spoke in perfect English, Enzell's blood ran cold.

"I know you are watching this," the creature said. "Good."

The creature pointed at the bloody scraps of his workers.

"This is to be your fate. Inadequate substance for those loyal to the gods. Your hearts, your livers, your spleens will be nothing more than fuel for us to continue our war against your pathetic species. This is not my first purge of abandoned slaves or evolutionary dregs. I am ancient. I walked this galaxy before your star was born, and I was there when your pathetic species was abandoned by the gods eons ago."

The creature looked around.

Enzell sat frozen in horrified fascination and waited for it to continue. He knew it was looking around for dramatic effect. He knew it was aware it was being watched, but how?

"This?" the creature said and motioned at the surrounding laboratory. "This is little better than a mud nest built by insects of the world you destroyed through your own incompetence and bickering. The gods bring unity, which is something your species craves. You are social creatures that cannot know the true value of belonging to something greater than yourselves. The gods give us that, and because your species has rejected them, we will render your species extinct like so many creatures from your sad, ruined home world."

Enzell smiled. The creature was subtle. Which was it? Was humanity abandoned slaves? If that was the case, was Earth really their home world?

"There is so much you do not understand about your species, your origins, or the nature of the galaxy. I know you are watching, and I know you are afraid" "

The face was alien, but there was no mistaking the grin which revealed the vicious teeth.

"You will provide us with entertainment as we eradicate you and everything your civilization built. When we are done with you, there will be less of the human race despoiling this galaxy than you can imagine. The worlds you call the tomb worlds will hold more clues and evidence of their passing than humanity. I will remember your species less than the other species we have purged."

How did it know it was being watched?

"I will leave you, for now. You call this game 'cat and mouse.' The cat can make countless mistakes, but the mouse can make only one. We can taste your soul, and you cannot escape us. We have never failed to purge a species. This purge has just begun, like thousands of purges before."

The creature put its helmet back on, hiding the hideous alien features.

"How do they know?" Enzell asked Tantalus.

"Unless they have some other extra sense we are not aware of, it must be extrapolation."

"It sounds very sure we are watching."

"Yes," Tantalus said. "This is not a new tactic used by the vanhat. However, in the past, only the Jotnar have demonstrated an ability for psychological warfare. These orja appear to be very different. Less controlled and more independent than others. There is virtually no indication they are vanhat based on readings from Russelman index sensors. Furthermore, they do not seem to notice Inkeris. This creature's ability to speak English is also very concerning. It could articulate very well and the cultural reference to cat and mouse was targeted. There is a lot to learn in this. These orja are different."

Enzell sat back and watched as the aliens finished. The last thing he saw them do was place a very well-aimed shot into every camera and sensor in his facility, leaving him completely blind. Were they gone? He would know the instant they opened the secret hatch to his elevator. It was not a straight drop either. It had been designed with numerous curves and loop backs, and there was a small nuke just below the facility so that if he desired, he could erase the facility and any tunnels leading from it. He had other escape routes from his bunker, but it was bothersome to be unsure if they were really gone. Another psychological attack perhaps? Were they there or had they gone, and how had they discovered *all* his cameras and sensors?

"There is no way they can access our networks from there?" Enzell asked.

"No," Tantalus said. "You have designed a read-only system. For them to intrude they would require actual two-way communication. Return traffic is not possible with the current technology in use. The systems in the lab receive only, they do not transmit. While theoretically it is possible for them to transmit an attack, they will not know if the attack is successful or how to pattern their efforts. Furthermore,

340 | WILLIAM S. FRISBEE, JR.

the bandwidth is limited and easily inspected for erroneous traffic. Those systems are one direction only."

Enzell nodded. That was how he had designed it, but he had hardware controls that would let him transmit.

He would save this information for now. He could likely slip it into the intelligence collection data streams in some way, but this might give him an edge against the false emperor and his coterie of flunkies. The question was, how could he use this new information?

"Continue analysis," Enzell told his AI slave. "I want more information. Details."

"Yes, sir," Tantalus said.

Could they compromise Tantalus?

Enzell looked through the data and pulled up several log files Tantalus didn't know it generated. Nothing seemed out of the ordinary, though. Tantalus had no secrets from Enzell.

He ran the log files through another system which would help him identify any anomalies.

* * * * *

Chapter Fifty-Two:
Mister Punchy

2nd Lieutenant Zale Stathis, USMC

There had been another breakthrough, and the ODTs followed Stathis as he led them through the habitat.

Dying plants and ruined buildings told Stathis this wasn't the first time this habitat had changed hands in the last couple days, and if he was honest with himself, it probably wouldn't be the last.

The Governance paranoia and methods of control were actually helpful. The Governance had designed the habitats so they could be more easily isolated and controlled. Stathis had thought nothing of it at first, just chalked it up to another way the Governance were stuck-up, controlling assholes. Each habitat was a self-contained city, and travel between them was discouraged. What little travel was allowed was tightly controlled through check points. "Ten-minute cities" was one reference he frequently saw used.

The ODT company following Stathis reached the Olga Check-point, and Stathis transferred command over to the local Legionnaire, a major.

"Fifteenth Company is yours, sir," Stathis said as the major came up to him. The major's SCBI was already sending commands to the different platoon commanders. Stathis' bodyguard squad, as he thought of them, took a knee, weapons pointed back toward the habitat.

"Thank you, Lieutenant," Major Pervoi said. He sounded tired.

Stathis wanted to ask if the major if he had everything under control, but that probably wasn't appropriate.

"Anything else, sir?" Stathis asked.

"Be careful heading back," Pervoi said. "They're up to something."

"What do you mean, sir?" Everyone knew they were up to something. The vanhat were forcing breakthroughs and coordinating attacks on the checkpoints. It was becoming more and more difficult to hold the line. Any attacks from the enemy outside the line usually coincided with an attack from inside the lines. The choke points were then hit from the front and back. Each time this happened a few more of them might get through the breach and disappear.

They were building up their forces inside the perimeter, but right now General Hui had two choices. She could fall back and cede control of most of the habitats to the enemy or she could do her best to hold the line while troops were deployed to sweep behind the lines to secure them.

An inner perimeter was being established that would push out to the outer perimeter and crush the enemy between, but that was going to be very difficult and costly to dig out the vanhat because they were sneaky bastards. One intelligence brief Stathis had seen recently indicated the vanhat were tunneling.

Pushing them off the Moon was becoming more and more unlikely.

"Just a hunch," Pervoi said. "They are becoming predictable; falling into a pattern."

"Predictable or not, sir, what they are doing is working," Stathis said. He was getting the same feeling. He liked a predictable enemy. The most dangerous enemies were the unpredictable ones. "I once had a gunny tell me that professionals are predictable, but the world is full of amateurs."

Pervoi remained silent.

"Good solid advice," Stathis said. "But he also said that you should never interrupt an enemy that is making a mistake."

"Who is making the mistake?" Pervoi asked.

"Major, I think we are. Somehow, somewhere."

The major tilted his head as he looked at Stathis, like he wanted Stathis's opinion. Stathis was tempted to say something stupid to get either a grin or rebuke from the major. You could always tell a lot about a person by the way they handled sarcasm and off-color humor, but Stathis wasn't sure if officers joked around that much, and Major Pervoi was a senior officer.

"How so?" the major asked as Stathis tried to think of something to say.

"They came to the Moon for a reason. Not Earth, not the Jupiter system, but here. The Moon. They either want to eat the emperor's face, or they're looking for something else."

"The control systems are under Zvezda Two," the major said. "Both are legitimate targets. Capturing or destroying either would be a major blow."

"Yes, sir," Stathis said, glad the major was picking it up.

"So, you think they're staging forces behind our lines to launch a major assault on Zvezda Two?"

How could he answer without offending or insulting anyone?

"It's what I would do," Stathis said. "But—"

"But what?"

"I dunno, Major." Something else was bothering Stathis. "I don't think that would be the only plan."

A pulse gave Stathis a brief migraine and he winced. Shrek came back online almost instantly as everyone rebooted their systems. The vanhat had just pulsed them with their EMP weapon.

"I hate that," the major said, turning away from Stathis. Everyone took cover and prepared for an attack, but there was no attack forthcoming. "They do that shit to screw with us. Those pee-holes are damned annoying."

"What impact does it have?" Stathis asked. He hadn't been present for many EMP attacks, but up here near the front lines, they occurred more frequently.

"Not much," the major said. "It ruins civilian cybernetics and trashes our non-military systems, but it doesn't seem to have much effect beyond that. It overloads our Inkeris for a few seconds, but we have a new update for them, so that if they crash, they instantly reboot. Always on. Not much time for the vanhat to exploit that. It's almost like they're just being pee-holes and trying to mess with us and civilians, though the civilians are getting hit hardest. There are fewer and fewer refugees making it through."

"Refugees?" Stathis asked. That didn't seem right.

"There are a lot of the orja," the Major said. "But civilians are pretty good at keeping their heads down and remaining unnoticed."

"You sure they're human?" Stathis asked, realizing what a dumb question that was. The vanhat were very different from humans, from their white cartilagelike outer skin to the shape of their heads. Even their walk was slightly different.

"We only allow humans through," the major said. "Pretty easy to tell the difference."

"But they were in areas without working Inkeris."

"We're watching for physical changes, talking to each one to make sure they seem sane. Doing what we can. If they are transformed vanhat, it isn't visible or obvious."

"We should set up confirmation at the refugee camps," Stathis said.

"The refugee camps are overcrowded chaos. Right now, the problem is making sure they have enough food, water, and air. Confirming identity is going to have to wait. Furthermore, the camps are too close to the lines, and we can't risk enemy hackers getting too close."

"Convenient."

"Is there something I need to know?" Pervoi asked.

"Is there?" Stathis asked Shrek.

"Where are you going with this?" Shrek asked.

"Maybe I'm just being paranoid, but there was this show about an AI that took over the world and snuck terminators into the resistance. These terminators were robots in human skin and could pretend to be humans. The resistance used dogs to sniff out these terminator units. It got super creepy when they sent a terminator back in time to—"

"You think they have terminators among the civilians?"

"These bastards are super smart," Stathis said, thinking about how they had tried to take control of the robots and turn them on the defenders at Zvezda Two.

"You don't have any dogs, do you?" Stathis asked.

"Pets?" Pervoi asked. "Only the most senior Governance administrators were allowed such luxuries. Especially here on Luna, where such a resource consumption could be considered a waste. There may be more cats than dogs. Why?"

"What if there are infiltrators among the civilians? What if they look and act human?"

"Are you being paranoid?"

"It isn't paranoia when they really are out to get you," Stathis said. "I've dealt with a lot of face-eating monsters. At one time, they were all human. These dudes are different. I'm just saying, maybe by letting in the refugees, we are making a mistake."

"You think we should turn away refugees?"

"No," Stathis said. That wouldn't work. How many innocent people would die if he gave that order? Would the major listen to such an order from a lieutenant, and what about all the other front-line bottlenecks where civilians were flocking?

"That is what a Governance officer would order if there was a risk," the major said. "For the greater good. Do you think there are infiltrators?"

"If there are, I'm sure they are already in the refugee centers," Stathis said.

"I'm working through the Legion network and seeing what we can do about setting up checks to screen the refugees," Shrek reported.

The major looked around, and Stathis saw a group of about nine civilians, refugees making their way through. They looked haggard. He saw the fear and terror in their eyes. Stathis didn't want to think about the horrors they had seen.

Except one old man. His eyes moved around, and he didn't have the same thousand-yard stare like the others. Maybe he had seen it all before, some veteran or something.

"You!" Stathis said, pointing at the old man. "Stop!"

Genuine fear flashed across his face.

"Problem," Shrek said, as a chill ran down Stathis's spine. Corporal Starkova, one of the team leaders now assigned to Stathis, gave an order to his fireteam and Private Metzenberg brought his SAW up and aimed at the old man.

Stathis didn't see a problem.

"Something is wrong," Shrek said. *"You may not have seen the micro-expression, but there was no transition."*

"So? I can understand him being scared."

"But there should have been. SOG watches for such things in a situation that would be labeled as abnormal. Usually, there is guilt or surprise. Fear is acceptable, but he did not look surprised until it was too late for a more suitable micro-expression to be displayed."

Stathis knew what micro-expressions were. The SOG understood them very well, and when he had practiced infiltration, he'd had to rely on Shrek to help him hide them. It was human nature to control their facial expressions. For most of their adult life, people practiced controlling their expressions. Micro-expressions were brief, involuntary facial expressions that revealed a person's genuine emotions. They appeared on a person's face before they could realize it and change their expression to what they want others to see.

To be singled out by a trooper should surprise and shock anyone.

"You sure?" Stathis asked.

"Abnormal," Shrek said. *"Not impossible."*

"Remember Mister Punchy aboard Station 402?"

Mister Punchy had been Stathis's name for Commissar Summers, one of his first encounters with a SOG commissar. Summers had seemed to enjoy punching helpless prisoners and had eventually turned and become one of the vanhat, demonstrating superhuman

348 | WILLIAM S. FRISBEE, JR.

strength and the ability to transform part of his body into a lethal weapon.

Stathis rested his hand on his sidearm as he approached. The sidearm would be better because he was pretty sure if this old man was a vanhat, he wouldn't have time to bring up his rifle. Mister Punchy had appeared completely human before he morphed into a face-eating monster and tried to claw Stathis.

Breaking the commissar's arm hadn't bothered him at the time, but Stathis would not break this old man's arm to check his reaction.

"Who are you?" Stathis asked, coming closer. Metzenberg and his team leader, Starkova, moved to a better position where they could fire on the old man and not endanger Stathis or anyone else.

"Should we search him, sir?" Starkova asked, and for a second Stathis didn't notice the young trooper was calling him sir.

What would searching Mister Punchy have accomplished?

Inching closer, Stathis prepared to draw his weapon.

"I know what you are," Stathis said. A bluff. "I know you serve the ancient gods. Time to serve the new gods."

Everything happened too fast.

The old man's left hand grabbed Stathis' wrist to keep him from drawing his sidearm as the other hand came toward his throat, already transformed into claws that Stathis knew could shred steel.

* * * * *

Chapter Fifty-Three:
Stathis

2nd Lieutenant Zale Stathis, USMC

Stathis knew he was about to die as the claws flew toward his throat. Hate filled the old man's eyes, right before they erupted in a spray of superheated gore. Another round ripped through his body, violently pushing the corpse away. Unrestricted now, Stathis drew his sidearm and placed another round in the collapsing body.

More fire erupted as another of the "refugees" ran toward Stathis, claws growing, hate filling the eyes. Blazer fire ripped into it, spraying the area with burning flesh and bone before it collapsed feet away from Stathis.

Weapons shifted to the remaining refugees, but they all fell to the ground, screaming in absolute terror.

"Check fire," Stathis said. He didn't want them to massacre the others.

"This is going to make things difficult," the major said, coming up to stand next to Stathis and look at the smoldering corpses.

"I don't even know who the new gods are, sir," Stathis said, taking a deep breath. He glanced over to see who had fired. Metzenberg and Starkova.

"Good job, gentlemen," Stathis said. A very officerly thing to say, but then he realized how he would have responded if some stuck-up officer had called him a gentleman. Damnit. He didn't want to insult them. "You guys rock."

"Thank you, sir," Starkova said. "The staff sergeant would have our balls if something happened to you."

There was a joke there, but Stathis couldn't think of anything. He had been so very close to dying.

"Yeah, well, I owe you," Stathis said, kneeling to look at the body more closely. "Face eaters strike again."

"*Unusual,*" Shrek said.

"*Unusual? Since we woke up from stasis we have been attacked by werewolves, vampires, demons, jackbooted thugs, and people that transform into monsters and you call* this *unusual?*"

"*The blood,*" Shrek said. "*It is more purple than red. Also, we are in an Inkeri zone and the claw hands should not be possible.*"

His SCBI was right. Stathis had seen bodies shredded by blazers. Mostly they were scorched, but not everything was burned by a blazer round. Sometimes the exploding flesh and bone caused other injuries, ripping apart muscle and bone, which caused bleeding and damage.

"*This is not normal for human blood, unless the blood is deoxygenated, not carrying oxygen,*" Shrek said. "*Furthermore, the organ placement doesn't seem right.*"

"*Something we can scan for as they approach our lines?*"

"*Some standard SOG civilian monitoring sensors might detect such abnormalities, but military sensors are not designed for such differentiation and clarity.*"

"*So, let's get some standard SOG civilian monitoring sensors.*"

"*They are extremely vulnerable to enemy EMP pulses.*"

"*So that is why they do that,*" Stathis said. He looked at the other civilians. "Do you know them?"

"No," said a short Asian woman as she clutched her two children closer. "They joined us a few hours ago. We don't know them. Please!"

"*Can we scan the others?*" Stathis asked.

"Not with standards sensors."

"Can't you recalibrate them or something? I thought you could work magic."

"Recalibration is possible, but perhaps you forgot how I mentioned increasing such sensitivity makes it more vulnerable to hostile EMPs? If we are pulsed, you will need replacement sensors because they will be completely burned out. I'm working with the SCBI network to find a solution."

"I will get bodies analyzed," Major Pervoi said.

"Thank you, sir," Stathis said.

"Why didn't you detect the absence of micro-expressions on the second one?" Stathis asked Shrek.

"Bad angle. I didn't see the face."

"Maybe that's something the troopers can watch for."

"It might not be the most reliable method," Shrek said. *"Regular humans may not have the ability to identify and assess such expressions."*

"The Legion can. And it's better than nothing."

"I will share this information with the others, but right now Legionnaires are needed to fight the enemy, not process refugees. Or will you volunteer for such duty?"

"Yeah. That would super suck. I would much rather fight face eaters and kick them in the teeth."

"Perhaps I will make that recommendation to Freya. The emperor may consider that duty a lot safer than running around like you are."

"Please don't," Stathis said. The gunny just might want to transfer him to a safer job.

"I won't," Shrek said, and Stathis was relieved. *"I'm a Marine, too, and would much rather be fighting than processing possible infiltrators."*

"Oorah," Stathis said. Sometimes with Shrek, he was just never sure.

"Now, we need to get back to Zvezda Two," Shrek said.

* * * * *

Chapter Fifty-Four:
Fighters

Captain Diamond Winters, USMC

The Weermag were persistent and unlike anything Winters had ever dealt with. Their ability to transition from Shorr space into lower Lunar orbit was extremely problematic for defensive operations. The larger ships could not be risked because the Weermag preceded their transitions with a volley of EMP missiles. Any Imperial ships in the vicinity would suffer. If the ships maintained a higher orbit, they moved faster and it was almost impossible for the Weermag to hit them, but then they couldn't maneuver fast enough to hurt the Weermag before they landed.

The Weermag also had jammers that interfered with automated systems, and Imperial engineers were still trying to figure them out. A functional Weermag ship emitted an energy that dramatically reduced the effectiveness of automated systems, like robots and auto-turrets.

Lunar orbit was a lot of territory, and while warships could maneuver, they could never maneuver fast enough. Winters was sure there were watchers planetside that could communicate with incoming vanhat so the gaps in coverage could be exploited.

The answer to that, of course, was Vanir-hardened drone fighters. The Republic fighters did not have human pilots so they could accelerate at speeds that would turn a human pilot to meat. They had enough redundant and hardened systems that provided resistance to the vanhat EMP. One weakness of the SOG-made fighters was that radio communication arrays rendered the drone vulnerable to EMP. The Republic fighters had a neutrino communication system, used heavily by the Aesir, which meant they could enclose the vulnerable components in a protective faraday cage. Vanir fighters still experienced failures but were far less vulnerable and could survive much closer explosions than SOG fighters.

Another significant problem was hacking attempts on Imperial fighters. Their radio communication systems made them vulnerable to that as well, and getting too close to the enemy caused them to self-destruct because the Imperial CAG lost control.

The biggest problem was that there wasn't an unlimited supply of Vanir-made fighters. The *Tyr* and the *Sleipner* were trying to make more but their manufactories had limits, and Inkeris were still considered top priority.

"Emergence," Brita reported.

Winters didn't waste time swearing. She had expected it because there was a gap, though a very small one. She watched the Vanir fighters accelerate toward the emergence. As usual, the first emergence was the EMP bombs.

This time something new slid out of Shorr space and at first it looked like it emerged and promptly fell apart. But then Winters saw they were enemy fighters. The first ship released almost twenty fighters that veered away from their carrier toward the Vanir fighters. The battle was about to change.

In seconds, the Vanir fighters were shattered wrecks scattered in orbit, part of a new debris cloud.

"They appeared to be AI-controlled fighters," Blitzen reported as Imperial warships boosted and began attacking with blazers and coil guns, laying down a barrage of fire.

More transport ships slid out of Shorr space and headed to the ground. At this range, their chances of reaching the surface were a lot higher.

"Paska," Brita said, and the *Eagle* accelerated hard once everyone reported secure and ready for hard maneuvers.

"Slippery bastards," Winters said, watching the vanhat drones slip out of the way.

"At this range, yes," Blitzen said. *"Their reaction times are good, but we can do better."*

"Small blessings," Winters said. *"We need to do better."*

Two enemy drones exploded. There was just too much incoming fire for them to evade, but other drone fighters were doing an admirable job of shooting down inbound Imperial missiles and shielding the transports that were bringing supplies and reinforcements to the hostiles on the ground. Blazers and coil guns couldn't be blocked, but the missiles that could send a cone of plasma or projectiles at a target were worse because they were closer and much harder to evade.

A squadron of Vanir drone fighters slipped into the chaos. They immediately started taking casualties.

"Can you take control of the fighters? Give them a better chance?" Winters asked Blitzen. The Vanir drone pilots were good, but obviously outclassed.

"Requesting control. I can help them dodge and evade, but not attack so easily. Incoming EMPs are disrupting targeting systems, and while there is sufficient bandwidth, I do not have the processor ability to do fight and evade."

"How about you evade and manage the systems, and I fight?" Winters said, remembering how ancient fighter pilots used to have two-person cockpits.

"Access request granted," Blitzen said. *"Converting your helmet view to VR of the fighter."*

"Brita, you have control of the *Eagle*," Winters said. Perhaps she should captain the vessel, but she also wanted to get up close and personal with the vanhat.

"Zen," Brita said, and the world around Winters changed. She was suddenly in formation surrounded by flashes of lightning. Incoming fire. Subtle changes in the ship felt like turbulence, but she knew it was Blitzen conducting evasive maneuvers.

Winters targeted the nearest vanhat fighter. She was familiar with Republic drone controls, so she knew the joystick in her hands controlled the drone and not the *Eagle* as she twisted it, causing the fighter to spin. She jammed the fire button and the vanhat drone exploded. A jerk and she thought a second drone had been hit, but it quickly stabilized.

Incoming fire cut toward her, and she slipped below it with Blitzen's help. She brought the nose back up, saw another enemy drone, and fired a burst from her blazer. She barely missed it, and it spun away as it tried to bring its nose back toward her.

Out of the corner of her eye, two fighters lit up, drawing her attention.

"They are targeting us," Blitzen reported, but Winters knew that before Blitzen spoke.

She spun her fighter and fired a burst at them, forcing them to evade and ruining their aim. A quick jink, and she fired another burst at a vanhat fighter.

Nearby, another Republic drone exploded.

"Space Legionnaires are linking in and controlling other Vanir fighters," Blitzen reported. Winters noticed a marked increase in the accuracy and effectiveness of outgoing Republic fire.

Now the vanhat fighters were suffering heavier casualties.

In minutes, the fight was over. The vanhat fighter carrier was a wreck smeared on the Lunar landscape. The transports it had been protecting had disgorged most of their cargo before being shredded by the Republic fighters.

The enemy weren't the only ones who could change and adapt quickly.

* * * * *

Chapter Fifty-Five:
Messages

Vanhat Commander – Kafasta

The tiny drone showed Kafasta what he didn't want to see. They had discovered the mbwiri infiltrators. He packaged that bit of information for burst transmission when the jamming let up long enough to get a transmission out.

The humans discovering the doppelgängers would complicate things, but Kafasta was sure there were already hundreds, maybe thousands, of infiltrators spreading out among the refugees. Tens of thousands of refugees had been allowed to "escape" the culling. Their only purpose was to act as cover for the doppelgängers. Now their usefulness might be at an end and the Weermag could finally eradicate those that had not infiltrated the human lines. He remembered another war where something similar had happened. A race of burrowing sentients that loved their tunnels beneath the surface of their jungle world.

Leaving non-combatants alive and un-slaughtered had been a difficult task, but Kafasta and the others had followed orders, carefully monitoring the pockets of survivors, coming close enough to terrorize them but not quite revealing the prey had been discovered. That had been a fun game, letting them think they had just narrowly escaped death. Of course, there had been the occasional stupid mentally deficient human, like the ancient Chutnika, that the Weermag were forced to kill. Prey did the dumbest things sometimes, and the Weermag took pleasure in removing such weaklings from the breeding pool.

The Chutnika were dead and gone, eradicated, their tunnels collapsed. Not even their bones still existed. They would only live on in his memory as a species that had been eliminated to appease the gods. The Chutnika had been small, and fighting through their tunnels had been difficult because the Weermag had to bend over almost everywhere. That was certainly a race that deserved extinction, like these humans, based on their Lunar facilities. Another race that liked to tunnel, though they were not as claustrophobic as the Chutnika had been. Still, why did slave races like to tunnel and cower?

Too many of these humans didn't fight for their life. Kafasta couldn't question the competence or ferocity of their fighters, but they appeared to be an exception to the rule. Killing them would leave the survivors defenseless.

Finally, the jamming eased, and they exchanged messages.

"The orders remain the same," Kafetan said, who, as his second in command, would receive the same data packets and authorizations. "This is dangerous."

"Agreed," Kafasta said. "The AIs will have a plan, though."

"I don't understand it."

"Neither will the humans."

"We are grinding ourselves against their forces and taking heavy casualties. We are letting the abandoned recover and become comfortable with the conflict. That is not in accordance with the Weermag code of war."

Kafasta realized why Kafetan was not in command, and it was Kafasta's duty to train the younger leader.

"Sometimes that is for the best. Let the enemy become comfortable, let them think they understand it. They too will think it has become a grind and will adjust their thinking to it. When they become complacent, we change the rules. They will not find all the mbwiri. I'm sure they have already infiltrated beyond the refugee camps."

"If only they had demons too," Kafetan said. Kafasta couldn't argue with that.

"Their ability to change would not allow their bodies to tolerate such implants. We cannot play with our prey and devour it too. Let the war run its course, and we will return to our long sleep until next time. Take pleasure in the frightened prey as they scream for mercy. We do not enjoy such pleasures in our tombs."

"This defiance is not normal," Kafetan said. His frustration was obvious.

"This defiance is normal for the prey of the Weermag," Kafasta said. "This is why the gods created the Weermag. We handle the most difficult prey. We are their serrated blade used to cripple and bleed the enemy, to destroy them for their insolence. We will make them suffer."

Kafetan remained silent, pondering.

"Do not rely on previous victories to prove future victories. Each battle must be fought to the best of our increasing abilities. We must not become complacent like our prey. We are the predators, and we will be victorious. The gods will continue to challenge us with greater enemies."

"We live for the hunt," Kafetan said. "I worry that these humans defy us so."

"The Weermag have never lost," Kafasta said. That was true. "Never. In all the purges, we have always been victorious. Do not think these humans stand a chance. We still have many more ships and troops waiting to enter the fight. We will build more, and we will swarm the humans like ponteen at feeding time if we must. We are warriors, we outnumber the humans three to one in this fight, and a hundred to one in the galaxy. We will not fail. Accept this challenge of your abilities. Rise to the occasion."

Kafetan's snarl was one of satisfaction. "The greatest trials bring the greatest rewards."

Kafasta would let the grub believe that. The fight was the greatest reward. The sweet victory of the last human being devoured was what Kafasta anticipated.

"We have our orders," Kafasta said. "We must strike elsewhere. Leave this outpost to think we have forgotten them so they will not be ready when a hunter company assaults them. Perhaps we will be tasked to block reinforcements and cut them from behind."

Kafasta watched a patrol move past the hidden Weermag. He saw the bodies of the mbwiri they carried on their four-legged robots. He was half tempted to give the command and wipe them out. They had no clue how close and how numerous his warriors were.

Let them have the bodies, let them study the mbwiri corpses. They would soon have more bodies to examine, Kafasta was sure. Wiping out this small unit would just be one of a thousand cuts, but it would reveal that the nearby outpost was in extreme danger, and Kafasta wanted to keep their presence a secret until it was time to wipe them out.

Patience was the virtue of the hunter.

While the hunter could make many mistakes and the prey only one, he savored the absolute power and precision of a perfect assault.

* * * * *

Chapter Fifty-Six:
Squadrons

Captain Diamond Winters, USMC

The virtual reality conference was the only real option at the moment, and Winters looked around her at the other officers. These conferences were becoming more common, and the SCBIs did a great job of making everything realistic.

"We need more Republic fighters," Captain Mamine said. He was a gruff Imperial Legion captain who was former Fleet. Winters wasn't sure if his attitude toward the Republic liaison was because he didn't like the Republic, or if he was just like that. Mamine scowled a lot, but Winters got the impression it was his personality and not his attitude.

"We don't print them on paper," Eversti Solja Saulson said, a thin, hawkish Republic officer. "We are making them as fast as we can, but they are being destroyed faster than we can create them."

"Transfer the tech codes to the Lunar facilities," Mamine said. "We can help make them."

"I'm not authorized for that," Saulson said. "That is proprietary Republic technology; the communication array especially."

"Can Imperial fighters be retrofitted?" Winters asked, but the second she asked, she knew the answer.

"No," Mamine said. "Republic fighters have better EMP shielding in addition to the comm array. The basic design of SOG—uh, Imperial

363

364 | WILLIAM S. FRISBEE, JR.

fighters has EMP hardening but not to the level of Republic fighters. The radio antenna is a serious weak spot for both EMP bursts and incoming hack attempts. Governance engineers knew there was only so much they could do. The Berus class three is built around the Aesir communication links and designed to integrate with Republic systems. Also, Imperial drones are not able to take advantage of the higher network bandwidth. We are working on an Ulfbert model which should work better for SCBI-equipped pilots, but they aren't ready yet."

Winters knew the Republic would not share the tech codes for their Aesir communicators, and to be fair, she wasn't sure she could argue that. What if the vanhat got that technology? She was hearing about more hacking activity planetside, and SCBIs were having to spend more time on network security. The vanhat had released a virus into the systems that was causing all sorts of problems. The Moon was not the bastion it had once been. Now it was vulnerable. It was being violated, and no place in the Sol System was safe from attack.

The Weermag were attacking the Empire in many ways, and the Empire still did not know how many there were, where they were coming from, or what they were fully capable of.

"We are fighting for the survival of the human species," Mamine said.

"Lunar facilities are not secure," Saulson said. "Republic communication systems, besides your SCBIs, are the only real advantage we have over these Weermag. Do you want them to capture the technology?"

Mamine scowled but didn't argue.

"What can we provide to the Republic to speed up production?"

Saulson shook his head sadly. "Taking over Inkeri production has helped, and we can concentrate more on the Beruses but our manufactories have limits. The tolerance required to manufacture some parts are the issue. Our engineers have designed a pairing mechanism that will completely prevent hacking because the drone fighter will have to be paired with a control node that is the only link. This will reduce the production times slightly and improve security dramatically but still there are tolerances we cannot escape. Our manufactories can print parts but are vulnerable to overheating and require regular maintenance. Simple physics is a limitation right now. We are trying to bring additional manufactories online, but that is a laborious process, and the battlestars were designed as warships, not manufactory ships. The support vessels are also working overtime. They are creating the more difficult parts. SCBIs are helping streamline the process, but there are limits."

Winters understood if Mamine didn't. Manufactories were not just 3D printers. They were automated lathes, smelters, fully automated factories that could produce almost anything.

"We can transmit shell specifications," Saulson said. "If Lunar factories could make the armored shell and drive components, we can concentrate on the comms and other internal systems."

"Weapons?" Mamine asked and Saulson looked at Winters.

"We are going to experiment with particle disruptor cannons," Winters said. "They are being made aboard the Republic ships as well. The technology from Quantico looks like it can be fitted on smaller drone fighters and will have a significant advantage over blazers because they are based on the particle cannon technology."

"Have they been tested?" Saulson asked.

"Not in combat," Winters said. "We have to be more careful putting them on manned systems because of the radiation they generate, but drones are an excellent candidate."

"Shouldn't we concentrate on combat-tested systems?"

"They will be modular," Winters said, reading the data Blitzen was feeding her. Mamine would be getting the same information. "An outer shell that can be opened to swap out modules with six hard points for the new Ulfberts."

Mamine nodded.

"We would like to retrofit the Berus and the new Ulfbert for dedicated SCBI and pilot control," Saulson said. "Squadrons can operate with the old American "Loyal Wingman" concept. A primary craft that is surrounded and guarded by other fighters. Each Berus, and eventually Ulfbert, fighter can be controlled by a pilot. Should that fighter be destroyed, the pilot can link to another of the drone fighters in the squadron. If a fighter is not actively being controlled, then AI will fly the fighter as a regular drone that will mimic and support the primary. We can train regular troopers with SCBIs to operate them."

"Excellent," Mamine said.

"Speaking of sharing technology," Saulson said. "It would help a great deal if you shared the SCBIs with the Republic."

"Above my paygrade," Mamine said, and Winters knew that came from Mathison. He was still in a pissing match with Admiral Carpenter and didn't want to give the technology to Carpenter who could fly off to deep space and fall prey to the vanhat. Winters was staying out of that. She understood Mathison not wanting to give that technology to Carpenter without some assurance the commander of the Republic task force wouldn't abandon Sol. Maybe that would change, but Winters had no idea.

Right now, the Wolf Legion, as it was being called, was proving extremely loyal to the emperor, and while the Republic was an excellent ally, Winters doubted they would stick around for the long haul.

She was surprised they were still here, to be honest. The Legion was more accepting of them, but other ex-SOG military forces were still extremely unfriendly to Republic forces.

"Either way," Mamine said, "we need more of them. A lot more. When paired with SCBI-equipped Legionnaires, they make a difference. We are also struggling to supply the pilots. We are barely ahead of production and even using regular ground troops as pilots we don't have enough."

"I know," Saulson said. "I know."

Winters would have thought that equipment would be in less demand than trained pilots, but she knew how thin the Legion was being stretched. They might be the only ones able to hold the Empire together against the Weermag.

"Transition," Blitzen reported. *"Another Weermag strike force transitioning into low orbit."*

"Paska!" Saulson said. "When are they going to run out of ships and troops?"

The meeting link closed, and Winters slipped into a drone fighter. There was already a Legion pilot commanding drones that were closer, but there was an opening for Winters, and she took it. That was another protocol that was developing. Whoever was in command of the squadron called the shots and other pilots joining the battle did so at the squadron leader's direction.

Spreading out below her were more Weermag ships and the drone she was controlling fell upon them like a swooping hawk, blazers firing. She had just missed the EMP pulses and the Weermag drone fighters climbed into Lunar orbit to engage the drones Winters was with.

Maybe she could get some sleep tomorrow.

* * * * *

Chapter Fifty-Seven:
Talking to the Enemy

Captain Duffy Sinclair, ODT

Sinclair knew they wouldn't break through as they attacked Zvezda Two, again. It was almost like they weren't trying, though they took heavy casualties. They also inflicted heavy casualties and defending Zvezda Two was not as easy as he would have liked. There were now a lot of troops stationed at or near Zvezda Two, and although the perimeter around the capital habitat had been pushed out, the vanhat were still sneaking in assault teams.

These vanhat were canny, absolutely lethal, and didn't just throw themselves into the weapons fire of the troopers defending the emperor.

"Incoming transmission," Finn said. *"Voice only."*

"From who?" Sinclair asked. Was there a nearby unit? Were they cut off and under attack?

"Unknown."

"Open link," Sinclair said, glancing at his XO. Most of the time only Governance officers had the gear to accept unencrypted and open-link transmissions, though ODT armor allowed it. The enemy could not transmit to his troops, which was a carryover. The Governance didn't like the enemy sending propaganda to regular troopers, and

officers were loyal enough to listen. Enlisted rarely, if ever, used it or monitored unencrypted channels.

"Humans," the voice said, and it obviously was not human. It was too deep, with something of a lisp. "We are the Weermag. The gods have decreed your destruction if you oppose us."

"We are opposing you," Stathis said. He must have returned and was doing rounds. Apparently, he didn't know Sinclair was linked in, too. "You have bad breath, which might be because of your diet. I hear veganism is all the rage. Have you tried that?"

"The gods have decreed your death."

"You sound like you desperately need a chocolate bar. Why tell us? You need to keep reminding yourself because you keep forgetting?"

"Your fear gives us pleasure," the Weermag said.

"Have you tried a candy bar? Simple minds, simple pleasures," Stathis said, and Sinclair smiled. "You might have to go somewhere else to get your rocks off. We're just going to curb stomp your skull. We're just waiting for the light to turn green and then we get mean. We are going to kick your ass, like stepping in poop on the grass. I'll put your heart on a cart, smash your face with my mace, and give your spleen to a queen."

The Weermag was silent as Sinclair tried to figure out what Stathis was up to. The young man certainly had a bizarre imagination and method of threatening the enemy.

"The Weermag will fail," Sinclair said on the link, letting Stathis know he was here. It wouldn't surprise Sinclair if other Legionnaires were listening in as well.

"Oh, uh, sorry sir," Stathis said. "Didn't know others got the killer rabbit's little threats. They're all threat and bluster. I remember talking to one of the Jotun, some sissy named Nasaraf. He talked a mean line, but in the end he got squished like the little bitch he was. I've also heard others. Lots of talk. They could take lessons in intimidation from a Marine gunny."

Sinclair smiled. He had heard some of those recorded conversations. That Stathis could make light of them eased Sinclair's apprehension a bit.

"So, Mister Wierdbag," Stathis said to the Weermag, "I'll let you talk with my captain. He's probably going to be even less impressed than me. He's a badass, and I think he's killed quite of few of you scum suckers. Quick question, though, is Wierdbag the name of your, uh, god-wannabe, or the name of your vanhat form?"

"Weermag is the name of our species. We have served the gods for many purges. We are ancient and this is our original form, a form of perfection and efficiency. While your species was still sludge in a primordial ocean, we were hunting the darkness, testing ourselves against the most dangerous creatures in this galaxy."

"That's cute," Stathis said. "Adorable really. We humans didn't evolve to the top of our food chain to become prey for some overexcited cannibal thugs. We are just getting warmed up while it sounds like you geriatrics are due for retirement."

"I agree," Sinclair said. Was Stathis going to turn the conversation over to him, or keep going? What was Stathis trying to accomplish? Sinclair wasn't sure he wanted to take over at this point. Stathis was entertaining enough. "As the lieutenant said, your species sounds like it's past due for retirement, and we will be more than happy to retire you."

"Thank you, Captain," Stathis said. "Can you Wierdbag's hurry with your attack? I want to have lunch in an hour. Lasagna is pretty

372 | WILLIAM S. FRISBEE, JR.

good, might even be some pizza. Maybe that's why you guys suck so much, your diet."

The link closed and a private link from Stathis came in.

"Sorry, sir," Stathis said.

"For what?" Sinclair asked.

"Said I would turn over the conversation to you but—"

"But what?"

"I dunno, sir, just trying to piss them off. Pissed off enemies make stupid mistakes, and I want them to hurry and launch their attack if they're going to do it. I hate it when I'm halfway through a good meal, and I have to let it get cold while I run off and fight bad guys. As a growing young man, I need my food, and Zvezda Two has some of the best chow."

"I think we can handle any attacks they launch," Sinclair said. "You go get lunch, Lieutenant. Welcome back. How are things out near the front lines?"

"Thank you, sir. The front lines suck, too. The wierdbags aren't talkative there, but we found some doppelgängers among the refugees."

"Doppelgängers?" Sinclair asked, and Finn displayed a report with video files on his cybernetic view.

"Yes, sir," Stathis said. "They can transform and look human. There was this one vanhat I met, a Commissar Summers or Willis. I forget. I called him Mister Punchy because he liked to ask questions with his fists, if you know the type. We thought he was human until he got all face-eaty."

No civilians or unvetted people were allowed anywhere near Zvezda Two. There wasn't enough data to show if they could get past Governance security yet.

"Are these doppelgängers human?"

"I dunno, sir," Stathis said. "Maybe they're capturing humans and taking their form? Or something like that. They aren't good with micro-expressions, so if you're quick you can catch 'em."

Something else to worry about. Obviously, Inkeris didn't stop them or do anything against the Weermag.

Could they get among his troops?

"I don't think they are a threat to troops, sir," Stathis said. "Yet. They have purple blood and their insides aren't human from what I've seen."

"Based on initial scans they can emulate human," Finn said. *"But beneath the skin they are alien. The full range of their capabilities is unknown."*

"I wouldn't want to be a civilian though," Stathis said.

Sinclair couldn't argue.

"A squad has arrived from Camp Lupine," Finn reported. Which was good news. More Legionnaires would definitely help bolster the lines. These were enlisted though, less ideologically indoctrinated than Legion officers, and Sinclair wasn't sure how he felt about that. The pipeline for Legionnaires was growing, but not nearly fast enough. Finn had told him that InSec was still strict about who was allowed into the Legion, but Sinclair just wasn't sure. The Governance military wouldn't change overnight.

Camp Lupine was what they were calling the newest facility for turning ODT, Fleet, or Guard troops into Legionnaires.

They needed to speed up.

* * * * *

Chapter Fifty-Eight:
Birds

2nd Lieutenant Zale Stathis, USMC

Stathis wanted another platoon. This was getting awkward. For weeks he had been fighting with warriors at Zvezda Two while "his" platoon underwent what was officially being called training and indoctrination at Camp Lupine, and now they were coming back to him. Shrek had just informed him they were on their way.

Sinclair had been using him as a fill-in platoon commander and executive officer. Stathis wasn't sure he enjoyed it. Shrek took care of most of the annoying administrative bullshit that kept most executive officers busy, but acting as Sinclair's deputy and commanding the company when Sinclair was sleeping or otherwise attending meetings or briefings kept him busy.

"They will be here tomorrow," Shrek said as Stathis walked the lines of Zvezda Two.

"They're going to hate me," Stathis said.

"Why do you think that?"

"Now they'll know what a fake I am. You gave me the edge that they couldn't match. Now they'll be just as capable."

"You underestimate yourself," Shrek said. It was Shrek's job to bolster his ego and encourage him. Stathis wasn't a fool. Soon he would be

just another guy with a SCBI among thousands. A private pretending to be an officer.

Stathis looked up at the ceiling. The birds weren't real; they were just images, a pity. He was on his way to a Guard barracks to review their training for a surprise "inspection." Beside him was Senior Sergeant Podgorni, a tall guy that got on Stathis' nerves, mostly because he was a head taller. He was acting duty staff NCO and had wanted to come along. Perhaps he was as restless as Stathis. The vanhat hadn't attacked in days, which could mean the patrols were more successful, but Stathis didn't believe that. They were planning something; he was sure of it. Noise makers, annoying little fist-sized robots that hammered at things and generated a lot of noise, made it impossible to listen for Weermag patrols or activity. They had hidden plenty of them in the area, which made it hard to find them.

Zvezda Two was a marvel of engineering. At the top, the radius was about a kilometer and a half, the bottom was a kilometer and it rotated completely once every twenty seconds, providing a full gravity. The "ceiling," which dipped down into the bowl, was a massive view screen that provided a view of a beautiful sky. Occasionally, a robot skimmed through the sky, cleaning off the viewscreen.

Walking through the habitat made Stathis feel like he was strolling through a park. There were plenty of "surface" structures, but most structures were buried in the bowl. There were a lot of tunnels, which was what service personnel and troops usually used, but Stathis enjoyed seeing the trees and bushes and odd little streams. It almost felt like he was back on Earth, and he found it soothing.

Usually.

He had lived with the platoon for so long, and he hadn't told them about Shrek. Now they would have their own assistants, and Stathis felt like he'd been keeping a secret from them. When they arrived, how could they not resent him not telling them? They would also learn that he had been a US Marine private before being assigned as their platoon commander.

"Wouldn't it be a good idea to assign them elsewhere and assign me a new platoon?" Stathis asked Shrek. Maybe a platoon that didn't know him so well?

"No. Every single one has requested to be re-assigned to your unit. The emperor has approved this."

Another decision the gunny probably hadn't thought out. He was too busy these days making big emperor decisions. The fact he bothered to involve himself in Stathis' career could be flattering, but Stathis wished the gunny would think things through a little more. Of course, he couldn't call the gunny or Shrek fools, but they probably didn't understand things as well as Stathis. They weren't "the man on the ground." Well. Shrek was, but Shrek was not the best with advice on social interaction. He was still having a hard time hooking up with Hakala, who was still aboard the *Eagle,* and the *Eagle* was in Lunar orbit trying to reduce the number of Weermag ships that survived to make it to the surface.

They had both been busy. She was spending more time as a drone operator than an HKT and Stathis could understand her dissatisfaction there. She was the physical, in your face, knee in your groin, knife in your ribs, type of fighter. Piloting a drone for long hours every day had to be mind-numbing and unpleasant.

"You think Hakala is gaining weight as a drone operator?" Stathis asked.

Shrek's pause indicated one of two things: he was checking or was surprised at this change in conversational direction.

378 | WILLIAM S. FRISBEE, JR.

"No," Shrek said. *"She is almost as fanatical about working out as you are. Saying anything like that in her presence may require you to spend time in the ICU. I would recommend against bringing that up."*

Statis looked up at the viewscreen sky. Those birds weren't real, and Stathis didn't think there were any birds alive on Earth. The only birds alive were in captivity.

"Weird, aren't they, sir?" Podgorni said. "Very distracting. There used to be actual birds that didn't live in cages and flew in the skies of Earth?"

"Yeah," Stathis said. "We had some rednecks in the Raiders that liked to hunt them and supplement our rations. They were so much better than MREs. Which was good and bad. If we were in the field for a short time, it kept the MREs from plugging us up, if you know what I mean. If we were in the field much? We weren't plugged up."

"Plugged?"

Stathis glanced over at Podgorni.

"Um. Constipated? MREs would get stuck and keep us from taking a shit if that was all we ate. Taking a shit after we got back from the field could be bloody and—"

Stathis paused. Perhaps Podgorni didn't need to know all that. That was history, and it reminded Stathis of things he would rather forget. Maybe that was the problem. Back on Base 402, he hadn't been plugged up enough? It had been an unpleasant experience running or moving tactically with his pants full of shit. These days he was fanatical about making sure the plumbing was hooked up right. So much so that he sometimes practiced hooking it up as a drill. Not a pleasant experience and not something he ever wanted someone to see, but as a lieutenant who people were supposed to respect and admire, he had to be quick and efficient in everything. There were things he had to avoid in the future.

"Understood, sir," Podgorni said, and Stathis caught him glancing up at the sky. "I've never seen a real bird except on a screen."

"Not even at a zoo or something?"

"Why go to a zoo? The Governance considered such things frivolous and unnecessary. People can see such creatures on view screens and get a better look. Seeing things live and in person? A waste of resources."

"That sucks," Stathis said.

Opposite the ceiling down in the center of the bowl was an island that didn't rotate. It led to the data centers, hydroponics, and other facilities that serviced Zvezda Two.

Walking around inside a bowl was stranger to Stathis than birds in the sky.

"Will the emperor ever restore Earth to its glory, sir?" Podgorni wondered aloud.

"Sure," Stathis said. "Eventually, I'm sure. Gotta kick the vanhat off, but I'm sure he wants to go fishing or camping. He would probably love to lead a regimental run up Mount Motherfu—um, high-ranking officers loved running in big formations; it gets their dick hard. I'm sure the emperor would enjoy a good run."

Podgorni glanced at Stathis.

"Mount Motherfu?"

"A less popular hill in San Diego, California," Stathis said. "I never spent much time there. I went to Parris Island for boot camp. It's where the real men go. We had bloodthirsty sand fleas, sand, and swamp, not hills. When I did squad leader school in Hawaii, we had this place called KT. Gods, I hated that hill. One time they made us go up it backward. Those were some sadistic bastards."

A thought occurred to Stathis. He came to a sudden stop and looked up at the birds. "Shit."

Podgorni stopped and brought his rifle up halfway.

"I was wondering why the vanhat hadn't attacked us in a while," Stathis said.

"Our patrols are pushing them out further, sir," Podgorni said.

"That is what they want us to think. These weirdbags are canny sons of bitches. What's above us?"

"A viewscreen?" Podgorni asked, looking up at the birds and clouds.

"And above that?"

"A lot of reinforced rock," Podgorni said. There was a pillar that rose up from the island to touch the ceiling and Stathis knew it contained some small service tunnels for robots, but there were facilities up in the ceiling, too. Not many, but some.

"Those bastards," Stathis said and then to Shrek, *"They're digging. We need to find out where they're coming at us from."*

"Explain," Shrek said, but Stathis knew Shrek understood.

"Those noisemakers are being used to hide their digging. They're almost ready so they're letting us think we've been victorious, so we'll start pushing out our patrols to look for them, but they're here."

"What do you mean?" Podgorni asked.

"The wierdbags are above us," Stathis said aloud. "Getting ready to attack."

Podgorni turned away and spoke into his link. Stathis saw alerts go out, but he wasn't sure if that was Shrek or Podgorni.

"You think they'll launch an attack or just drop a nuke on us?" Stathis asked Shrek. He would drop the nuke if they just wanted to kill the emperor and destroy the Zvezda Two data encryption controllers.

"We need to evacuate," Shrek said.

"No shit," Stathis said, scanning the ceiling. How much time did they have?

Aesir robots began pouring out of hidden hatches, their weapons aimed at the ceiling. Stathis knew he was going to look like an idiot if he was wrong. He wanted to look stupid and get busted to private. If he was right, he really hoped the emperor didn't promote him.

* * * * *

Chapter Fifty-Nine:
Diversion

2nd Lieutenant Zale Stathis, USMC

Stathis wanted to point his weapon at the ceiling, but there was a lot of it, and they could come through almost anywhere.

"We are evacuating the emperor," Shrek said. *"There is a ninety percent chance you are correct."*

"Why didn't you figure this out?" Stathis said, trying to figure out the best place for a lieutenant to be when vanhat fell from the ceiling. In all the movies, the lieutenant would be right below where the enemy attacked and would probably be the first to die. Or the lieutenant would be cowering in a bunker or something. Didn't the guy discovering the enemy always die first in movies?

A Marine lieutenant should be where he could best control the battle that was about to begin. How did you fight a ceiling, though?

"That was a creative leap," Shrek said. *"We've been over this haven't we? I'm very good at data analysis and extrapolation. You are more of a creative thinker."*

"I think outside the box. Yeah, I remember. But this isn't a box. This is a big bowl buried in the Moon, and the enemy wants to eat our faces."

"You are the lieutenant. Quit whining and do lieutenant things."

"Great. What lieutenant things? What does the manual say to do about face-eating weirdbags about to pour out of the ceiling and kill you?"

"What do you think?" Shrek asked, and Stathis scowled. A teaching moment? Shrek could be as bad as the gunny sometimes.

"We don't know where they're coming down," Stathis said. They could break through the ceiling almost anywhere, and it didn't have to be just one place. They also didn't have to attack; just create a hole big enough to drop a nuke.

"And?"

"Establish mutually supporting strong points that can cover the evacuation of the emperor and staff," Stathis said. *"Establish a line of retreat. Establish a spearhead to lead the emperor out of this trap and keep him secure."*

"Good, but you aren't alone."

"Yeah," Stathis said. *"Delegate."*

Stathis opened a link to Captain Sinclair. "Captain? I'm going to establish a couple of strong points here in the main chamber. If you want to take the ready platoon and evacuate the emperor through tunnel Zulu I think that is the safest route out right now."

Tunnel Zulu was an auxiliary tunnel that led halfway around the Moon. Dug through the mantle, it was a secret escape route. The Weermag might suspect it, but Stathis doubted they could do anything about it. It was also monitored and patrolled.

"Wilco," Sinclair said.

"Main entrance is under attack," Shrek reported. *"It may be a diversion."*

"The diversion you are ignoring is the main attack," Stathis said.

"What?" Sinclair asked.

"Um, sorry, sir," Stathis said. "My SCBI informed me the main entrance is under attack and says it is probably a diversion. I was just quoting one of Murphy's laws of combat that, um, never mind."

"I will have some troops sent to reinforce the entrances," Sinclair said. "You secure the main habitat chamber."

Stathis looked around. That was a lot of territory to cover.

"Aye, sir," Stathis said. There wouldn't be enough troops.

"If I was a wierdbag face eater, what would I do?" Stathis asked Shrek. *"No shit your pants jokes."*

"You would launch a multi-prong attack designed to achieve your objective," Shrek said. *"The diversion at the main entrance doesn't make sense, though."*

"What's the objective? Killing the emperor and destroying the data center can be done by dropping a nuke on us. Why launch an attack?"

"Secondary entrance is now under attack. Colonel Baker is sending forces there to reinforce."

"Shit," Stathis said. *"What if that's what they want? Launch several attacks and try to get the emperor to retreat into an ambush?"*

"Sharing the data with other SCBI and officers."

"They get the emperor, our resistance crumbles, and they capture the data center and decryptors. Shit."

"You sound paranoid," Shrek said.

"It is not paranoia when they really are out to get you."

A section of the ceiling began flashing and moving.

"Heat differential," Shrek said, and Stathis fired at it as it moved away from him.

"What the hell?" Stathis said as his blazer fire ripped apart the viewscreen and the damage also moved away from him. Like a tear in the sky flying away. *"Why is it moving? How are they doing that?"*

"The ceiling is not moving," Shrek explained. *"You and the view on the screen are moving. You are in a bowl, remember?"*

More weapons reached up and blazer rounds cut into the ceiling and rock.

Stathis could see where that part of the ceiling would make its circle and come back to him.

"Only one fireteam fire," Stathis said and designated a cluster of robots controlled by a team of Praetorians. The others obeyed him and ceased fire. "We don't want to do their work for them and dig them out with our fire."

Did he have to say that and explain it to the people here? It should be obvious, but lieutenants were supposed to state the obvious, weren't they? Or was that the platoon sergeant's job? Other troopers from Sinclair's company arrived, and Stathis pointed them to locations where they would have a good viewpoint to cover the rest of the habitat.

Overall, the habitat wasn't huge, but it was when you were trying to make sure weapons covered every square meter.

Another spot brightened on the ceiling, and Stathis assigned another team to fire at it.

The blazer rounds could pierce two meters of rock depending on the type of rock. Stathis didn't know what the Weermag were using to dig their tunnel, but it probably wasn't blazer proof, and if they could delay them from breaking into the main habitat that would give the gunny time to escape, or at least break out of the trap he was about to end up in.

"I hear you figured out the Weermag before they attacked. Good job. You doing okay, Lieutenant?" asked Mathison on a direct link. Stathis was flattered the gunny would take the time.

"Doing good, Gunny," Stathis said. "Um, Emperor." He would have to settle on one or the other someday. Why hadn't the gunny told him? "They're attacking all the entrances and trying to go all airborne and drop on us from above. Gonna be like shooting ducks in a barrel."

"Fish in a barrel, dumbass," Mathison said. "Keep your head down. Baker's evacuating me, and I don't want any stupid heroics."

"Aye, Gunny," Stathis said. "You get out of here. I've got your back. If I don't make it, maybe you and Skadi can name a little gunny after me?"

"Shut up, Stathis," Mathison said.

"Aye, Gunny," Stathis said. "Quick question, though. Did you figure out when the wedding is? Or where?"

"I haven't asked her," Mathison said.

"Dude, Gunny, you gotta ask her sooner instead of later, you know."

Another spot on the ceiling began heating up, and Stathis got a bad feeling. The spots were too far apart for the Weermag to just be changing things around a little bit. There were at least three tunnels coming down. The Weermag had been busy. Stathis marked it for another fire team.

"Since when did I start taking relationship advice from you?" Mathison asked.

"Since you got too busy doing emperor things and forgot to think with your dick occasionally. That's important too, you know. I have plenty of experience thinking with my dick. There was once this place in Papua New Guinea that—"

"Stathis," Mathison said, that warning in his voice.

"Sorry, sir," Stathis said. "Let me rephrase that as a fancy pants lieutenant. You need to think about the continuation of your dynasty and the welfare of your subjects. You have many duties, Emperor Mathison, and your people need more than your wisdom."

"Shut up, Stathis, and keep your head down. Don't make me regret promoting you to first lieutenant any more than I am."

The link closed.

The first breakthrough finally opened, and bodies fell through.

No, they weren't bodies. Bodies didn't return accurate fire as they fell to the ground.

Stathis hoped Mathison had made it to the tunnel. These Weermag were tough, dangerous bastards, and he could already tell there were a lot of them.

Wait.

Had the Emperor just promoted him to first lieutenant? That meant he would posthumously be promoted to captain.

Cool.

* * * *

Chapter Sixty: Breakthrough

Prime Minister Wolf Mathison, USMC

The unions on Earth were complaining again about long hours, and Mathison was considering an orbital bombardment. He could now understand despots who finally got sick of people and ordered tanks and soldiers to open fire. Arguing with the worker unions on Earth was like arguing with a narcissistic toddler. Six hours a day was not overworking someone, and they didn't need an increase in pay for working eight. People were starving, and the vanhat were destroying transports faster than they could be built or salvaged.

Everyone thought they were critical to the war effort and refused to seriously acknowledge the war didn't revolve around their individual contribution.

"Those union sons of bitches live in their own little worlds," Mathison said, growling as he closed the link. He didn't enjoy having to rely on Feng and InSec to "encourage" people.

"They do," Skadi said, pushing back from her desk. "They are discouraged from traveling and are fed a bunch of propaganda. Furthermore, they are pressured by authorities to avoid thinking for themselves and obey. 'Compliance is kindness.' They have been told how critical and important they are for too long."

"Don't they realize we are losing Earth? Now maybe the Moon?" Mathison asked. He knew the answer, of course.

"Of course, they do," Skadi said. "But they are scared. Scared people find comfort in patterns. They want to resist these changes and problems, and they are resisting the only way they know how."

"They shouldn't be resisting the people trying to save them," Mathison said. One of the things he liked about her was she could be devil's advocate and take an opposing view to help him see all angles.

"That is all they know. Paska!"

Mathison checked her display.

"The Weermag are breaking through the main lines. This appears to be a major assault. They have tunneled around some bottlenecks and the lines in sectors Aarne and Berta are collapsing. This is a major push."

"What do you need from me?" Mathison asked.

"We might need to commit Aesir to holding the line," Skadi said. "This is getting bad."

The door slid open, and Colonel Baker came in as an alert flashed on Mathison's cybernetic display.

"The Weermag are launching an attack," Baker said. Behind him a team of Praetorians entered, weapons at the ready.

Mathison made a point of looking around. Of course, they were. But here? Zvezda Two?

"So, what's new? Have they made it in?"

"Maybe," Baker said and pointed at Mathison's helmet. "I need you to armor up. I think it would be best to evacuate you to site Beta."

"Evacuate? I thought you and your Praetorians had the situation under control."

"Lieutenant Stathis suspects the Weermag are distracting us and tunneling down. They are—"

A red alert flashed across Mathison's display. He slipped on his helmet, then pulled his rifle from the holder on the side of his desk. Skadi was doing the same.

"The lieutenant thinks they're tunneling and could drop a nuke on our head."

Mathison wanted to swear. He had a meeting with the Lunar Steel workers union in an hour. He didn't know what he was going to promise them. A firing squad was tempting, but that wasn't the kind of emperor he wanted to be, so he had to figure something out. His meeting with the transport union on Earth had not gone well, and he had skipped breakfast.

"I thought you had pushed out the Weermag," Mathison said.

"War is a democracy," Baker said. "The enemy gets to vote, too. Do you want me to drag your ass out of here?"

"No," Mathison said. He was confident Baker would have his Praetorians try. Baker was nervous.

"You need to hurry," Freya said. *"He is right."*

"Why didn't we have any warning?"

"The Weermag have been using decoys and sporadic attacks to mask their activity, it appears. Their attempt to break out of the stalemate might also be a diversion. Lieutenant Stathis suspected they were up to something and realized they might tunnel down. He shared the data with Shrek and additional analysis indicates a high likelihood."

"You didn't figure this out?"

"Based on general data? No. The Weermag are exceptionally subtle. They appear to have implanted AI assistants as well, and this is giving them an advantage we are not used to dealing with. The precision and techniques they are using

were not intuitive or easily deduced without that leap. It is a very creative method if the lieutenant is correct."

Mathison followed Baker into the basement to the escape tunnel. There were plenty of Praetorians around and they looked ready to shoot anything and everything. How the hell could the Weermag get at him?

"Breach detected," Freya said. *"Lieutenant Stathis is deploying troops and engaging the Weermag. Additionally, attacks on the perimeter entrances are picking up in tempo. These are more than just raids. Colonel Baker has already alerted the reserves. He is not overreacting."*

Running away from a fight didn't feel right.

"Stathis figured it out?" Mathison asked Freya.

"Affirmative. Though might be too late."

"It's not too late," Mathison said. It would be too late when he was dead, or the nuke went off.

Down in the subbasement, there were six tube cars designed to speed through the escape tubes to other parts of the Moon. Mathison had known they were here but had honestly never expected to use them. Zvezda Two really was buried deep inside the Moon's mantle. An infantry attack might be the only way to attack it without ripping apart the Moon itself, and Mathison was sure if the Weermag could, they would.

Every report he had received on the Weermag had made Mathison realize they were the vanhat elite, or if they weren't, then humanity was going to get a really nasty surprise, assuming the Weermag weren't victorious.

On Earth, the vanhat forces continued to grow in strength and commanders were resorting to orbital strikes with alarming frequency, but those vanhat weren't a fraction as scary as the Weermag.

Now he was going to have to evacuate and leave Zvezda Two. The center of his power. The place that had become his comfort zone.

"Open a link to Stathis," Mathison told Freya.

"He is busy and about to face a Weermag assault from above."

"He can multitask."

"Link open," Freya said.

"I hear you figured out the Weermag before they attacked. Good job. You doing okay, Lieutenant?" Mathison said. Stathis was thinking, and that might have saved them all.

"Doing good, Gunny," Stathis said. "Um, Emperor. They're attacking all the entrances and trying to go all airborne and drop on us from above. Gonna be like shooting ducks in a barrel."

"Fish in a barrel dumbass," Mathison said. Stathis was distracted and nervous. He was doing a good job of hiding it, but Mathison could tell. "Keep your head down. Baker's evacuating me, and I don't want any stupid heroics."

Mathison remembered defending and then evacuating a different bunker on another planet. There Stathis had come back for him. Mathison owed the young man.

"Aye, Gunny. You get out of here. I've got your back. If I don't make it, maybe you and Skadi can name a little gunny after me?"

"Shut up, Stathis," Mathison said. That was a line of thought he didn't want to follow. Skadi would certainly have something to say. He knew Stathis had his back, but who had Stathis' back? Mathison was sure that if he slowed down, Baker was going to club him and drag him away by his feet. The ex-Delta Force operator was mean enough as it was.

"Aye, Gunny," Stathis said. "Quick question, though. Did you figure out when the wedding is? Or where?"

That was something else Mathison didn't want to think about. It was easy to find another problem to focus on, and Mathison knew he was avoiding it.

"I haven't asked her." He would have to unless he could find another solution. What if she said no? She worked beside him every day, almost every waking hour. Why would she want to spend more time with him? If he was going to ask her, it should be a special occasion. Dammit. Was he really thinking of asking her? How could he arrange something special? It wasn't like he could just look up from his desk and ask. Well, yeah, he could, but it should be more special than that.

"Dude, Gunny, you gotta ask her sooner instead of later, you know."

"Since when did I start taking relationship advice from you?" This was the absolutely wrong time to be discussing this. What was Stathis' problem? Leave it to the young man to state the obvious in the most annoying way at the worst time possible. Wasn't he supposed to be fighting for his life?

"Since you got too busy doing emperor things and forgot to think with your dick on occasion. That's important too, you know. There was once this place in Papua New Guinea that—"

It wasn't his dick he had to think with. He didn't like being pressured into it. Not by Stathis, not by Feng, and not by Admiral Carpenter. He remembered Stathis getting in trouble for something in Papua New Guinea. Had he ever been punished for that?

"Stathis," Mathison said. How could he get the lieutenant to think about his job and not Mathison's sex life? Of all the things to discuss.

"Sorry, sir," Stathis said. "Let me rephrase that as a fancy pants lieutenant. You need to think about the continuation of your dynasty and the welfare of your subjects. You have many duties, Emperor Mathison, and your people need more than your wisdom."

Stupid lieutenants. Stupider privates. Perhaps now it was time. Stathis wasn't acting like a stupid, bright-eyed, bushy-tailed, timid little second lieutenant anymore. Not that he had ever acted like that, but Mathison had watched him around the other Legionnaires and Captain Sinclair. It was easy to forget that Stathis had once been a dumb ass private and the unending source of headaches and stress.

"Shut up, Stathis, and keep your head down," Mathison said. "Don't make me regret promoting you to first lieutenant any more than I am."

"Promotion noted and being processed," Freya said as Mathison closed the link.

"Is he going to be okay?"

"I don't know. Depends on the Weermag. Are they going to assault us through those breeches or just drop a nuke? Even if they conduct an assault, his chances are slim."

If they dropped a nuke, Mathison knew his chances were non-existent.

"He'll make it," Mathison said with a confidence he didn't feel. *"How far along are we from moving the decryptors and other critical pieces?"*

Which was the real problem. Zvezda Two wasn't home because it was where he racked his rifle.

"There is less reliance," Freya reported. *"If we lose it, it will still be a blow to the Empire. But unless they capture it, it won't be a fatal blow. We should be able to destroy it if looks likely."*

Small victories.

Mathison got into the tube car, crammed in tight with several other troopers. Baker was doing his job and didn't give a damn about

396 | WILLIAM S. FRISBEE, JR.

Mathison's comfort as he tried to stuff as many troopers in the little tube car as he could manage. The extra troopers would be additional armor and cushioning around him at the very least. Skadi was put in another tube car, which made sense tactically, but Mathison thought it was annoying. If he was going to be stuffed into a vehicle like clowns stuffed into a clown car, he would prefer Skadi be one of them rather than a bunch of guys. Not that a woman would be any softer in armor. Mathison didn't really know his Praetorians that well and if they had not been in armor, he would be able to smell their breath and be able to tell what they had for breakfast.

He could marry worse, a lot worse. Maybe better. Some mouse of a woman for bearing children would work when Skadi said no. They had a good working relationship, and Mathison didn't want that to change. Skadi was his equal in so many ways. A battle buddy, someone who would kick him in the teeth if he crossed a line, someone who understood boundaries, someone he knew he could trust with his life. Literally. She had his back and understood him. Though he had shot at her in the past. Hopefully she wasn't still looking for payback.

He didn't want some mousy woman, but Feng was probably already interviewing women for the role.

He wanted to ask her, but if she said no, that would be depressing. As if he didn't have more important things to worry about.

The tube car started up and entered the tunnel where it barely fit.

"This feels like running away," Mathison said on a private link to Skadi.

"We are running away," Skadi said. "But we deny the enemy their tactical objective in the most brutal way possible. We are taunting them and making them waste resources."

"We're losing people," Mathison said. "Those are valuable resources too."

"They are losing more. Stathis and Baker are giving them hell. They will fail to wipe them out, but we will be victorious. This is not even a tactical retreat. This is snatching the prey out of their jaws and telling them to eat paska."

Packed in this tight was worse than what he used to call "asshole to belly button." The Marines had used what were called cattle cars to move people around. Basically, nothing more than trailers where Marines were packed in so tightly, they couldn't sit down. This was worse because he was pretty sure in cattle cars Marines hadn't been pushed up against the ceiling and lying on people's heads. This was some serious clown car shit. Who said emperors always traveled in comfort?

Which didn't make it feel any less like running away in Mathison's mind, but Skadi was right. She also had more experience retreating from the SOG, though she wouldn't think about it in those terms. She'd been fighting a numerically superior enemy for over a hundred years and never given up, never surrendered. The SOG had feared her, dedicated a task force to hunt her down. In the end, she had won. There was inspiration to be gained from that.

The problem was that the vanhat were not the SOG. Would this failure embolden them, or did they even care?

It was going to take almost an hour to get to their destination, and Mathison knew there was no getting comfortable. Changing the view of his helmet display let him escape the claustrophobic feeling of being squeezed into a small space in a small car in a tube that was hurtling through a little tunnel under billions of tons of rock.

Would he have to worry about his guards freaking out? Would now be the time to get to know his guards or would it be awkward having a conversation with someone whose elbow was pushing your head against the side of the car, or the guy whose rifle butt was poking you in the ribs?

"So, where are you from?" Mathison asked the closest guard, the one pretty much sitting on his knee.

"New Kursk sir," the man said. A habitat on the Moon. A local guy. This was going to be a long ride.

"It's a trap!" someone said on the main link.

Mathison felt the tube car hit something.

* * * *

Chapter Sixty-One:
The Emperor

Vanhat Commander – Kafasta

The first of their rail cars slammed into the ambush and was nearly vaporized by the mine, but the other cars were not as close as he had expected. The others were not in the kill zone and stopped where he did not want them to. These humans were not as predictable as he liked.

These humans were lazy, and Kafasta wondered how they had climbed their way back to sentience so quickly after the last purge. Or perhaps it was incompetence more than laziness? It couldn't be competence.

Sonar scans, scout drones, and data analysis had shown there were two secret exits from the human leader's bunker. This was the only one with high-speed transportation, thus making it the one they'd most likely use. The secret rail was a mostly bored tunnel, but in this section, it exited the human-made tunnel and traveled along a lava tube for several kilometers before sliding back into a human-made tunnel.

The plan had been to let the humans exit the tunnel, travel along the rail, and then enter the second tunnel. The first transport being vaporized would collapse that route and cause the following cars, which likely held their leader, to stop. Kafasta's troops were positioned nearby so they could then wipe out the guards and, if possible, take the human emperor prisoner.

That, combined with the capture of his bunker, would throw the humans into disarray, disrupt their ability to contain the main invasion force, and break the stalemate. Having their supreme leader captured and the equipment to trigger their brain bombs under vanhat control would paralyze the human forces throughout the system. Furthermore, the brain bombs could be triggered, and the automated defenses shut down. Humans were such fools. This pathetic race wouldn't last much longer. Kill the head, the body dies. So simple and elegant. That was the flaw of top-down leadership.

The worst-case scenario would be the death of the emperor, but the demons could create some convincing video of his capture and cooperation.

The ancient gods wanted their leader alive, and that was the biggest problem he faced.

The Weermag had learned how to track humans based on their Inkeri generators and that was the only reason he had known his ambush was facing failure. The other cars were too far back. Their retreat to Zvezda Two was blocked, but he had planned to use the lava tubes to escape with his prey, and most of his force was concentrated near the far end of the tunnel, where he had expected to trap them.

This contingency had been planned for, but the force guarding against escape from the other tunnel was not a large one. If only their prey had traveled another kilometer or two through the lava tube.

Damned lazy and incompetent humans were ruining his plans.

Giving the command, his troops headed back toward the other tunnel where the humans were debarking to engage his rear guard. If they bunkered down to wait for reinforcements, then troops from the main invasion could reinforce his fighters. The prey likely had rein-forcements coming, but Kafasta didn't worry about them.

"They are attacking!" Kafetan said.

"They are resisting," Kafasta said.

"No," his demon whispered. *"The humans are attacking. Your rear guard may not hold."*

"Your analysis indicated they would bunker down and wait for reinforce-ments," Kafasta told his demon.

"The analysis was flawed. The bodyguard commander has likely been overrid-den by the chaotic and unpredictable emperor."

Kafasta despised the demon. It had made the analysis, but now it was not accepting its own flaw and error.

Would the ancient gods understand, or would they blame him?

"Faster!" Kafasta urged his troops. The rear guard had expected to face a small force and was supposed to fight a short action, not a sustained battle. The demon's analysis had indicated there would be a human rear guard which would attempt to attack the main force and free the emperor from the trap.

Didn't these damned humans follow their own doctrine and pro-tocol? They were attacking his rear guard. If the humans got past them, they could flee into the lava tunnels and that would make it very hard to track them and capture their leader. Their doctrine, their profes-sionalism, should make them realize how dangerous that could be, es-pecially with the main invasion force breaking through the lines.

Stupid, lazy, annoying, unpredictable, unprofessional humans! How did they accomplish anything?

* * * * *

Chapter Sixty-Two:
Ambushed

Prime Minister Wolf Mathison, USMC

The car slammed to a stop and Mathison thought they might have hit something. He was seeing stars from whatever had hit him in the face. Someone's helmet or elbow?

"Debark! Debark! Debark!" someone yelled. "Get the emperor to safety!"

It was the dumbest thing Mathison could imagine. Safety was where?

"What's going on?" Mathison asked Freya.

"The tube car system uses part of the lava tube system," Freya said. *"We are in one such lava tube. The Weermag have tunneled into it and set up an ambush. They have destroyed the lead car, but the second and third have deployed troops. Fighting is becoming more intense. Rear guard is detecting damage to the tunnel behind us."*

"Damage?"

"Analysis indicates charges have either collapsed the tunnel or a Weermag force has breached the tunnel and may come up behind us."

"So, it's a trap?"

"Apparently," Freya said. *"Stathis warned us of this. Colonel Baker felt there was no choice."*

404 | WILLIAM S. FRISBEE, JR.

"Shit," Mathison said. Walking into a trap was never good, but still being surprised by it was worse.

"We have communications with Imperial forces and reinforcements are on the way."

Which didn't mean shit. The Weermag could bottleneck the reinforcements and keep them from arriving just as easily as the humans had bottlenecked the main Weermag forces. Tunnel warfare was nasty for so many reasons.

"What's the plan?" Mathison asked.

"The colonel plans to bunker down and wait for reinforcements," Freya said.

"Hell no." That would surrender the initiative to the enemy, and that was exactly what they would expect.

"We may not have the firepower to break out. There are forces in front of and behind us," Freya reported. *"The tube car rail comes out of a human-made tunnel into the lava tunnel at an angle, but the lava tube is full of Weermag."*

It wasn't full of Weermag like the clown car had been, Mathison was pretty sure.

"They'll expect us to hunker down and wait for reinforcements," Mathison said on a link to Baker. "They're sure to have planned for that."

"Get back in the tunnel," Baker said, coming on the link.

"No," Mathison said. "That's what they want. Professionals are predictable."

"Professionals are predictable for a reason," Baker said. "Gravity only works one way."

"Pick a direction and push," Mathison said.

"I'm the one in command of your security. You are the protectee, I am the protector, Emperor Mathison," Baker said. "In this, you do what I tell you. If we survive, you can have me replaced."

Baker was wrong, Mathison could feel it, but he understood the ex-Delta operator well. As a Marine Raider, he had done bodyguard work for some warlord in Africa so long ago. The protectee always thought they knew better, but the fact of the matter was that the protectee didn't spend all his time planning escape routes and evaluating the tactical situation of keeping the protectee alive. In this case, the protectee spent most of his time at the macro scale, planning Fleet operations and economies.

This was different, though. This protectee had been on both sides of that relationship, and Mathison knew that hunkering down and waiting for reinforcements was a terrible idea. That was what the Army did; wait for reinforcements to stomp the enemy flat with superior firepower and tactics.

Marines weren't so smart and preferred to create chaos they could exploit. That allowed a smaller force to do damage completely out of proportion to their size. Of course, sometimes that meant the smaller force got wiped out. Mathison was smart enough to know that.

But what would the Weermag expect?

"How well do the Weermag know us?" Mathison asked on a link with Skadi.

"Damned well," Skadi said. She had worked with the military forces more than Mathison had. "They have SCBIs, though they may not be as good as ours, and they have very good analysis programs. Without the Legionnaires to counter them, they would run circles around us. Their coordination and psychology of warfare is exceptional."

Would there be chaos the detachment could exploit, or did they have to hunker down?

"How far away are reinforcements?" Mathison asked Freya.

"A half hour if they don't run into resistance," Freya said.

That was too damned long. This fight could be decided in a few minutes, and they would run into resistance.

Mathison was pulled out of the tube car, and he saw blazer fire flash overhead. The lava tube was not pressurized, so there was no sound as the Praetorians pulled him along. Mathison helped as he could, but they kept him down and pulled him back into the tunnel the tube cars had come out of.

Inside the sealed car, he hadn't known about the lava tube. He had thought it was a carved tunnel all the way from Zvezda Two to their destination.

"What do you think the Weermag expect us to do?" Mathison asked Freya. If he knew what they expected, he could try to do the opposite.

"I estimate time is on their side," Freya said, which wasn't what Mathison had expected.

"It shouldn't be."

"The attack on Zvezda Two was preceded by other attacks in other sectors. There have been breakthroughs in multiple areas. General Hui has her hands full. The attacks started a half hour ago."

Mathison didn't like the timing at all. Too much too soon. Could the entire offensive have been launched to influence him? Was the attack on him and Skadi an attempt to disrupt or assist the new offensive or was it designed to make him run into an ambush?

Thousands of people were dying.

"We need to break out of this," Mathison said, opening a link to Baker.

"We are good," Baker said. "We can hold out until reinforcements arrive."

"No, we need to punch out. If they pin us down, we're going to get swarmed."

"We have reinforcements coming."

"So do they."

"If we break out," Baker said, "we could run into more enemy troops, and we'd be going in the opposite direction of our reinforcements."

"The Weermag will expect us to hunker down and wait."

"Time is on our side, not theirs."

"I disagree."

"I'm in command of your safety."

"I'm overriding you."

"You can't."

"Then I can start shooting."

"God damned crayon-eating jarhead. We need to hunker down."

"Damned dogface soldier. We need to break out and get mobile. That's an order."

Baker changed links, and the surrounding Praetorians checked their magazines. Two stood beside Mathison and the others moved forward. The rate of fire increased, more rounds were coming in at them, but Mathison felt confident more rounds were headed toward the Weermag.

Mathison couldn't hear the commands, but he saw the Praetorians shoulder their weapons and move out of cover toward the Weermag blocking their escape.

He saw some Praetorians take hits and go down, but the majority made it out of his view around the edge.

In seconds, his two bodyguards and Skadi's two guards urged them both forward. Obviously, the attack was successful so far.

Baker was going to kick his ass later, but right now they were moving.

* * * * *

Chapter Sixty-Three:
Proposal

Prime Minister Wolf Mathison, USMC

Mathison realized he needed to get out and run more. Being chained to a desk trying to govern the Empire was making him fat, and he was now out of shape. He needed Stathis to thrash because proving himself better than the young man forced him to work harder. They were running from the battle and the lava tube was not a nice smooth corridor that was easy to traverse. Without the light gravity of the Moon that allowed them to navigate drop offs and sudden curves that would go up or down, they would have been trapped. They all had food paste and water, the bare minimum needed to survive. They would probably run out of ammunition before they ran out of the nasty, unappetizing paste which they could only eat by attaching to their helmet.

The lava tubes were a maze, and the Weermag bombardment had somehow collapsed numerous tubes, even this far down.

Baker was ahead of Mathison, leading the way, and next to him were Skadi and her two Praetorians. They were down to about twenty Praetorians, and Mathison felt guilty knowing how many they had started with. It had been over forty, and he knew some had stayed behind to buy them time. It would be at the cost of their lives. Brave bastards.

410 | WILLIAM S. FRISBEE, JR.

A real leader would know the men who were dying for him, and Mathison knew he had failed at that. If he survived, he would have to change that.

"We're getting further and further from reinforcements," Baker said. Shouldn't he be a little less insolent toward his commander?

"The Weermag haven't overrun us," Mathison said. There were at least a hundred hot on their trail. The Praetorians were almost out of claymores, which was a surprise to Mathison. Since when did the palace guards include mines as part of their kit?

"The last explosion might have collapsed the tunnel a little," Baker said. "That will slow them down, but they like to blow shit up as much as Marines, and they have more demo than we do."

"Contact front!"

That was bad news. How the Weermag had got so many troops this far down was a mystery. But things were about to get bad if they couldn't punch through the force in front of them.

More Imperial forces were in the lava tubes, but not all of them had Aesir communication links, and Mathison knew things were going to get worse unless he could get out of these tunnels and into a more secure area. So far, they had encountered no one except Weermag, who had to be having problems because of all the jamming and radio interference.

Mathison quickly learned that whoever the SOG had tasked with mapping these lava tubes had done a terrible job of it. A lot of tubes had been simply ignored. Laziness or incompetence, Mathison didn't know, but mapping would have to be done because there would be no other way to root out and purge the vanhat presence.

An explosion ahead made Mathison look up at the ceiling. This wasn't Earth, but there was gravity, and that gravity could pull the ceiling down on them. Cave ins would still be fatal. At best, they would crush whoever was below. At worst, they would be trapped and at the mercy of the Weermag.

This area looked more like a cave than a lava tube and was wider.

Mathison saw movement ahead, and Freya flagged it as hostile. In the blink of an eye, he was firing. The Weermag soldier twitched and died. There was another explosion and chunks of the ceiling fell, providing some cover and spreading dust into the thin atmosphere like smoke.

Freya showed him the outlines of his Praetorians and observed enemy troops. There were a lot of enemy troops, and the number of his defenders was decreasing.

Blazer rounds flashed past. Retreat might not be an option. His stomach was growling, but he couldn't bring himself to eat one of the food tubes. They could be trapped here for the rest of their brief lives if they couldn't push through.

Another explosion told Mathison the Weermag weren't trying to capture him alive. Nearby, a Praetorian was crawling, one leg gone and blood spurting. The bleeding stopped, but the trooper kept crawling. Where he was going or what he was doing, Mathison didn't know. Hopefully, his automated tourniquet had done its job.

Mathison moved to help the Praetorian when another explosion threw him back. He saw Skadi's icon on his heads-up display flash amber.

Mathison almost forgot the trooper as he looked over and saw Skadi was down. Another trooper was pulling her behind a fallen boulder and her shoulder armor looked dented.

Grabbing the legless trooper by the handle in his harness, Mathison jumped toward the boulder where Skadi was.

Behind the boulder, Mathison knelt and left the injured trooper where he was protected from enemy fire. Hopefully, more boulders wouldn't fall, but right now he was more worried about Skadi. He pulled up her suit diagnostics and saw her shoulder armor had a breach and was being sealed by automated systems. Not serious.

Skadi shook her head as if to clear it, and Mathison took the opportunity to pull a grenade from the fallen Praetorian's rig. Standing, he pulled the pin and hurled it at the enemy. Freya helped guide it and the augmentation in his armor made it a lethal projectile as it slammed into a Weermag coming out of the tunnel. The grenade slammed into the alien's head, maybe breaking it as the creature fell backward, and the grenade sailed on.

Ducking back down, he looked at Skadi.

"Paska, paska, paska!" she said. Her helmet turned to him. The visor was up, and he saw her looking at him. She looked like she was in pain.

"If you are kneeling, it better be for a better reason than to help me up. I don't need your help to stand. Back off."

Now Mathison was embarrassed. It was bravado on her part. She didn't look like she was doing too well, but she was regaining her senses. Sometimes she could be damned annoying. What would Stathis say? He always had some smart-ass comment. As a gunny he knew he shouldn't be trying to think of what a private would say. He was kneeling. Something about kneeling being a Marine firing position? Too much bravado. Stathis could say some real stupid shit, too.

"Will you marry me?" Mathison asked and held out the ring from the grenade pin.

Then he realized who he was talking to, not just a comrade at arms, but to Skadi. Once he said the words, he realized he couldn't take them back. He had meant to be funny. Anyone else would have laughed, but Skadi? Mathison froze. Blazer fire and explosions erupted around them as he stared at her in shock.

Her eyes went from the ring to him, and Mathison wasn't sure what was there, but it wasn't anger.

"Yes, of course," she said. "I kind of expected a nice dinner and fancy surroundings, and a much nicer ring, since I understand that is your custom, but considering how we met... Did you arrange this excursion just to propose?"

She had said yes? Was she joking too?

"Well, yeah. We both needed the excitement and exercise."

"I've been waiting for you to propose. I would have proposed but figured that might hurt your ego."

Mathison stared at her as she took the ring out of his fingers and tucked it into a pouch. It would be too awkward to fit on her armored glove.

"It would have been better at a fancy dinner where we could kiss," Skadi said. "You jarheads like your traditions, don't you?"

"Um..."

"You can call off the battle now," she said. "I said yes. Let's get to safety. This armor needs to be removed and repaired."

Her removing her armor suddenly took on a lot more meaning. Had she meant it when she said yes?

The explosions and weapons fire increased, and Mathison ducked. She was joking, right? Turning the joke back on him. Wicked. They would laugh about this later. They probably weren't going to escape this. Mathison knew she had a sense of humor, but what if she wasn't joking?

Shit. He wasn't ready for this. He wondered if Stathis had found any instruction manuals on the topic.

The firing slowed, then stopped.

"Cease fire! Cease fire!" Baker was yelling on the all-hands link. "Friendlies."

Mathison looked over the boulder and saw Imperial ODTs pouring into the lava chamber. It became immediately clear why the Weermag had been pushing so hard. They had been caught between two

Imperial forces. Identifiers showed they were from a line ODT regiment so they wouldn't have Aesir comms. His suit linked in with their network. Mathison hated to think they were safe now, but this company pouring into the chamber was the lead element, and they were down here to save him and Skadi, his fiancée?

"You could have asked me a lot earlier," Skadi said, using his still outstretched hand to pull herself up. "I really would have preferred a nice dinner over this."

Medics moved forward to help the wounded Praetorians and ODTs. A Praetorian medic arrived next to Skadi.

Mathison didn't know what to say.

"The wedding better be more traditional," Skadi said. "My dad will not join us in a firefight, you know."

She was still holding his hand as she looked at him. Now he saw something he had never seen in her eyes. A smile.

"Now, about dinner?"

Mathison still wasn't thinking straight and handed her a tube of the nasty food paste.

"Sir?" Baker said. His tone told Mathison there was bad news. How could there be bad news? Skadi had said yes.

"There has been a nuclear detonation in Zvezda Two."

Stathis!

* * * * *

Chapter Sixty-Four:
Away

1st Lieutenant Zale Stathis, USMC

S tathis didn't recognize the voice in the link because of the static and jamming, but it let him know they had at least partially won.

"The emperor is away," the voice said as Stathis continued to fire at vanhat dropping from the holes above. One victory today. The vanhat had failed in their attempt to kill the emperor. That was the important thing. Keeping them from capturing the decryptors should be easy because he could have them destroyed.

"Lieutenant Stathis," a voice said. The link said it was a Legionnaire major. "You need to withdraw. We are leaving robots behind to cover your retreat."

Stathis looked around and realized he was probably the only human still on the surface shooting at the vanhat. An icon on his display showed the evacuation route.

"The robots can hold," Shrek said. *"The major is planning to destroy the decryptors."*

"Then we lose control of all the platforms," Stathis said. Didn't people know that?

"Not completely. There has been an initiative to set up alternate command centers and integrate SCBI control by Legionnaires."

"But the face eaters have SCBIs."

"Precautions are being taken," Shrek said, but Stathis was skeptical.
"You need to retreat now. You are the last."

"Why am I the last?"

"Because you are not in any direct chain of command."

"Oh." Stathis turned and sprinted toward a set of stairs leading toward an evacuation point. Around him, the weapons fire continued unabated.

A single blazer round slammed into the ground nearby, but Stathis leaped through the door before more rounds came his way.

Running down the empty corridor, Stathis expected to encounter vanhat intruders at any moment.

"They've broken through," the major said. "They're inside and taking out the robots. We are running out of time. We cannot let them recover the decryptors under any circumstances."

Stathis tried to run faster. It wasn't far.

"Hurry!" Shrek said, and Stathis knew he would not make it.

The major had orders to detonate a low-yield nuclear device to destroy the decryptors and data center if the vanhat could not be stopped. That device would also kill everyone in Zvezda Two. The major had his orders. He couldn't allow the vanhat to get too close because then their SCBIs could plant a virus or some other nasty into the system.

* * * * *

Chapter Sixty-Five:
Escape

1st Lieutenant Zale Stathis, USMC

The explosion threw Stathis across the cabin. He saw stars as he slammed into the wall. Someone was screaming, and Stathis checked his display. His shoulder was dislocated.

His armor flexed, the strength augmentation providing feedback, and Stathis screamed as his shoulder was relocated.

"Sorry," Shrek said, as Stathis blinked back the tears. *"A relaxed body takes less damage and—"*

"Are we going to die?" Stathis asked.

"No. We barely made it. The detonation has sealed the tram tube behind us."

Stathis looked around the cabin. Not everyone had survived, and Stathis gritted his teeth. His arm hurt like hell, but he saw one trooper with a broken neck. Flexing armor would not fix that.

After the initial silence, the groans and screams began. The tram had stopped, trapped in the tunnel by the explosion.

"We will have to travel three kilometers on foot to the next substation," Shrek said. *"It is unknown if the vanhat have made it that far. The front lines are collapsing and the Weermag have breached multiple locations."*

"If a nuke didn't kill me, then the Weermag can't," Stathis said. They needed stretchers. He looked for the major and swore. The trooper

with the broken neck *was* the major, and his life signs were non-existent. He was the only officer present.

"We survived," Stathis said aloud, and several helmets turned toward him. "The fight isn't over yet. We have three kilometers to go, and we have to move fast. The vanhat have broken through, and they are coming this way. If we don't stay outside their front lines, we are going to die. We need stretchers. We aren't leaving anyone behind."

Stathis checked his ammunition levels. Not good.

"Get as much ammunition as you can carry, too, but the living are the priority right now."

"Wilco," said an ODT, and was echoed by others.

Stathis directed people to separate the dead from the wounded, the mobile from the immobile and hoped they could move fast enough.

The Weermag had broken through, and Stathis knew they couldn't be contained now. Soon the Imperial forces would be surrounded.

Good. That meant the Wolf Legion could attack in every direction. He was tired of this defensive garbage. He wanted the enemy to try to contain a US Marine and see how much they liked it. The gloves were coming off.

"They have us surrounded," said an ODT sergeant. He had to be checking the reports.

Chesty Puller had said something when the Marines were surrounded near the Chosin Reservoir.

"Good," Stathis said. "They won't get away this time."

# # # # #

About the Author

Marine veteran, reader, writer, martial artist, computer consultant, dungeon master, computer gamer, dreamer, webmaster, proud American, and, best of all, dad.

Growing up in Europe during the height of the Cold War and serving as a Marine infantryman through the fall of communism shaped Bill's perspective on life and the world. When most Marines were out trying to get lucky he was studying tactical manuals. Years later, he shared much of his knowledge to a website for writers of military science fiction.

These days, he's brushed off the pocket protector and is a top-gun computer consultant.

Learn more at http://www.WilliamSFrisbee.com and join his mailing list here: http://williamsfrisbee.com/mailing-list/.

* * * * *

Get the **free** Four Horsemen prelude story **"Shattered Crucible"**

and discover other titles by Theogony Books at:

http://chriskennedypublishing.com/

* * * * *

Meet the author and other CKP authors on the Factory Floor:

https://www.facebook.com/groups/461794864654198

* * * * *

Did you like this book?
Please write a review!

* * * * *

The following is an
Excerpt from Book One of Abner Fortis, ISMC:

Cherry Drop

P.A. Piatt

Available from Theogony Books

eBook, Audio, and Paperback

Excerpt from "Cherry Drop:"

"Here they come!"

A low, throbbing buzz rose from the trees and the undergrowth shook. Thousands of bugs exploded out of the jungle, and Fortis' breath caught in his throat. The insects tumbled over each other in a rolling, skittering mass that engulfed everything in its path.

The Space Marines didn't need an order to open fire. Rifles cracked and the grenade launcher thumped over and over as they tried to stem the tide of bugs. Grenades tore holes in the ranks of the bugs and well-aimed rifle fire dropped many more. Still, the bugs advanced.

Hawkins' voice boomed in Fortis' ear. "LT, fall back behind the fighting position, clear the way for the heavy weapons."

Fortis looked over his shoulder and saw the fighting holes bristling with Marines who couldn't fire for fear of hitting their own comrades. He thumped Thorsen on the shoulder.

"Fall back!" he ordered. "Take up positions behind the fighting holes."

Thorsen stopped firing and moved among the other Marines, re-laying Fortis' order. One by one, the Marines stopped firing and made for the rear. As the gunfire slacked off, the bugs closed ranks and continued forward.

After the last Marine had fallen back, Fortis motioned to Thorsen. "Let's go!"

Thorsen turned and let out a blood-chilling scream. A bug had approached unnoticed and buried its stinger deep in Thorsen's calf. The stricken Marine fell to the ground and began to convulse as the neurotoxin entered his bloodstream.

"Holy shit!" Fortis drew his kukri, ran over, and chopped at the insect stinger. The injured bug made a high-pitched shrieking noise, which Fortis cut short with another stroke of his knife.

Viscous, black goo oozed from the hole in Thorsen's armor and his convulsions ceased.

"Get the hell out of there!"

Hawkins was shouting in his ear, and Abner looked up. The line of bugs was ten meters away. For a split second he almost turned and ran, but the urge vanished as quickly as it appeared. He grabbed Thorsen under the arms and dragged the injured Marine along with him, pursued by the inexorable tide of gaping pincers and dripping stingers.

Fortis pulled Thorsen as fast as he could, straining with all his might against the substantial Pada-Pada gravity. Thorsen convulsed and slipped from Abner's grip and the young officer fell backward. When he sat up, he saw the bugs were almost on them.

* * * * *

Get "Cherry Drop" now at: https://www.amazon.com/dp/B09B14VBK2

Find out more about P.A. Piatt at: https://chriskennedypublishing.com

* * * * *

The following is an

Excerpt from Book One of the Echoes of Pangaea:

Bestiarii

James Tarr

Available from Theogony Books

eBook, Audio, and Paperback

Excerpt from "Bestiarii:"

"Mayday Mayday Mayday, this is Sierra Bravo Six, we've lost power and are going down," Delian calmly said as Tina screamed from the back. He and Hanson began frantically hitting buttons and flipping switches. "Radio's dead, I've got nothing." He had to yell it so Hansen could hear him over the wind.

Mike's eyes went wide. He felt his stomach come up into his throat as the helicopter dropped and began rotating. "Shite," Seamus cursed and smacked the button to drop the visor on his helmet.

"Keep transmitting," Hansen told his co-pilot. "Damn, I've got no electronics, can we do a manual re-start?" He stayed on the stick and the collective, trying to control the autorotation.

Delian had been hitting every button and toggle switch possible. "No, I don't think this is a short, it looks like everything's fried. Mayday Mayday Mayday, this is Sierra Bravo Six, we are going down." He told the younger pilot, "You know what to do. Keep it level, auto-rotate down, try to control the rate of descent. Time your glide. You see a place to land?"

The helicopter was spinning to the right as it fell, which tradition-ally was the reason the pilot was the right stick. Hansen looked out the window as he fought the controls. "We're in the mountains, nothing's flat. I've got trees everywhere. Hold on back there!" he yelled over his shoulder.

The helicopter began spinning faster and faster and Mike found himself being pulled sideways in his seat. The soldier on the door gun lost his footing and floated up in the air, then was halfway out the open door, one hand still on the mini-gun, restrained only by his tether as the G-forces made Mike's face feel hot. He vomited, and the bitter fluid was whipped away from his face. The world outside the open

430 | WILLIAM S. FRISBEE, JR.

doorway past Todd was a spinning blue/green/brown blur. Tina was screaming wildly. The wind was whistling around the cabin.

"We've got smoke coming from the engine," Delian said, peering upward. "What the hell happened?"

"Brace for impact!" Seamus yelled at the cabin, and wedged his boots against the seat opposite.

"Coming up on the mark, keep it level," Delian said calmly. "Get ready for the burn!" he yelled over his shoulder at the passengers. He switched back to the radio, even though he thought it was a waste of time. "Mayday Mayday Mayday, this is Sierra Bravo Six—"

"If they work," Mike heard the pilot respond, then suddenly there was a roar, and he was pressed down in his seat, getting heavier and heavier. The helicopter was still spinning, and out the open doorway and windshield there was nothing but a blur of greens and browns. Mike got heavier and heavier, and Tina stopped screaming. Then the roar stopped, and they began falling again, pulling up against their seatbelts. Tina opened her mouth to scream once more, but before she could draw a breath the helicopter hit with a huge crunch and the sound of tearing metal.

* * * * *

Get "Bestiarii" now at: https://www.ama-zon.com/dp/B0B44YM335/.

Find out more about James Tarr at: https://chriskennedypublish-ing.com.

* * * * *

Made in the USA
Middletown, DE
14 October 2024

62590525R00239